MURDERED SLEEP

MURDERED SLEEP

a Dade Wyatt mystery

R.A. Harold

Station Road Press
Montpelier, Vermont

Murdered Sleep
R. A. Harold

Published by Station Road Press
Montpelier, VT 05602

Cover photo: "Market Space & Penna. Ave., Washington, D.C., 1901," Library of Congress Prints and Photographs Division.

Author photo by Wayne Fawbush

ISBN 978-0-9831609-5-3

for Christine and Donald Brooks,
most welcoming of Washingtonians,

and in honored memory of
Morris King Udall

CHAPTER 1

National Theatre, Washington, D.C., April 2, 1906

One red hand holding up a gore-clotted dagger, the other dripping blood, Dade Wyatt edged into the dimly lit bedchamber. "I have done the deed—" he stopped, his gaze snapping to the window. "Didst thou not hear a noise?"

"I heard the owl scream and the crickets cry," whispered Julia Marlowe, a wild-eyed Lady Macbeth. A guttering candle threw their trembling shadows on the wall. "Did you not speak?"

He started back from her in growing horror. "When?"

"Now."

"As I descended?" His eyes swept the room, flicked back upwards to the staircase.

"Ay." She stared, fixated, at his dripping hands.

He held up his free hand as if a horrific thought had just struck him. And felt a seam of the too-short costume rip under his arm.

Silence fell between them.

The Porter and Macduff shifted restlessly in the wings.

Wyatt stared at Mrs. Marlowe, but Lady Macbeth still wasn't saying anything.

Because, he realized, the next line must be his.

His mind was a frozen fog. What scene they were in? What was supposed to come next, what had they been talking about?

He stood there while a clock in his head ticked off the seconds. Runnels of sweat coursed down his back. His face burned. The spirit-gummed goatee itched unbearably.

In her Lady Macduff costume, Giovanna Treadwell stared at him from the wings with mouth half-open and held up her hands as if trying to pray the lines into his head.

Where had the prompter gone?

Nothing.

Red hands, a dagger. Of course! The murder just done. Something about—another chamber. Servants. No, grooms, not servants. Who were asleep, weren't they? Yes. "The, uh, grooms did sleep," he ventured. But Lady Macbeth just stared at him, frowning in puzzlement. "Then one—"

Offstage, the Porter and Macduff exchanged concerned looks. Another pause, while his brain locked and froze deeper. In the darkened house, a couple of cleared throats, shiftings in seats.

He took two panicked steps to stage left and, despite the red oozing down his wrists, touched the back of a chair, as if discharging static electricity. An old trick that sometimes worked. And the line broke loose, tumbled out of him in a rush.

"Hark! Who lies i'th'second chamber?"

"Donalbain," Mrs. Marlowe hissed back, eyes widening in relief.

He had it now. He stared at his own bloody hands. "This is a sorry sight."

A smile flickered on Lady Macbeth's face as Mrs. Marlowe responded. "A foolish thought to say a sorry sight."

The scene moved on to Macbeth's horrifying realization. "Methought I heard a voice cry 'Sleep no more...Glamis hath murdered sleep...Macbeth shall sleep no more.'" Wyatt's voice was loud and high-pitched, as if to cover the racing beat of his heart. They finished the rest of the scene without incident, but he couldn't get his heart to slow down.

He followed Mrs. Marlowe into the wings. "I'm so sorry—"

Her rich, deep laugh rang out. "That's why we call them rehearsals, silly! You're doing rather well, considering." A flirtatious finger reached up and smoothed the edges of his mustache. Her smile deepened the almost masculine cleft in her chin, and he smiled in his turn. If playing opposite America's leading Shakespearean lady was a challenge, it was also going to be a pleasure.

Until now, Wyatt had been playing the well-intentioned but ineffectual Thane of Ross, a middling part. But Mrs. Marlowe's lover and leading man, Edward Sothern, had fallen ill with pneumonia in Baltimore, and Wyatt was his understudy. Stumbling over Macbeth's lines and struggling to learn his new stage placements, he was finding Julia Marlowe's gratitude and forbearance almost burdensome.

The sudden promotion unsettled him. Lines didn't come as easily as they had in his youth, and opportunities for frozen panic abounded. He'd forgotten the physical demands a role could make—the cramped limbs of a Richard III, the long, frequent and occasionally dangerous sword fights of the Histories. It would take every ounce of energy and concentration he had to be ready for their opening night at the National.

Still, it was soul-satisfying in a way he hadn't felt since he'd left his work as a security agent and resumed his stage career. Now, with Sothern's illness and his own move into the lead, he felt the old serpent of artistic ambition uncoiling in his chest. Convenient for the character he was playing and, like any good actor, he was prepared to use it.

If he could only get the bloody lines down.

He closed his dressing-room door and leaned his head against it, letting his muscles go slack and breathing slow. When he turned to his dressing-table, he found an ivory envelope there with a familiar monogram and his own name in a slapdash scrawl. He thumbed it open. Congressman Warren Dodge, his friend and former employer, requested Mr. Wyatt's company on Wednesday for luncheon at Willard's.

Washington Post, stop press edition, April 4, 1906

CENSURE VOTE UNLIKELY IN VERBAL ASSAULT ON HOUSE FLOOR

Congressman Latham of New York, Victim of Colleague's 'Astounding' Character Slur, Pronounces Procedural Remedies Inadequate

Members of the House of Representatives expressed "shock and outrage" in the wake of an astounding statement made on the House floor this morning by Robert L. Nielsen, the Populist Representative from the Second District of Wisconsin.

The statement came in response to remarks by Representative Richard Latham, R-New York, concerning an amendment proposed by the Member from the Badger State.

Described by one shocked hearer as "as vicious an assault on a gentleman's character as has ever gone unchallenged," Nielsen's statement, which in the interests of maintaining the journalistic standards of a family newspaper will go unreported here, can fairly be characterized as offensive in every particular.

A breach of this nature is unquestionably grounds for censure and possibly even expulsion, according to a source close to the Committee on Rules of the House. However, Representative Latham stated in response to a reporter's inquiry that such a procedural action "could not but aggravate the damage of the offense." He declined to elaborate as to what he would consider a more suitable penalty, but was heard to state that "Nielsen shall pay for this, make no doubt of that."

Representative Latham is a six-term veteran of the House and the Vice-Chairman of its Committee on Appropriations. Mr. Nielsen is in his second term and serves as the junior minority member of the Committee on the District of Columbia. His public statements concerning what he has characterized as unfair treatment of the Negro race and of the "downtrodden workers" of the United States have brought him into frequent conflict with the House leadership including, on a number of past occasions, Mr. Latham.

"They left out the most interesting stuff, it appears." Wyatt's face emerged from behind the *Washington Post* with a look of amused inquiry.

Warren Dodge stirred his coffee. "No question Bob Nielsen went too far," he shrugged. "But Latham won't hear of a censure vote, and I can't say I blame him." He nodded to the vigilant waiter to refill Wyatt's cup and attacked a flaky slice of the Willard's famous apple tart. A buzz of excited conversation rose from knots of dark-suited men at the tables around them.

Across the expanse of snowy linen, Wyatt found himself unable to suppress a smile, albeit a sleepy one. The rehearsal had gone late, but he hadn't seen Dodge since arriving in Washington and was curious about how the man the press referred to as a "pulp and paper baron" was adjusting to life as a junior Congressman from New York.

Wyatt saw his own smile reflected in Dodge's wide grin. "I dare say you would find it amusing," Dodge said. "No love lost and all that." Indeed, Congressman Richard Latham of Corning, New York, was a man Wyatt hated as much as he was capable of hating anyone.

"Care to fill me in?"

Dodge leaned across the table, lowering his voice. At the neighboring tables, men in expensive suits conferred, some Dodge's Congressional colleagues, others prominent lobbyists. "We were debating one of Nielsen's more, ah, quixotic floor amendments—"

"What about?"

"Lord, what was it?" The planes of Dodge's bony face sharpened with the effort of recollection. "—a minimum *wage*, that was it. Of all things."

"Don't we have one?" Wyatt asked innocently.

Dodge scowled and went on. "So the Speaker Pro Tem recognizes Latham, who starts in about—how did he put it? 'the right of an industrialist to dispose of the fruits of his capital as he sees fit.' A view with which I'm inclined to sympathize."

Wyatt suppressed another smile. Dodge seemed to enjoy his designation in the New York press as a "wealthy industrialist" almost as much as his Congressional title.

"And Nielsen's nostrils are starting to flare. He bounds to his feet, the Chair recognizes the Member from Wisconsin, and the rest is—very much off the record."

"A personal insult, the *Post* said?"

"He dashes the hair out of his eyes—the man should find himself a good barber—and shouts—" Dodge leaned farther over the table and dropped his voice to a whisper, "'Fruits of capital, Mr. Speaker? The meanest alley-whore of the gentle-man's acquaintance'—and trust me, he laid particular emphasis on the possessive—'comes by her living more honestly than he, for her labor is her own!'"

Wyatt choked on a mouthful of cake and guffawed into his napkin, dabbing the corners of his eyes. "Lord! I would have bought tickets to see that," he finally managed.

"They call a recess, of course, and Latham stalks off to the cloakroom, looking apoplectic, as you can imagine—"

"Good thing they've outlawed dueling." Wyatt flicked a crumb from his mustache. Morose delectation was an unworthy but highly enjoyable sentiment. Richard Latham had disowned his daughter Rose when she married Wyatt, a penniless fellow actor. He'd had no contact with Latham in twenty years, not even when Rose died, but he felt the injury afresh with the mention of the man's name, and his smile faded.

"The worst of it is," Dodge added, "that everybody knows that the alley-dwelling trollops he referred to are, without excep-tion—"

"Negroes," Wyatt finished. "I imagine that would have set him off."

Dodge grinned. "I wouldn't like to be in Nielsen's shoes. Latham has a lot of power, and he's not known for making idle threats."

Wyatt glanced back at the newspaper. "'Nielsen shall pay for this…' Wonder what he's got in mind?"

CHAPTER 2

Wyatt awoke in the darkness of his hotel room to find his lover on the window-seat, gazing through parted curtains into the gray light of approaching dawn. He switched on the spindly bedside lamp.

She let the book she was holding fall and turned towards him, bronze curls rippling to her small waist, the customary laughter in her great dark eyes displaced with something which might have been sadness or guilt or regret but which to Wyatt's eye held a tinge of fear.

"What is it, Giovanna?" He kept his voice gentle; in the last few days she had begun to startle easily. He picked up his pocket-watch from the bedside table. "It's five o'clock."

She shook her head. "I just can't sleep." Her voice was deep and rich for a woman's. It had charmed him from the wings before he even saw her.

As colleagues in the Sothern & Marlowe troupe, they were breaking the rules: she was a married mother of two, a fellow actor. Wyatt's move up to villain-protagonist gratified him professionally but concerned him for Giovanna's sake. Her sweet, sly sense of humor and near-Elizabethan capacity for wordplay masked a sensitive temperament, and as the touring company moved from Philadelphia, Wilmington, and Baltimore to Washington, he had noticed an emerging skittishness. He wondered if she was pulling back from him now that the run was almost over. Or whether, despite all their precautions, she might be— no, that couldn't be. He'd have seen signs of it...

His own stomach gave a sudden leap. Tonight was opening night; no more room for error. "Is it us? I know it's an adjustment—me moving into the lead—"

He saw the old mirth flash momentarily in her eyes. "Macbeth's changing you already. He'd have to, I suppose. It's just—it takes a little getting used to."

"Is that all?" he laughed. "You know what Mrs. Fiske says—you have to feel what the character feels. But it's only a play, love." She had a point, though; it was hard to shake off Macbeth's single-minded ambition, his dark distrusts, his need for conquest. Macbeth was a warrior who couldn't let go of being at war. Wyatt, who'd once charged up Kettle Hill with Theodore Roosevelt as a Rough Rider, knew what that felt like.

Giovanna was doubling roles as the First Witch and as the doomed, angry Lady Macduff, left to the murderous mercies of Macbeth by her warrior-husband. That lady's acerbic response to her fears suited Giovanna's sparkling wit, which as a rule showed to better advantage in the Bard's comedies, but this tour had given her a chance to display a rich emotional range that embraced tragedy and romance as well.

Wyatt had little guilt about cuckolding Giovanna's real-life husband Thomas Treadwell, a touring actor in his own company. A magnet to women and a well-known Don Juan, Treadwell, as his wife well knew from the theatrical gossip mill, was currently involved with his twenty-year-old leading lady. He would drop the girl, of course, at the end of the run; he always did.

He slid from the bed and walked barefoot to her across the worn Turkey carpet, taking both her hands in his. She smiled up at him, the warmth in her gaze dispelling his doubts.

"I miss the children. And I don't know how it's going to be with me and Thomas, now that—" she turned again towards the window.

"—both of you have something to hide?"

She stared at him, wide-eyed, and flushed, a hand flying to her throat. The response puzzled him. They had talked freely, even humorously, of this as her first infidelity and how it had begun to balance the scales between her and her husband. Theatrical standards were, after all, notoriously lax in such matters.

Their time together would end with the return to New York. She was determined to keep the home intact for her children. But there might be other tours together… He would miss her. Perhaps she would miss him too, more than she was letting on. Of her feelings for Treadwell—

"Let's not think about it yet." He pulled her to her feet and folded her in his arms, lifting her gently off the floor. She was so light, as if her bones were hollow as a bird's, so small in the circle of his embrace. "We've got better ways to use our time." He bared her slender throat with one hand and bent to kiss it, felt her gratifying shiver of response.

Later, as she slept deeply by his side, he woke to a sharp rapping on the door. She gasped and began to sit up but he stroked her hair. "I won't let anyone in." He had long since come to an understanding with the Johnson Hotel's house detective, a profitable arrangement for that gentleman.

At the door, a bell-boy proffered a familiar looking cream-colored envelope on a silver tray. Once more Wyatt recognized Warren Dodge's crisp monogram.

"Sorry to disturb you so early, sir," said the bell-boy. "But the man downstairs is waiting for a reply."

Wyatt held up a finger and closed the door, tearing open the envelope. He frowned, perusing the jagged black scrawl. "Nielsen murdered, Latham falsely suspected. Need your counsel. Carriage at hotel entrance 8:30."

Lips drawn into a tight line, he reopened the door and handed the boy a quarter. "Fetch me a copy of the *Post*. And—" he hesitated, then drew a breath, "tell the messenger I'll be there as requested." The boy nodded and turned down the corridor.

Giovanna blinked up at him from the pillow. "What was that about?"

He let the breath out. "That Congressman friend I had lunch with. Trying to drag me back into my old line of work."

She sat up. "But we open tonight—"

"Don't I know it."

After the door closed behind him, Giovanna sat up in the bed, shivering in spite of the lacy wool shawl she drew around her shoulders. She hated concealing herself from Wyatt, the man whose touch had brought her the most unalloyed joy of her life. The deep brown eyes that sought hers across the stage at curtain calls, the kindness—it was an odd word, but it suited—of his touch on her bare flesh. They'd been so unguarded with each other until the play's run brought them to Washington, where she was known. Or used to be known.

That was the fear that woke her before first light with her heart pounding: that one night she'd walk onto the stage and someone who'd made his way into the audience would stand up and tell everyone who she really was. And then her life would fall apart like a sandcastle in an incoming tide. What would she tell the children? How could she explain it to Wyatt?

It was silly. It wasn't going to happen, it couldn't. In the busy, rational daylight, she knew this, but in the silence of night, when her defenses were down, she couldn't shake the fear. She had to get hold of herself, she had to go on stage and not think about it, concentrate on her lines. Use her fear to fuel Lady MacDuff's mortal foreboding, that with her husband's exile her own life and her children's lives were forfeit to the savage tyranny of *Macbeth*. Lose herself in the weeds and weird pronouncements of the First Witch. After all, there was the costume and the makeup, and the stage identity: Mrs. Thomas Treadwell. That's who she was now. If she kept acting it, it would become the truth. It had worked until now.

CHAPTER 3

Washington Post, early edition, April 6, 1906

MEMBER OF CONGRESS FOUND BEATEN TO DEATH NEAR FOGGY BOTTOM RESIDENCE; INQUEST SET FOR TODAY

Police Say "No Suspects as Yet" in Brutal Slaying of Wisconsin Representative

The body of Robert L. Nielsen, a second-term Member of Congress from Wisconsin, was found on a street near his home early yesterday morning by two Negro operatives returning from the night shift at the Heurich Brewery. Nielsen had sustained massive head injuries and, according to Detective Commander Ian Macalester of the District of Columbia Police, "There is no doubt that he was the victim of foul play." Police declined to comment on the nature of the murder weapon, but there are unconfirmed reports that a gentleman's walking-stick was found near the scene of the crime.

As reported in a stop-press edition of this newspaper on Wednesday last, Nielsen was described by colleagues as the offending party in an altercation on the House floor in which he is said to have offered a "grave insult" to a senior member of that body, Representative Richard Latham of Corning, New York.

The District police also declined comment as to whether Mr. Latham was being considered as a suspect in Nielsen's death, but an unnamed source told the Post that he has been requested to remain in the Washington area pending additional investigation of the heinous crime.

The District of Columbia Medical Examiner will conduct an inquest this morning, but there is little doubt of the coroner's returning a verdict of homicide.

"You can't be serious, Warren. You know what that man is to me." Wyatt rose from his chair in front of Dodge's mahogany desk and stalked towards the door.

"He needs an investigator to find out who killed Robert Nielsen. He didn't." Dodge glared at him, his unruly red hair glowing like a corona in the spring light from the window behind him.

Wyatt came back and flattened his palms on the desk. "You can't know that."

"He was elsewhere when Nielsen died."

"Then why hasn't he said so?" Teeth clenched, Wyatt stared out the window towards the slums and alley dwellings of East Capitol Street, trying to quiet the pounding in his ears. Below him, a platoon of Negro gardeners unloaded pots of daffodils and scarlet tulips to be dug into the borders of the Capitol's East lawn.

Dodge creaked back easily in his swivel chair. "There's a lady involved."

The brutal death of the crusading Populist had appalled his Congressional colleagues and shocked Washington out of its April giddiness. Nielsen had been found on the street outside his rented Foggy Bottom house, his head bloodied and broken in an attack that inevitably recalled the assault by Congressman Phillips Brooks on the abolitionist Sumner fifty years before. His very public altercation of the previous day on the House floor with the arch-conservative Richard Latham had ended in what Latham had pronounced an abominable insult.

A mortal insult, perhaps?

After Rose had defied him and married Wyatt, Richard Latham had cut off all communication between his daughter and her family. Rose had died of consumption eight years ago—could it really have been that long already? Wyatt's attempts to inform his in-laws of their daughter's grievous condition and obtain financial help for her treatments had been met with stone-cold silence.

And now Warren Dodge wanted his help to save a man he loathed. With his opening night as Macbeth only hours away.

"It's absurd. He should hire a Pinkerton—they do it for a living."

"The fellow he talked to there promised he'd find him some Negro crook from the neighborhood to pin it on as a robbery gone wrong. Latham didn't find that reassuring."

"It was his walking-stick, wasn't it?" Wyatt hissed the words, turning back with his hand on the doorknob. "The man's a murderer. He let his own daughter die—"

Dodge rose and held up a restraining hand. "That was bad, Wyatt. But it wasn't murder. Latham knows I don't always see things his way, but he's helped me get my feet on the ground here. He's been decent to me. And more importantly I know he didn't do it."

"Decent to you. What does that mean?" Wyatt's deep brown eyes blazed at Dodge, his wide, normally generous mouth beneath the thick, silky mustache twisted with loathing.

Dodge looked uncomfortable, a unique event in Wyatt's experience. "Among other things he's, ah, actually put me in the way of one or two business opportunities. Real estate, I mean. This town is starting to grow—"

Wyatt shook his head impatiently. "That doesn't mean he didn't kill Nielsen."

"He's told me where he was that night. But he can't be public with it."

Wyatt snorted. "A woman, you said?"

"A lady." Dodge's tone was uncharacteristically conciliatory. "A lady who can't afford a hint of scandal."

"How convenient."

"It's not at all convenient. Quite the reverse. An alibi no gentleman could consider using."

"He'll hang for it, then. I'll shed no tears."

"Adultery isn't a capital crime." Dodge, as Wyatt well knew, had reason to have pondered that question. "Nor is disowning your child. Though he was wrong to do so."

Wyatt let out a breath and came back to the chair. "I've just taken over one of the most demanding roles in the repertory. I'll be lucky if I have my lines down tonight. Pinkertons aside, you could find a dozen good investigators to do this. Ask Macalester. He's running Homicide here now."

"I did. He suggested I get hold of you. Which I'd been inclined to do anyway." Dodge ran a hand through his thinning hair and swiveled his chair to face the window. As a freshman Congressman, he had drawn a tiny Capitol office far from the grandeur of his Park Avenue townhouse, morning light being the only compensation for its inferior eastern view. "Your judgment's as sound as any man's I know. And you got me out of that business on the island with my hide intact."

"And I've been out of the investigation game since then, as you'll recall." Wyatt closed his eyes on the painful memory. It was almost three years since a suspicious death at the Dodges' summer place on a Vermont island had threatened to blast Dodge's political career in the bud. The murderer had been brought to justice during a long-coveted visit from President Roosevelt. But the denouement had been tragic.

"He's terrified, Wyatt. They found one of his canes in a clump of bushes near the scene, covered in blood—Nielsen's blood, presumably. He's got a very public motive, he's known for his bad temper—and he knows what you did on the island. He'll pay you well."

"His money's no good to me now!"

Dodge's nostrils flared, but he kept his tone even. "I'll pay you, then. Do it because—" He swiveled his chair back towards the window and took a deep breath. "I'm asking it as a personal favor."

Wyatt was intrigued. Warren Dodge wasn't a man to ask favors of anyone. "Have they locked him up yet?"

"No. The papers have it right for once—they've questioned him, sent the cane off for examination, told him not to leave town. The police chief's not anxious to put a sitting member of the House in jail for murder. Particularly one with Latham's seniority—and influence over the D.C. budget."

"We've got a few days while they go through the usual formalities." Dodge's voice eddied through the whirlpool of emotions in Wyatt's gut. "Talking to the neighbors, who heard what, that sort of thing. You won't have much time, but if you get started right away—"

"Before or after my opening night as Macbeth?"

"I'm well aware of that. We saw you as Ross in Baltimore, by the way."

"You didn't mention it at lunch."

"A week ago Tuesday. We looked for you at the stage door afterwards, but it appeared you and Lady Macduff had some business to discuss." Dodge gave Wyatt a penetrating stare, though there was a slight twitch of the lip. Wyatt felt himself redden but didn't take the bait. "So, you've got your days free, am I right? Shows in the evening?"

"It might surprise you to learn that actors have no more free time than anybody else." Wyatt drew in a deep breath. Dodge didn't need to hear about how exhausting a performance could be, how it took two or three hours afterwards to wind down enough to sleep, how hard it was to be functional before noon. "Look, if you're so convinced the fellow's innocent, I'll talk to him. Though I'd sooner eat dirt."

"Good. I've made you an appointment—"

"You presumed a good deal."

"Calculated risk; I'm good at those," Dodge grinned. "And I've booked you a suite at Willard's. Get you out of that rat-hole they keep for traveling actors."

"Ah—no, thank you," Wyatt said, reddening further. "We all stay together on these runs. Makes for—better camaraderie, that sort of thing."

Dodge's grin widened. "Suit yourself."

"Besides, I haven't agreed to this yet, and there's every chance I won't. And there's the matter of figuring out who did it if Latham didn't."

"Nielsen manufactured enemies by the dozens. There weren't many in the House who liked him."

"Nobody likes a conscience."

"You've got that right," Dodge said. "But political dislikes don't tend to end up murderous, merely ruinous. I'm guessing it was something more personal."

"Getting in the way of somebody's business opportunities, for instance?"

Dodge bristled, but mastered himself. "Could be, I suppose. He's got—he had—a few bills in committee that would've throw a monkey wrench in the works of some big development projects."

"Including Latham's?"

"Yes, and any I would have got involved with as well." Dodge's candor was one of the things Wyatt valued in the friendship. "It's one reason I hesitated about signing on with the Columbia Heights project—"

"Something Latham was getting you into?"

"Well, he introduced us. Local developer named Dunagin, very successful. Brilliant, really."

"Were Nielsen's bills going anywhere?"

Dodge shrugged. "Likely not. Latham, among others, would've put the kibosh on them before they could hit the House floor, even if they got out of committee."

"What do we know about Nielsen's private life? He wasn't married, was he?"

Wyatt saw Dodge register the "we" and suppress a smile. "To his causes, I suppose," Dodge said, pouring a cup of coffee from a silver pot and holding it out to him. He waved it away. His nerves didn't need any more jangling.

"He was widowed some years ago," Dodge said. "There was talk of a lady-friend, a journalist for some muckraking rag. No idea how serious it was—maybe just allies in the Good Fight. But she might be worth talking to."

"He was killed near his lodgings, the paper says."

"South of K Street, a neighborhood they call Foggy Bottom." Dodge said. "Not the most savory part of town, Germain tells me. Watch yourself down there."

"You brought Germain down with you?"

"A colored steward's a reassuring sight to the Washington gentry when they visit. Seriously, though, he's helping us get the new house to rights and then he'll go back to New York. Sends his regards."

"When's the funeral?"

"Tomorrow morning. At the Unitarian Chapel. You'd want to go anyway. Isn't the murderer always supposed to show up at his victim's funeral?"

"Lots of people show up at funerals. Look, in the unlikely event I agreed to do this, I'd want a good-sized retainer."

Dodge opened his desk drawer and handed him a pale green sheet of paper. A bank draft. "That get you started?"

It was an absurdly large sum. But perhaps, Wyatt reflected, not large enough for what Dodge had asked him to do. He handed it back and turned towards the door. "Hang onto it. I'll let you know what I decide."

Jolted to half-consciousness by the Johnson's muddy coffee, Wyatt stumbled out into the April morning. He had survived opening night, which was as much as could be expected in the circumstances. He hadn't missed any lines, the applause at the end seemed warm enough, but he hadn't lost himself in the character as he did when he really knew a part. The exaltation that accompanied a really good performance, the feeling any serious actor craved like a drug, still seemed a long way off. Even with Giovanna's warmth at his side, his sleep had been shallow, his mind reverberating with what Dodge had asked him to do.

Washington was in exuberant bloom, beds of bright tulips everywhere, tree branches pink-frothed with blossoms of apple, cherry, and plum, bobbing lightly in the breeze. He made his way to the church through the wooded paths of the Mall, almost being run over by several members of the fashionable equestrian class who used the area to exercise their pedigreed mounts and be seen by one another. He turned towards the White House and up to All Souls Unitarian on L Street. It was a famous old congregation, active in the abolitionist movement around the Civil War. A man of Nielsen's sensibilities would have found welcome there.

When he reached Pennsylvania Avenue, he recalled with not a little irony the triumphant veterans' parade in which he had been persuaded to ride when Roosevelt's famous regiment, sick and depleted from tropical fever, returned from Cuba. Rose's condition had worsened in his absence, as he should have expected, the long struggle ending mere weeks afterward. He had finally, he thought, put it all behind him, but Dodge's summons of the previous day had reopened the old wound. Anger surged in his chest. Dodge's request was monstrous. His own acquiescence, however tentative, even more so.

Robert Nielsen might have been unpopular with his colleagues, but his funeral had drawn a full house. The nave of the small church was packed with prosperous-looking men in unseasonable black suits; Wyatt recognized Speaker Joe Cannon and Vice-President Fairbanks. Few wives had accompanied the House members, however, and the gathering had a notably masculine air. Wyatt installed himself in the lightly populated north transept. A dubious-looking array of idlers and curiosity-seekers around him pointed and whispered, along with corvid clusters of ladies of a certain age, as familiar an accompaniment of funerals as the black-plumed horses drawing the hearse. Reporters jostled one another for aisle seats opposite the political notables, no doubt hoping to catch some on the way out for some ill-advised speculation on their colleague Latham's involvement in Nielsen's death.

The old Lothario himself was in evidence; chin held defiantly high, leaning heavily on his walking-stick, Latham strode in with his wife on his arm. Mrs. Latham looked pinch-faced and old in a dull black silk which did not suit her. Wyatt shrank back in his seat. Two or three reporters made a feint towards Latham but were repulsed by a scowl and a peremptory wave of the hand. Wyatt felt a fleeting twinge of sympathy for the besieged Congressman. No doubt the jackals had been camped outside his home too.

Heads swiveled as the choir began a mournful rendition of "O God, Our Help in Ages Past" and a somber sextet of men bearing Nielsen's simple oak coffin on their shoulders began a slow, swaying march down the flagged aisle. A short, solid figure in a black robe emerged from a door in the sanctuary wall and stood waiting to meet them, serene and silent. Ulysses G. B. Pierce was a preacher of distinction, his sermons already published though he had been the church's chief minister for barely three years. He looked around the congregation with a gaze that seemed to Wyatt at once knowing and infinitely forgiving, the look of a man who understood and sympathized with human frailties while rarely being tempted himself. As the strains of the hymn died away, Pierce stepped forward to lay a hand on the coffin, set on a low bier.

A loud rustling and murmur of voices in the south transept distracted the minister and the congregation: a crowd of several dozen Negroes, mostly dressed in shabby but well-kept Sunday clothes, began to file into the pews, led by a sallow-skinned, angular young woman with steel-framed glasses whose eyes, Wyatt could see from across the narrow sanctuary, were red-rimmed and swollen. But she held her head high on a long, slender neck, staring at the minister and congregation as though daring anyone to remark on the group's presence. A buzz of whispers spread through the black-suited worthies in the nave, looks ranging from stunned curiosity to frank hostility. The Reverend Pierce inclined his head graciously to the newcomers and, with a mild gesture, silenced the whispers. He ascended to the pulpit, and his "Dearly beloved" pointedly included the occupants of the south transept.

It began as a standard enough eulogy for a Congressman, Wyatt thought, but it was enlivened by Pierce's obviously close acquaintance with its subject, his sympathy with the man's causes, and his shock and outrage over the manner of Nielsen's death. "Robert Nielsen's militant spirit," he intoned carefully, "did not endear him to all who knew him, as the manner of his death so clearly suggests. Nonetheless, we will remember him as a man of courage and conviction, doing the work of God in this wicked world on behalf of the poor and the oppressed. And we pray that God will find it in His heart to have mercy on the benighted soul who committed this grievous act—"

"We do no such thing!"

In the collective gasp that followed, the bespectacled young woman who had led in the group of Negroes was on her feet in the aisle of the south transept. Pierce turned a surprised but benign gaze on the interloper, who stared back at him and then stepped out into the body of the church.

"God forgives the sinner who repents and owns his deed." Her voice, low-pitched and resonant with conviction, carried easily throughout the church. "But when that sinner takes refuge in the trappings of his high office, the community must call him to account! Richard Latham, you will answer to God for this—" her voice quavered but she took a deep breath, "—this good man's death, and to the law of man as well! Why is this murderer still at large?"

There were murmurs of "Amen," and "Say it, Sister," among the poorer-looking Negroes, offset by hisses of outrage in the larger congregation. "Who is she?" "How dare she come in here—"

Wyatt's gaze flew to Latham, sitting rigid and clench-jawed among his House colleagues, his blue eyes ablaze with indignation. He half-rose from his seat but was restrained by his wife's hand on his sleeve. As abruptly as she had risen, the young woman returned to her pew, biting her lip, her shoulders heaving, on the verge of another bout of tears. What had she been to the murdered man?

Pierce's mellifluous voice brought the crowd's attention back to the pulpit.

"The ways of God are not man's ways," he said mildly, "nor is divine justice to be equated with that fallible product of man's. God sees into the hearts of men, and perhaps only God will ever know who took our brother Nielsen's life and why." He went on, knitting up the torn fabric of his sermon while giving respectful acknowledgment to the righteous anger of the young woman and the dark-faced community for which she spoke. Pierce was well suited to a ministry in Washington, Wyatt thought, glancing at Latham again. Spots of anger still burned in the Congressman's cheeks but, search as he might, Wyatt could see nothing of the "guilty thing surpris'd" in the face.

But the young woman was surely convinced. Wyatt scrutinized her from his vantage point: half a head taller than Giovanna, a long, almost equine face, hair of an indeterminate brown wisping out from under a small-brimmed black hat at least three years out of fashion, as was the black cotton sateen of the dress, the sort favored for wear in offices and other places where young women earned an underpaid but respectable living. The eyes, when she took off the glasses to wipe them, were large and of a luminous gray, the mouth wide under a slightly hooked nose, almost sensually full, exotic in a face that otherwise brought to mind the ascetic. Her bosom, modest in both coverings and proportions, heaving still as she tried to master the emotions that had led to her remarkable outburst, a fatherly-looking Negro man in tweeds patting her hand and murmuring with kindly sympathy in her ear.

With the end of the service, reporters buzzed among the House members streaming out, looking for quotes. The young woman and her entourage were leaving the south transept, forming the rear of the crowd streaming down the nave behind the coffin-bearers. Wyatt contrived to slip into the stream of mourners at a point where the main body melded into the more unorthodox group behind.

"...no surprise, really," a portly senior Congressman a few rows ahead was saying. "Sort of common-law wife...Stanstead, I think, Lucy or some such...partner in crime on all that rabble-rousing he did with the Negroes..." the speaker caught a faster current in the crowd and moved out of Wyatt's hearing range. Latham and his wife drifted into range and Wyatt dropped back a few steps.

"...would surely have done better to set a moral example for those poor Negroes," Mrs. Latham was hissing into her husband's ear, "instead of providing more fodder for scandal..."

The procession moved down the church steps. The coffin was being loaded into a glass hearse drawn by black-plumed horses for the journey to the Baltimore & Potomac station, where a train would take Nielsen's body back to Wisconsin for burial. At the other end would be a sister and her family; no parents were left to grieve the untimely loss of a son. The only funeral flowers being placed on the coffin were two small wreaths, one each from the House and Senate, Wyatt presumed, and a modest spray of red roses and fern tied with a white ribbon. Wyatt followed the gaze of the young woman, her eyes once again awash with tears, and guessed it to have come from her.

The coachman adjusted his old-fashioned top hat and flicked his whip. The horses began a slow trot, the stream of mourners easily keeping up as the mourning-coach and a few other conveyances of dignitaries and elders made its way towards the Gothic spires and turrets of the Baltimore & Potomac station. The new Union Terminal, all marble magnificence though not yet complete, gleamed white in the spring sunlight.

Wyatt let himself drift along with the crowd. The young woman's outcry intrigued him. What perversity of mind was leading him to doubt her conviction that Latham was Nielsen's killer? He didn't doubt for a minute that the old Casanova could have enticed some woman with sufficiently low standards into giving him a convenient alibi. Or his wife, for that matter. Still, surely he'd have had more sense than to use a cane that was unmistakably his as the murder weapon.

Perhaps there was more history between Nielsen and Latham than was generally known. Perhaps this strange young woman, if she had indeed been Nielsen's paramour, knew something that would clinch Latham's guilt once and for all, something Wyatt could throw in Dodge's face to force him to face up to the fact that the man who'd done him a few political favors was a liar and a murderer.

He waited to approach her until the funeral guests had retreated to Willard's for the customary luncheon. The Negroes had melted away, no doubt back to the work from which they could ill afford to take time off.

She stood alone, then, on the platform, watching the funeral train till it dwindled to a westbound speck and disappeared. She removed her glasses and polished them on her skirt. In profile she was more striking, the skin more olive than sallow, the hook-nosed face reminiscent of some image from an ancient Greek coin, at once regal and tragic. In her dull black dress and rigid posture she seemed contained, encapsulated.

"Miss…Stanstead?" Wyatt doffed his black homburg. She turned towards him with a look of bleak reserve and began to walk back down the platform.

"I'm not talking to the press."

"I'm not a journalist. I am a—an investigator. My name is Dade Wyatt. I have been asked to look into Mr. Nielsen's death."

She frowned. "I've already had several interviews with the Detective Bureau. Please, it's not a good time—"

"I, ah, don't work for them," Wyatt said.

Her head jerked up quickly and her eyes flashed scorn and fury. "I see—that monster has hired you to help him evade the consequences of his crime." She swept past him towards the waiting-room. "You'll forgive me if I don't wish you success."

CHAPTER 4

Alexis Germain, Warren Dodge's Creole steward, dropped the wallpaper sample he was holding and stared in wonder at his employer's back.

"Did I just hear you say you asked *Wyatt* to investigate this?"

Dodge turned from the stepladder where he had unrolled another sample against the wall. "I think the dark green's better with the gold. That maroon is oppressive—though I suppose Augusta ought to have a look at it."

"It's *your* study." Germain picked up the fallen roll and twirled it absently in his hands. "But Miz Dodge does have a good eye." Dodge had bought a trio of four-story brick townhouses, built on speculation and not quite complete, on Belmont Road in the not-as-yet fashionable neighborhood just north of Dupont Circle. The middle house would be a temporary Congressional home until he and Augusta found something more stately in an older and more prestigious neighborhood. Transplanted daffodils and hyacinths were already blooming in the small garden, but the place was unfinished and smelled of new paint.

The house was coming along more slowly than Germain liked. He'd hoped to be back overseeing Dodge's Manhattan household by now, listening to Caruso and Patti on his new Victor phonograph in his own little book-lined lair.

"Wyatt's not all the way in yet," Dodge was saying. "But he will be once he's convinced Latham didn't do it. He won't be able to resist finding out who did." He climbed down from the ladder and handed Germain the unfurled wallpaper.

"They don't pay him enough at that Shakespeare company?" Germain's hands automatically rolled up the wallpaper.

"They're at the end of the run. You'll see him, he'll have it down cold—" He stopped, flushing, clearly having forgotten that as a Negro, Germain wouldn't be allowed into the National Theatre. Slender and olive-skinned, a head taller than his employer, Germain had the exotic good looks of his mixed blood, the blood that had barred many doors to him in his native Louisiana and still did so in the capital of a supposedly enlightened nation.

Germain raised an eyebrow, but left it at that. "Seems to me the man's finally gotten healed up. This could tear him right open again."

Dodge poured two mugs of coffee from a carafe on a newspaper-covered table and handed one to Germain. "I hadn't looked at it that way," he admitted, perching on the edge of a paint-splattered stool. "He's still nursing a grudge against Latham, no question."

"Hates his guts, you mean." Germain sipped his coffee. "Wouldn't you?"

"Wyatt wants to think Latham's money could have saved her. Maybe it's easier to blame somebody else than think about the things you could have done differently yourself."

"The gal's dying, and her father won't even answer a letter." Germain put down his cup and began folding up the stepladder.

Dodge shrugged. "He's a difficult man. But Rose was a difficult woman at times. I wonder what I'd do if Amy got mixed up with—"

"You wouldn't have sent her to Miss Willard's if you wanted her to come out a dainty li'l lady," Germain laughed, shaking his head.

"She's dissecting frogs these days. Thinks she wants to be a lady doctor. Her mother's afraid she'll turn out unmarriageable."

Amy Dodge, Germain reflected, wasn't likely to be troubled by that thought. "Anyway, how's he going to manage Macbeth and all that too—*if* he's crazy enough to agree to it?"

"He doesn't have a day job," Dodge grinned. "He may need some help from you. This Nielsen fellow was a bit of a hero to the colored community around here. Somebody there may know something about who else had it in for him."

Germain frowned over the stepladder. "You're forgetting I'm a stranger here myself. And I need to be getting back to New York soon."

Dodge's eyes circled up to the unpainted egg-and-dart molding of the high ceiling and down to the study doorway, which as yet held no door. "At the rate this is going, you'd best plan on another month here. Somebody's got to ride herd on this crew. Take the train up for a day or so if you're worried, but the staff can get along without you a while longer."

Germain stifled a sigh. Dodge was the best employer a man could ask for, as a rule, but sometimes he pushed things. "Suppose we wait and see how Wyatt and his wife's daddy get along, before you go signing me up as a side-kick detective."

"Getting along is a bit much to hope for," Dodge grinned. "Temporary toleration's probably the best he can manage."

"You haven't known this man Latham long," Germain said. "Why are you so determined to save him?"

Dodge looked up at him and shrugged as if surprised by the question. "He didn't do it."

Wyatt was talking to Louisa Stanstead's retreating back.

"I have been asked, not retained—"

She turned back to him, shaking her head. "That travesty of a funeral! Not one person—" she turned her head away and rummaged in a small reticule for a handkerchief. When she spoke again, her voice quavered. "Not one bore Robert the least good will—" she buried her face in the linen. Wyatt stood silent as she composed herself, resisting the temptation to place a friendly hand on her arm.

She steadied her voice with a great shudder. "If not for those loyal colored friends, Robert would not have had a friend in that whole church. Not those hypocrites from Capitol Hill, nor my sensation-seeking colleagues, much less the *hirelings* of his murderer—"

Wyatt reeled inwardly, but kept his composure. "You're a journalist?"

She flashed a grim smile, and Wyatt saw in her face the light that must have drawn Nielsen to her.

"A lady reporter, yes. A muckraker, a scandalmonger—I've been called many things. But the one thing I've never been called is Robert Nielsen's wife. And that I was, in all but name."

She stared defiance at him, spun on her heel and hurried away. The waiting-room door slammed behind her and he was left alone on the platform. He hesitated a moment and strode after her, half-blinded by the sunlight reflecting off the great windows of the waiting-room.

When he opened the door, the ticket-agent was scrambling out of his booth. Louisa Stanstead had fallen backwards in a heap on the plush carpeting between the rows of chairs. Her spectacles hung at a crazy angle from one ear. Wyatt ran and dropped to her side. She was deathly pale, but breathing. He waved the anxious ticket-agent away. "Fetch some water and a damp cloth."

The man nodded and vanished into the station. Wyatt took her wrist and felt for a pulse. It seemed slow but steady. Her eyelids began to flutter.

"Miss Stanstead?"

"What happened?"

"You fainted. The ticket-man's bringing some water."

"I felt so light-headed—it was like a tunnel—" She began to sit up and seemed to think better of it.

"Best if you lie still, for a few minutes," Wyatt said. "Let the blood come back to your head. Here." He pulled a plush cushion from a nearby chair and gently tucked it under her head.

The ticket-man came back with a glass of water and Wyatt helped her sit up enough to take a few sips. He dabbed the wet cloth gently around her neck and forehead, tucking the stray spectacle-stem back behind her ear. Passengers began trickling into the waiting-room. She looked around in alarm and started to get up.

"It's all right," Wyatt said. "Just a faint," he said to a pair of elderly matrons bearing down on them.

Louisa Stanstead sat up and braced her elbow against the cushion, taking a few slow breaths. "I think I'm all right now."

"Let's get you into a chair," Wyatt said. "Take my hands and get up very slowly. There—put your head down for a minute."

With the water-glass in hand, he watched her. The curve of her back in its thin black jacket, the hands wrapped around the upper arms, seemed terribly vulnerable. When she raised her head, he said, "It's been a devil of a day for you. I'll wager you forgot to eat this morning."

She nodded. "I'm sorry to put you to so much trouble. Mr., uh, Wyman."

"Wyatt," he smiled. "If you feel up to moving, let me buy you a cup of tea. We needn't talk about—anything you don't care to."

She hesitated, came to a decision. "That's kind of you." She stood up slowly and allowed him to take her arm.

"Will the station café be all right, or would you prefer something more private?"

She gave him a wintry, sideways smile. "I've caused a great deal of scandal already today. What's a little more?"

Louisa Stanstead sat across the marble-topped table from him in the dim café, the cup of tea cooling in her hands, taking a nibble at intervals from the stale-looking raisin bun he'd bought her.

"You are a private detective. A Pinkerton man?"

"I was, briefly. I'm an actor. For a while I earned my living as an investigator."

She peered at him through her thick lenses and nodded. "You have the looks for it. Acting, I mean." There was no hint of flirtatiousness in her tone; it was a simple observation. "I've not heard your name."

"I'm with the Sothern & Marlowe troupe. We just arrived in Washington a few days ago."

She smiled. "Robert and I love Shakespeare—" her voice caught and she looked away for a moment. Wyatt remembered all those moments after Rose died, when he talked of what *we* like, what *we* did, before he'd remember there was no more *we*. She cleared her throat. "We were going to have a night out together. To see *Macbeth*. Are you in it?"

"Yes. We opened last night."

"This man who asked you to do this—he must be a good friend, if you're spending your daylight time in this fashion. Or perhaps it's a small part?" She seemed genuinely curious, not out to insult.

"It is a good friend. And it all seems too neat—Latham's cane at the scene, for instance." He saw her head drop and she bit her lip. "I'm sorry—"

She shook her head. "I'm going to be living with this for a long time."

"Of course, people who murder, particularly in anger, aren't necessarily thinking clearly," he said. "But I understood you to say Mr. Nielsen may not have been popular with his colleagues—"

He was relieved to see her laugh. "If you get tired of acting, Mr. Wyatt, you should take up diplomacy."

"The thing is," he said, "I knew Latham well, years ago. He's arrogant and vengeful, no doubt—but surely he could have killed anything of a legislative nature that Robert—Mr. Nielsen—cared about. Wouldn't he be more likely to take his revenge that way?"

She took a thoughtful nibble of the bun and chewed for a moment. "They'd already tried putting Robert on the D.C. Committee. Thinking he'd find nothing to interest him there! I suppose Latham could have got the Speaker to put a hold on all Robert's bills, and move him to the Committee on the Disposal of Obsolete Government Records—" she stopped and frowned. "You know, it is hard to think a man like Latham would have the guts to murder someone himself."

Wyatt pushed his coffee mug aside. "If that's so, the man we're after is an opportunist. And presumably isn't fond of Latham either."

"Or the woman. Don't the police always suspect the wife?"

"With a few exceptions," Wyatt smiled, "I've found the police lacking in imagination."

"You seem a nice man, Mr. Wyatt. How did you mix yourself up with someone like Latham?"

Wyatt shrugged and picked up the coffee-mug again. "I married his daughter."

Her eyes widened, then narrowed. "And blood is thicker than water?"

"He disowned her. They never spoke again."

"But you reconciled after her death."

"Far from it!" Wyatt stared at her, puzzled. "How did you—"

"You'd have said, 'They haven't spoken since.' So—why, then?"

"Well, not because he's family," he smiled over the rim of his coffee mug. "A mutual friend—that good friend I mentioned—called in a favor. I said I'd talk to the man, but—"

"You have as much reason to hate him as I do." She seemed unsure all of a sudden.

"*If* he killed your—Mr. Nielsen."

"Who else could it have been?" She half-rose, then dropped back and buried her face in her hands. "Oh, God! I'm just as responsible for Robert's death as he is."

Wyatt's hand on her shoulder brought her head up. "If we hadn't quarreled that morning," she whispered, "Robert wouldn't have been so angry, and wouldn't have said what he did on the House floor. And he'd still be alive." She stood abruptly, shaking off his hand, and gave him a bright little smile. "Well, that's no concern of yours. Thank you for the tea, Mr. Wyatt. I'm late for a meeting." She took a great, ragged breath. "His work will *not* die with him."

Wyatt nodded. "May I call on you, if I—"

She opened her hands and gave him a weary nod, then turned and hurried out of the café. He sank back into his chair and stared after her. He would give a great deal to know what that quarrel was about.

CHAPTER 5

In the cheerful light of a spring Saturday, there was nothing sinister about the murder site. A brick-paved sidewalk heaving with roots and weeds, a tight little row of neatly kept, plain-fronted brick houses forming a continuous line. Trees just showing the first pale green dots that would become leaves in another two weeks, with gas streetlights at widely spaced intervals.

The closest the police had come to a witness, Dodge had told him, was an old Negro woman who lived in a second-floor apartment at the corner off 24th and I Streets Northwest. Nielsen's body had been found in the odd little triangle formed by the south arc of Washington Circle, 24th Street Northwest, and New Hampshire Avenue, in the borderland between Foggy Bottom and the beginnings of the embassy district. Mrs. Washington had heard scuffling and thumping, raised voices, a cut-off cry, near her window around eleven o'clock. But she wasn't about to go out and investigate—and besides, the noises could have come from Snow's Court, a disreputable alley at the back of her building, where "folks gits up to all kinda things, day and night," as the lady had told the police. In any case, she'd had no telephone to summon help.

When the two Negro workers returning from their night shift at Heurich's brewery found the Congressman's body in the triangle, Nielsen had been dead for several hours. The men had done all that police could have wished; one ran to the precinct house while the other stood guard over the body. The police had found Latham's silver-knobbed cane, caked and sticky with blood, in a nearby clump of bushes.

The door to Mrs. Washington's apartment, shared with the downstairs neighbor, was opened by a plump younger woman, who scowled when he explained the purpose of his visit.

"Police done talked to Mama already. She told 'em everything she remembers."

Wyatt held his homburg deferentially. "I don't doubt that, ma'am, but sometimes details come back to a person after a time. If I could just talk with her for five minutes—"

"She sleepin' now. Come back another time. Tomorrow, maybe." She closed the door in Wyatt's face with great deliberation. He was a white man, a stranger. Perhaps if Germain had been with him…

He made his way west to Nielsen's small rented house. It was clapboard rather than brick, just north of I Street on 25th Street Northwest. If she had indeed been his wife in all but name, this was Louisa Stanstead's home as well. It was one of those neighborhoods unique to Washington, most of the houses fronting the streets belonging to whites, with warrens of alleys in the interiors of the blocks, inhabited by the sorts of poor black folk who had accompanied Louisa to Nielsen's funeral.

Recalling Dodge's warning about the neighborhood, he made his way past Nielsen's house and into the narrow mouth of Snow's Court, which proved to be a labyrinthine blind alley with numerous branches. He drew only passing glances from the women scrubbing heavy, sodden sheets against washboards and dull-eyed men in undershirts and gallused trousers, sorting through piles of rubbish in the middle of the alley for metal, wood and other salvageable items that might garner them a few pennies. The screeches of children at play and the colicky wails of babies echoed off the alley walls.

Tin-roofed brick houses no bigger than gardening huts huddled together on either side of the alley, their rickety wood porches sticking out into the cobbled passage, leaving barely enough room to walk. The day's warmth intensified the stench of rotting vegetables and slops and over-used wooden privies. He wondered whether even Germain would make any headway here. No one would mistake him for a brother in poverty.

"You lookin' for somebody, mister?" A graying man with a slouch hat and a day's growth of stubble rose from the stoop where he'd been sitting and limped towards him, a pile of whittled wood-shavings falling at his feet. His tone and expression held neither challenge nor friendliness.

Wyatt tipped his hat. "Name's Dade Wyatt. I came by hoping to talk with Mrs. Washington—" he waved his arm back towards the alley entrance, "but Miss Washington tells me that she's not, uh, at home at the moment."

The man's brow's knit in something between curiosity and disapproval. "What you want with ol' Miz Washington? You work for the landlord?"

Startled at first, Wyatt broke into a smile. "Good heavens, no. I didn't know she had one. I'm a, uh, Congressional investigator. I've been asked to look into the recent murder." Did Congressional investigators ever looked into murders? He didn't know, but hoped his interlocutor didn't either.

The man's sardonic laugh showed a brief flash of yellow teeth against his tawny skin. "Which one? Had two of 'em here in the last month. Weren't no question of who did it, though."

Wyatt raised his eyebrows in polite inquiry.

"Do-mestic disputes, guess you'd call 'em."

"This happen a lot here?" Wyatt said, as if asking about milk deliveries.

"Don't know as you could say that," the man replied thoughtfully. "Had been pret'near a year since the last one. Folks crowded in like this, though," he swept a well-muscled arm in a half-circle, "bound to cause friction. Summer 'specially. Fistfights, mostly, maybe break a bottle on the head here and there. Most folks just keeps their heads down and tries to get by."

Wyatt took a stab in the dark, studying the man's face and seeming to remember something.

"Weren't you at Congressman Nielsen's funeral?"

The man's eyes narrowed. "So happens I was. That what you came here to ask about?"

"I thought I'd seen you before. That's the murder I'm looking into."

The man gave a short laugh and turned away. "That case, I can't tell you nothin' about it. 'Cept he was a righteous man and it ain't right what happened to him."

"You were one of the gentlemen with Miss Stanstead."

At the mention of Louisa's name, the man turned back and considered him. "Come on over here and set a minute." He limped back to the stoop and brushed a few curls of wood from the top step, sat down and extended his hand, which was callused and strong in Wyatt's grasp. "Name's Joseph Franklin. Wyatt, you say your name was?"

"That's right. Pleased to meet you."

"What you got to investigate anyways? Didn't they find that fella's cane and all?"

Wyatt squinted in the sun making its way over the roofs of the buildings opposite. "He claims he was somewhere else at the time. If that's so, somebody might have set him up. Did you know Mr. Nielsen?"

Franklin scratched the back of his neck, tipping his hat forward into his eyes. "He come back here, time to time, bring his laundry to Ella's over there. Talk with folks."

"What about?"

"Oh, you know, him bein' on the D.C. Committee and all, livin' just around the corner, seein' how folks lived back in here. Thought something should be done, you know? Got no sewers here, just the pumps for water, landlords charge nine, ten bucks a month and you see what you get for that."

"He was from Wisconsin, wasn't he? Why did he care?"

Franklin's guffaw was rich and resonant. "Way I've heard it, they marked him for a troublemaker his first term. Had him on the Judiciary Committee first, bein' a lawyer, but then he starts puttin' in bills to give ladies the vote and such, so they bust him down to the D.C. Committee, where they figure he can't make no trouble and it won't help him with the folks back home. Next thing, he's got bills in to give ever'body in D.C. the vote, and two Senators just like it was a state."

"Couldn't have been very popular in the House, then."

Franklin raised a shrewd eyebrow. "Well, you'd know more about that than I would." He picked up a stick and resumed his whittling.

"I only go up there when they call me in," Wyatt improvised. "What did people hereabouts think of him?"

Franklin stroked his stubbly chin. "When that man decided he was in the right about somethin', he wouldn't let it go. He'd be tryin' to help, you know—get some clean water in here so the li'l babies wouldn't be dyin' from the typhoid. Miz Conklin over there—" he nodded towards a bony, dark woman sitting on a doorstep, limp-armed and staring at the ground, "she los' her youngest a couple weeks ago. Mr. Nielsen come by to commis'rate. He was like that. Righteous. And after he started walkin' out with Miss Louisa, well, then, we figured he was all right. You talk to her?"

"A little bit, after the funeral." Wyatt shifted the brim of his own hat to shade his eyes. "She seemed to be taking it pretty hard. She said she's a reporter?"

"She is now. Got hired by some charity committee to come down to the alleys and write reports about the conditions. But nothin' got done, so she quit workin' for them folks and started writin' for the papers. Sometimes the *Star*, sometimes onea them muckraker magazines, you know?"

"*McClure's? Collier's?*"

"Yeah, onea them. She's even put stuff in the *Washington Bee.* That's the colored folks' paper 'round here," he said proudly in reply to Wyatt's inquiring look. "'Honey for our friends, stings for our enemies,' is what Mr. Chase says. Anyway, Miss Louisa's good people. We was layin' bets on when they was gonna get married."

"People here liked them?"

"Well, he wasn't the easiest fella to like, you know? But he wasn't like some that come around tryin' to get us off the demon rum and savin' our souls an' such, when you can tell they'd be scared to be left alone here for five minutes."

Wyatt smiled. Nielsen must have known, and pitied, a good many of the "alley-whores" he'd taunted Latham with.

"Wait a minute," Franklin said, standing and dusting off his trousers, "lemme ax you somethin'. Why would y'all believe that Latham fella when he says he didn't do it? Ever'body knows what happened in the House that day."

Wyatt rose, dusting off his pants in his turn. "Fair question. Some of my, ah, colleagues are checking out his alibi. If it turns out he's telling the truth, we need to be looking for somebody else. Who maybe tried to set him up on top of it."

Franklin shrugged as if to acknowledge the fairness of this.

"Mr. Franklin, can you think of anyone around here—any of the local folks—" he didn't say 'colored'—"that Mr. Nielsen might have done some injury to, or caused them some trouble?"

Franklin chuckled. "Not 'less you count Costello—" He broke off, looking as if he wished the words unsaid. Wyatt stayed silent.

Franklin hesitated. "Aw, it ain't nothin'. He was sweet on Miss Louisa before she and Mr. Nielsen got together, that's all."

"Is he a colored man?"

"Now don't you take nothin' from what I said. That didn't make no difference to Miss Louisa. No disrespect, but we think she might have a li'l bit of colored blood herself, somewhere back there. Seemed like he was courtin' her for a while before she met the Congressman."

"And Nielsen moved in on him?"

Franklin shrugged. "Poor fella's unlucky in love, know what I mean? A mite too serious for his own good, maybe. Back when he was in high school he was walkin' out with a pretty li'l gal. Miz Wilbur's daughter. But she done disappeared up north— ain't nobody heard from her in years. Might be passin', she was light enough for it—" Franklin stopped and his expression grew sober. "He's a good man, Costello. He teaches history over at the M Street School now. Takes his job real serious. Workin' hard to advance the race. I shouldn't a said nothin' like that about him."

"You were saying Miss Louisa—ah, Miss Stanstead and Mr. Nielsen were trying to improve conditions here?"

"Tha's right."

Wyatt's arm swept around to take in the alley dwellings. "Who owns these buildings, do you know? Maybe he didn't like Nielsen interfering in his business. Making things difficult for him."

Franklin grinned. "I told you that, I might bring trouble on my own self."

"But you do know a name," Wyatt pressed.

"Truth is I'm not sure. Places have changed hands a few times." He took a deep breath and blew it out. Wyatt waited. "Last I heard it was somebody Dunagin. You didn't hear that from me. Anyways, they send a couple goons around every month to collect the rent, is all I know. Irish fellas, they sound like. Nobody you wanna mess with. I sure don't."

Wyatt pulled a dollar piece and a visiting card from his pocket. "Point taken. Mr. Franklin, I appreciate your time. May I—"

The man's eyes widened. He started to shake his head, but changed his mind and pocketed the coin. "I ain't sellin' nothin' here. Just answerin' a few questions. Hadn't been I got turned down at the slave market this mornin', I wouldn't take it." He laughed at the shocked look on Wyatt's face.

"Over on Washington Circle, where they come to pick up day-laborers from the neighborhood—that's what we call it. They think I'm too old for a hard day's work. Some day they'll be right, I guess."

Wyatt turned towards the mouth of the alley. "I'm obliged to you. If you think of anything else that might help, will you get in touch with me?" He pointed to the card in Franklin's hand, where he'd crossed out his New York home address and penned in the name and address of the Johnson Hotel. It was far from luxurious, but he wondered if the man had ever seen the place.

"Mr. Wyatt," Franklin called after him. He stopped and turned towards him.

"If that ol' white man didn't kill Mr. Nielsen, folks 'round here would take it as a favor if you'd find out who did."

"If I do, I'll come back and let you know." On his way back around the cut-off corner of 24th and I Streets, Wyatt looked up at the second-floor window from which the old woman had heard the attack on Nielsen, just in time to see a hand withdraw and a curtain close.

CHAPTER 6

Giovanna Treadwell froze in her steps at the look on Wyatt's face when he strode backstage that evening. "What's wrong? What's happened?"

"We'll talk later," he said through gritted teeth, his hand on his dressing-room door.

She grabbed him by the arm. "Please. Just tell me—so *I* can settle."

"Oh, Mrs. T!" Frederick Lewis, the young actor who'd replaced Wyatt as the Earl of Ross, rushed up to her. "You're here! May we run the lines again?"

Wyatt nodded curtly to him and ducked into his dressing room, slamming the door behind him. Giovanna turned to Lewis and took in a sharp breath. "Of course, Fred. Green room or stage?"

Her heart hammered in her chest. It was bad enough to think about walking out on that stage and not knowing who might be sitting out there in the dark waiting to expose her. Had someone said something to Wyatt?

He had known it wouldn't go well from the moment he approached the wrought-iron gates of the faux-chateau off Connecticut Avenue, walking slowly since he was a few minutes early. The hollow churning in his gut, recalling the last time he'd been face to face with Latham. The scene seared in his memory: Latham denouncing him, before his weeping daughter, as a "degenerate actor who has seduced her into his own degraded style of living and turned her against her own family."

Rose's back had stiffened at that. She'd stopped the tears with a great intake of breath and told her father that it was the family who'd turned against her, seized Wyatt's arm and pulled him out of the house she'd grown up in, never to return.

In the filtered light of his study, Latham's face showed the passage of twenty years, his silver hair thinner than it had seemed at a distance in the church. But there had been enough traces of his fine, aristocratic features in Rose to give Wyatt a fresh stab of loss at the sight of him. To his relief, Latham behaved as if they had never met, and did not offer to shake hands.

"What do you need to know?" He folded his arms on an inlaid Louis XV desk, the shelves of tooled leather books behind him completing the picture of patrician elegance.

"Your movements after six o'clock on the evening of the murder. And your opinion as to how your walking-stick came to be at the scene."

"You believe me to be innocent, then?" Latham's eyes were cold, but there was a hint of eagerness, perhaps desperation, in the question.

"I doubt you'd have been foolish enough to leave such evidence behind. Perhaps you can identify others likely to have harbored as warm a grievance against Nielsen as your own."

"As to that," Latham considered, "he had few friends on the Hill, a handful of those Populist rabble-rousers and bleeding-heart reformers—"

Wyatt produced a small notebook from his jacket pocket. "I'd want those names too."

"—but until that day, his insults and slanders had been largely of a less—ah, personal, more political nature."

"Whoever did this—if it wasn't you—was determined to tie you to the crime, and may also be presumed to have a grudge against you as well as Nielsen." Wyatt rose from the velvet-upholstered chair and paced the parquetry floor. "I should think one grudge may be personal and the other political."

"That's logical enough," Latham said.

"It was also someone with ready access either to the House cloakroom or to wherever you keep your walking-sticks at home."

"I generally kept it in the cloakroom, but as I was—somewhat distracted on my way out of the Chamber that day, I took it home and left it in the umbrella-stand there. In the vestibule of the side entrance, where tradesmen and servants are coming and going constantly. The—ah, stick was a gift from…an old friend," Latham added, reddening.

Wyatt sat and let his gaze bear down on Latham's face. "The same friend who constitutes your unusable alibi?"

Latham's nostrils flared. "No."

"Might this…old friend have any reason to wish you ill?"

"Absolutely not," Latham growled. "The friend has—uh, it is nothing to do with the matter at hand."

"We can't make many such assumptions."

"Understood." Latham poured himself water from a crystal carafe but offered Wyatt nothing.

"Any of your household staff have a grudge against you?"

Latham frowned. "They are as well paid and fed as any in this town, especially for Negroes as most of them are. The usual problems with shiftlessness and malingering, nothing a good thrashing with a riding-crop won't take care of. A stable-boy who put my Arabian away without a proper rub-down, that sort of thing."

"Does he still work for you?"

"Went back where he came from down South, I was told. If I were you I'd concentrate on Nielsen's so-called friends in the House, or some of those do-gooders he ran with who haunt the halls urging their social schemes. With the low morals of that lot, there'll have been some jealousies occasioned in the course of exercising their free-love prerogatives."

Wyatt arched an eyebrow and stared. "Low morals."

"There's nothing that crowd wouldn't countenance—marriage with Negroes, sodomy, open adultery—well, for that matter, you might start with that doxy of his. The harridan who vilified me at the funeral—maybe she did him in once she realized he wasn't about to marry her when he could get it for free."

"And what about the 'doxy' you claim as an alibi?"

Latham shot to his feet, fists clenched, face scarlet. "How dare you!"

46

Wyatt rose, shaking his head, and opened the door. "Nothing's changed," he said, his voice deadly calm. "I don't know why I thought it should. Go hang for all I care." The slam of the study door echoed behind him and rattled the brass-potted *aspidistras* in the marble foyer.

He vented the ferocity of his encounter with Latham in that night's performance. It heightened Macbeth's anger towards Duncan for naming Malcolm his heir, sharpened the ruthless edge of his instructions to the murderers of Banquo, energized the final great duel with Macduff. He had the lines down now, and in the dark wings between scenes he let his mind drift back to Nielsen's murder. He knew Latham hadn't done it. It would be someone else's job to find out who did. And yet—

He watched Rowland Buckstone stride on stage as Banquo at the beginning of Act 3, musing on Macbeth's unlikely ascension.

> "Thou hast it now: king, Cawdor, Glamis, all
> As the weyard women promised, and I fear
> Thou played'st most foully for it—"

Nobody likes a conscience. His own words to Dodge, the day after the murder. Banquo was a threat to Macbeth because he knew what he must have done to gain the crown...wasn't someone who served as a conscience in your life more likely to start as an ally than an enemy? He joined Buckstone on the stage, sent him off for his fatal ride, and began his own soliloquy:

> "Our fears in Banquo stick deep,
> And in his royalty of nature reigns that
> Which would be feared...
> And under him my genius is rebuked..."

There it was again, the reason Macbeth had Banquo killed: an inconvenient conscience. Had Robert Nielsen known something about someone that they couldn't bear to have known? Something Nielsen's self-righteous nature couldn't or wouldn't keep hidden? Someone he knew, for instance, 'passing' for white— and what was it that Mr. Franklin had said about Louisa having *a li'l bit of colored blood herself?* Wyatt's mind momentarily blurred and he nearly lost the line. Registering alarmed glances from the two Murderers waiting for their entrance in the wings, he hastily pulled himself back into the monologue, filing the uncomfortable thought away.

The lines held; the power of emotion he'd longed for was there, thanks in no small measure to his encounter with Latham. But it nearly undid him in the last act, when Macbeth learned of his wife's death and delivered his great monologue.

"She should have died hereafter," he began. And nearly stopped: his Rose *should* have died hereafter. Richard Latham, who might have changed her mortal course, chose not to. The last letter he'd sent the man: *My wife, your daughter, is dying. I haven't the money to take her to a sanatorium.* Returned unopened.

With a great heave of his chest, he went on. "Tomorrow, and tomorrow, and tomorrow creeps in this petty pace from day to day…" Those lost years after she was gone from him. Easier, now, but it had all come back.

When he came offstage, his tears making runnels through the greasepaint, Mrs. Marlowe was beaming at him in the low light, tears sparkling in her own eyes. "Well done!" she whispered. "Now that's what I call great acting!"

CHAPTER 7

After the hurried change out of her First Witch costume, Giovanna checked her embroidered cap and medieval plaits in the dim backstage mirror and tried to slow her heart. In the quiet of the wings, surely the others must hear it pounding. Wyatt, as arranged, had drawn out his speech at the end of the prior scene, which gave her a few precious seconds. The small boy playing Macduff's doomed son, Billy Harris, gave her a dubious look as if he, too, feared the intruder in the audience. Giovanna swallowed and smiled at him. A child of a famous acting family, he was doing so well for such a little fellow. He'd be carried offstage to be murdered by Macbeth's hired assassins, screaming and kicking out in terror. When they put him down, he'd run into a faraway corner and dissolve into giggles. He reminded her of Jamie, her eight-year-old. Who had his father's wavy hair and chestnut-brown eyes, his mother's quick tongue and teasing humor. Freckles, too, in the summer…

There was a tug at her hand and a child's version of a stage whisper. "We're on, Mrs. T!"

She smoothed the kirtle of her gown, feeling her hands damp on the silky fabric, and followed him out. Stage fright had never been like this.

Wyatt sat at the dressing-table wiping off Macbeth's beetling eyebrows with cold cream. The rose scent of the stuff was nauseating, but nothing worked better on greasepaint. He closed his eyes, reveling in the feeling of having been lost in his character, slowly coming back to earth after a riotous curtain-call. A feeling he hadn't had in a long time, though a small corkscrew of fury and grief, the fury that had energized him, still lay at the pit of his stomach from his interview with Latham.

Behind him, the door opened almost soundlessly. His eyes flew open and he saw in the mirror a tall, hooded figure slip into the room and shut the door behind it. He whirled and stood, grabbing it by its cloaked arms.

He heard a gasp and the hood fell back to reveal the face of a woman he had never met. A long, aquiline nose, creamy olive skin, deep-set, dark-lashed eyes, the pupils dilated to black pools—with agitation, passion, or fear?—yet withal an impression of strength and command as she faced him down.

"Forgive me, Mr. Wyatt." The voice was low, the accent exotic. Spanish? Italian? "Richard told me how to find you."

Behind her, there was a soft tap on the door and it began to open again. Giovanna's head appeared around it, her hair loose and free from its medieval cap. His arms dropped and the woman hastily pulled the hood up, turning away to hide her face. Giovanna's dark eyes took in the scene at a glance. "Oh!" Her hand flew to her mouth. "I—" It came out as a little sob. Before he could say anything, the door slammed shut and she was gone. Heart sinking, he heard her footsteps hurrying down the corridor.

"Sit down," he said, grim-faced. There was a chair beside the door and she sank into it. He sat slowly back on his stool. "You're Latham's alibi."

He studied her face. A beauty in the grand style, perfect bones. The hair pulled back in a twist, deep brown, maybe black. Not much past forty, surely. He'd seen this face somewhere. A picture in the newspaper? His glance fell to her hand, where a great rose-tinted diamond sparkled in the low light. Her opera-cloak was of fine dark wool lined in black satin.

"I am—I was—with him that night. Mr. Wyatt, you must help us."

"I already told him—"

She held up a hand. "I know. We must talk. I cannot stay—the coach is waiting." She thrust a program into his hands. "An autograph, please—for appearance's sake. Come privately tomorrow. Bring your friend, Mrs. Dodge. Please—for the sake of our countries."

Our countries? In a half-daze he rummaged for a pen, found one and scrawled his name across the front of the playbill. She pulled a visiting-card out of a tiny purse and handed it to him.

Mme. Isabel Barros Alves Almeida e Pereira de Lima. 14 Lafayette Square.

Now he knew why she looked familiar. The woman who sat before him was the wife of the Brazilian Ambassador. Whose country was soon to host the Third Pan-American Conference, upon whose success Theodore Roosevelt's foreign policy would depend.

The angry words he'd thrown at Latham came back to him. *The 'doxy' you claim as an alibi.* He felt himself turning scarlet under the greasepaint.

Shaken, Giovanna accepted Fred Lewis's arm for the return to the hotel. She'd never seen Wyatt like that, all cold, barely controlled fury. Had he found out something about her? No, that couldn't be, surely, he had only gone to visit that man, the Congressman accused of murder, where would—but why was he with a woman in his dressing-room? She was well-dressed, wealthy-looking. There were always people at the stage door, hoping for an autograph or proffering an invitation to a private supper—but Wyatt had never let one of them into his dressing-room before, she was sure of it. Something must have happened, someone must have said something…she wouldn't go to his room tonight. She couldn't bear it if he turned her away. And he wouldn't come to her, he'd been too concerned about her reputation…dear God, it was going to be a long night.

A soft knock on her door roused her from the half-doze she'd fallen into in the room's faded armchair. She'd left the bedside lamp on; the small clock next to it said 1:30. She rose and, with her heart thumping, opened the door.

"Where have you been?" Wyatt whispered.

She pulled him in and closed the door quietly behind him. "Who was that woman?"

He laughed softly. "That was no woman. That was the lady in the case. I'm sorry—I wanted to explain after, but you'd gone, and—"

"Fred walked me back. I, ah, didn't know how long you'd be."

Wyatt ran his hand through his hair. "Giovanna! How could you think—"

She collapsed onto the bed, found a sob welling up in her throat. "I didn't know what to think. You were so angry when you came in for call—"

"Good Lord, you thought that had something to do with you?" He sat next to her and put an arm around her shoulder.

She pulled herself upright and looked at him. "People say things sometimes," she said. "Someone sent Mr. Sothern a note saying that he should watch out for Mrs. Marlowe because a 'loose woman' like her was bound to have several lovers…" It sounded feeble. Julia Marlowe had laughingly told her of Sothern's amused reaction to the anonymous missive, which they both believed had come from Sothern's estranged wife, Virginia Harned.

Wyatt stroked a stray lock of hair from Giovanna's forehead. "Do you think I could believe it for a minute if anyone tried to tell me you were a loose woman? Don't you think I know what it's costing you, being with me like this?"

"But you were so angry, and then there was that lady—I didn't quite know what to think."

Wyatt smiled and kissed her on the forehead. "Do you want to hear all about my horrible day, or shall we leave it till morning?"

Afterwards, as she lay peaceful in the circle of his arms, his mind drifted to their first days together, early in the run. Her room at the Statler in Buffalo was across the hall from his, and for two nights in a row—he always slept lightly, away from his own bed—he'd heard her door creaking open in the small hours. An assignation? He hadn't seen any evidence of an intimacy with anyone else in the cast, and actors were attuned to such things.

Curiosity and his old investigative instincts had overcome gentlemanly restraint on the third night. Donning a dressing-gown, he opened his own door as quietly as possible and watched her back retreating down the hall to the service stairs. He set out behind her, matching his slippered steps to hers. Down, down, down the dimly lit staircase for five floors, always keeping out of sight in case she heard something and looked up. She went all the way to the basement and he saw a door open, the light in the room beyond almost as dim as the stairwell's, and he realized she'd gone into the hotel's kitchen. The unlatched door swung shut behind her, but after waiting a few moments he saw a wedge of bright light; she must have opened a refrigerator. He ventured his head around the door. She was removing a carton of eggs and a block of cheese, which she laid carefully and quietly on a counter near the stove.

"Good Lord," he thought, "she's cooking!"

She pulled a metal bowl from a shelf and cracked an egg into it. As she reached for a second one, he leaned forward a little more and lost his balance, stumbling to recover it, and she heard him. She shrieked and the egg smashed to the floor. The game was up. He pushed the door fully open.

"It's all right, Mrs. Treadwell. It's only me. Wyatt."

Her hand clutched at the top of her dressing-gown. "Mr. Wyatt!"

"I'm so sorry I startled you." He stepped towards her.

The fear in her voice gave way to indignation. "You nearly gave me heart failure. What are you doing down here? Did you follow me?"

He looked suitably sheepish, but ignored her second question. "Um, ah, the same as you, I expect. I came foraging for something decent to eat. I am terribly sorry." He went to the sink, found a dishcloth, and swooped down to her feet to wipe up the broken egg. "Please—I'll clean this up. It's my fault."

She let her shoulders drop. "I'm so sick of hotel food! I've been avoiding dinner before the show, and then I get so hungry I can't sleep."

"Me too," he said, "I thought I'd take a chance and see if I could rustle something up. I never thought I'd get nostalgic for my own cooking."

"A man who cooks!" she said, eyes wide in intrigued mockery.

"It's the lot of the impecunious bachelor, I'm afraid."

"A man like you?—" she checked herself. *A man as attractive as you*, he read in her look. Through the gap in her dressing-gown he saw a froth of lace framing an intriguing swell of bosom.

So rare to see a woman without her imprisoning corsets...he blushed and cleared his throat. He'd been staring.

His eye roamed with another kind of lust around the ultra-modern kitchen's gleaming surfaces. "Nice setup they have here. Is it, ah, safe this time of night? I was worried about getting caught."

She smiled then, a crooked smile with mischief in it, the first offstage smile she'd given him. "Well, you did! A good thing it was I who caught you, wasn't it?—" she broke off and resumed in a lighter voice. "I, ah, actually had a little chat with the sous-chef when we arrived," she said. "I was raised in the restaurant business, you see, and I've been known to—"

"Invoke professional courtesy?"

"That's a good way to put it. He said as long as nothing's out of place in the morning..."

"Well, then," he said, "may I offer my own services as a sous-chef?" He opened the refrigerator and ducked in. "Here's some onion and pepper somebody's already cut up. And look!" He yanked a mostly-full bottle of Graves out of a terra-cotta wine cooler. "How did the staff let this get by them?"

Over the omelet and wine, she'd told him about her childhood in Paterson, New Jersey, as the daughter of immigrants, about her parents and brother lost in a shipwreck coming back from a visit to her grandparents in Genoa. How she'd grown up around her father's cooking, watched him work, begged to learn. But after they were gone she wanted to get away from all the memories, she'd done well in school plays, and...

Drifting towards sleep now, he leaned over and stroked her hair. Funny how he'd never meant to fall in love, as if you could control that. Why had she had to be married? They could have made a good life together. Did he have any right to wish that they still could?

CHAPTER 8

Wyatt found Warren Dodge at his breakfast table on Monday morning, leafing through the *Washington Post*. Peering over half-moon glasses, Dodge gestured him to a spindly-looking chair upholstered in celadon brocade and nodded to a maid to pour coffee for him.

"Croissants are good," he offered. "Reviewer is singing your praises here." Wyatt's hand went up in a forestalling gesture, but Dodge didn't see it.

"'The substitution of Mr. Wyatt for Mr. Sothern in the title role is no occasion for disappointment. He brought an energy and force to the portrayal of the Scots arch-villain that outshone even the redoubtable Mrs. Marlowe in the role of his consort.' Not bad."

Wyatt dropped into the chair. He never read his reviews, even those he'd been told were good ones, while the run was still going. "I had a good night. What else did they say about the ladies?"

Dodge scanned the page and frowned. "'Mrs. Marlowe, of course, has never been equaled in the persona of the 'fiend-like queen'. As Lady Macduff, however, the saddest of Macbeth's victims, Mrs. Treadwell gave a somewhat stumbling performance—'"

Wyatt winced. Sunday had been an off-night for Giovanna; he should have known better than to share the details of a murder investigation with a woman of her sensitive and sympathetic nature. Now she was all worried about the poor lady in the case. She'd made him promise to talk with the ambassadress again before throwing Latham to the wolves. "I'd planned to give it up, Warren. The man is more than flesh and blood can stand. I should never have agreed to consider it—"

Dodge's brow furrowed and cleared. "Oh! You mean Latham, not Macbeth. Well, you weren't expecting him to change his spots, were you?"

Wyatt helped himself to a croissant from a femininely styled white and gold buffet. Dodge caught his glance and his nostrils flared. "Allard *et fils*. Found in all the *best* houses, or so Augusta tells me."

"The lady in the case paid me a visit after the Saturday show, after I'd more or less told Latham to go to the devil."

Dodge looked alarmed. "So you know who she is now."

"And why it matters so much to keep her out of it. She told me to come and see her. Are she and Mrs. Dodge on calling terms?"

"She's a bit beyond freshman Congressional wives, though we met her at a reception. She's never come here, but then we're hardly ready for visitors." Workmen could be heard hammering on the ground floor below, which led to a brick patio and a walled garden backing onto a cobbled alley.

Dodge sighed. "You won't take Latham's word for it?"

"Even if I did, I'd need to know the details. I'd rather get them from a witness."

"It's asking a lot." Dodge drained the last of his coffee.

"You've no room to talk on that score."

Wyatt and Augusta Dodge arrived at the Federalist portico of the Brazilian Ambassador's residence on Lafayette Square, and were quickly shown upstairs.

Senhora Isabel Barros Alves Almeida e Pereira de Lima rose to greet them. In the daylight Wyatt could see that she was about his own age, but with her flawless skin and slender figure in dark blue silk overlaid with black lace, she could have passed for someone much younger. A china tea service sat on a low table before the brocade divan to which she gestured them; there would be no servants to interrupt this conversation.

"Mrs. Dodge," she began, "I am happy to see you again. Mr. Wyatt, I apologize for my untoward, ah, intrusion of the other evening." The tone was chilly, distant, the accent lightly Latin with, he now realized, a British cast; her husband's last posting had been the Court of St. James.

Wyatt murmured a demurral. What must it have cost a woman of her stature to have come to him? He doubted she had even disclosed her liaisons with Latham to her Catholic confessor—even the seal of the confessional might not have felt safe. Her willingness to trust two relative strangers with a secret that could destroy her was testament to feelings for Latham that Wyatt couldn't begin to appreciate. As he understood the codes of the upper crust in such matters, Latham could have expected that she'd abandon him to his fate rather than risk her reputation.

He declined the tea she was about to pour for him, inwardly cursing whatever social arbiter had designated that loathsome brew as the beverage of gentility. "With respect, Senhora, I do not believe I am the person to help Mr. Latham."

The hand that set down the teapot shook a little. "So he told me," she said. "But he believes otherwise. Because of his friends—" she indicated Augusta with a nod and an open hand, "who told him what you did for them. And because he feels you are the only man he could trust to—to navigate the situation. And he told me something else."

Wyatt raised an eyebrow but kept his face neutral.

"He told me he had misjudged you, Mr. Wyatt. He thought you were a fortune-hunter. That you would go away when he threatened to disinherit his daughter. But you did not."

Wyatt's astonishment was reflected on Augusta's face. Senhora Pereira was shaking her head sadly. "Pride, I suppose. It is a great sin, but—once you have embarked on a course, you cannot always turn back. Even now—"

Pride. Wyatt had swallowed his for a time. Rose, for her part, refused even to try to contact her father. Pride could be fatal… Latham wasn't about to ask his pardon, to tell him to his face that he'd been wrong, that he regretted his daughter's death. But it was a concession of sorts.

He sighed and shook his head. "If I were to go forward with this, I would have to know as much as possible about the circumstances of that evening—Mr. Latham's movements, and so forth."

Senhora Pereira's back stiffened. "I can vouch for his presence in my—ah—private suite between the hours of nine o'clock and four in the morning. Does this not cover the time during which this Nielsen was killed?"

"Most likely," he told Senhora Pereira. "But there are questions nonetheless. For example, was Mr. Latham in possession of a walking-stick when you and he—er—"

Augusta Dodge rustled uncomfortably on the divan. In deference to her errand, she had chosen a gray silk rather more subdued than her accustomed palette for afternoon calls, which ran to peacock blues and tawny golds. Wyatt shot her a quick look.

"My husband is in Sào Paolo for the last two weeks." The words came out in a rush. "In consultation—with the Foreign Minister and others, to prepare for the Pan-American Conference in Rio. And to consider the terms of the Pan-American Treaty." She rose and paced distractedly towards the long velvet-draped windows, her fingers at her mouth in a charmingly girlish gesture. She turned back to face them. "You see how God punishes sin—" Her voice broke and a heart-stabbing little cry came out. "To let Richard die for what he did not do would be a far greater sin. Yet if I tell, my husband's ministry—" she broke off, and the dark eyes which Wyatt had thought cold were now stormy.

"Again with respect, Senhora," he said, "you are not the first lady of high rank in Washington who has—er, found herself tempted into a circumstance—"

"But they are experts at it," she said bitterly, "I know those women. Their husbands are buffoons, or pompous—what is the word, windbags. Who traffic with courtesans behind their backs. I have betrayed the kindest of husbands, a man revered by all—"

The Brazilian Ambassador was an eminence, a hero of the abolition movement in his young manhood, a man of letters, a patriot. But this clean-burning flame of a woman—whose resemblance to a dark-haired version of Rose was stabbing his heart—needed a man who would match her passion. She was the heiress of an aristocratic family from Rio, twenty when they married, an ideal political match for the then-forty-year-old Pereira, if not a soul-mate. But Latham?

As if reading his thoughts, she said, "We had met at one or two diplomatic functions. But nothing—untoward occurred until we encountered each other one day in Rock Creek Park, where I often ride Aurelius—my horse. Richard likes to ride there also— he keeps a fine stable, as you may know. We fell into conversation…"

She closed her eyes. "Do you know what it is to be hungered for? To be desired? Do you know the thirst that it feeds in the soul?"

Beside him on the divan, Augusta's silks rustled again and she cleared her throat. The mystery wasn't in this woman's attraction to Latham, but in the absence of consuming desire for her on her husband's part. Giovanna's face flashed before him, and he understood why, after he'd told her the bare bones of the situation, she had urged him to "for Heaven's sake help that poor lady." Senhora Pereira was no highly placed courtesan, no bored aristocrat of loose morals.

He gave no answer, and she expected none. She sat down heavily in her blue armchair.

"A stairway leads down from my room at the back of the house to a door. That door leads to the garden, which you can reach by a gate at the side of the house, or by another in the alley which runs behind. The servants had the evening off and I knew they would not return until very late. Even my lady's-maid was walking out with her young man, though I was concerned for her reputation—" she broke off with a rueful laugh. "Richard came to that back door. I remember the clock was striking nine. He carried with him his walking-stick, yes. Gold, with a lion's head."

Wyatt straightened up. "Not silver?"

"No. I have seen him with a silver stick, with a knob, on other occasions, but I think this gold one is special for him. I gave it to him."

"Indeed?" Augusta leaned forward, clearly absorbed.

"He carried it whenever he—came to see me. Even when he paid formal calls in the afternoon, with his wife. It was his way of telling me, you see—what he felt for me. Our secret."

"And he took it with him when he, ah, left you."

She nodded. "About four, four-thirty, I am not sure exactly, but I know it was after four."

Wyatt wondered whether Mrs. Latham would confirm the time of her husband's return, but that would do nothing for his alibi. Recalling with a fresh stab of pain her complicity in Rose's banishment, he had no doubt she would swear Latham was at her side all night if he required her to. He found himself wondering what Senhora Pereira's lustrous black hair would look like, loosened from its pins and braids, cascading down a creamy slope of back…Richard Latham knew. The anger of that thought brought him back to business. Robert Nielsen's pocket-watch had been smashed in the assault. That placed the time of death at 10:45 p.m., with confirming evidence still to come from the medical examiner.

"Did Mr. Latham talk about the incident in the House involving Nielsen?"

"All he said was: 'I have had a most unpleasant day, my dear, of which I shall spare you the details.' I had not seen the evening papers, so I had no idea of the incident to which he referred." The blue velvet armchair almost matched her dress; Wyatt had the sensation that she was dissolving into it.

"That was all?"

She smiled sadly. "Except something about how being with me was balm to any wounded heart."

"Was he angry, or upset, when he came to you?"

"Disturbed, yes. Agitated, I would say. But in control of himself. A little weary. He is not a young man—" She poured tea for herself and refilled Augusta's cup.

Augusta's eyes darted to Wyatt's as if seeking permission. "How long previously had you made this, ah, assignation?" she asked gently.

"Just after my husband left for Brazil." A touch of shame had crept into her tone. "Circumstances did not permit Richard to come sooner."

What gyrations this couple had gone through for their liaisons. Even with a preoccupied husband on her end, it couldn't have been easy. Wyatt remembered an enameled snuffbox he'd seen somewhere, which bore the legend, *All life is sweetened by risk.* He remembered the fierce joy of that charge up Kettle Hill with Roosevelt. Perhaps it was true.

"And he left—around four, did you say?"

She lowered her eyes. "He fell asleep for a while. I myself could not sleep, so I read a little. Then he woke while it was still dark and said he must leave me. He was so careful for my reputation—" She covered her mouth and her eyes brimmed with tears. "When he had gone, I sat until it was light, asking God to forgive me for what we had done, vowing it would be the last time." She took a deep breath and gave a little laugh. "And of that, at least, God has made sure."

Wyatt, who had made his own failed bargains with God, felt a flash of sympathy. And then he thought of the old proverb that revenge was a dish best served cold. What if Senhor Pereira had somehow learned of his wife's betrayal?

"Senhora—were you and your husband acquainted with Mr. Nielsen?"

"I recall that he was presented to me at our New Year's reception. He seemed a strange and unpleasant fellow to me, though he did express admiration to my husband for his role in our country's emancipation movement. They seemed to like each other."

The timing didn't work. Whoever had killed Robert Nielsen had capitalized on the incident on the House floor. Ambassador Pereira had been five thousand miles away, beyond the reach of news which in any case was of no particular concern to his country.

It suddenly occurred to Wyatt that Latham could have placed his trust in a hired killer, even someone from his own household. Someone who, in the unscrupulous fashion of his kind, had stolen Latham's cane and left it at the scene to ensure himself an ongoing source of blackmail revenue. But could even Latham have slept peacefully at his lover's side, knowing that someone was carrying out his order to kill? Possibly. There was no one capable of more evil than a man convinced of his own righteousness.

"Senhora, did you ever have any contact with any of Mr. Latham's servants? Employees?"

"No—he was very careful in that way. I received a few brief notes from him, always sealed—they could easily be thought to be notes of thanks for a visit or a dinner. He and his—his wife dined here several times. Because of his position, my husband thinks him an important man to cultivate." She smiled wanly at the irony. "Mrs. Latham herself called only last week."

"How did he get here, when he visited alone?"

"His coachman would drop him at Willard's. Then he would dismiss the man, telling him he would be out late and would ride home with a colleague, something of that sort."

Perhaps Latham had pressed his coachman into service as an assassin. He might already have been paying the man off to keep silent about his assignations. Unsavory as the prospect was, he'd have to find out more about Latham's household staff. He would take Dodge up on his offer of Germain's help…

…which meant that, in spite of Richard Latham, he was putting himself back on the case. He sighed and shook his head, cursing himself inwardly for a fool.

"So, none of his servants were likely to have known of his visits to you?"

Fear flickered again in the ambassadress's eyes. "They might have suspected something," she acknowledged, "but nothing, I think, that would trace him back to this house—to me. I am told that within a short distance of Willard's there are many, ah, houses of entertainment—" Wyatt saw Augusta grimace in sympathy with the shudder of revulsion that crossed the Senhora's face at the thought of being likened to such company. He thought of the insult Nielsen had thrown at Latham, the barb about alley-whores; Latham's tastes, clearly, were nothing if not expensive.

"As for my own servants," Senhora Pereira went on, "the servants' quarters are at some distance from my boudoir…"

They had been playing a high-stakes game with consequences that spanned a hemisphere. They were lucky not to have been caught out. He thought of the beautiful Queen Anne of France, whose honor the Three Musketeers had defended, and of her lover, the shallow, contemptible Duke of Buckingham, so unworthy of her. He cared not a whit for what would happen to Richard Latham. But this woman's frailty had put the future of her eminent husband—indeed, the fortunes of their country and its relations with the United States—in jeopardy. If he could satisfy himself that Latham had not simply hired out the deed, he would do all he could to save Senhora Pereira. He laughed inwardly at the image of himself as D'Artagnan.

"Please, Senhora, say no more. I am sorry for the trouble this has brought you. And—" he glanced at Augusta, whose expression was neutral though there seemed to be a glint of amusement in the gray eyes, "I will do everything that may be done to prevent your having the slightest involvement in this wretched matter."

"And you will save Richard?" Her hands wrung together as if in prayer. "Only do that, and I will let him go with all my heart and be no further source of trouble to him."

"Madam," Wyatt said earnestly, "no man could consider your company as anything but a privilege."

"Smitten, were we?" Augusta shot him a sideways smile on the doorstep and he felt himself redden.

"Well, at any rate, the old roué can't be accused of poor taste."

Augusta opened a gray parasol that perfectly matched her dress and took his arm. They walked through the tulip kaleidoscope of breezy Lafayette Park towards the White House. "You believed her, I take it."

"Didn't you?" Wyatt said, surprised, before he caught Augusta's lips twitching in a vain attempt to suppress a laugh. "I don't doubt he was with her that night. But that doesn't mean he didn't pay someone else to do it. Someone who thought far enough ahead of him to take his cane and leave it at the scene, by way of—"

"—ensuring himself an annuity for life," Augusta finished. "How sordid. One can't entrust servants with anything these days. Will you take me to tea at Willard's?"

Wyatt grinned. "People will talk."

"I certainly hope so. At my age, one has so few opportunities to be talked about, and how else to distinguish myself from the common herd of Congressional wives? A promenade along

Peacock Alley with a handsome leading man ought to just about clinch it."

Wyatt's blush deepened. What if Giovanna heard about this? But Augusta, like her husband, was an old friend. And, he had to acknowledge, one he'd never found particularly attractive... Giovanna would be pleased with his new role as knight-errant, a welcome change from the slaughterer of women and children he became most evenings at eight. But he had tonight off; there would be dinner with Germain, and a chance to learn more about Nielsen's death.

CHAPTER 9

Louisa Stanstead pulled down a majolica pitcher from a shelf in her kitchen cupboard. "You've decided to take the case, then."

"The more fool I," Wyatt smiled. He watched her fill the vase from the tap and strip the ribboned tissue from the bouquet of daffodils, forget-me-nots and white carnations he'd brought. The flowers transformed the homely yellow pitcher into a vessel of beauty.

She bent over the carnations, her gaze abstracted for a moment. "Blameless love following the beloved to the grave," she said. "You know, don't you, that the word 'daffodil' is derived from 'asphodel'?"

"You know your mythology."

"And my Language of Flowers. They're lovely." She looked up at him. "You're a kind man, Mr. Wyatt. And a thoughtful one. I was about to make coffee—"

"Oh, please, I wouldn't—"

"Oh, it's not on your account, believe me! I'm in great need of a stimulant," Louisa said. "I've been half-asleep on my feet all day."

Grief was exhausting, like a bad case of influenza. It struck him with a little stab in the heart that he was remembering how it felt rather than feeling it directly. Progress, he supposed.

He followed her into the kitchen, watching her as she scooped coffee into the basket of a battered-looking percolator and lit the gas with a kitchen match. She took a great sniff from the canister. "I feel more awake already! Tell me—are you convinced Latham is innocent?"

Wyatt didn't answer right away. "Not entirely," he said. "But he does seem to have an alibi that will hold up. Enough for me to agree to an investigation—for now."

She looked at him as if expecting a further explanation. When he offered none she said, "Please sit down, Mr. Wyatt, and ask your questions, and we'll get this over with soon, I hope."

Wyatt took a chair at the rickety kitchen table and pulled out his notebook. "Fair enough. You mentioned a quarrel with Mr. Nielsen on the morning before his, ah, statement on the House floor. I take it he didn't return here in the evening?"

"No. When he stormed out of the house that morning, it was the last time I—" her voice quavered. "The last time I saw him alive."

"Can you tell me what it concerned? The quarrel?"

"He asked me to marry him."

Wyatt laughed. "Those aren't usually fighting words."

"We'd lived as man and wife this past year and more." Her voice was soft with grief and memory. "No church could sanctify our union, we agreed on that, I thought—" she broke off abruptly and took a long, shuddering breath.

"Take your time."

"He wanted to marry me in the church," Louisa went on. "He'd talked to Reverend Pierce about it. It pained him for me to be an object of scandal, he said. Not to be invited with him to dinners, not to be received. Robert, of all people, caring about such things!"

"It sounds as if he was concerned for your happiness."

Louisa nodded sadly. "I realize that now. But I threw it back at him. 'Marriage is for controlling property and enslaving women, you said. How could you wish that for us?' I asked him. 'Shall I become your legal appendage?'"

She bit her lip, lifted her head and looked straight into Wyatt's eyes. "How I've wished those words back. They killed Robert as surely as the villain who struck him."

"I don't understand—" Wyatt rose and poured them both coffee.

"He was so angry and hurt. 'Appendage? Is that what my love and regard mean to you?' He stormed out of the bedroom. 'I must go or I shall say something I'll regret,' he said. And the door slammed behind him. And that," she said, "is the last time I saw Robert alive." She took off her glasses, and the tears fell on the planks of the kitchen table.

"I'm so sorry." Wyatt's nose retreated into the strong, aromatic coffee. He resisted the urge to put a hand on her shaking shoulder.

She peered up at him, her eyes red-rimmed. "If he hadn't been so angry, he wouldn't have said what he did to Latham, and he'd still be alive, and…" Louisa gulped a mouthful of coffee.

"Even if political forms of revenge wouldn't have satisfied Latham," Wyatt said, "if he wanted your—Robert dead, I think he would have hired someone, and he'd have waited a while until the memory of that public insult had faded. I doubt he would have been so careless as to leave a weapon at the murder scene that could so clearly be traced to him."

Louisa knit her brows. "Unless they met again that night, after Robert's meeting, or he followed him to the house to demand that he retract his words publicly, and their quarrel broke out afresh."

"What meeting was that?"

"The organizing committee for the new YMCA—the 'colored YMCA,' as my press colleagues insist on calling it. Their monthly meeting at the Strivers' Hall on U Street. They usually go until ten or so," she said, anticipating Wyatt's next question.

From what he'd learned of the man, throwing himself into a meeting would be just the way for Nielsen to numb his bruised feelings over Louisa. Someone who was there might have seen him leave. Or might have followed him.

"Regarding a renewed quarrel—I don't think so," he heard himself say. "The Congressman seems to have been struck down before he had a chance to defend himself, or make any attack of his own. And if Latham was cold-blooded enough to lie in wait for him, and take him unawares, he'd surely also have thought to use a weapon other than a walking-stick that could be traced to him."

Louisa was staring at him. "Is that why he hasn't been arrested?"

"I haven't talked to the police. But they'll have thought the same thing, surely." Wyatt didn't want to believe what he was telling her. He wanted to help her run Latham to earth and see that he got what he deserved. But Senhora Pereira had no reason in the world to tell him what she'd told him, except that it was the truth.

"So Mr. Nielsen had not been home at all that evening."

She closed her eyes and shook her head as a fresh wave of grief washed over her. "I assumed he was still angry with me. That he might wish to stay away until he could—ah, master his feelings. Robert did have a temper—we both did, really—we'd quarreled once or twice before, and I knew he had the meeting—so I wasn't too concerned at first. And him lying out there *dying*. All alone—" She drew in a sharp breath. "If your theory is correct, that means—"

"It means someone wanted Latham taken down as well as Nielsen. Two birds with one stone."

"How odd. They couldn't have been more opposite, politically speaking." She warmed up his coffee from the pot and he nodded thanks.

"It's also possible the murderer seized a convenient opportunity, and simply didn't care whether he implicated Latham or not."

"But he'd have to have taken some risk to get hold of Latham's cane—"

"—and that is suggestive," Wyatt finished. "Do you know who would have been at the meeting with Mr. Nielsen? They may have information about when he left and with whom and so on."

"Or be added to your list of suspects," Louisa said sharply. She pushed herself up from the table. "No, you're right, Mr. Wyatt. Someone may know something useful. Come back around five. I'm hosting a meeting of the Alley Relief Committee, and many of them would have been at the YMCA meeting as well."

So much for his one night off from the theater. Wyatt smiled and rose in his turn. "That would be most helpful. I wonder— might I ask an additional favor? I have a good friend, a colored man, who's new in town. I think you'd like him. He hasn't had much of a chance to meet people yet—"

"Bring him along, by all means," Louisa smiled. "If he's good-looking and single, he'll have plenty of friends in no time."

Wyatt reached for his hat. "Forgive my asking, but—will you be all right?"

Her face clouded. "Actually, I'm on a hunt for new lodgings. I won't be able to stay here without Robert's share of the rent." She looked around the shabby but cheerful kitchen. "I will miss it, but maybe it's best now…"

"I'm sorry for that," Wyatt said. One more small, sad instance of how murder wrecked the lives of the victim's survivors. "Thank you for your time, and for the good coffee."

"You've unsettled me, Mr. Wyatt. In one way it would be a relief if it weren't Latham, if Robert's anger with me hadn't provoked him into doing something that led to his murder. But I want someone to pay in kind for what happened to him. Much as we both despise Latham, I suppose we must give him a fair trial before we hang him."

"Spoken like a true journalist," Wyatt laughed.

"Come in, Wyatt," Warren Dodge said in the falsely affable tone he reserved for the early stages of business deals, waving him towards a chair beside the desk. One other chair in his tiny Capitol office was already occupied by a big dark-haired man on the youthful side of middle age who regarded the newcomer with a noncommittal smile that held, unless Wyatt was imagining it, a trace of annoyance at the interruption.

"May I present my friend Dade Wyatt," Dodge said. "Wyatt, this is Cornelius Dunagin, whose real estate firm is well known in the City." The man whose development project Dodge was thinking of investing in, Wyatt remembered. And something else—something the man Franklin had told him. The slumlord of Snow's Court?

Dunagin rose and turned to shake Wyatt's hand. He was tall, with a wrestler's build and ruddy complexion, and a crushing handshake to match. His suit was dark and conservative in cut, the better, perhaps, to offset something feral, even mechanical, in the pale gaze that scanned Wyatt as their hands connected.

"Wyatt's inv—" Dodge started to say, but Wyatt shot him a look that stopped him in mid-word. "Uh, in town with Sothern and Marlowe."

Dunagin's eyebrows went up. "Indeed! An actor, are you!"

Wyatt nodded and tried for a smile.

"Your name's new to me, I confess. They're doing *Macbeth* at present?"

"Wyatt's taken over the lead." Dodge said with almost fatherly pride.

"Has he indeed? The Countess and I shall certainly have to come, now that I've met the leading man."

"That's Mr. Sothern, who was taken ill," Wyatt said quickly. "I'm his understudy."

"I'm sorry to hear he's ill, but I dare say you're up to the challenge."

"We were, ah, just talking about the demise of Congressman Nielsen," Dodge said. "And Mr. Latham's present difficulties."

"A bad business," Wyatt said. "Did you know the men?"

"Who didn't?" Dunagin chuckled, resuming his seat. "Nielsen, God be good to him, has been a scourge to honest businessmen since he set foot in the District. As for Latham, as Dodge here knows, we have—a number of common interests. I'm sorry for his trouble." The accent strove for British but overlaid a vowel-strangled version of Irish. A Belfast native, Wyatt guessed.

"You don't believe him capable of the murder, then? The press seems to."

"Of course not. Latham's quick-tempered and he's not a man to cross, but he is a gentleman."

"So he'd have someone else do the dirty work if he wanted murder done."

Dunagin's sidelong smile at Dodge held a hint of exasperated sympathy. "Sounds as if you've been spending too much time in your character, Mr.—Wyatt, was it? I don't think him at all capable of such a heinous act."

"It doesn't matter what I think," Wyatt said, "I'm only an actor. But the police have him in their sights, and the evidence so far seems to be against him."

"You've taken quite an interest in our local affairs, I see."

"Not every day a Member of Congress is beaten to death, is it? Sounds to me as if this Nielsen made a lot of enemies in the business community hereabouts."

Dodge was watching the exchange like a spectator at a tennis match.

"I can't think of anyone who'd stoop to murder." Dunagin's tone had slipped towards patronizing.

"I've taken something of a personal interest in this," Dodge interposed. "You know Latham's been a friend and benefactor to me since I came to Washington—indeed," he said, turning to Wyatt and then back to Dunagin, "it was he who introduced us."

"This Commander Macalester, who's running the investigation," Dunagin said, "Down from New York, isn't he? Is he any good?"

Wyatt sent Dodge another warning look and a quick head-shake.

Dodge shrugged. "I may have met him at one or two City functions. Roosevelt likes him, I've heard—Latham will need all the help he can get. Perhaps you'd know of injuries done by Nielsen to others—or of circumstances in which he might have been an obstacle to someone's vital aims."

Dunagin chuckled. "Oh, I've been around boardroom tables where there were idle comments about hiring a pack of thugs to do away with the fellow. As you must know, Mr. Wyatt, as another friend of my friend Dodge," Wyatt saw Dodge's eyes slip sideways at the description, "the speculator's game is rife with obstacles—meddlesome civil servants, overcautious bankers, obstinate neighbors and so forth. Nielsen was merely one more ant at the picnic, if larger and more persistent than most. If I were the police I'd be looking among the, ah, Negroes he seemed so fond of."

"From what little I've heard of the man, it's hard to imagine a Negro who'd stand to lose much by his continued existence, whereas—" Wyatt let his hands fall open and smiled ingenuously.

"Oh, now, you mustn't mistake the hyperbole of the board-room for the stuff of penny-dreadfuls. We have many ruthless entrepreneurs in the City, but they limit their weaponry to lawyers and contracts."

"As a rule, no doubt." Wyatt's bland smile could not entirely conceal the hostility he felt welling up. "But it sounds more likely to me that someone like Nielsen would have been attacked by a white man. The Negroes seem to have held him in high esteem, judging by the news reports."

Dunagin rose with deliberation and strode to the hat stand, removing an immaculate top hat. "*Belinda* will be out of the boat-yard next weekend," he said to Dodge. "We're hoping you and Mrs. Dodge will join us soon for a day or two on the Chesapeake." Dodge nodded but didn't reply.

"I'll call on you another time on the matter we were discussing." Dunagin gave Wyatt a cold little bow and left the room.

"Dear me," Wyatt said. "I appear to have offended the gentleman."

Dodge gave up the attempt not to smile and stood, stretching himself like a cat. "You did me a favor, coming in when you did. I need time to think about whether go in on this Columbia Heights scheme, and he's pressing me for an answer."

"Interested in being a land baron as well?" Wyatt enjoyed Dodge's half-pleased reaction to being described in the press—accurately enough—as a pulp and paper baron. "Mr. Dunagin didn't strike me as your usual candidate for a business partner."

"He's damn good at what he does," Dodge said. "Latham and others tell me he hasn't taken a loss on a development yet. Remarkable for that trade. I'm not ruling it out. For a mere hundred thousand, he tells me, I'll become one of Washington's leading men in business. "

Wyatt, who had never owned property in his life, grinned. "Sounds like a bargain to me."

"He might just be right—land and building costs are nothing here compared to the City's. It's tempting."

"Thanks for not letting the cat out of the bag, by the way."

"Oh—that. Well, the look you gave me would've turned a lesser man to stone. I take it you're on the case?"

Wyatt scowled. "Mrs. Dodge will have told you about the meeting. I don't see how as a gentleman I can refuse at this stage. Stop grinning at me like that."

Dodge made an insincere attempt at a straight face. "I take it you didn't want Dunagin knowing what you're up to?"

"Not yet at any rate. Puts people on their guard." *Especially a man like him*, Wyatt didn't add; there was something disquieting about that cold gaze. "You think there was anything to that business of Nielsen having enemies all over the Chamber of Commerce?"

"More of an attempt to smokescreen Latham, who I think he half-suspects of actually having done it. But there's no question Nielsen was stymieing a lot of people's plans. Including Dunagin's, come to think of it."

"Didn't realize the District of Columbia Committee had that much power."

"If Nielsen had lived and been re-elected—and he was popular back home—Cannon was all set to banish him to the Antipodes. The Committee on the Disposal of Obsolete Government Records."

Precisely the punishment Louisa had envisioned, Wyatt remembered. "Would anyone ever *want* to be on that?"

"Surprised he hadn't done it already," Dodge went on, "but he'd probably figured the D.C. Committee would be punishment enough, since it would deprive Nielsen of a venue for raking pork back into his district. He obviously had no sense of what mattered to a man like Nielsen."

"This opens up some interesting avenues. Where do I find records of bills introduced into the D.C. Committee?"

"House Clerk's office. But you're more likely to find sore points in the bowels of the D.C. Government. Since the Committee approves the appointments of the three Commissioners, Members can exert a lot of leverage by threatening to oppose re-nominations."

"So Nielsen may have been putting pressure on the Commissioners—"

"To deny permits for subdivision schemes like Columbia Heights. In fact, that's one reason I'd hesitate about an investment with Dunagin. Nielsen was trying to get Macfarland—the chairman—to put forward an ordinance that would deny new development permits to anyone who owns properties out of compliance with building codes."

"Which Dunagin has a few of?"

"Heard of Snow's Court?"

Wyatt nodded. "Not far from where Nielsen was killed. A real hellhole. I went by there looking for witnesses."

"Rumor has it Dunagin owns most of it."

"The locals think so too," Wyatt said.

"From what I hear, places like that go up for a hundred dollars apiece, rent out to Negroes for eight and a half to ten a month. You can't beat that return on investment."

"But can you sleep at night?" It was out before Wyatt could stop it.

CHAPTER 10

When Wyatt came to drag him away from his duties, Germain was supervising the installation of a bathtub with claws that would have done justice to a Chinese dragon.

"Will you stop in Foggy Bottom with me before we go to the restaurant? I'd like your impressions of Miss Stanstead. And the people around her."

Germain grinned. "The colored people, you mean." He took his tan derby from a hook and followed Wyatt down the front steps. "She gonna stay down there after all this?"

Wyatt shook his head. "She won't be able to afford the place now." It had rained briefly, and the evening air was moist and flower-scented, the dying light a soft molten gold. In the iron-fenced gardens they passed on their walk down to Dupont Circle, tulips were giving way to lilacs. Their sweetness took him back to his childhood in Ohio, where lilacs had bloomed around the farmhouse door, just as in the Whitman poem he loved.

Louisa's door was opened by a young Negro woman in a striped shirtwaist, the soft swelling of mid-pregnancy evident under her neat gray skirt. Wyatt tipped his hat and introduced himself and Germain.

"Oh, yes, Mr. Wyatt. Miss Stanstead was telling us about you." There was a touch of cool reserve in the smile on the young woman's round, pleasant face, which warmed when she turned to Germain. "I'm Mrs. Wilbur." She gave them both her hand. "I do some housekeeping for her and Mr.—" She bit her lip. "She had to step out for a minute, but won't you come in? She just went to get some milk for the coffee—here she is now."

Louisa came up the brick walkway behind them, a milk-bottle in her hand. She greeted them with a pleased smile. "Ah, you did bring your friend!"

Wyatt made introductions, explaining that Germain worked for Congressman Dodge.

"You're most welcome, Mr. Germain. Do come and meet everyone—Mr. Charles Weller from Associated Charities is here. We've had our prayer and our—our little weep over Robert, and we're all agreed the best way to honor his memory is to carry on with our work. His work. Mr. Germain, since you're a new arrival, this will be a chance to enlarge your circle of Washington friends." Germain smiled and nodded his thanks. They followed her and Mrs. Wilbur down the corridor to the small parlor, which was full of people.

A respectable-looking group of Negroes, mostly light-skinned, the men in suits, the ladies in walking-costumes and feathered bonnets, sat listening to a deep-voiced speaker, which heightened Wyatt's discomfort with arriving late and being ushered into a roomful of complete strangers. Grateful for Germain's company, he let Louisa make room for him on a piano-stool while the speaker continued. Curious glances came their way, the women's registering appreciative appraisal when they fell on Germain.

Wyatt's ear caught the drift of the speaker, a tall, boyish-looking white man in a dark blue suit. "As we all know, Miss Stanstead's report of last year on the conditions in the alleys, a first-rate piece of work—" Weller gestured towards Louisa, who nodded acknowledgement, 'has gone largely unheeded in the halls of Congress. As for Mr. Nielsen's amendment to deny new building permits to the owners of these hell-holes until they repair them, its few remaining supporters lack the seniority, the committee positions, and the necessary zeal to advance it. The best we can hope for this time is the condemnation bill, which will at least require the demolition of the most unsanitary of the alley slums. Yes, Mr. Templeton?"

A graying man in a tweed suit rose, concern and anxiety shining in soulful eyes that seemed out of keeping with his burly physique. The same avuncular-looking man who had been at Louisa's side during the funeral ceremony, Wyatt remembered.

"What is the point of forcing our poor brothers and sisters from their homes—however miserable and squalid—if there is nothing to replace them?" Wyatt felt as much as heard the tremor of emotion in Templeton's rich baritone. "Where are they to go? Can we not use the occasion of our tragic loss," he inclined his head towards Louisa, "to unite our allies on behalf of Mr. Nielsen's amendment?"

Weller smiled sadly and shook his head. "The developers' money speaks louder. Those hovels yield them ten dollars a month. Why, several Members and even one or two Senators are sleeping partners in their building projects in Northwest." Wyatt and Germain exchanged uneasy looks.

A woman of about Wyatt's age, hair upswept in an elegant pompadour and wearing a dove-gray walking suit, paced into the center of the room. "That's Lady Mollie—Mrs. Terrell," Louisa whispered. "She started the National Council of Negro Women."

"Mr. Weller, Mr. Templeton." Mrs. Terrell opened a graceful hand to each. "I incline to the view that we should seize the moment and try for the greater goal." Templeton gave her a grateful, almost relieved smile; speaking in public seemed to have unsettled him.

"Did I hear you say, Mr. Weller," Mrs. Terrell went on, "that the condemnation bill's passage is all but assured?" Weller's arms were folded over his chest, but he nodded assent. "Then we have little to lose by mobilizing our allies on the Hill—the faithful remnant—to attach Mr. Nielsen's amendment. And to defeat the marriage ban as well. Clarence Wilbur, as our legal expert here, can you summarize that odious bill's provisions?"

The slim, fine-featured man with one arm around Mrs. Wilbur rose and lowered his eyes in demurral. The name sounded familiar, and Wyatt thought he had seen him before, but couldn't place him. "I'm only an insurance attorney, Mrs. Terrell—but the bill is fairly simple. It would be illegal for a white and a Negro to marry in the District. It voids any such marriages, makes any offspring illegitimate and bars them from inheriting, and provides for up to ten years in prison for the couple and the officiant. It applies to all the U.S. territories as well—Oklahoma, Arizona, New Mexico, Alaska—"

"Who counts as a Negro?" someone asked.

"Anyone with one-eighth or more of Negro blood."

There were murmurs and shaking of heads. An angular, elderly woman in a plumed black hat rose to her feet, pillar-straight in her severely tailored black cutaway suit. Her yellowish skin was so pale that she would have been taken for white in any but this gathering. Wyatt thought at once of Oscar Wilde's Lady Bracknell, though he detected none of that redoubtable matron's mordant humor in the stern lines of the mouth and nose.

"Mrs. Templeton." Weller gave a deferential little bow.

"Thank you." She glared at the broad-shouldered Templeton who, Wyatt noted with amusement, shrank from his mother's eye. "Mr. Weller, I am of your opinion regarding the condemnation bill. We would do well to take this opportunity to rid our city of some of the loafers and criminal elements whose behavior hinders the advancement of our race. And while we are about it, let us expand the committees of volunteers who venture into these dens to instill some degree of civilized Christian behavior in their unfortunate offspring."

A short, dapper man with a fringe of graying hair and a fine Guardsman's mustache stood, adjusted his immaculate white cravat and stared defiantly at Mrs. Templeton, who had several inches on him. "Well, ma'am, advancing the race by eliminating members of the race seems like a dubious bargain to me."

Louisa elbowed Wyatt and passed him a newspaper, folded up to reveal the masthead: the *Washington Bee*. She drew a finger under "Calvin Chase, Publisher."

"Admittedly they're an embarrassment to us all," Chase went on, "and we wish they'd just go back to the plantations, since they're generally a lot blacker than we are. But we're all darkies as far as the white world is concerned"—he gave Weller and Wyatt a 'present company excepted' look—"so I say we make common cause with our alley-dwelling brethren, as your son suggests, and work for Mr. Nielsen's amendment. *And* the defeat of the marriage bill."

Wyatt heard a stifled snort beside him and turned to see Louisa burying her face in her handkerchief. She resurfaced and bit her lip, merriment dancing in her eyes.

Charles Weller gave an eloquent shrug. "I don't dispute the rightness of that course, Mr. Chase, only the practicality. But as Mrs. Terrell says, we'd risk little harm to the condemnation bill."

"If she's willing, I shall ask Miss Stanstead to prepare an article for the next edition of the *Bee*," Chase said, smiling towards Louisa, who returned the smile and murmured her assent.

"And we can all start making our Congressional contacts," Mrs. Terrell added, sealing the collective agreement. Mrs. Templeton's chest puffed up with suppressed indignation, but she resumed her seat.

"I have a special announcement," Mr. Chase said, his eyes alight with pride and pleasure. "Dr. Dubois will be giving a talk next Thursday on the proceedings of the Atlanta Conference. He's been gathering statistics on the health and physique of the Negro American that will give the lie to those so-called scientific studies about the Negro's mental inferiority. Good ammunition for our visits to the Hill."

"And I have one more announcement," Louisa said. "Friends, this is Mr. Wyatt—and Mr. Germain, who works for Congressman Dodge of New York. Mr. Dodge has asked them to look into Robert's death—"

Uneasy murmurs rose the group, which Louisa quelled with a gesture. "It was easy for me to conclude that Richard Latham killed him," she explained, looking a little abashed, "perhaps too easy, and perhaps what the real killer intended. Latham is a despicable man, but it is possible he is the wrong man for this murder." She looked over at Wyatt, "If we don't explore other possibilities now, and Latham is acquitted—on the evidence—" her voice quavered, "the real killer might never be found." She swallowed, closed her eyes and looked away. "—and I couldn't bear that!" The last words came out in a rush. There were more murmurs now, and a few skeptical, nearly hostile looks in Wyatt's direction.

He smiled his thanks to Louisa. What an admirable woman, a truly decent woman. In her circumstances, he might have told an investigator like him to go to the devil. Louisa urged those who had been at the YMCA meeting to tell Wyatt all they could about what they'd seen of Robert Nielsen that evening. It was an awkward moment; something he learned from these people might point to one of their own as a killer, though as his gaze swept the room it was hard to imagine anyone in this painfully respectable group of earnest altruists in the role of murderer.

Louisa's introduction of Germain as a new arrival in Washington was markedly more social. The group relaxed, the matrons visibly sizing him up as an eligible match for their daughters.

Wyatt realized that not one of these people knew—or would care—about his own real-life work as an actor. Since the National Theatre refused to admit Negroes, none of them—or only the very lightest-skinned, if they were feeling bold enough—would ever see him perform. He flushed, scanning their faces, feeling angry and ashamed. He should have refused to have anything to do with the place…he'd conveniently forgotten its retrograde practices when he signed on for the Sothern & Marlowe touring season. That would have been easy enough when he was playing Ross, but now that he was in the lead—what hypocrisy. Too late to boycott the place now. Ambition and principle seldom kept easy company; Macbeth himself was the ultimate exemplar of that.

CHAPTER 11

Giovanna settled into the gilt brocaded chair the waiter held for her and nodded her thanks. Mrs. Julia Marlowe, resplendent on her night out in ice-pink ruffled silk and a wide-brimmed hat trimmed with ostrich plumes, ordered a bottle of pink Mumm's to match her costume and sat back, scanning the Willard's Art Nouveau dining salon with the ambivalent air of a celebrity who wishes to dine in privacy but hopes nonetheless to be recognized and whispered about. Her face alone would have assured comment: the deep brown eyes illuminated by candlelight, the perfect bowed mouth, the rich, dark hair, the chin with a hint of a cleft. And that stage presence which Giovanna envied so, the sense she gave of one born to be seen and admired, the confidence and grace she radiated in all of her roles.

"Well, I don't know about you, my dear, but I for one am ready for this tour to be over! Going mad on schedule every evening has become something of a trial—and I've been so worried about poor Edward."

"Oh, how is he?" Giovanna had quite forgotten about Edward Sothern since Wyatt had taken over the lead.

"But he seems on the mend, and your Wyatt is doing so well, though I'd never tell Edward that—Giovanna, that buttercup yellow is luscious on you. Wherever did you find it?"

Giovanna smiled up at the young, white-gloved waiter who was filling her flute with rosy bubbles, a colored man with close-cropped hair and an air of kindly dignity beyond his years. If Wyatt was hers, why was he off tonight chasing after criminals for a man he despised, when they had so little time left together?

Her own fault, perhaps…she had felt sorry for the man's lady-friend, whoever she was…

"You're lucky, in a way," Mrs. Marlowe was saying in a stage whisper, as if reading her thoughts. "There's no wife complicating the picture. Edward's been trying to get free of that Harned harridan—ha! I like that—for years now and she won't let him go. Shall you divorce, do you think? Treadwell won't object, surely? Or is it just a *petite affaire* for the length of the run?"

Giovanna spluttered and barely managed to swallow her champagne. "Dear Julia, what on earth makes you think I would—"

"Shhh! Ahem—I'm told the *homard en croute* is exceptional, is that so?"

"We're pleased to think so, ma'am." The waiter had returned with menus, and stood aside smiling while they made their choices.

When he had gone, Mrs. Marlowe leaned confidentially over the table. "Oh, my dear, you didn't think you could keep it secret, did you?" She held up a forestalling, lace-gloved hand and let out a silvery laugh. "Please—don't worry! I'm sure Edward and I are the only ones who know, and it's only because we had a—shall I say clandestine phase of our own before he finally broke with Virginia. If I weren't such a fool for Edward, I'd be a little jealous—Mr. Wyatt has grown rather dashing since he began playing the villain, don't you think? Tell me *everything*."

Giovanna felt her face grow hot. "Really, Julia, I—"

Mrs. Marlowe sat back, her head slightly cocked and a knowing eyebrow raised.

"I could never leave Thomas. There are the children." Giovanna twisted the napkin in her lap. The waiter arrived with their terrapin soup.

Mrs. Marlowe gave her a sympathetic look. "Ah, the children. That, alas, has not been a consideration for me. Of course that would make a difference. But what are you going to do? I think you must have another little secret that even Wyatt doesn't know yet. One that could change everything?"

Giovanna's soup spoon clattered into the bowl, sending thick green gobbets onto the tablecloth but not, thankfully, onto her yellow dress. She took a deep breath and forced a smile, dabbing ineffectually at the stains with her napkin. The waiter, with a look of understanding sympathy that positively terrified her, replaced the napkin.

"I can't imagine what you mean." What she couldn't imagine was how Mrs. Marlowe might have found her out.

"I'm known to be rather observant," Mrs. Marlowe smiled, still keeping her voice low. "And for the last couple of weeks you've been worried about something. Perhaps you're a little—late?"

Giovanna stared at her, then broke into a laugh and shook her head. "Oh, goodness, no!" She spooned in a mouthful of the soup. "Though if I keep eating like this, I'll gain enough weight to have it thought so. This is quite heavenly, isn't it? I'm so glad you brought me here—I'd been looking forward to parading down Peacock Alley in my new gown. There was a handsome fellow in a naval uniform who was watching us—"

"The blond one, you mean, with the charming mustache?" Mrs. Marlowe preened. "He was pretending to admire my *rivière*—"

"And was patently more interested in what it was clasped around," Giovanna laughed, with an admiring glance at the circle of diamonds on her companion's snowy bosom. "Dear Julia, how do you stand it?"

Julia Marlowe's laugh stopped abruptly and she leaned forward again. "Divorce isn't so awful, you know. If you're an actress, it's more expected than not. Though I confess I still feel bad about poor old Taber. Consumption, you know, four years after—just like Wyatt's wife—" she rummaged in a pink-and-crystal reticule and blew her nose delicately with a snowy linen square, emerging with a conspiratorial smile. " It's not as if Treadwell's going to want to keep the children from you."

"Look what's happened with the Corey case," Giovanna protested. "They say he'll go to Reno, for a divorce. Miss Gilman's name is being dragged through the mud—"

"Mabelle is an actress," Mrs. Marlowe replied reasonably. "Publicity is publicity, and being a home-wrecker with the President of U.S. Steel will only help her career in the long run. As for Treadwell's finding out, you've been perfectly discreet. And

I can give you at least four names for an action on grounds of adultery."

It sounded so cold and businesslike. Giovanna could think of more than four names, but she couldn't imagine hauling Thomas into court for a divorce suit. He might treat her more like an adored pet than a grown woman, but adoration in a husband wasn't something to be overthrown lightly. A tomcat, perhaps, but he'd been faithful in his fashion...he had always come back to her...

"Besides," Mrs. Marlowe added, "one has only to look at Wyatt to see that he truly cares for you. And Wyatt's a one-woman man. I knew him when Rose Latham was alive."

"Did you really?" Giovanna utterly failed to keep her tone casual. She'd been so curious about that part of Wyatt's life, one of the few topics that were off limits between them. "What was she like?"

Mrs. Marlowe took a sip of her champagne. "She was lovely. Golden-haired, tall, seraphic—eyes blue as gas-jets—though I wondered, sometimes, how Wyatt lived with that intensity. And whether it was related to the disease. Consumptives run that way, you know."

"How was she as an actress?" Giovanna thought of Dogberry's line about odorous comparisons, but she had to know.

"What would I say...single-minded. Impossibly high standards. She *immolated* herself for her art. She was on stage that very last night—a hemorrhage from the lungs, that's what took her. In mid-soliloquy—it was ghastly. He was out with some men friends. She slipped away just as he got to the bedside." Mrs. Marlowe's eyes filled. "It's taken him years to recover, my dear. And the way his eyes shine when he looks at you—"

Giovanna lowered her eyes and bit her lip. Maybe Wyatt did love her—the woman he thought she was. Not just as a diversion for the length of the run; a real love, a love that could last. And she could love him that way too. The thought was new, and terrifying.

CHAPTER 12

At the end of the Alley Relief meeting a courtly, ascetic man with the long face of a Velasquez grandee strode up to Wyatt and wrung his hand. He proved to be the Reverend Francis Grimké, pastor of the 15th Street Presbyterian Church, and a man of note judging by Germain, who clearly viewed the introduction as an honor.

"I hadn't thought there was much doubt about the identity of Bob's killer. But I suppose this Latham fellow's co-sponsorship of that detestable marriage bill doesn't equate to murder."

Wyatt's nostrils flared. "Latham is sponsoring that bill?"

"As the child of a slave and her white master, I take that matter somewhat personally. You seem surprised, Mr. Wyatt." The minister included Germain in his smile.

Wyatt shook his head. "The word would be horrified. Perhaps appalled. But, no, not surprised."

"Then why on earth would you be trying to absolve the man of this crime?" asked a younger man who now stood at Grimké's elbow, his tone somewhere between amazement and challenge. Handsome, mahogany-skinned, with a fine, almost arrogant Arabic nose, he held a hand in his trousers pocket a little too casually, as if he'd been advised to try to appear more at ease than was his habit.

Louisa interposed to smooth over the awkward moment. "Mr. Germain, Mr. Wyatt, This is my good friend Mr. James Costello, who teaches at M Street."

Wyatt had heard that name recently...from Franklin, the man in the alley. Costello was the man who had been 'sweet on Miss Louisa' before she and Nielsen became a couple. "My goal is to help bring Robert Nielsen's killer to justice," he said in a conciliatory tone. "I'm not out to absolve anyone."

"You understand, Mr. Wyatt," Grimké said, "people here may be reluctant to tell you anything that might put their friends under suspicion. The police here are all too ready to pin crimes on any Negro who happened to be near the scene at the time—even 'respectable' ones like us."

Wyatt nodded. "I do understand, Reverend. I've also got no interest in manufacturing suspects."

"What's your field, Mr. Costello?" Germain asked with friendly interest. "You wouldn't by chance be a historian?"

Costello broke into a smile. "Did Miss Stanstead tell you that? I do teach history. I have been making a study of our Afro-American heritage, but I'm not sure that makes me a historian."

"Well, now, you might be interested in some things I brought with me when I left N'awlins," Germain said. "I did a bit of research on the *gens de couleur*—the folks I came from." Wyatt watched him cut Costello out from the little knot of people and take him to a corner, where they began an earnest conversation. From time to time Costello's eyes darted around the room, searching out Louisa with an expression of hunger, sadness, and—was he imagining it? a trace of hope. What had Mr. Franklin from the alley said? *Unlucky in love…*something he and Costello had in common.

Calvin Chase of the *Washington Bee* was at Wyatt's elbow. "I'd sure like to know what you find out, Mr. Wyatt. We'd all rather think that Latham fellow did this."

Wyatt smiled. "Understandable. Were you at the YMCA meeting, Mr. Chase?"

"Usually after the program, folks hang around and chat for a few minutes. I did myself that night. Sometimes I pick up a good story that way. But I don't remember seeing Bob after the meeting adjourned. Nor when he left, or with whom."

"I dare say you can tell me—who were some of Mr. Nielsen's allies on Capitol Hill? Other men you'd think of as friends of the race, for instance?"

Chase frowned. "What's that got to do with a murder investigation?"

"Maybe some of them have been threatened. And may themselves be in danger from whoever—"

"Ah! I see. Well, come on over here—get yourself some more coffee and I'll see if we can't help you out." Chase gestured to the sofa. Wyatt returned from the buffet with fresh cups for both of them. "Now, you know, Mr. Nielsen got Mr. Weller to take him and some other Congressional folks into the alleys. So they could see the conditions first hand and report back to their Committees. He even had a couple of Senators—George, who's the fella with the white hair and big mustache?"

Templeton, who'd been pointedly introduced to Wyatt by his widowed mother as George Templeton, *Junior*, perched on the arm of the sofa. "Senator Foraker, most likely. The other one was William Warner, I remember. From Missouri. Real gentleman, face like an ol' hound dog."

"That's him," Chase beamed. "We ran a piece on him a while back. Told him he ought to run for President. Roosevelt's no friend of the race, you know," he said in response to Wyatt's look of surprise. "Thinks white folks need to be reproducing more so they don't get outbred by inferior stock like us."

Wyatt felt himself blush, and grinned. "I for one haven't been much help to him so far. What about Nielsen's House colleagues?"

"Who's that one, going bald, a little goatee—John Lacey from Iowa—and Birdsall, the big man with black hair, looks like a prizefighter—he's from Iowa too," Templeton said. "Chair of Judiciary. Kicked up a fuss when the Speaker took Nielsen off his committee."

Germain and Costello rejoined them. "I heard he might put in a bill to re-enfranchise the Negroes down south," Germain said. Wyatt had a twinge of recollection: disfranchisement was the reason Germain had left his beloved New Orleans. Black people had been deprived not only of the vote but of most forms of legal protection, and lynching had become a spectator sport.

"But Birdsall wasn't at all happy with Bob," Chase put in. "He got a bill out of his committee to force the train companies to get rid of the Jim Crow cars once they cross the Virginia-D.C. line.

Cost him a few chips, I can tell you. And Nielsen sank it with some crazy floor amendment about banning the cars altogether, that didn't have any more of a prayer of passing than I do. Wasn't the first time, either. Lord deliver us from our friends, Mr. B. said."

Legislative frustration seemed a flimsy ground for murder, but Wyatt filed the names away. Mrs. Wilbur came back into the room, untying her apron. She dropped into a rocking chair and put her feet on a small embroidered stool. "You all talking about Mr. Nielsen?"

"Mrs. Wilbur," Wyatt said, "you kept house for him—you'd know him about as well as anybody. What was he like?"

The young woman's cheerful face dimmed. "Mr. Nielsen was a fine man, and a true friend of the race." She hesitated, and Wyatt nodded encouragement. "But he wasn't the most—amiable man you'd ever meet. He didn't like something, he'd speak right out, and not in a whisper either. You know St. Mary's Episcopal, about three-four blocks from here?"

Wyatt had admired the little gem of a Negro church, designed by the noted architect James Renwick, with its Tiffany windows and elegant brickwork. He nodded.

"Well, he takes the Reverend Taylor to task in the paper, says that instead of spending money on what he called 'self-glorification,' they should have used it to help the poor folks in the alleys right in their backyard. Like Judas did in the Bible."

"Now, honey—" Clarence Wilbur had come into the room.

"You know what I'm talking about, Clarence. When Mary Magdalene buys that fancy pomade and washes Jesus' feet with her hair, and Judas says what a waste it is, they could have spent that money on the poor. Some folks think he had a point, too." She folded her arms and rocked back in the chair.

Clarence Wilbur stood smiling over his wife and massaged her shoulders. "I'm glad Reverend Grimké's left already."

Judas. Wyatt was struck by the comparison. Usually you thought of him as the betrayer, the false friend, but in that Gospel passage Judas was the purist, the zealot offended by money spent on luxury instead of ministry. That sounded a lot like Robert Nielsen. Or was there someone, some cause, that Nielsen had betrayed—or threatened to betray? His wounds—some had not bled, made after he was already dead—suggested some extraordinary eruption of emotion.

A hired killer would have done the job and left, most likely tossing the weapon into the nearby Potomac. And a racial bigot, even one with a lynching mentality, would have shrunk from implicating a political ally like Latham by using his cane as a murder weapon…he thought again about Mr. Franklin's comment about 'passing.' And about Louisa Stanstead herself having "a li'l bit of colored blood." What if Louisa was lying about the nature of their quarrel? He didn't want to think that. Surely someone passing for white wouldn't devote her time and energies to the welfare of colored people, much less live among them.

Louisa approached him and Germain. "Did you learn anything useful, Mr. Wyatt?" She looked weary, and grief still drooped at the edges of her eyes. Early days to be hosting company, picking up the fallen torch or not.

"I got some of the information I was after from Mr. Chase."

She smiled. "I do enjoy him. He's a true journalist—rank and position mean nothing to him, and he has a real nose for hypocrisy."

"He certainly put Mrs. Templeton in her place. I don't envy that son of hers."

Louisa shook her head. "Such a nice man. Do you know, he's one of the top men at the Strivers' Mutual, and she treats him like an utter failure? He has to live in her house, to save money, because of his little boy. It's so sad—they don't know what's wrong with him, but he's never grown properly, and he's always sick. The medical bills must be killing George, I'm afraid, though he never talks about it."

Germain frowned. "His mother looks well-to-do."

"She has pots of money, Mr. Chase says. But she never forgave Mr. T. for marrying the boy's mother—she was so much darker. A plantation girl from down South. Mrs. Templeton thinks Negroes should better themselves by marrying light-skinned women like her, or even white women. And then when his wife left him and the child, it was nothing but 'I told you so's'. She calls poor Branford a 'degenerate' and says he ought to be put away in an idiot asylum, so she won't give George a dime."

Wyatt had a pang of fellow-feeling for George Templeton, begging in vain for a cold-hearted parent to help him save a life that should have been as dear to her as to him. He thought of Tomás, a child of desperately poor immigrants he'd met in the slums of the lower East Side. Dodge and he had virtually adopted the boy, Dodge sending him to Dr. Trudeau's sanitarium to cure him of consumption. He couldn't imagine Tomás's grandmother, if he'd had one, holding back a cent if it would help him get better.

George Templeton had a son, damaged yet beloved. Thomas Treadwell had a son with Giovanna. Banquo had a son, Fleance—it wasn't just dynastic considerations that prompted Macbeth to want both of them dead, he realized, it was envy. The fruitless crown, the barren scepter…his own life so far, fruitless and barren. What would it be like, to be a father, to have a son of his own? With Giovanna…

He brought himself back. "Miss Stanstead—how goes your search for a new place? Can any of these friends help you find something?"

Mrs. Wilbur reappeared in the doorway. "Louisa? Lady Mollie wanted a word with you before she leaves—"

Wyatt and Germain stood. "We'll let you get back to your guests," Germain said. "This man owes me a steak dinner."

"I'm glad you came by. We'll talk soon." Louisa gave them a grateful smile. "It looks as though I may not have to move after all."

CHAPTER 13

The spring air had cooled considerably with nightfall and Wyatt was glad of his wool jacket. "Interesting way to spend your night off," Germain mused as they crossed the Rock Creek bridge towards Georgetown. "That was a fair sampling of the Black Four Hundred there."

Wyatt sniffed a hyacinth blooming in a planter atop the bridge abutment. "You mean like Mrs. Astor's Four Hundred in New York?"

"Lady Mollie—Mrs. Terrell—she's a national heroine to us colored folks. She's on the speaker's circuit all over the country. All we needed was Dr. Dubois and we'd have had everybody who's anybody in the Movement."

"Well, he's due in town next week. What about Booker T. Washington? You told me he's had dinner with the President."

Germain's guffaw tipped his derby far back on his head, making Wyatt realize how much he had missed his friend's rich laugh and his company. "Lord, no, he's on the other side. See, some folks think segregation's something we just have to adjust to. Washington started his school down in Georgia to train us as mechanics and tradesmen, which is acceptable even to the Southern white man—'less somebody gets too successful at it, and then he's likely to find his premises burned down. Separate and not quite equal's good enough for him."

"I didn't know that."

"But Dr. Dubois says we have to send our best and brightest to the white universities, to uplift the rest of the race. Take our rightful place someday. He went to Harvard himself, first Negro ever to get a doctorate there. What I hear, Nielsen and those other Congressmen Mr. Chase was talking about, they see things Dubois's way."

Wyatt followed Germain through the low door of the old tavern. They ordered schooners of beer from an aproned waiter, who told Germain it was good to see him again.

Wyatt raised his ice-cold glass in a salute. "So, what's this Strivers' Mutual Miss Stanstead was talking about? Sounds like an insurance company."

"That's right. The Strivers' Mutual Advancement League and Benevolent Society. 'By the Negro, For the Negro,' that's their motto. 'Strivers' is what we call the folks who are trying to advance themselves and help the race. They're a good, solid company. I thought I might talk to them about some life insurance, matter of fact."

Wyatt wondered if Germain's relationship with Laura, a willowy Creole courtesan he'd met in New York, had become more serious. Germain read his thought, and his eyes clouded.

"Haven't seen my lady-friend in a couple of months now. Wonder if she's gonna remember me, by the time I get back there."

"*La donna è mobile*?" Wyatt smiled. "From what I saw, she seemed to be pretty serious about you."

Germain stared into his glass. "I'm gonna need to be able to offer her something more than a room in the house and pickin's from the kitchen. Been thinking about getting a little place of my own, living out. Might have to go up to the east nineties, though—I'd stay closer by if I could find a place that would—"

Rent to a colored man, Wyatt finished the thought.

"Problem isn't so much finding a place," Germain went on. "It's findin' a place in that New York society. Hard to get any of the colored gentry in Manhattan to give you the time of day, 'less you got "Van" in front of your name."

"Dutch Negroes?" Wyatt's eyebrows lifted.

"You'd be surprised. Some of 'em with pedigrees as long as any old member of the Knickerbocker Club. They're not much on *arrivistes* from the South—nor on ladies who are a little vague about their previous occupations. I'd like to give Laura a good life, Wyatt, but I don't want her havin' to live a lie."

Wyatt grunted sympathetically, having contemplated romantic pursuit of one of Laura's fellow *filles de joie* before being preempted by a wealthy old Dutchman. Living a lie, it occurred to him, was what actors did for a living. It took prodigious amounts of mental and emotional energy, but it came and went with the parts and the costumes, and it was socially acceptable. Concealing one's past—whether as a courtesan, a colored man, or a killer—would be a full-time job, and an exhausting one. He wondered if he'd met Nielsen's murderer already.

Germain's voice jolted him out of his reverie. "Mr. Dodge said he saw you in Baltimore. Seems to think you got somethin' going with a lady from the cast—"

"That was Lady Macduff," Wyatt said quickly. "We had a scene together at the time, when I was playing Ross."

Germain looked at him steadily. Wyatt felt himself redden and dropped his eyes. "It's none of Dodge's damn business," he snapped. Germain kept looking at him.

His shoulders sagged. "It's no good. She's married."

"People get unmarried. 'Specially actors, or so I'm told. This just a flash in the pan till the run's over?" Germain raised an eyebrow, as if he knew the answer.

"Well, it started out that way." Wyatt looked up and saw Germain read the pain in his eyes.

"How married is she?"

"There are children. He's a womanizer, like a lot of leading men, but not bad otherwise, I gather."

"She feel the same way you do?"

"Sometimes I think so. But—"

"It's harder for a woman. Still," Germain blew a speck of foam off a fresh beer, "never hurts to ask." There was that eyebrow again. "You should introduce me sometime. Seein' as I won't get to see her onstage."

"I wish I'd thought about that when I signed on for the tour—"

"Ain't up to you to solve the world's problems, *mon ami*." Germain smiled. "Not that I don't appreciate the thought."

"I was going to take her to the Smithsonian," Wyatt said. "Have you been there yet?" He was fairly sure the national museum couldn't be segregated.

"You gonna have time in between actin' and investigatin'?"

"I'll make time. I won't let this business deprive me—" he cleared his throat and said in a lighter tone, "Speaking of matters of the heart, what'd you think of Costello?"

"Bright fella—a real scholar. School's lucky to have him. If he weren't colored, he'd be teaching at Harvard, same as Dr. Dubois ought to be."

Their steaks arrived, sizzling on cast-iron platters beside baked potatoes split open and running with butter. "Looks to me like he's still a li'l sweet on Miss Stanstead," Germain added. "She could do a lot worse. You thinking he might've decided to—get rid of the competition?"

"He doesn't look the type," Wyatt conceded, "but sometimes it's the respectable, repressed ones you have to worry about. They hold things in till they can't stand it any more, and then they explode. What'd he have to say about Nielsen?"

"I got the impression he didn't much care for him. But he didn't want to, you know, speak ill of the dead. He did say he thought the man sometimes did the cause of the race more harm than good, always spoilin' for a fight."

"That could be jealousy talking," Wyatt said. "But first things first," he went on through a mouthful of baked potato. "There's somebody in Latham's household I'd like you to talk to."

"Is this somebody that was at that YMCA meeting?"

Wyatt reddened and put down his fork. Without a great deal of apparent effort, the people at the Alley Relief meeting had managed to get him off that track. He smiled ruefully, not blaming them. In a similar situation, he'd probably protect his friends too.

CHAPTER 14

Yﾟou've spoken to the Latham fella, then?" Commander Ian Macalester of the District of Columbia's Metropolitan Detective Bureau, looking as much like a wire-haired terrier as Wyatt remembered, caught Wyatt's appraising look from his perch on the edge of a battle-scarred desk.

"Aye, right enough," he said, rapping the monstrosity with his knuckles, "I thought Mr. Roosevelt would have laid on some fancier digs when he lured me down here. Put not your trust in princes. But we're due to move in a couple of weeks—my new office is quite grand, I'm told." Macalester, formerly an inspector in New York's Central Detective Bureau, had helped Wyatt and Germain run a murderer to earth in Vermont, earning the President's admiration in the process.

"The visit with Latham wasn't pretty," Wyatt said. "There's some history."

Macalester thin lips pursed and he swung his short legs back and forth against the desk. "I heard about that from Dodge." His Glasgow burr hadn't faded after more than thirty years off the boat.

"Fortunately for him, I have other avenues for satisfying myself on the question of whether he killed Nielsen. Germain's helping me with one last item in that regard."

"Now that would be a most helpful thing to the Metropolitan Police." Macalester hopped down and rifled among the papers on his desk for a notebook and pen. "Seein' as we've been on the verge of arresting him for the past week."

"I wondered why you hadn't." Wyatt stood to stretch the numbness out of his backside. Police chairs seemed designed either to discourage long visits or to put suspects in such a state of unease that they'd confess to anything to be allowed out of them. From Macalester's windows he could see the Baltimore & Potomac station, where Robert Nielsen's body had begun its long journey home and where President Garfield had been fatally shot, and east of there to the half-built Union Station which would replace it, blazing white in the morning sun.

Macalester sighed. "He's not much of a flight risk, I'll admit. And I wouldn't have cared to be on the receiving end of Speaker Cannon's wrath had we taken him in right away. The Force's budget is thin enough, God knows. The NYPD looks a cushy billet by comparison, promotion or no promotion. So what've you got?"

Wyatt left out the details of Latham's alibi but assured Macalester that he had talked at length with its source. "There's a lot at stake here, Commander. If he had to use the alibi, the State Department wouldn't be happy."

"He might've thought of that before—ach, well, I dare say the fella wasn't expecting he'd be needing one. Assuming he didn't do it, for argument's sake."

"You get any Henries from the walking stick?" Wyatt, and Macalester were coming around to accepting Sir Edward Henry's bizarre notion that a man's fingerprints were unique identifiers. He allowed himself a moment of *schadenfreude* at the image of Latham having his fingers rolled in ink by some oaf of a policeman.

"Latham's, of course," Macalester said. "We were fly about it, got a comparison set off a glass he'd used," he added, demolishing Wyatt's pleasant little fantasy. "But we fingerprinted everybody else that might've touched the cane legitimately—got matches for two House cloakroom clerks, and the parlormaid at home, none of whom seem to've had anything against Nielsen. A partial print from Nielsen as well. He clutched at it briefly, it seems, before—" They both winced at the thought.

"Nothing else?"

Macalester returned to his perch on the desk. "It was a wee bit tricky, because of the dried blood. But I'd say our man—or woman—must've worn gloves. Don't look at me like that—if a woman got one good swing in at the right spot, she could have rendered him helpless and finished him off."

"I suppose. They'd be stained, then—the gloves. The murderer's clothes too."

"Like as not. Latham's valet showed our detective the coat and trousers he came home in that night. Not a spot on them. However," he grinned crookedly, "there were traces of some expensive scent, which also means the clothes hadn't been cleaned, and that argues in his favor as well. You've talked to Nielsen's young lady?"

Wyatt turned back from the window. "You'll have heard about her outburst at the funeral. After I talked with her, she was less sure it was Latham. But she didn't offer any ideas about who else might have done it." He didn't enlighten Macalester about Louisa's quarrel with Nielsen; he wasn't going to do the police department's work for them.

"So, what do you think?"

"What's that phrase you coppers use—*cui bono?* Nielsen was getting in the way of some big development interests, I hear. Trying to force them to fix up their slum properties before getting new permits."

Macalester looked skeptical. "With a votin' majority of the House and Senate investing in Washington real estate? I exaggerate but slightly—seriously, I can't see him having got far with that."

"Profits delayed, profits denied, maybe?"

Macalester tapped the pen on the notebook. "I'll wager it's somebody Miss Stanstead knows. You and Germain were at her house, you say—how fares that excellent chap, by the way?"

"Homesick for New York. The work on Dodge's new townhouse is dragging on."

"So who'd you meet at the soirée? Anyone with an obvious reason to kill Nielsen?"

"Not unless you count romantic rivalry."

"It's happened before, laddie, as we both know."

"I'd talked to a fellow who lives in Snow's Court, the alley behind Nielsen's house. He let slip that Miss Stanstead had a suitor before she took up with Nielsen. I met the man last night—a colored man, teaches history at the M Street School. Do you know of it?"

"'deed I do, and an esteemed institution it is." Macalester's eyes, which Wyatt had seen turn cold as ice-chips when grilling a suspect, were warm and alight with interest. "It's the pride of the Negro aristocracy hereabouts—the equal or better of any white school. Not an easy place to get hired. You must be highly educated and the soul of respectability."

"Doesn't sound like a place that would harbor killers," Wyatt said. "But this Costello is worth a closer look, and Germain can help me there. Your people got anyone else in their sights?"

"Well, we've a difficulty. As you know, Nielsen associated with coloreds of all levels of society. Which might have let him in for trouble with his Southern colleagues who object to such things— they're a powerful lot hereabouts, and they're making headway, I'm sorry to say. There's that Milton fellow from Florida who's given to conniptions over the fact that whites and Negroes in the District are allowed to marry with impunity, as he puts it. In his constituency, that would get the colored half of the couple strung from the nearest tree."

"Milton," Wyatt remembered, "he's the one who introduced the marriage bill—the Washington Negroes are up in arms about it, and of course Nielsen would have fought it tooth and nail."

"I can't see this Milton for a killer himself. Why would he implicate Latham, who's a co-sponsor, for one thing? But those that elect him and his ilk would be happy enough to work over a fella they would judge to be—what's the malodorous term they have? A 'nigger-lover.' As a warnin' to the rest. Take a seat—you're makin' me nervous with your pacing."

Wyatt plopped back into his chair. "Wouldn't they have strung him up, if that was their aim? And in a mob, to boot?" There had been all too many newspaper accounts of this degenerate form of mass entertainment. "And while we're on the subject, your heels against the desk—"

Macalester stopped drumming his legs in mid-swing. "Ach, stringin' up a white man, and a Congressman, might be a bit beyond even the likes of them. And they're not likely to have used

Latham's cane, him being a co-sponsor of the bill and all—he's one of them, as they'd see it."

"So, what's the difficulty you were speaking of?"

"I've had the devil's own time trying to get a couple of Negroes onto the detective force. Men with the education and, I'm sorry to say, the lighter skin are far more likely to aspire to some more socially acceptable pursuit, like teaching. The ones with native intelligence that I'd happily take a chance on, I can't get past the Chief. He can't see Washington society standing for colored men prying in their midst. But it would be very handy in a situation like this."

"Germain can help you there. If Dodge wants me to help Latham so badly, I dare say he can spare him for a bit of nosing around in the colored sections."

Macalester beamed approval. "A right useful fellow, Germain. Send him round for a wee blether. We don't want Latham languishing under suspicion—*if* he didn't do it—nor do I care to subject myself to the barbs of the yellow press, and the colored press, for that matter, for not having run him in yet. Which, absent a break in the next few days, the Chief will probably have to do within the week."

"That's not much time." Wyatt rocked back in his chair and put his feet up on Macalester's desk. "You never told me you were leaving New York. Mrs. Baird didn't mention it. What do you hear from her?" Wyatt's New York landlady, a Highlands native, had been friends with Macalester since her arrival in America.

"Well," Macalester's face turned wistful, "what I heard from her was, 'We'll not be seeing you for a while, then.' That was after I asked her to marry me, so she could come with me, and she turned me down."

The chair legs thumped back to level. "But I thought—"

"Aye, well, so did I," the Scotsman said, shaking his head. "I thought we had an understanding, you might say. But she said she couldn't be leaving New York—who'd take care of her tenants?"

Wyatt felt a guilty flush that was not justified in the circumstances. He'd never asked anything of Mrs. Baird—not directly, anyway—though she had looked after him for months after

Rose's death, and otherwise kept a motherly eye out for him over the years. Macalester caught his look and smiled.

"It's not on your account or anyone else's, laddie. Marie's quite set in her ways after all these years as a widow, and I'm not sure how she'd do with a husband about the place, never mind moving to the swamps of the Capital." Wyatt was startled by the use of his landlady's given name. It hadn't occurred to him that she had one.

"I'll just have to set my sights on some wee lassie in her forties lookin' for a rich old husband. And as for you, young fella, how d'you like being a terrible murderer yourself? Though I've always inclined to the view that Macbeth was the victim of slander."

Wyatt grinned. "Being a countryman of his, you're in a better position to know than I. I just do what Shakespeare tells me to, and the sword-fights are fun."

"Did you know that his Lady was the rightful heir to the Scottish throne, usurped from her by her cousin Duncan? Who was killed by Macbeth in battle, by the bye, which is much more sporting than murdering him in his bed."

Wyatt beamed. "Really! That explains a good deal—I'll pass it along to Mrs. Marlowe. She'll be pleased. She's always saying that Lady Macbeth is misunderstood."

"But it also illustrates a fundamental principle of homicide investigation—look at the family first."

"You think Miss Stanstead—"

"Can you rule her out?" Macalester was giving him the ice-chip gaze again.

Wyatt shook his head reluctantly. "Not yet. I'm meeting her later. And before you ask, I'm not making any assumptions." He rose and headed for the door. "I can get you some show tickets, unless that would constitute bribing the constabulary."

"That depends on how good your performance is, now, doesn't it? Let me know what Germain finds out—about whatever you've set him onto."

"Commander," Wyatt turned back with his hand on the doorknob, "it's good to see you again."

"Aye, right enough," Macalester said gruffly, waving him out.

CHAPTER 15

Since Latham could not be informed of plans to investigate his coachman as a potential murderer for hire, Wyatt had adopted a favorite disguise of a bearded Scots workman and spent a morning as a casual laborer in the flowerbeds of Latham's mansion. He learned that the coachman, like most members of the servant class in Washington, was a black man—a huge, well-muscled fellow who would have had no trouble dispatching Nielsen. Armed with the man's description, Germain buttonholed Willis, who was Warren Dodge's coachman, and suggested an evening out.

Willis was too pleased about being turned loose for the evening to question his new boss's suggestion of Bullock's, a favorite after-hours watering hole for coachmen, where he had once taken Germain in what now seemed a successful attempt to ingratiate himself with the keeper of the household keys and accounts.

"Homey li'l place," was all Germain offered for explanation. "Nobody puttin' on airs there."

Bullock's occupied a square brick house on the Georgetown waterfront that had been the office for a tobacco warehouse a half-century ago. It was low-ceilinged, dimly lit, and hazy with blue smoke, redolent of the grainy smell of the nearby flour mill and the muddy reek of the Potomac. Willis was a wiry little man who would have done well as a jockey, and he moved easily among the burly crowd of horse-handlers, too small to be a challenge to anyone.

"I got the first round." Germain signaled the bartender, a cadaverous white man with a droopy mustache, for two porters, looking around with an expression of friendly curiosity.

"Hey, br'er, never seen you in here before." As luck would have it, it was Latham's coachman, a big handsome devil all right, instantly recognizable from Wyatt's description of his gray-flecked side-whiskers and glossy chocolate skin.

"Been here a couple times with my man Willis there. Name's Germain."

"Tyler."

They shook hands and Germain signaled for another beer. He surveyed Tyler's huge hands and bulging forearms. Certainly capable of beating a man to death, and he wouldn't even have needed a stick.

"Willis?" Tyler looked over to where the smaller man was accepting a cheroot from a lanky man in overalls. "Yeah, I know him. Drivin' for that new Congressman—what's his name? Dodge. Willis say he a good man to work for. You a driver yourself?"

"Steward for Mr. Dodge. Just down from New York City for a while, get his new place to rights. Be headin' back in a month or so. We up to our ears in paint and wallpaper, but I thought I'd take me a night off."

"Just got off myself."

Germain took a swallow of porter. "You a driver?"

Tyler leaned his elbow on the bar and sipped foam pensively from his glass. "For now."

"Contemplatin' a change?"

"Might not have a choice. Man I work for's named Latham. You heard of him?"

Germain frowned for a moment. "Rings a bell." He allowed his eyes to open, round and white-rimmed. "You mean the one in the papers? Supposed to've killed that other Congressman fella?"

"That's the man. What he gonna need a driver for, he locked up in jail, or fried in the 'lectric chair?"

"Man! He an' Mr. Dodge be friends." Germain was rather enjoying the descent into working-class patois. "He helped him out last session when he'd just got here. You think he done it?"

"Lawd, no. I been drivin' the man all the time he been in Washington, lemme see, twelve years now. He got a temper an' he can hold a grudge, but I don't see him as no killer. 'Sides, he beat that fella to death, he'd'a got blood all over his clothes, an' Prentiss—that's his valet—say he come home in the same ones he went out in, an' not a speck on 'em. Which you could not do if you done beat somebody to death. Just a li'l trace of some high-class perfume or other, heh, heh."

"Sounds like he got him a li'l *doudou*, like we say in N'awlins," Germain said.

"Li'l piece on the side? That don't do no harm."

"Depend on the lady," Germain grinned in response and held up two fingers for the barkeep. "Heard they got some down offa Pennsylvania Avenue…"

"Well, you gots to look out for yourself, that's the truth. But you lookin' for a little fun, brother, I don't mind tellin' you I got just the place." He went on to describe with great gusto the acrobatic attributes of one Minerva Jones, "'least, that's what she call herself," a high-yaller gal at Miz Melba's on the corner of 13th and D Northwest.

"Well, I might just take myself on down there sometime," Germain said, all beery geniality and hail-fellow-well-met, "I'm mighty obliged. You tell her your name, so I can tell her who sent me?"

"You crazy?" the big man guffawed. "She just calls me Henry. You tell her Henry that was there last Tuesday sent you."

Germain furrowed his brows. "You was there the night of the killin'?"

Tyler looked sheepish. "I took the coach on home like Mr. Latham said. Knowed he wouldn't be home for a while, so I went on out again, figured I'd have myself a little fun, same as he was doin'. Oooweee! That gal kept me goin' all night, heh, heh, heh." He slapped Germain on the back and ordered two more beers.

"Wasn't you afraid of runnin' into him down there?" Germain caught Willis's eye and signaled the bartender to pull another beer for Dodge's little coachman.

"We don't zactly move in the same circles, you know what I'm sayin'. Ladies I can afford can't afford no perfume like what came home on *his* clothes."

"They done found his cane there, though." Germain took a thoughtful pull on his fresh pint. "Think somebody in the house mighta wanted to get him in trouble?"

"Well, they's a few that might be happy enough to get Mr. Latham in trouble. He'd fit right in as an overseer on a South Georgia plantation. He done whupped onea the stable boys upside the head with his ridin' crop, poor fella—but see," the coachman looked at Germain shrewdly, as if beginning to wonder why he was asking all these questions, "ain't nobody in that house woulda hurt Mr. Nielsen. They all knowed he was a true friend of the race—and we don't got too many of them left."

"You drive the missus around too?" Germain asked casually. "My man Willis, he take Miz Dodge all over town on her visitin' calls."

"She don't go out much. Got one or two charity things, sewin' circles for fallen women, suchlike. She go to church a lot. Ain't been the same since she lost that gal, what I hear below stairs. Only worn black for near on seven years now. No wonder he messin' 'round."

"What happen to the gal?" Wyatt's wife Rose. Germain kept his tone offhand.

"She was long gone by the time I come around. What I hear, she was somethin' to look at. Like a angel, Beulah said—that's Miz Latham's lady's maid. Run off and married some dirt-poor actor, papa disowns her, don't allow her mama to make no contact. That's what I mean about him holdin' grudges. So that gal, she gets consumption and dies without her folks ever seein' her again. Shame. What I heard, the husband sent letters, telegrams, nothin' doin'. She was a only chile an' now they got nobody."

Germain felt a catch in his throat. This was the other side of Wyatt's story. "Mmm-hmph-hmm. That when Miz Latham took to wearin' black?"

Tyler nodded his head. "Mr. Latham, he acted like nothin' happened. But the missus, she done never got over it."

"Sure is a sad story." Germain drained the last of his porter. "Now, look here, brother, anything happen to Mr. Latham, you come on by an' I'll see if I can't keep my ears open, somebody lookin' for a good driver."

"Be innocent of the knowledge, dearest chuck," Wyatt said with a sardonic smile, catching Lady Macbeth under the chin and kissing her, "till thou applaud the deed." Under the heavy wool tabard, his hand found the hilt of his sword, which he fingered uneasily while delivering the rest of the speech. It had wobbled during the fight scenes for the last few days. So had Sydney Mather's Macduff sword, and the properties people hadn't yet found them substitutes. He had an uneasy vision of one of their blades whirling free of its haft during Macbeth's final duel with Macduff, flying out into the audience like a lethal whirligig, leaving a path of bloody gashes in its wake. It was an unlucky play, after all.

"...Light thickens, and the crow makes wing to the rooky wood...So, prithee, go with me." He put his arm around Mrs. Marlowe's waist and hurried her off the stage. His hired murderers came in from stage left to wreak his bloody sentence on Banquo. Giovanna, perched on the edge of the props table in her Witch costume, gave him a quick smile and disappeared into the wings. Behind a screen in the dim backstage light, the wardrobe mistress got Julia Marlowe into Lady Macbeth's silky banquet gown and came out to throw an embroidered robe over Wyatt's head to replace his tabard.

Mrs. Marlowe emerged from behind the screen and took Wyatt by the elbow, nodding towards the props table.

"She's in love with you," she whispered into his ear.

"What?" he hissed back.

"Seriously. We talked at dinner."

Wyatt's glance flew wildly between Mrs. Marlowe and the action on the stage. Banquo was yelling at his son Fleance to flee from the assassins cutting him to ribbons.

Mrs. Marlowe's hand was on his arm. "Oh, she didn't say so, of course. But a woman can tell. I would be bloody, bold and resolute, if I were you." She leaned in, confidential, like an ambitious wife telling her husband how to dispose of his enemies. He scanned her face in the dim light, wondering if she were joking.

"Propose marriage to her, silly boy!" she hissed. "Treadwell's got dozens more where she came from, and I *know* he won't fight her on the children."

The scene lights dimmed as the assassins dragged Banquo's inert, bleeding corpse from the stage. Once in the wings, Rowland Buckstone came back to life and sprinted off behind the screen for his Ghost costume, a silvery-white, red-slashed version of the one he had been slaughtered in. A stagehand stood by with a huge white powderpuff for his hair.

Wyatt shook off the tumult Mrs. Marlowe's words had aroused in his heart and forced himself back into character, grabbing her by the elbow and leading her back onstage to the soon-to-be-haunted feast. "You know your own degrees: sit down. At first and last the hearty welcome…"

Marriage to Giovanna. Making a life with her. He hadn't allowed himself to contemplate the possibility.

CHAPTER 16

Washington Star, Evening Edition, April 11, 1906

POLICE MUM ON SUSPECTS IN CONGRESSMAN'S DEATH

Congressman Latham Rumored 'Prime Contender,' But No Move Yet To Arrest

A spokesman for the Metropolitan Bureau of Detectives today declined "to speculate" on whether an arrest might be imminent in the brutal slaying of Congressman Robert Nielsen of Wisconsin, which occurred in the night hours between April 4th and 5th. Nielsen was found beaten to death a block from his Foggy Bottom residence on Thursday morning last.

An altercation on the House floor earlier on the day of his death, culminating in what a colleague characterized as an "unforgivable insult" to Representative Richard Latham, a senior member from the Corning-Elmira district of New York, led to speculation that Latham's arrest on suspicion of Nielsen's murder was imminent. However, a full week after the discovery of a bloodied walking-stick bearing Latham's initials in a shrubbery near Nielsen's mangled corpse, Latham appeared unconcerned.

"I am sorry for the man's death, I know nothing whatever about it, and therefore have nothing to say," he told reporters outside his 16th Street home this morning. Asked by a reporter how his walking-stick came to be the murder weapon (though this has not been confirmed by the Office of the D.C. Medical Examiner), Latham declined comment. There are unconfirmed reports that he has engaged the services of Arthur O. Partridge, the well-known criminal defense attorney from the firm of Partridge, Gibb and Howland of this City.

A female associate of Nielsen's who was engaged with him in a variety of activities promoting the uplift of the colored race is reported to have publicly denounced Latham as the murderer during obsequies at All Souls Unitarian last week, though a colleague of Latham's opined that he "wouldn't give any weight to the rantings of an obviously hysterical female."

A source close to the investigation, who insisted on anonymity, said in a reference to Police Chief Richard Sylvester that "Latham's the prime suspect, no question. It's a matter of the Chief's working up the guts to let us make the arrest."

In a booth at the White Coffee Cup, Louisa Stanstead leveled her gaze at Wyatt over a mug of black coffee. "You're wondering if I did it myself."

"The police are," he said. "You've not been questioned yet?"

She laughed and shook her head. "I assumed some delicacy of feeling might account for the delay."

"That would be uncharacteristic." He noted the dark circles below her eyes. "The homicide commander, who's an old acquaintance, has the quaint notion that a murder victim's nearest and dearest are the likeliest suspects."

"I have no alibi." She clacked her mug on the table.

"None whatever?"

"And what's worse, after trying to sit up for him, fretting about our quarrel, hoping to make amends—I fell asleep on the divan over a weepie from the lending-library. It's how I relax—" She gave him a twisted little smile, took off her steel-rimmed glasses and polished them with her napkin. "If I'd stayed awake—if I'd gone out to look for him—" She turned her head away. "I still have the book too, it was overdue even then."

"I dare say they'll forgive the fine in the circumstances," Wyatt smiled. "There was no one else around the house at all? Mrs. Wilbur?"

"She lives two streets away. There was a knock on my door— half-past five or so, not quite full daylight. A policeman. Someone had told him where Robert lived, that's what woke me up. I'd loosened my stays, but I was still in my clothes—I must've looked a fright, even before he told me what had happened."

Perhaps that was why they hadn't hauled her in for questioning yet. The perverse thought occurred to him that, with a little more attention to dress and grooming, Louisa Stanstead could be rather attractive. Without her spectacles, her gray eyes were rather fine, the brows arched delicately above sculpted cheekbones. Her gallantry of spirit and her humor reminded him of Giovanna, which brought a pang of pity; the Lady Macduff scene had fallen flat again last night. If Mrs. Marlowe was right, maybe it was the thought of their imminent parting…

"Were you truly angry with Mr. Nielsen over the proposal?"

"I'm a hypocrite," she shook her head with a sad smile. "I would have married him, in the end. I claimed to want nothing to do with marriage and its patriarchal overtones, but the truth is that I took against it—" she stopped and bit her lip.

"Go on," Wyatt said gently.

"To insure myself against the absence of offers." She raised a hand to forestall his protest. "I had myself convinced it was the way I wanted things. So I had to refuse him. I think he made his offer in part because we were fodder for gossip. He couldn't be indifferent to the effect it was having on my reputation."

"But the ladies of your circle—" Wyatt began.

"—are mostly women of color, and necessarily more tolerant of unconventional domestic arrangements."

Latham's hateful speculation about Louisa killing Nielsen for refusing to marry her when he could "get it for free" came back to Wyatt in a rush. "Miss Stanstead—Louisa—is there anyone else who can attest to the Congressman's having made you a proposal on the morning before the murder?"

She shook her head with a rueful smile. "It could have been my spinsterish fantasy as far as the world is concerned—" She looked up suddenly.

"What is it?"

"He had a ring-box with him, in his pocket. He took it out and opened it when he asked me to marry him."

"Do you know what he did with it after you…ah, refused him?"

The pain that washed over Louisa's sallow face wrenched his heart. "He dashed it to the ground," she whispered. "The box with the ring. It might have rolled under the tallboy in the parlor—I haven't had the heart to look for it…"

"Let me come with you," Wyatt said, realizing the value of a witness in such a situation. "But there's one more thing I must ask you about, though it belies your assertion that you're not an attractive woman. There was someone else who cared for you, before Mr. Nielsen—"

She flushed and gripped the edge of the table. "Where did you hear that?"

"One of the colored gentlemen from the funeral told me that you'd had a suitor—you introduced us, in fact. Mr. Costello?"

Her flush deepened. "Who is trying to drag poor James into this?"

"Jealousy is a common motive for murder."

"And colored men are of course more passionate and vengeful in such matters," she said sardonically. "We have Shakespeare to thank for starting that. But it won't do, Wyatt—James values his respectability above everything, poor man. He's achieved so much—got a fine education at Howard, gained a position at the most prestigious colored school in America. For a while I thought I might be able to love him."

"Until?"

"I realized it wasn't so much me he wanted as a light-skinned wife who would cement his social standing."

"That sounds harsh," Wyatt said, wondering why Louisa had said "light-skinned" rather than "white."

"Oh, it's possible things would have come down to marriage eventually," a reminiscent smile came like winter sunshine, "he has that lost puppy look—you want to take him home and feed him and tuck him in. I think James saw me as a mother figure. He lost his own quite young. And he may have been encouraged in the knowledge that by many definitions, I am a Negro myself."

She laughed at Wyatt's astonished reaction.

"My great-grandparents on my mother's side met at Oberlin, which you may know was a hotbed of abolitionism back then."

Wyatt nodded. "I grew up near there. On a dairy farm."

110

"My great-grandmother had been a slave—a nursemaid in a New England family, not terribly dark skinned by all accounts. The family got religion at some point, freed her and paid for her education—she was still quite young—and then she met my great-grandfather, who was an abolitionist. So you see, if that bill of Milton's were to become law, Robert and I would have been forbidden to marry, since I'm one-eighth Negro. Which most of my colored friends know, by the way."

"But you and Mr. Costello—" Wyatt began.

"—who would have been forbidden to marry if I were white, could marry with impunity under the terms of the bill. A bill which he opposes with all his strength."

It would have been a cold-hearted murderer who acted on the basis of that little equation. "How long is it since you've seen him?"

"Privately? Oh…weeks and weeks. He came to the funeral. He didn't try to approach me, but I saw him on the edge of our group. I really should be going—"

"I need to know how things ended. Between you and him."

"They never really began. He used to call on me, when I lived over in Georgetown. I would offer him tea, we'd talk about history or literature, sometimes he brought flowers or a little plant. I was flattered by his attentions, which were the first in my experience. He's a nice-looking man, as you saw—I assure you I've been attracted to darker-skinned men than he—but I couldn't feel for him what he felt for me, and then I met Robert. He was there one evening when James came by—this was before Robert and I set up housekeeping. I'm afraid it was all too obvious to poor James that he was—what's the expression? A third wheel, and he quickly took his leave."

"Did he seem angry or upset?"

She shook her head. "He just looked…sad. Those big brown eyes…you're not seriously thinking he might have killed Robert?"

Wyatt offered her his arm for the walk back to her house. "I've only met him that once. I don't know what to think. But he'd have an obvious motive."

The look she gave him as they paced down the street was full of anxiety. "Wyatt, he values his good name above anything. You mustn't take that from him. I should hate to see him suffer more than the pangs of despis'd love I've already visited upon him."

"Speaking of visits—has he made any private calls on you since Mr. Nielsen's death?"

"He asked Nettie—Mrs. Wilbur—whether he might come around for a condolence call. I asked her to discourage it if she got the chance. Though knowing James, that's all it would be—at least at first. He'd die before he could be accused of being un-mannerly." She smiled sadly. "I'm afraid that's another thing I found tiresome about him."

They were halfway around Washington Circle when Wyatt stopped and turned to Louisa. "You've not told me the truth, Miss Stanstead. About why you refused Mr. Nielsen."

"I beg your pardon?"

"You wanted to spare him the political embarrassment that would come if it were revealed that he had a colored wife. I think that rather noble of you."

She dropped her eyes. "Not exactly. But it would have compromised him on the marriage bill—the idea of a personal interest. He would have been ridiculed in the press and among his colleagues."

"Did he know of your—your heritage?"

She smiled. "Of course he did. From the beginning."

On his knees, he retrieved the little red velvet box from the dusty corner where it had rolled. Filaments of spiderweb came away with it; it had sat there for some time. He brushed them off.

"Open it," she said. "I can't bear to."

It was a small square-cut emerald with a baguette diamond on each side, set in filigreed white gold. She drew in a sharp breath and began to cry.

"It's lovely." Wyatt handed her the box.

"It belonged to his mother," Louisa said. "It was so old-fashioned of him—quite unlike him!"

"Love changes people." Wyatt laid a hand on her arm. "I assume his sister in Wisconsin can vouch for the ring—and I think the police will agree that it supports your story of that morning's events. And I believe that Mr. Nielsen would be very happy to see it on your finger."

With shaking fingertips she lifted the ring from its white velvet slit and slipped it onto the middle finger of her left hand. "His mother's hands must have been larger than mine," she murmured. "This was her wedding-band. Don't you think his sister should have it—" She collapsed on the divan and covered her face with her hands.

Which was where Mrs. Nettie Wilbur found her a few moments later when she came into the kitchen with a basket of groceries. " 'Ouisa, you here?" She dropped the basket and came into the parlor, shooting Wyatt a glare at the sight of her friend's shaking shoulders.

"It's all right, Nettie—" Louisa held out her hand with a watery smile. "Look what Mr. Wyatt just found for me, where Robert had—ah, dropped it that morning."

Mrs. Wilbur grasped her hand and examined the ring. "See, I knew it! I told my Clarence—we were picturing the two of you here, settled down, maybe even a little one—" her hand strayed to her own rounded belly, and her gaze turned sad. "You having any luck looking for a new place?"

Louisa brightened. "I hadn't told either of you yet! Do you know what my dear Robert did? He took out an insurance policy with the Strivers' Mutual, not long before he was—before he died. Mr. Templeton came round and told me about it. It will give me a small annuity—just enough to let me stay here, with what I make at my writing. And keep on a little household help." She smiled up at her friend, who squeezed her hand warmly. "It's a great relief, I must confess."

Wyatt's brow furrowed. Insurance was an all too frequent motive for murder. "And he'd told you nothing of this?"

Louisa caught the change in his tone. "Mr. Templeton was puzzled by that too. He asked me for copies of the policy, but I haven't been able to find any. It doesn't matter—they have the

113

originals at the office. He brought me the first check himself. What a dear, kind man he is."

Wyatt made a mental note to talk with George Templeton and gain his impressions of what Nielsen might have told his lover about the insurance policy. An annuity was a weaker motive than a large lump sum, and there seemed nothing venal about Louisa Stanstead. But Macalester would grasp at the detail like a terrier on a trousers-leg.

"What did Mr. Nielsen's will say?" The question came out more abruptly than he'd planned, but Louisa only smiled.

"There wasn't one," she said. "All he owned was the family homestead in Madison, that had been left to him and his sister by their parents. So he didn't need to will it. They were—there's some legal phrase for it—joint tenants? She'd get it automatically if he..." she bit her lip. "I've never been to Madison. I never saw his home. Where he came from. I wish..." she shook her head.

CHAPTER 17

Commander Macalester looked up from the medical examiner's report, his sharp blue gaze meeting Wyatt's over half-moon glasses. "Our medico here," he tapped the paper with the back of his hand, "says that the bruises on Nielsen's limbs and torso are peri-mortem at least, if not postmortem, and furthermore, seem *not* to have been inflicted with an instrument capable of producing lethal injury." He rose and poured Wyatt a mug of tarry-looking coffee and some equally opaque tea for himself.

"The cane didn't kill him." Wyatt frowned over the rim of his mug, elbows on knees in a well-upholstered leather chair. Macalester's new office in the District Building was as much of an improvement as promised, with polished wood floors glowing at the edges of an Oriental carpet and a view of the White House from his massive rosewood desk which might have induced delusions of grandeur in a weaker man. The coffee, however, was the same police-issue swill he'd had on prior occasions.

"It's unlikely, according to the good doctor Blaisdell. He says the depressed fracture that produced the hematoma—the build-up of blood at the brain-stem that killed him—was most likely produced by something thicker and heavier. A cosh, say, or a baseball bat."

"Cosh—is that Scottish for a sap?"

"'Sap' is American for idjit, I thought." Macalester rose and came around behind Wyatt's chair.

"I'll try not to take that personally," Wyatt grinned. "Bludgeon, then, or slung-shot. But there was blood on the cane."

"There were two potentially fatal blows." Macalester proceeded to use Wyatt's head to demonstrate the injury sites. "One was to the temple—delivered from behind and to the right, our man says. Splintered the temporal bone, opened the scalp, hence all the blood. The other struck the left parietal bone, at the back here, leaving a depressed fracture—which suggests a powerful set of arms, you might note."

"Or a practiced swing with a baseball bat."

"Maybe so. It's harder to conceal than a cosh, but it's the favorite weapon of some of our local plug-uglies for hire. Or street thieves, for that matter, though he still had his wallet. One or the other of these blows rendered him unconscious and produced the subdural hemorrhage that killed him. Combined with the nature of the bruises on the rest of the body, this suggests that—"

Wyatt bounced in his seat. "—he incapacitated Nielsen with the sap, or the bat, then whaled about his unconscious or dead body to make it look as if there had been a fight. The blood on the cane would have come from the scalp wound."

Macalester assumed his habitual perch on the edge of his desk, a pose which reminded Wyatt of a garden gnome. "We can rule out anyone with medical expertise as our perpetrator, it's fair to say. What I think he intended to look like defensive bruises," he reached back for the report and peered at it over the glasses, "were all over the wrists and arms—on the distal as well as the proximal surfaces of the forearms." Macalester demonstrated by crossing his own arms above his head. "Whereas if you're raising your arms to ward off blows—"

"—the blows should be on the insides—the proximal surfaces," Wyatt finished. "So we've got premeditation, if a bit clumsy, and a calculated attempt to set up Latham as the killer."

"As you say, it points to staging." Macalester folded his arms and nodded approval of his student's deduction, which annoyed Wyatt exceedingly. "Blaisdell also tells us the evidence points to someone right-handed and a wee bit shorter than Nielsen."

Wyatt grunted. "That doesn't help much, Nielsen being six foot one." Cornelius Dunagin, he remembered, was Nielsen's height or even taller. "Were those two blows enough to cause death?"

"Either one could have, Blaisdell says. The poor fella probably didn't know what hit him. Just as well. Our murderer was lucky too—the first one probably rendered Nielsen unconscious."

"That'll be some comfort to Miss Stanstead," Wyatt said.

Macalester gave him the ice-chip gaze. "Assuming she didn't do it herself, which with these findings isn't out of the question."

"You have to admit it's unlikely," Wyatt said with some asperity. "Who's in the market for the services of these plug-uglies you mentioned?"

"The usual criminal element—it's a common way of settling territorial disputes. We also hear of the occasional shady businessman whose interests are interfered with, upping the ante with his opponents."

"Someone like Cornelius Dunagin?"

Macalester looked surprised. "The real estate baron? Never met the man, but far as I know he's respectable enough. Haven't heard of any criminal acts—" he paused.

"But you have heard something."

"Not directly, just rumors. Nothing we could tie him to—or anybody else, for that matter. Tenants getting roughed up over unpaid rents, and so forth. No complaints filed, though."

"I met him at Dodge's office. Now I think of it, he was asking Dodge if he'd known you in New York. Dodge was smart enough not to tell him anything."

"Well, now. Why would he want to know that, I wonder—" Macalester's eyes narrowed. "You're not thinking he might've done for Nielsen?"

"Or hired it out."

"And left Latham's cane at the scene? And what might he have against a business partner who, from all we've heard, has brought him lucrative introductions to the upper crust?"

"I'll be looking into that."

"It's time I laid eyes on this Dunagin chap," Macalester said, "and found out what's caused you to take against him so quickly." He hopped down from the desk. "But I can hardly just drop in for a spot of tea, being a policeman and all. Seems to put people off."

"He said he and his wife—he calls her the Countess—would have to come and see the play, now that he's met me. And arguably I was a little rude to him at Dodge's office. What say I send them a pair of complimentary tickets for tomorrow night—he can think of it as a peace-offering—and get you a seat with a good vantage point—"

"Dear, dear!" Macalester shook his head, "D'you realize what tomorrow is?"

Wyatt was about to shake his head, but stopped. "Friday the thirteenth." He wasn't prone to superstition, but something about the convergence of that date and a performance in the Scottish Play sent a shiver up his spine. "Well, it can't be unlucky for everybody."

"Send me a ticket, then, but with a bill, if you don't mind. Can't be gettin' accused of graft and corruption this early in my tenure."

"Bring a lady with you—you'll blend in better."

Macalester scowled. "Are you saying I look like a flatfoot?"

"Most people don't go to the theater alone. And your picture will have been in the papers, right? So if you're by yourself, anyone who recognizes you might get the idea that you're, ah, working."

"There may be something in what you say," Macalester nodded. "I'll see if my faithful clerk Miss Blumenhofer will join me, tell her it's part of a clandestine investigation."

"Good. And if I'm on the wrong track about Dunagin—"

"We're back to your asymmetrical theory. Someone has a personal grudge against Latham and a political grudge against Nielsen. Or the other way round—someone who shared Nielsen's politics."

That led back to Louisa, or to one of Nielsen's reformist colleagues—or, Wyatt realized with a sinking heart, to someone in the Negro community Nielsen had worked so hard to help— who in killing the Congressman would bring discredit on his cause and double the damage of his death. He'd rather think about greed as a motive and someone like Cornelius Dunagin as the killer.

"Are you off Latham's trail, then?" That was, after all, his only job here: to clear Latham of suspicion. The double duty was exhausting. The day-time he'd relied on to recharge after a performance was taken up with investigation. If he got Latham out of the sights of the police, he could go back to being a stage villain, and to thinking about what to do about Giovanna. Mrs. Marlowe's backstage confidences had awakened a hope he hadn't dared acknowledge.

Macalester shook his head. "Not by a long shot. Blaisdell admits the cane still could have been the murder weapon, or that Latham could have used a handy brick or rock, for instance, to strike the fatal blows. He might've killed him in cold blood, then set up the scene to look like a fight—"

"Not leaving his own cane, surely!"

"Odd how that argues his innocence, isn't it? But he may have been surprised in mid-battery and dropped it in yon clump of bushes—where we had a right rummage before we found it, so if it was a plant, it wasn't the most obvious one."

Ambivalence, Wyatt wondered, or perhaps remorse. Someone not inured to violence, who killed with the first, surprising blow, more interested in dispatching the victim efficiently than enjoying his suffering. But why implicate Latham?

"To answer your question, no, we're not putting Latham in the clear," Macalester said. "We've more than enough evidence to indict him and, in the absence of a likelier suspect, I'd not be surprised if the U.S. Attorney decided to go forward at the first of next week, what with the press breathing down our necks. So you'd best bring us a credible alternative, and right soon. In between slaying challengers to your Throne of Blood, and whatever other ways you have of amusing yourself."

Wyatt caught up with Dodge between House committee sessions and gave him a digest of his encounter with the Alley Relief Society. "Nielsen was pushing an amendment—which sounds a lot like the permit denial ordinance you were talking about," he remembered. "There's a bill coming out of committee that would require the District to condemn all the unsanitary dwellings and see that they're taken down. Nielsen wanted to add that provision to it."

"Fighting on several fronts. Good strategy on his part." Dodge waved him into his office and sent the clerk for coffee.

"The Alley Relief group plans to keep pushing for it. Think they'll get anywhere?"

Dodge shook his head. "They'll be lucky if they get the condemnation bill."

"If you're still seriously thinking about going in with Dunagin," Wyatt said, "you'd better check up on whether he owns Snow's Court. That's as close as I get to giving a man like you investment advice." He paced back and forth in front of Dodge's desk, tugging on the strands of his mustache, and stopped. "If he does own it—or other places like it—Dunagin's got as much reason as anybody to have wanted Robert Nielsen gone, doesn't he?"

Dodge's look was incredulous. "You're not thinking *he* might've killed Nielsen?"

"Depends. Could Nielsen really have had an effect on Commissioner Macfarland's chances for reappointment?"

"It's not so much that—Macfarland's a God-fearing sort, for Temperance and woman suffrage and such. He'd have been sympathetic to Nielsen's pleas for improving the lot of the Negroes. Not a crusader himself, but susceptible to pressure. Which has now been conveniently removed."

Wyatt planted his palms on Dodge's desk. "Can you string Dunagin along for a while longer? Tell him you're interested, but you want to do some—what do the lawyers call it—due diligence? It would give me more time to poke around, see if I find any links to Nielsen's death."

"That's asking a lot. He wants an answer right away. I've put him off as it is."

"If he had anything to do with it, that's the last partnership deal you'll want to put your name to. Have you had him to the house?"

"I've been giving out that the Belmont Road place is merely a cheap alternative to a hotel suite until we get the new place built on 16th Street, and not a place to entertain guests. Which is true enough—"

"And?"

Dodge looked at the floor. "I don't know that Augusta can learn to like him. Said he had the air of a *parvenu* the first time she met him. And I'm even less sure about the wife."

"Was that the Countess he was talking about?"

"He married up, by his description. A Madame—what was it—Kóhary? Some sort of exiled Hungarian aristocrat. Welcomed at all the best diplomatic receptions, he assures me. You can imagine the effect *that* had on Augusta."

"What precisely is his business relationship with Latham?"

Dodge stuck his thumbs in his waistcoat pockets and stared out to the slums of East Capitol Street, where several of the city's worst alleys lay, as reformers were fond of noting, in the very shadow of the Capitol. "They're partners in a couple of deals. Latham's been the front man for him with some other partners—his money's quite a bit older. They find that reassuring."

"So if Latham's nailed for Nielsen's death, Dunagin loses a major draw for his development schemes?"

"Well, I probably wouldn't have received him if Latham hadn't paved the way," Dodge admitted. "Latham has already lined him up with half a dozen major investors, who may well go south if he's indicted—unless—"

"Unless what?"

"Unless they're already signed on, and it's too late to matter. But even then, if Dunagin did have something to do with Nielsen's murder, why try to implicate Latham by leaving his walking-stick at the scene?"

Wyatt flopped back into a chair. "That I don't know. But there's an old rule of thumb I remember you telling me: when you see a situation you don't understand—"

"—look for the profit motive," Dodge finished. "Think there's anything to his idea of looking among Nielsen's Negro associates?"

"Can't rule it out yet," Wyatt said ruefully, "but I'd rather start with him. How did Germain make out with Latham's coachman?"

"I left him this morning with an ice-pack on his head, having made the supreme sacrifice of getting drunk with the man to loosen his tongue. He's convinced the fellow spent the night of the murder with some trollop on Pennsylvania Avenue. You may persuade him to run that one down while you're commiserating with him."

CHAPTER 18

"The coachman's clean," Germain told Wyatt, whom he had enlisted as factotum and pack-mule for a visit to the Centre Market on Pennsylvania Avenue. Wyatt didn't mind; the cavernous, turreted red-brick confection halfway between the Capitol and the White House was the crowded, bustling heart of the city, with the buzz of buying and selling at seven hundred vendors' stalls underlain by the rattle of delivery wagons on the cobblestones of B Street, washed shiny by a spring shower, to the rear. Earthy smells of newly picked radishes, leeks and lettuce and the pleasantly dry, bitter scents from heaped banks of daffodils, iris and tulips competed with the salty tang of oyster stalls and rank, rich aromas of cheeses from the surrounding Maryland farms. It was a relief to be among ordinary things, ordinary people with ordinary concerns.

He wished suddenly for his own small kitchen in his Upper West Side apartment, for a few cooking-pans and a colorful heap of this wonderful fresh food spilling out of the market-basket he now carried. He thought of making dinner for Giovanna there, opening a bottle of claret…the thought of their imminent parting squeezed his heart and pulled him back to threading the narrow aisles in Germain's wake, catching up with him at a butcher's stall hung with gutted, headless carcasses.

"If Tyler needs an alibi," Germain went on, "he can get it cheap and quick from Miss Minerva Jones. Or anything else he'd like cheap and quick. She was more than happy for twice her usual fee to tell me what all she did to him last Tuesday night, and for how long. I told her I was one of those fellas that just liked gals to talk dirty to 'em," he explained in answer to Wyatt's quizzical look. "She said it was a waste, but it was my money." Germain's rich laugh floated over the heads of the butchers, who were cutting a bright red loin of beef to his specifications. "Seems he high-tailed it down there as soon as he took Latham's coach back home, stayed till two-three in the morning. One of her regulars, evidently."

"Hmm. 'Clean' isn't the word I'd have used," Wyatt grinned.

"But it gives him an alibi. Something else he told me," Germain's voice lowered and Wyatt had to strain to hear him in the surrounding cacophony. "Your wife's mama? Miz Latham? Took to wearing black when Rose died. All she's worn ever since. Word below stairs is she wanted to get back in touch with Rose after she married you, and he wouldn't let her."

Wyatt stared at him, his throat constricting, thinking of the pinch-faced woman by Latham's side at Nielsen's funeral. How he'd despised her. "He made her choose between him and Rose." He felt his eyes fill. "The bastard. I should let him rot—"

"He didn't do it, Wyatt. And there's nobody else in that house that would've, now we know it wasn't Tyler. So unless he kept a thug or two on the payroll for when somebody did him an injury, you'd best be looking elsewhere."

Wyatt closed his eyes. Senhora Pereira shimmered in his mind, blue-robed, like the imperiled Queen of France, graceful, nervous fingers hovering at her throat. It was as good a motivator as any. He'd be her d'Artagnan, rescue her from the danger in which her passions had placed herself and her country. Unlike her lover, she was worth saving.

Germain dropped several large packages wrapped in butcher paper in Wyatt's basket and they moved on to the seafood stalls.

"I've got another favor to ask."

"You ask a lot, *mon vieux*."

"I know. But there are things you can do a lot better than I. This one won't be as entertaining as Miss Minerva Jones, I dare say."

Germain raised an eyebrow. "Ooookay...?"

"Find out where James Costello was on the night of the murder."

"Oh, man. You serious, Wyatt?"

"Nielsen stole his lady-friend. At least, he may see it that way."

"*Maybe* that would make him mad enough to kill him. Like we were saying, it's the respectable ones that go off the rails sometimes. But beating him to death? I can't see that. Too messy. Poison, maybe, or shooting him." Germain turned to the shellfish vendor, who was handing him a lidded pail filled with ice and oysters. "Here, hold this while I pay the man."

Wyatt balanced the pail on the rim of the basket. "Who knows what a fellow will do when he goes off the rails?"

"But getting Latham's cane to do it with—that's too much planning ahead. Anyway—I'll see him on Sunday. They're having a memorial service for Nielsen in the Howard University chapel. You should come too." Germain reclaimed the bucket of oysters.

"Won't it go better if it's just you? They'd know the only reason I was there was to snoop around."

"Well, that's most of the reason I'd be going. "Cept for trying to worm my way into respectable Washington society." Germain blinked in the bright spring sunshine beyond the market's archway.

Wyatt laughed. "The way those ladies were eyeing you at Miss Stanstead's meeting, I doubt any worming will be necessary. I guess I'll come along at that, keep you out of trouble."

In eighth row center at the National Theatre, Commander Macalester ran a finger under the stiff collar of his dress shirt and squirmed a little in his unaccustomed tailcoat. His ancient but serviceable top hat had been consigned to the cloakroom. Banquo's Ghost had just made his appearance; Wyatt's Macbeth seemed to shrink under his horrible, gory smile. Absorbed in the scene, as was the plump and bespectacled Miss Blumenhofer rapt in her Sunday frock at his side, Macalester nearly forgot that this was the last before intermission, his best chance for a good look at the Cornelius Dunagins, who would be in the first mezzanine box at stage left. Wyatt had invited them backstage afterwards and had suggested Macalester's stopping by for a "coincidental" introduction.

He rose with the crowd as the curtain fell, glancing up and around in what he hoped was a casual way. His gaze landed on the mezzanine box, where a woman in garnet silk trimmed with black lace was being helped into an opera cloak by a big man with dark, wavy hair who matched Wyatt's description of Dunagin. The man looked up as if he'd felt himself being stared at; for half an instant his eyes met Macalester's and he stopped moving as if spell-bound. Macalester stood for a frozen moment of his own, stifled a gasp and quickly turned away. The man in the mezzanine box had a face he knew. The face of someone who'd been dead for twenty years.

He poked Miss Blumenhofer in the ribs. "You've just been taken ill. We have to go." She gave him a wild-eyed, devastated look, but professionalism prevailed; she slumped against him. Her eyelids fluttered and she seemed to grow pale. With Macalester supporting her by the elbow, the two made their way quickly to an aisle and through a velvet curtained doorway to a side lobby. With trembling hands Macalester pulled a small notebook from his breast pocket, scribbled a note and folded it in thirds, addressing it to Wyatt. There was a silver half-dollar in the pocket, which he extracted and pressed into the hands of a startled usher along with the note. "Get this to Mr. Wyatt right away," he said. "He'd asked us backstage after the curtain, but my niece is unwell." The usher nodded and disappeared.

Macalester slipped out of a side entrance and put the disappointed Miss Blumenhofer into a hackney, promising to explain later and thanking her profusely. Heart pounding, he made his way rapidly a few doors down to the District Building. Only in the safety of his darkened office did he realize he'd forgotten to retrieve his top hat.

On no account mention me to Dunagin, Macalester's note read. *Meet tomorrow my office 10 a.m.* Wyatt crumpled the note in his hand and tossed it into a wastebasket just as a knock came on the green room door. He opened it to reveal Cornelius Dunagin and a woman in garnet silk trimmed with black lace. "Please, come in."

"My dear, let me introduce you to the star of the show," Dunagin said, all smiles. "Mr. Wyatt, my wife Countess Antonia Kóhary."

Wyatt, still in the bloodstained armor in which he'd been slain, bowed deeply. "An honor, madam. Forgive my disorderly appearance."

"Oh, you were marvelous!" she said in a husky contralto. "The best I have seen in the role, I *assure* you. And I have seen many times—the Scottish play, I think I must call it?"

Wyatt inclined his head and suppressed a smile. Something about the woman's deep, dark eyes and aquiline nose made him think of the vampirical brides of Count Dracula who'd attacked the young lawyer in his sleep, in that otherwise forgettable potboiler he'd read on a train.

"Come and have supper with us at the Raleigh, won't you?" Dunagin said. "The view from the top floor's spectacular. Dodge and his wife will be there—they've been to a recital or some such. Suggested you join us. And some of my business colleagues as well."

"They would simply *love* to meet you," the Countess purred.

Wyatt was about to demur when it occurred to him that Dodge had suggested the outing as a chance to observe Dunagin and other potential suspects at close range. And if Macalester was anxious to avoid the man, it could only be because he'd seen in him something that alarmed him.

"Very kind of you," he said. "Perhaps for just a little while. Shall I meet you there in half an hour?"

Closing the door behind them, he sighed and sat down to remove his stage makeup. He'd been looking forward to spending the rest of the evening with Lady Macduff. He hoped she'd understand.

CHAPTER 19

The morning sun on Macalester's desk revealed a litter of grainy photographs scattered among Wanted posters. He looked up sharply as Wyatt was shown in.

"You left at intermission. What's this all about?"

"Resurrection, it appears," Macalester said. He pulled out a half dozen of the pictures, all of them evidently police booking photographs dating from some time past, and three of the posters. "Take your time and tell me if any of them look familiar."

Wyatt grabbed the pile and sat, scanning the photos rapidly, then slowing down. "Something about this one, I—" His head shot up. "A younger version of Dunagin?"

Macalester nodded with grim triumph. "My thought exactly."

Wyatt read the faded handwriting on the back of the photo. *Patrick Joseph O'Donoghue, 10/17/84 alias "Dandy Pat".*

"He looks about eighteen or twenty here," he said, "which would make him about—"

"—about Dunagin's age," Macalester said. "Only thing is, Dandy Pat is supposed to have died the year after that. They pulled his bloated body out of the East River."

"How'd they know it was him?"

Macalester took the photo back. "The clothes on the body were the ones he'd last been seen in—everything matched the description we had. He'd been in the water too long to go by his face, but the height was about right, and a ring on his finger, a big chunky thing he used like a set of brass knuckles. Thing is, we'd been about to arrest him for a particularly nasty set of murders."

"And it was your case."

"Aye, it was. And it haunts me to this day. He was a senior lieutenant in the Whyos—you'll have heard of that gang?"

"On the wane, last I heard. Had a couple of run-ins with them over the years."

"Indeed!? You're tougher than you look, laddie."

"I didn't meet up with the smarter ones. What was he wanted for?"

"Seems a young lady, quite young in fact, that he'd marked for his own had got tired of waiting for him to come home nights and resumed her former, ah, profession." Macalester stood and began prowling the room, tapping the photo with the back of his hand. "He traced her to a place on Mott Street, went in with guns blazing, so to speak, left her and a customer and two of her colleagues like a pile of butcher-meat on the floor. I'd never seen a crime scene as bad, till the Black Hand massacre."

"Any witnesses?"

"One poor wee chambermaid who cowered in a linen-cupboard and managed to stay quiet. Just a glimpse through a crack, but she knew the fella all right. She stayed in that cupboard for hours, afraid he'd come back and find her, then ran all the way to the station-house. In between fits of hysterics, she told us who it was. We'd half the force out looking for him—known haunts, associates, bolt-holes, train stations, docks—not a sign of him, and no one who'd seen him afterwards. Or not that they'd admit to, despite our best efforts at persuasion."

"Until the body turned up. And you were sure it was him?"

"Well, we'd no fingerprinting in those days, of course, but it seemed the logical conclusion. We reckoned one of the ladies' 'protectors' must have done for him, maybe even somebody he came to looking for a hidey-hole. He'd been whacked unconscious and dumped in the drink—while still alive, apparently, there being water in the lungs. And now..."

Wyatt wasn't used to seeing Macalester in a state of uncertainty, much less the fear that shadowed his face now. "It's technically a cold case, right? Still open?"

Macalester nodded. "That's right, since we never convicted anybody. There's still an evidence file somewhere—"

"It sounds as if *he* did away with somebody—someone who looked like him—and switched identities."

Macalester sighed. "Wouldn't have been anybody known to the police. His cohorts were all accounted for, and closely questioned at that. But then, dozens of people disappear in the City every day."

Wyatt sprang to his feet. "Immigrant ships."

"Eh?"

"The gang's turf was down near the tip of the Island, right? What if he got hold of somebody coming off a steamer through Castle Garden, befriended him, got him drunk at some waterfront dive, say, and—"

"If you don't watch out, you'll turn into that villain you're playing," Macalester grinned but quickly turned sober again. "We examined all the embarking steamer passengers from that night on, and for the next week. He couldn't have got away that way—"

"But not the *dis*embarking passengers. What if there was an Irishman—an Ulsterman—named Cornelius Dunagin on one of the ships that came in that day?"

Macalester's eyes went wide. He reached for the telephone on his desk and barked into the mouthpiece. "Miss B., get me Commissioner Watchorn at Ellis Island. Right away. That's where all the ship manifests are now—what didn't burn up in the '97 fire, anyway," he explained, hanging the earpiece back on its stand.

"What if you find something?"

"There's no statute of limitations on murder, laddie. If we find someone by that name within a day or so of Dandy Pat's disappearance—well, we shall have to proceed with great care. Dandy Pat was a very dangerous young man. And if you're right—"

"—that makes Dunagin a likelier possibility for the Nielsen murder as well. Would also explain why he was asking Dodge about you the other day."

Macalester looked stricken. "It does, doesn't it?"

"I must say he gave every indication of civilized behavior last evening. After the second round of champagne, even Augusta Dodge seemed to be softening on him. Though not so much on the Countess, come to think of it. His wife," he added in response to Macalester's puzzled look. "Countess Antonia Kóhary, late of

Hungary, we're told. I don't think Augusta was buying the pedigree."

"Not surprised to hear that," Macalester managed a smile. "I don't suppose you probed him for *his* pedigree?"

"I've found it useful at times to give the impression of being a cheap drunk," Wyatt smiled in his turn. "Got all confidential about having been a star-struck country boy dazzled by the lights of New York, then asked him if he'd grown up on a farm himself, back in Ireland. And how come he didn't end up in New York like all the other Irishmen I know. Had to kick Dodge under the table to keep him from jumping in."

"Good thing you've long legs."

"Came in through Baltimore in '85, he says—had a job as a shipping clerk waiting for him. The company paid his passage. I thought that was illegal."

"Not at that time."

"Says he got restless after a few weeks," Wyatt said. "Took a little jaunt to see the Nation's Capital and got work here as a junior clerk for a realty company. Which he now owns, he was pleased to tell us. This Dandy Pat was also an Irish immigrant, I take it?"

Macalester nodded. "Came in as a lad of eleven or twelve and started getting in trouble right away. Family was from the Dublin slums but they might have started elsewhere."

"Dunagin says he's from Armagh. That's in Ulster, isn't it?"

"What's his accent like?"

"You'd be a better judge. To me he sounds Northern Irish trying to sound English," Wyatt said. "Not sure I could tell if he was from somewhere else."

"He'll have been counting on that, if he is an impostor," Macalester said. "Not so many Irish here to trip him up."

"Any chance of fingerprints in the case file?"

Macalester frowned. "What good would that do at this stage?"

Wyatt reached into his jacket and carefully drew out something wrapped in a linen napkin. He set it down on Macalester's desk and unwrapped it, holding the napkin only at the corners. It was a champagne flute. "I'm developing criminal tendencies at that. I pilfered this from the Top of the Dome—the Raleigh's supper room."

"Dunagin's, I take it?"

Wyatt nodded. "I'm probably not the first to have made off with a souvenir."

"Well, now!" Macalester grinned. "What made you think of doing that?"

"Your note. You'd clearly been spooked by the sight of him, so I figured there might be something criminal there—and a set of prints couldn't hurt."

"You'll make a policeman yet," Macalester said. His phone rang, startling them both. He seized the earpiece. "Ah, thank you. Yes, please—put him through." He looked up at Wyatt. "It's Watchorn. Good man."

CHAPTER 20

Washington Bee, April 14, 1906

HEINOUS MURDER OF CONGRESSMAN NIELSEN MAY LEAD TO DEMISE OF HIS LEGISLATION ON BEHALF OF THE RACE

The murder of Representative Robert Nielsen of Wisconsin is already manifesting repercussions to the disadvantage of the District's citizens of color. A true friend of the race, the Congressman was brutally done to death—some would say assassinated—on 24th Street in Foggy Bottom a week ago last Tuesday. Though his bloodied cane was found at the scene and he had a well-publicized, bitter altercation with Mr. Nielsen just before the latter's death, no charges have yet been filed against the powerful Representative Richard Latham of Corning, New York, a co-sponsor of the infamous "anti-miscegenation" bill recently introduced by his colleague Milton of Florida.

This bill, which would deprive citizens of the District of the right to marry whom they choose, if one of the parties has one-eighth or more of Negro blood, had passed the Judiciary Committee but was referred to the District of Columbia Committee last month at the vociferous insistence of the late Mr. Nielsen, who called it "an affront to human decency and an insult to the Constitution," with a view to, as one observer said, "bottling it up there for the duration."

While Mr. Nielsen's objections had thus far kept the bill from being taken up, the Bee has learned that Representative Campbell Slemp, Vice-Chairman of the Committee, has been heard to opine in the halls of Congress that there being now no "vocal" opposition to the bill, it may see Committee action as soon as next month.

A deputation of Washington's leading citizens of color, led by Mrs. Mary Church Terrell, Mrs. Anna Julia Cooper, and the Rev. and Mrs. Francis Grimké, intends to make its way to Capitol Hill in the next few days and attempt, as Mrs. Cooper put it, to "persuade the Committee members to put a stop to this insulting and retrograde measure."

Representative Nielsen also introduced into the D.C. Committee last session a bill of particular interest to our less fortunate citizens of color, which would deny new building permits to companies owned or controlled by landlords whose current District properties fail to meet basic standards of safety and decency. Mr. Nielsen had taken it upon himself to learn of the appalling conditions in which the City's alley-dwellers, now largely people of color, are forced to live while paying extortionate rents to absentee landlords.

Mr. Nielsen's ardent support for this measure is said to have been on the verge of succeeding in bringing the bill up for debate and a vote in the Committee. It had garnered the co-sponsorship of such notable friends of the race as Congressmen John Lacey and Benjamin Birdsall of Iowa, despite reported past disagreements about legislative tactics between Mr. Nielsen and the latter gentleman.

Sadly, it appears that with the death of Congressman Nielsen this progressive and essential measure may have reached its high water mark and that its support is ebbing away. The community leaders who will lobby to prevent passage of the aforementioned "marriage bill" also intend to use the occasion of their visit to urge members of the D. C. Committee to incorporate Mr. Nielsen's amendment into the condemnation bill.

Perhaps if concerned citizens of color will also communicate their views to the District Commissioners, those gentlemen may be willing to use their not insubstantial influence with the District Committee to restore momentum to this measure. It would be indeed tragic if the killer of this noble advocate for the cause of the colored man is also able, by means of his foul deed, to destroy Mr. Nielsen's great work and his legacy.

Wyatt looked up from the settee in Giovanna's room. "Assassination," he said, pain crossing his face.

"Since when have you taken to reading the colored press?" she smiled at him in the mirror of the dresser where she was arranging her hair.

"When a politician's killed, especially a crusader like Nielsen—his ideas and initiatives die too. It's not just murder—it can change the course of history."

She turned on the stool to face him. "Did he matter so much?"

"The colored folk seem to think so." The back of his hand tapped the page. "They don't have many friends left on Capitol Hill—Nielsen was abrasive and far from well-liked, but he did more on their behalf than anyone else there, if only because he wasn't afraid to speak his mind."

Assassination…Wyatt had the guilty reflection that it wasn't always for the worst. He had been in attendance on President McKinley on that ill-fated day in the Temple of Music. Though the shots of the assassin still haunted his dreams, he thought that on balance the country was better for Roosevelt's leadership. McKinley, good and decent as an individual, had been a pawn of the corporations…

Giovanna's voice recalled him to the present. "Are you making any progress?"

Wyatt smiled. "The trouble with crusaders is that they make so many enemies. It's hard to know where to concentrate. There's a slumlord I've got my eye on—Nielsen was clearly getting in his way. But it may be I want him to have done it, because I took a dislike to him the minute we met."

"What about the lady friend? The reporter?" He heard an edge in Giovanna's voice. Jealousy?

"It's where you start, naturally. She doesn't have an alibi. But she seems genuinely grief-stricken. They'd quarreled that morning, and she blames herself for the foul mood that let Nielsen to insult Latham as he did."

"What about?"

"The quarrel? He was urging her to marry him, she says. After having given her to understand he shared her socialist-anarchist

134

views on free love and such. They'd been, ah, co-habiting for some time. She took the proposal as retreating from his principles, that he was becoming ashamed of her, and told him so."

Giovanna laughed. "Now, that's an original way of rejecting an offer of marriage. It would have come in handy on a couple of occasions."

Wyatt froze, thinking of Julia Marlowe's backstage whisper. There: the subject had come up; he had his cue-line.

> *If it were done when 'tis done, then 'twere well*
> *It were done quickly...that but this blow*
> *Might be the be-all and the end-all here,*
> *But here, upon this bank and shoal of time,*
> *We'd jump the life to come.*

He took her hands in his. "Not surprised to hear you were so much in demand, Madame Treadwell." *Now might I do it pat, and now I'll do it...* He swallowed and looked at the floor. "I've been wondering, actually—about whether you might, ah—"

She blinked at the gravity in his face and pulled away from him with a high, nervous giggle very unlike her usual deep, hearty laugh, took out a tiny pocket-watch and smiled up at him. "If you're about to make a proposition, my liege, there's just enough time for the bloody tyrant to ravish poor Lady Macduff before we're due at the Easter breakfast."

He rallied from the blow and smiled back at her. "Or vice-versa." He drew her to him, starting to untie her lacy shawl. "You'll have to do your hair again."

"There is one thing that doesn't ring true, though," she mused as his fingers began to run through her curls and massage her neck. "Have you ever known anyone to stand on principle like that when her heart was truly in the other's hands?"

"Meaning that—?"

"—that either she didn't really love him, or there was a deeper reason for her refusal."

Wyatt chuckled. "She'd found out they were brother and sister separated at birth?"

Giovanna punched him in the arm and smiled up at him. "No, silly. But ideals or not, it's no trifling thing for a woman, even these days, to forego her reputation when she's given a chance to make it right. I wonder if the lady-friend isn't hiding something."

"As it happens, the thing that could damage her the most—and I think the real reason she refused Nielsen—is something she's been quite open about, at least within the colored community. Miss Stanstead tells me she's one-eighth Negro."

Giovanna pulled away from him. "She—she *admitted* to that? But that means—"

"That if this bestial bill passes—the one Latham, among other troglodytes, has been urging—she couldn't legally have married Nielsen. She didn't want to put him in an awkward position, where he could be accused of wanting to defeat the bill out of self-interest."

There was another strained little laugh. "That's rather noble of her. Would you have suspected, by looking at her, that she was, uh—"

"Part colored? I'm not sure. Her complexion's on the olive side, but if I'd had to guess at her ancestry, I might have said Jewish or Levantine. Surely it doesn't matter."

She took another step back. "Perhaps not to you."

He stared at her, not quite sure what he was hearing. "When I started meeting Southerners, they'd try to tell me, 'You haven't lived with colored. They're not like us.' Well, I've been around a lot of them since then, and I don't see much difference, except most of them are poor and we treat them badly."

Her gaze held him for a long moment. "My dear, I think you actually believe that—"

Wyatt had a happy inspiration. "Actually, I've got a good friend I'd like you to meet. He's Congressman Dodge's steward. And he's colored, as it happens." Perhaps Giovanna hadn't met many colored people. Immigrant communities were often rather insular, and she might have spent her childhood among the Italians of Paterson without having been exposed to many Negroes. Meeting Germain could be a good start on broadening her horizons. And a little part of him, he realized, wanted to share the wonder of her with someone before she was gone, to let a friend see them openly as a couple, if only for an afternoon.

"But he can't come to the theater, can he?" she said quickly.

"We could meet him at the Smithsonian. Take an afternoon off. He hasn't seen it yet either."

"Really—how long has he lived in Washington?"

"Brand new here. He's from New Orleans originally. He runs the Dodges' household in Manhattan. He's only here to get them settled in their new town-house."

Giovanna's brow cleared. "Well, can you really get away from this investigation business?"

"For one afternoon, and the company of friends," *friends I must part from soon*, he did not add, "Richard Latham will have to get along without me." He smiled and reached for her.

She came back into his arms with a small sigh. "Hold me, Wyatt."

"What's the matter, love? Please—tell me what's been troubling you so."

She smiled, shaking her head. "I was thinking about Thomas. What if someone's told him…"

Wyatt drew her closer. "'Present fears are less than horrible imaginings,' as an acquaintance of mine often says. You think he'd want to force the issue, when he has all the young ladies he wants and the added prestige of being married to the most promising young Shakespearean actress of her generation?"

"Men are different that way," she said. "He might think it's all right for him, but…" Her head drooped on his chest. "The children—what would happen if we…"

"Well—what *if* we?" He held her at arms' length and tilted her chin so that her eyes met his. "I know what we've said right along. Just here and now and when the run's over, it's over. But—have you given thought to leaving him? He'd have to let the children go with you."

She searched his face, her expression an odd mix of pleasure and regret, her voice when it came out timid and small. "What are you saying to me?"

"What I'm saying, my darling, is—"

She took in a sharp breath and clapped her hand over his mouth. "No! Please—don't—don't say something we'll both regret. It's not—it's just not…" she bit her lip and shook her head. Tears brimmed over and fell, sparkling in the lacework of her shawl.

He searched her face. "I'm sorry—I thought perhaps—forgive me. I pushed too far. I didn't mean to upset you."

She turned away, but he took her shoulders and brought her back to face him. "Giovanna, what is it? You've been fretting since we finished in Baltimore. Thomas is half a continent away. You're not worried about the big show?" There was to be a gala performance that evening in honor of the Easter holiday, with the First Lady and several Cabinet officials in attendance. "You've got Mrs. Mac done to a turn. They wept for you in Baltimore." He heard the lie in his voice. Her performances had been flat since they got to Washington.

She gave him a tight little smile. "No. I'm just being silly. You're right." She took his hands and towed him towards the dark-columned bed. "Let's make the most of the time we have left."

After he had gone to dress for the breakfast, Giovanna lay wideeyed and fully clothed on the disheveled bed, arms curled tight around each other, watching the gold of early morning fade into full daylight. Wyatt had been on the verge of asking her to leave Treadwell and marry him. Only her hand on his mouth forestalled it. How had it come to this? The affair had begun as a delightful diversion. A good-looking man, passionate but gentle, had given her his undivided attention—and, it now appeared, his undivided heart. A man who wanted to love her completely for who she was.

Or, rather, who he thought she was.

It had been easy with Thomas, all these years. She had known from the time they met that his path was strewn with discarded lovers. She was the one, with her exotic beauty and sparkling repartee, who'd finally brought the notorious Lothario to the altar, who'd made a loving father of him. When she realized before long that she had tamed the leopard, but not changed his spots, she bore it with grace. Her secrets would be more damaging than his if they saw the light of day in a divorce action, and in any event, she'd enjoyed their times together. He was a fun-loving, perpetually youthful man who played with his babies like a big brother and dreamed up games to entertain them. He entertained her too; that was his genius, after all. If something was missing, that trust that allows lovers to be entirely naked with one another, to see and accept one another whole—well, what was that against a thriving career, a pair of lovely children, a beautiful home and a dashing husband who could always tease her out of the blues?

More than she'd ever thought possible. She turned on her side and wept.

CHAPTER 21

It was an odd speech for a eulogy. James Costello's rhetoric in praise of Robert Nielsen was as polished as any of his predecessors' in the pulpit of the Rankin Chapel, but it had the generic quality Germain recalled from the Catholic funerals of his New Orleans youth; any number of names from William Lloyd Garrison to Booker T. Washington could have been interchanged for Nielsen's.

When the service was over, Germain gave his arm to his neighbor in the pew, an elderly woman. Filing out behind the thick, slow-moving crowd, she regaled him with the contents of Costello's article in the *Voice of the Negro* about the Niagara Movement: a group of colored Americans had gone across the border at Buffalo last year to hold a meeting in protest of "Mr. Washington's" policies of accommodation, and promised to unleash a "mighty current" of protest to improve the lot of the race. She leaned over Germain to nod approvingly at Wyatt. "It's nice to see a white gentleman at an event like this."

"I'm sorry for the occasion of it, ma'am," Wyatt said. "Mr. Costello is certainly an impressive speaker."

Germain introduced Wyatt to the lady, a Mrs. Hutchins.

"He is a fine young man, isn't he? One of the coming men of the race. Were you a friend of Mr. Nielsen's?"

"Er—admirer would be a better term," Wyatt said. "I come from his part of the country. The Midwest."

"Well, there you are, we have a few gentlemen left in Congress from there who are true friends of the race." Mrs. Hutchins sniffed loudly into a lace-edged handkerchief. "And to lose Mr.

Nielsen…hardly anybody dares to speak up for us any more. All these lynchings, now—what did they fight that war for?"

It was a good question.

"A lot of colored folks in the South these days are worse off than slaves," she went on, "getting worked to death as leased convicts. And then you got Mr. Nielsen cut down in his prime for trying to do right by us, his murderer walking around, nobody laying a glove on him." Mrs. Hutchins' nostrils flared. "It was that Latham fellow and everybody knows it."

"You ain't gonna be popular for removing Latham from the suspect list," Germain told Wyatt at the reception.

"I'm not, am I? Look, about Costello—"

"I'll try and find out where he was."

Wyatt nearly choked on a cucumber sandwich. "I thought you brought me here because you didn't want to do that yourself."

"I got a feeling this killing was personal." Germain inhaled a small creampuff. "What is it Mr. Dodge says? Sex and greed, the two great motivators of mankind. I'll bet he was at that YMCA meeting Nielsen spoke to just before he was killed. Along with a lot of the folks here. Lemme see if I can find out where he went afterwards."

"Why, it's Mr. Germain, isn't it? From Louisa's. How good of you to come!" Lady Mollie Terrell, in a black walking-costume and matching plumed hat, broke away from an admiring circle of what must be her former students. "How are you settling in?"

Wyatt, spotting Louisa Stanstead alone in a corner, tactfully withdrew. Germain responded in kind to Mrs. Terrell's warm hand-clasp.

"Doing fine, ma'am, though the finish work on Mr. Dodge's house is a trial. Your husband's address was very moving—he must have known Mr. Nielsen intimately." Robert Terrell, a Harvard *magna cum laude* and Howard Law School valedictorian, had recalled the fiery Nielsen's tenderness in caring for a little Negro boy attacked by a gang of white street Arabs.

"It's still such a shock. They were both on the committee for the new YMCA, and the Strivers' Board as well. To think we were among the last people to see him alive."

"That's right, you were at that YMCA meeting. You might've known how he was getting home, or seen somebody leaving with him, or following him out?"

Mrs. Terrell smiled sadly. "My husband and I left before Bob did, but it was a lovely spring night—I'm sure he'd have walked home from the meeting. He never took a trolley even in bad weather. He'd have gone down U to 16th, most likely, then down New Hampshire Avenue to Washington Circle. It would have been easy for someone to follow him, if they knew he was speaking at the meeting. Whether or not that person had attended the meeting himself," she added significantly. "Oh, here's Mr. Costello—he might remember something. James, you did a lovely job. Bob would have been pleased."

Germain joined Mrs. Terrell in praising Costello's speech, which won him a careful nod of thanks.

"Mr. Germain wanted to ask you about the YMCA meeting. The night Bob was killed, you know."

The young man's face flickered in a one-sided smile. "Am I a suspect now?"

Germain groaned inwardly. "We were hoping somebody from the meeting might have noticed something—ah, unusual. Like someone who didn't belong there, or who left early, perhaps, or hung around late. It's possible Mr. Nielsen was followed as he left, and attacked as he got near his home."

"Why follow him all the way to Foggy Bottom?" Costello asked. "Wouldn't a determined killer—if it wasn't Congressman Latham, which still seems the most obvious solution to most of us—have attacked him as soon as they reached some isolated spot?" His frown of concentration was deepening to a scowl.

"Unless it *was* Latham, it's clear that whoever murdered him wanted Latham set up as the killer. Latham wouldn't know about his meetings and would expect to find him near his home."

"It wasn't a large contingent that night…the usual group, wasn't it, Mrs. Terrell? Mr. Bowen, Mr. Pittman—he's to be the architect for the YMCA building—Washington's son-in-law." A tone of dismissal in the last, whether for Booker T. Washington or his son-in-law Germain couldn't tell. "A couple of people from the Strivers', since they were hosting. Clarence Wilbur and George Templeton, and the new man—Roy DeYoung. Talk to Clarence—he probably locked up afterwards. Mrs. Cooper, of course." Mrs. Anna Julia Cooper, a Sorbonne graduate, had succeeded Robert Terrell as principal of the M Street School. "I left just as the meeting adjourned, so I can't help you much," Costello added.

"Of course, you had school the next day...?" Germain hoped he'd elaborate. Costello merely nodded and lifted an eyebrow.

"I was much impressed by your article in the *Voice of the Negro*," Germain said. "I was thinking of our discussion about the parallels between the Roman and American republics. Would you be interested in some classical texts for the school library? I find myself with some duplicates—a nicely bound set of the Collier's series—Herodotus, Livy, Tacitus, so forth, if that would suit."

"It would suit admirably!" Costello beamed. "We're always struggling for good material. The library is particularly thin in history and the classics. Since you've read my article, Mr. Germain, you know that I reject out of hand Mr. Washington's contention that our Negro youth are good for nothing but being taught to be tradesmen and servants."

From the man's sincerity and warmth, Germain knew better than to take the reference as a personal slight, but wondered whether Costello was this socially tone-deaf on all occasions. He felt a momentary pang at the loss of his Collier's set, which was not in fact a duplicate, but consoled himself with the thought that he was doing his part for race advancement.

"Why, my students at M Street are as accomplished in Latin and Greek as any college man of Harvard or Yale..." Costello went on as they walked together down the steps of the reception hall. He was as much of an enthusiast, Germain reflected, as Louisa Stanstead, though without that lady's wit and humor.

"Perhaps you'd like to join us on Thursday for a literary evening," Costello was saying. "Do you know Mrs. Fleetwood?"

"That wouldn't be Mrs. *Christian* Fleetwood?"

"The same. You may have a chance to shake the hand of one of our first colored war heroes." Sergeant Major Fleetwood had been awarded the Medal of Honor in 1865 and had later, as a commissioned Major, commanded a National Guard battalion. "But Mrs. Fleetwood is an institution herself. Head of nursing at the Freedmen's. And her Thursday Evenings at Home—well, you'll meet anyone worth knowing in literary circles hereabouts. And this week will be something special—Dr. Dubois will be there to talk about the Atlanta Conference. I'll introduce you to Mrs. Cooper—perhaps she'll talk you out of some more of your library."

CHAPTER 22

Macalester scanned the coffered dome and golden stone arches of the Library of Congress Reading Room. "Magnificent, isn't it?" He sidled into the chair across from Wyatt's, halfway around a mahogany crescent of desks.

"Glad you suggested it," Wyatt whispered. "I've never been here myself." The desks were arrayed in three elegant arcs around a circular podium where librarians took patrons' book request forms and sent them down to the stacks by pneumatic tube. Light spilled down from the dome's oculus, illuminating a sparkling waterfall of dust-motes that fell on their desks like a mythological shower of gold.

"Got another 'phone call this morning from my good friend Watchorn." Macalester's eyes gleamed with grim triumph. He pulled a notebook from his jacket pocket, looked around at their fellow patrons and lowered his voice. "Seems one Cornelius Dunagin, twenty-one years of age, late of Armagh, came through the Castle Garden immigrant processing center on the evening of May 19, 1885."

"Which—let me guess—was the same time Dandy Pat O'Donoghue went on the lam."

"The *very* day, laddie. According to the records, this Dunagin had a position waiting for him at the importing firm of Oxford, Wye and Sons—"

"—in Baltimore. And they'd hired him sight unseen?"

"Well, that wasn't in the immigration records, naturally. However, I had an enlightening conversation by long distance with one J.W. Philpott, a venerable gentleman from the sounds of him, who was then, as he is today, the chief clerk at said firm."

Wyatt rocked back in his chair.

"They were on good terms with some counterpart firm in Belfast," Macalester went on, "and somebody there placed an advertisement on their behalf for a couple of junior clerk positions. All done by correspondence, and the long and the short is that they offered a job to a young fellow named Cornelius Dunagin, on the strength, Mr. Philpott tells me, of the neatness and elegance of his hand. Paid his passage to New York and his railway ticket from there to Baltimore."

"But if O'Donoghue had used Dunagin's railway ticket, he'd have been—"

"Spotted at the turnstiles, or so we'd have hoped. Either he got by us, or he got to Baltimore some other way. But someone got there, one way or another. Here's the funny thing, though—Mr. Philpott says that he didn't stay with them long, since his handwriting proved to be quite inferior to the sample he'd sent."

"How did Dunagin, or whoever he was, explain that?"

"Apparently hung his head sheepish-like and said he'd had a friend write the sample for him, because he was so eager to emigrate and get work with a good firm. They put him on a sort of probation, but he gave notice a week or two later and that was the last they heard of him. I do enjoy witnesses with elephantine memories."

"They didn't go after him for the passage-money?"

"Oddly enough, he paid it back when he gave notice," Macalester said. "I asked Mr. P. where a presumably impoverished Irish lad would've come by the thirty dollars in steerage fare, and he said the chap told them he'd got it as a loan. So as far as they were concerned, they were quits."

"Smart thinking on his part—they might've pursued him for it. Wonder who he knocked over to get that thirty dollars." Wyatt rocked back in the chair, frowning. He straightened up and the chair legs banged abruptly on the floor, drawing a glare from a bookish-looking young woman a few seats down.

"Car float."

"What?"

Wyatt dropped his voice. "How O'Donoghue could've got out of New York that night without getting nabbed. There are dozens of 'em going back and forth in the harbor every day. Freight cars being ferried across to Jersey City and Hoboken and Perth Amboy, who knows where else. All he'd have had to do was sneak onto one, keep out of sight for the length of the ride, catch a passenger train from Jersey. You didn't have the Jersey stations covered, did you?"

"Not right away," Macalester said. "We sent them descriptions the next day, but—you know, that could have been it."

"It would've been a rocky ride—depending on the tide, I've seen those things cranked up and down five or ten feet at the transfer bridges."

"Desperation's a powerful thing," Macalester said. "In any event, we have two problems: proving it's him, and reeling him in."

"Don't forget figuring out whether he killed Nielsen, or had it done. And keeping you safe, in case he did recognize you—"

"I'm afraid there's little doubt of that. I'm glad I thought to take Miss Blumenhofer along, otherwise he might be wondering how I just happened to be there on the night you sent him tickets."

"He may be wondering that anyway."

"She was fair disappointed to be yanked away at the intermission," Macalester said ruefully, "especially when I was a bit vague about explaining things later."

"I'll get her a couple more tickets—and no objections from you, please, since you used her so ill. She can take another lady-friend along and bring her backstage afterwards."

"I'll take a wee train trip up to the City," Macalester said, "right away, in fact—confer with the current Detective Bureau chief, let him know what we've found. Even if we haven't the evidence yet to nail him on—"

"—the NYPD should know, so you're not the only one who does," Wyatt finished. "You'll take an armed escort on the train? I'd come myself if I hadn't the, ah, prior commitment for the evening. If you're right about this fellow—"

"I can look after myself, laddie—" Macalester began with some indignation, but under Wyatt's stare he shrugged and added, "it wouldn't be a bad idea at that."

"If Dunagin has somebody tailing you, he'll report back the *fait accompli* and you'll be safer. What happened to Dandy Pat's supposed body, by the way?"

Macalester's brow furrowed in recollection. "It wasn't claimed. Confederates he had, but not friends—nobody wanted to pay for a burial. It'll have gone to Hart's Island."

"The potter's field. But since it was identified as O'Donoghue— would they know where he's planted?"

"Probably. There's a registry. Why'd you ask? There won't be much left of him."

"If you're right, and the NYPD can track down some of the real Dunagin's relatives back in the Old Sod—"

"Ah!" Macalester beamed. "Roentgen rays!"

"Maybe there'd have been some distinguishing feature—a deformation or a healed fracture. Something the relative would know about but Dandy Pat wouldn't."

"Worth a try," Macalester said, looking impressed.

"You've got the champagne glass?"

"You anticipate me. We'd taken a lot of stuff from his last known digs, and I was planning to have a look in the evidence locker," Macalester said. "We weren't fingerprinting then, of course, but you never know. Resourceful of you," he added, "picking up that goblet. If you weren't such a convincing villain, you'd make a decent policeman. We'll see what we can do."

Wyatt and Giovanna made their slow way down the National Museum's Hall of Ethnography, where costumed figures stood frozen in mid-action in their glass display cases. Here was a group of Eskimo hunters about to harpoon a glassy-eyed seal who seemed oddly serene in the circumstances, an Algonquin squaw tending her papoose, a Ubangi woman proudly displaying her twelve-inch lip-plate.

From the display of red-robed Masai herdsmen, a head seemed to detach itself and float into the aisle.

Giovanna jumped back with a little cry. Germain, in a gray suit with a bright red waistcoat, smiled at them and tipped his hat.

Wyatt broke into a grin. " They let you out after all! Mrs. Treadwell, may I present my good friend Alexis Germain—"

With a slight, trembling hesitation, Giovanna offered Germain her hand.

"Sorry to have startled you, ma'am," he said, taking it with his own measure of hesitation. Colored men, Wyatt reflected, weren't often asked to shake hands with white women, even up North.

"Please," Giovanna was saying, "since you and Wyatt are such good friends, I—ah, hope you'll call me Giovanna."

Germain glowed. "That's kind of you. And I'm Alexis."

"Have you been here before? There's so much to see—"

"Quite the endurance test, for all its marvels," Wyatt smiled. "What do you say we visit the café for something restorative before we tackle the Hall of Architecture? Their coffee won't be as good as yours—he's from New Orleans," he told Giovanna, "and he does some sort of voodoo with—chicory, is it? Never had anything like it."

The Smithsonian's coffee was by no means up to Germain's standard, but it came in well ahead of the sludge on offer at Macalester's office, or at the National Theatre. Giovanna, who despite her slender frame had an irresistible sweet tooth, delightedly plunged into a new treat on the menu: a hot fudge sundae, a concoction of vanilla ice cream and thick, warm chocolate sauce.

"It's all the rage in Los Angeles," the soda jerk said, topping it with a mound of whipped cream and a cherry and setting it before her, beaming with professional pride. "It made its way here pretty fast, I must say."

Giovanna took a spoonful and closed her eyes in bliss. "I can see why." She was in a dusty-blue ensemble today, a light spring wool with puffs at the top of the sleeves and a matching tricorn bonnet awash in plumes. That and the sundae combined for a girlish look that melted Wyatt's heart. He looked over at Germain, who was gazing at her intently while doing justice to a large slice of apple pie à la mode. It was early in the year for ice cream, but the three were in a festive mood, like children playing hooky from school. Other groups of diners, who seemed to have segregated the cafeteria into white and colored sections by unspoken agreement, stole curious and, in the case of the whites, occasionally hostile glances at the trio.

Germain was detailing the horrors of painting egg-and-dart molding when Giovanna let out a gasp. "Oh, look what I've done!"

A blob of fudge had fallen on the edge of her sleeve. She started to dab at it with her napkin but Germain leaned forward with a restraining hand.

"That'll only make it worse. Here—" he handed Wyatt the unused knife he'd been issued with his pie. "Get under the spot and lift off whatever you can." He called the waiter over and asked for a glass of seltzer and a sponge. After they had the stain down to a faded light brown, he said, "Now, if you'll go to the powder room and take the coat off, you should be able to sponge a little soap onto it and get most of it gone."

They watched her hurry off to the ladies' washroom, Germain following Wyatt's gaze after her.

"Beautiful woman," he said. "Gonna be able to let her go?"

Wyatt's wince of pain made him wish the words unsaid. "I was advised that if I proposed to her I'd have a good chance of being accepted. But when we got near it, she backed me away."

Germain folded his arms and waited.

"I think she cares for the husband—other than being an incorrigible Casanova, he sounds not a bad fellow."

"That's a pretty big 'other than,' *mon ami.*"

Wyatt shrugged. "I don't know how much to push her. She's been jumpy since we got here," he added, his face troubled. "It's affecting her performances. She says she's worried about the husband finding out about us. But it seems like more than that to me—as if something happened to her here once, in Washington, something she doesn't care to confide in me about. Or not yet, anyway."

Germain had a very good idea of what that secret was. He wondered how, or whether, he should tell his friend what had been apparent to him from a few moments after he was introduced to Giovanna: his friend's lady-love was a colored woman passing for white.

CHAPTER 23

After escorting Giovanna back to the Johnson, Wyatt climbed the steps of Washington's City Hall, spirits drooping as he contemplated the stale-smelling office and the cheery, plump clerk in the green eyeshade who stood before him, waiting for his request. He used an old trick, telling the clerk that he had a cousin in Virginia who looked just like him. The clerk beamed and allowed that he was himself a Leesburg man—"that's as in Thomas Lee, sir, not Francis Lightfoot Lee, as is commonly supposed, but his father."

After a few more historical disquisitions, the clerk cleared his throat. "But you didn't come here for genealogy. What can we do for you today?"

"I have been asked to make a confidential inquiry," Wyatt began, "on behalf of a potential investor in the Columbia Heights scheme."

The clerk squinted behind his thick glasses. "The Dunagin proposal? We've got half a dozen fellows with big plans for that neck of the woods."

"Dunagin, yes. We'd heard some talk there might be, ah, delays on some of the permits, depending on some bill that's before the D.C. Committee—"

The clerk gave a low, snorting laugh. "Yes sir, I know the one you're talking about—Nielsen's amendment. It would've kept us from giving out permits if the company had compliance problems on its existing properties. Dead as he is, if you ask me."

"Were you expecting it to pass?"

"Might have," the clerk shrugged. "Commissioner Macfarland thought it was a good idea. So did Mr. West, and Nielsen was pushing them both pretty hard to tell the Committee they wanted it to go through. But the other Commissioner's dead set against it, and now that the pressure's off, I expect they'll let it go.

"Thing is," the clerk went on, leaning his elbows on the counter and giving Wyatt a confidential look, "it's been a real nuisance in the office here, because the effective date would have been the first of January last. Retroactive, you know. So things have been backing up while we waited to see how the bill was going to go."

"You've had to hold back on issuing building permits?"

"There were only a few that would've been affected. But your man Dunagin there stood to lose more than most, see. Fact, I think the Nielsen fella wrote that bill to get at him in particular. We've had a lot of complaints about his properties. And of course there's been a lot of noise in the colored papers about the alleys, which he owns a lot of." The clerk leaned even farther towards Wyatt, who obligingly leaned into the counter and allowed himself to be whispered to.

"I think it was that woman friend of the Congressman's, the reporter lady, that got him going on all this."

Wyatt gave the clerk a blank, wide-eyed look.

"You didn't know about her? You'd better, if your man's investing in real estate in this town. A real rabble rouser, that one. She worked for the Alley Commission for a year or two. When she finished her report and they wouldn't jump to it and do everything she called for, she quit and went off to be a—what do they call it? A special correspondent for some of the local rags. Colored ones not excluded, I might add." The clerk's eyes narrowed shrewdly. "Your man in Congress himself?"

"Why would you think that?" Wyatt kept his tone casual.

The clerk laughed. "That's why the amendment wouldn't have made it in the end, Nielsen or no Nielsen. I'm not telling any tales out of school when I say half the Senate and a quarter of the House are speculating in Washington property. Roosevelt putting us on the world map like he is, this town's on the verge of amounting to something."

"And some of them are partners with Mr. Dunagin, you say?"

The clerk's eyes hooded. "I didn't say anything of the sort." Then he dropped a broad wink. "But I don't mind telling you,

I think that Columbia Heights deal is a safer bet than it was a week ago."

"Well, that should come as a relief to the sleeping partners."

"More to Dunagin, I'd say. Their money's in escrow till he gets the permits. Don't tell me your man was thinking of handing it over outright?"

"They—ah—had discussed an escrow arrangement, of course," Wyatt said hastily, wondering what an escrow was exactly. "But, naturally, you don't want to be tying up the money when it can be working harder for you elsewhere, so to speak."

"'Course not," smiled the clerk. "You can tell Congressman Dodge things should be moving along nicely from here."

Wyatt froze. "What did you say?"

"Little bird told me he might be making inquiries."

"And this little bird asked you to let it know if this Congressman—what'd you say his name was—did?" Wyatt reached for his wallet and took out a ten-dollar bill. The clerk's smile broadened. Wyatt folded the bill in quarters and slipped it through his fingers into the clerk's doughy hand. "My client's privacy is of great value to him. He'd much prefer this visit went unrecorded."

The clerk winked again. "What visit?"

"Good man," Wyatt said.

He trotted down the City Hall steps and out into a drizzly spring evening. Was there a building permit officer anywhere, he wondered, who wasn't on the take? That Dunagin had been keeping tabs on Dodge's, and others', inquiries wasn't a big surprise, but it confirmed Wyatt's fears about the man's thought process. He wondered whether Macalester had made it safely to New York, and what he might find in twenty-year-old evidence files.

If Wyatt asked him how he could be sure, Germain couldn't explain it to him. It wasn't so much a sixth sense as a recognition of pattern—the way someone spoke and carried herself, a tension held in the body. The same doubled, semi-conscious sense you got from watching an actor on stage, that you were inside the frame of a performance, however brilliant and convincing and moving the performance might be. And Giovanna's was exceptionally good.

Lots of people were passing these days, sometimes just for an evening out so they could go places that were supposed to be exclusively white, sometimes for a lifetime, which meant becoming somebody else. Passing was the only way left to a colored person to have a decent life in America any more, if you were lucky enough to be light-skinned and European-featured. He had a few old friends among the *gens de couleur* of New Orleans who had crossed the line, who couldn't acknowledge him when they met.

With that deception you bought a decent future for yourself and your children. The way things were going for the race, you'd almost be crazy not to, if you could live with the broken ties to family and community. The white world had made up its mind to keep Negroes in poverty and subjection, and recently they'd found new weaponry: a lot of scientific jargon about cranial dimensions and jaw angles and limb ratios that only "proved" the case if you accepted the idea that Negroes were inferior to begin with. With that as underpinning, they were piling on the laws to make it all official.

He pulled his mind back to the kitchen table and the week's menus he was perusing with the cook. She was a large and affable woman with Creole roots of her own, who had more or less been bequeathed to Dodge by his Congressional predecessor.

"Mr. Dodge promised he'd be home in time for dinner tonight," he told her. "He told Miz Dodge he hadn't had your pork chops in marmalade sauce for a while. Might think about that instead of the chicken."

"He sure can eat for a skinny fella," Cook observed. "They gettin' some asparagus in the market already—think he'd go for that?"

Germain made his way back upstairs. He liked Giovanna, was instantly attracted to her himself. She and Wyatt looked good together. If what they had going was just an affair, ending with the tour, there'd be no need to say anything.

But Wyatt wanted to marry the lady, and if she was inclined to accept him, he deserved to know the truth. If any white man was capable of absorbing such a blow, he'd put money on Wyatt, but finding out after the fact that he'd been lied to in a systematic way—what ground would a marriage have to stand on then?

He didn't envy Giovanna her dilemma. The price of passing for a lifetime was high—cutting off a whole world of people who knew and accepted you for what you were. And if you came back onto your home ground—he'd bet serious money Giovanna had been raised in Washington—you'd always be looking over your shoulder for someone with enough of a meanness towards you to call you out. He wasn't about to do that—no decent man would—but Wyatt would have to know soon. It was up to her to tell him.

Congressman George Pearre of Maryland, a pleasant, aristocratic-looking man about Wyatt's age, polished his gold-rimmed spectacles on a handkerchief and regarded Wyatt across a handsome oak desk. As vice-chairman of the District of Columbia Committee, he had been one of Nielsen's close allies on behalf of the City's Negroes.

"I thought it was an open-and-shut case for Latham—do you seriously think it could have been anyone else?" He raised an eyebrow in polite inquiry.

"A man like Latham, sir, has any number of canes to choose from. Does it seem likely to you he'd conveniently drop one with his initials on it at the murder scene?"

"If the murder were an impulsive act arising out of a resumed quarrel," Pearre said in a tone that reminded Wyatt that the man was a lawyer, "I suppose he might have panicked when it was done, and thrown down the weapon. It was found hidden among shrubs, was it not? At some distance from—poor Bob's body?" At this, Pearre's voice caught and he redirected the snowy handkerchief to his eyes. "Forgive me, Mr. Wyatt—the public Robert Nielsen was a scourge to the powerful and corrupt, but he was a kind friend to me. I have no love for Richard Latham and I would be glad enough to see him punished for Bob's death."

"As might someone who seized the opportunity of the quarrel. Congressman, I must ask you about two matters before your District Committee—Mr. Nielsen's amendment to the condemnation bill, that would deny building permits to owners of properties in violation of the codes, and the mixed marriages bill."

Something in Pearre's kindly face shut down. "Ah—I fear that the condemnation bill will come out without Bob's amendment. It just doesn't have the momentum, since his—since we lost him. The votes just aren't there—"

"But Commissioners Macfarland and West were both in favor of it, and you yourself had spoken on its behalf—" Wyatt stopped. The look he saw on the Congressman's face was fear. "There have been threats?"

Pearre took off his glasses again and twisted the stems in his fingers. "Oh, ah, no, not threats exactly—"

Wyatt kept his gaze steady. "Congressman, you may rely on my discretion."

Pearre's eyes dropped to the floor. After a long moment he sighed and pulled open the middle drawer of a credenza behind him. "I will need to rely on it, I assure you." He pulled out an envelope and handed it to Wyatt. "This was in my letter-box at home last Tuesday evening. A week after Bob's death. Thankfully, I found it before my wife did."

Taking out his own handkerchief, Wyatt shook a sheet of letter paper out from the envelope and held it by the tip. The message had been typed and was unsigned. *Mrs. Maxwell's husband might be troubled were he to learn of her prior history,* it said. *You would be well advised to reconsider your support for the Nielsen amendment. A concerned friend.*

Wyatt looked up. "Mrs. Maxwell is my wife's younger sister," Pearre said. "When she was still quite young, she, ah, ran off briefly with a railwayman. There was a marriage—or something like it. She realized her mistake within days. The fellow was abusive and a drunkard. She came home. We had it annulled. But there was a, a miscarriage." Pearre blushed. "No one knew, we thought. Including the Reverend Maxwell, whom she married three years later, and by whom she has four lovely children. The family hasn't spoken of it since it happened, but—"

"Someone snooping around might have come upon some old gossip."

Pearre nodded. "He'd have had to snoop pretty hard. Hired a Pinkerton or someone of that sort. No one saw it delivered," he added. "I believe that others of my colleagues who strongly supported Bob's amendment must have received similar—communications. Each has told me that he can no longer support Bob's bill—for personal reasons."

"This is vile. Have you taken it to the Capitol Police? Attempted blackmail of a sitting Member—"

The Congressman shook his head. "Please—it's all I could do to have shown it to you. I cannot let this—this person, whoever it is—destroy my sister-in-law's life. Her husband is a good man, but somewhat, ah, self-righteous. If he came to know of this—" he shook his head, "don't you see? I can't take the chance."

Wyatt's fists clenched. So Nielsen's amendment would die, and the assassin—or assassins—would accomplish their aim. "Do you know if Mr. Nielsen received such a note?"

"It wouldn't have been the first time, if he did. He never took such things very seriously, and it seemed so much empty blustering until the...you might ask Miss Stanstead."

Wyatt caught a tone of respect and even affection when Pearre mentioned Louisa. It occurred to him that Pearre was the first white man he'd met who'd referred to her in that fashion.

"He told me he planned to make her his wife, Mr. Wyatt. Whatever their Goldmanite philosophy, it pained him that she wasn't received in society—my own wife included, I'm sorry to say—'It just isn't *done*,' she said."

"Your colleague Latham suggested that Miss Stanstead killed him because he *wouldn't* marry her."

Pearre's face twisted in dislike. "Had he said that to my face, I should have knocked him down. Believe me, if I thought for one instant that Lou—Miss Stanstead had anything to do with Bob's death, I should be howling for blood—" He stopped and stared at Wyatt for a moment, who nodded encouragement.

"You don't suppose that Bob had received a letter of this sort, with some threat to make an open scandal of Miss Stanstead? That it's what made him decide that they should marry—to protect her?"

Wyatt considered. "Their relationship seems to have been fairly well known."

"Among their friends and allies, yes—but it wasn't exactly public. Had it been so, her work on behalf of the Negroes might well be compromised—and it mightn't have sat well with his constituents either, if word got back to Wisconsin."

Wyatt replaced the letter in its envelope and laid it on the desk.

"This note," Pearre said, "it rather tends to exonerate Latham, doesn't it? I realize he has development interests, but it seems unlikely that as a prime suspect in Bob's death he'd have the brass to be sending out this sort of thing in the wake of it."

Wyatt scratched his chin. "I understand your need to, ah, do as you must regarding the amendment. Perhaps in your position I'd do the same. But may I take the note? It may prove important in tracking down our man. I will be cautious, I assure you." He wasn't altogether convinced about the Henry method, but it might at least tell who had and hadn't touched the paper. And if Macalester got a decent set of prints off the champagne glass… otherwise, there wasn't much hope for identifying the author of a typed missive.

But Pearre looked alarmed and shook his head. "I'm sorry. I just can't take the chance."

Wyatt wasn't sure he'd have handed it over either. But he had other possibilities. "Mr. Pearre, what do you think will happen now with that other bill—the one Mr. Nielsen so vehemently opposed?"

"The marriage bill. Or the miscegenation bill, as its proponents call it…" Pearre looked away for a moment. "We haven't the votes in Committee to keep it bottled up—and too many other things to spend our capital on," Pearre finished rather lamely, then smiled. "Well, one good thing comes out of this—Latham's in no position to push for this outrage on the floor, as long as there's a chance of his being under indictment. Not to mention Bob's allusions to, ah—alley-ladies, which three hundred and ninety-odd memories would recall vividly the moment Latham rose to speak for the bill."

"Has there been anything of this sort," Wyatt pointed to the envelope, "regarding the marriage bill?"

"A few rantings from the usual lunatic fringe, nothing we don't get on a dozen bills every day."

Which meant, Wyatt reflected, that the author of the notes was someone with very direct interests in Washington real estate: Dunagin, or some associate of his paid for dirty work. But if Dunagin was responsible for Nielsen's death, why would he deliberately implicate his business partner?

CHAPTER 24

Wyatt learned by the end of the week of three more notes delivered to Representatives Birdsall, Lacey, and Smith, all Iowans. The dirty laundry threatened with public airing ranged from a feckless son's impregnation of a hometown girl to a mother addicted to morphine and confined to an insane asylum to a brother's failed investment in a firm with criminal ties. None of them would hand over the letters, though Wyatt could see that they had all been typed, as Pearre's was.

John Chaney of Indiana, whom Calvin Chase had characterized in a *Washington Bee* editorial as "one of the purest and strongest men of the Republican Party," was his last stop. An affable, white-haired man who resembled an older version of the Prince of Wales, Chaney was a first-termer.

"We have very few Negroes where I come from, Mr. Wyatt. But I learned from Bob that everything that ghastly war was fought for seems to have been undone—my mother lost two brothers, and she never got over it." Wyatt thought of his own father, a Methodist minister and fervent abolitionist, who'd gone off to war when his second son was still an infant. He had never come back. For all practical purposes, he and his father had never known each other.

Chaney turned and stared out his window which, like Dodge's, faced the alley slums of East Capitol Street. "Since they stuck me on the D.C. Committee as a lowly freshman, I took my cues from Bob. He led us on tours of the alleys near his home—" Chaney turned abruptly from the window and shook his head. "These poor people are worse off than slaves.

Those little children—not a hundred yards from the Capitol, no school, no medical care whatever—"

The typed note Chaney had received threatened to inform his wife and the *Terre Haute Tribune* about the Congressman's "improperly intimate relationship" with his "particular friend" and one-time law partner who now lived and practiced in Washington.

"What will you do? About this note?" Wyatt was resigned to hearing Chaney bow out as the others had.

Chaney's lips tightened into a firm line. "Jack Strothers is a brother to me and I don't mind who knows it. We've shared rooms on business trips and patronized steambaths and a few other things that some people consider questionable. My wife has known him longer than I have and holds him in as much esteem as I do. He's family to us. They'd have to do better than this."

"It doesn't have to be true to damage you."

"I couldn't live with myself if I abandoned Bob's cause now. I will press on for his amendment and for the defeat of the marriage bill. But I must own that I don't expect to succeed."

Wyatt rose. "May I take this note? It would be most helpful to our investigation—it may be possible to trace it to its source."

Chaney's smile was almost mischievous as he handed over the envelope. "When you find the scurrilous rogue who sent it, I'd like to have a little chat with him."

"The new Chief of Detectives," Macalester was saying, "is a convert to the fingerprint theory." He and Wyatt were strolling the tangled paths of the Mall towards the Washington Monument grounds. Tree branches were turning lime green and fuzzy in the lazy Saturday light, and the spring breeze wafted scents of moist earth and new-sprung grass into their nostrils.

"Fella named Woods," Macalester added, "taught English to Roosevelt's boys at Groton. He's got chaps going through the old O'Donoghue evidence. He'll let me know if they match anything to the prints on yon glass I took up with me. "

"Anything, ah, untoward on the journey?"

"Thugs jumpin' out of the bushes and such? Happily, no. The couple of well-armed gorillas I took with me might've put them off," Macalester smiled. "But don't worry; I'm still watching my back. Any luck on the Hill?"

"Letters," Wyatt said. "Of the poisonous variety. Sufficient to discourage most of Nielsen's allies from pushing his amendment to the condemnation bill."

Macalester stroked his chin as he walked. "First I've heard of things getting to their level. A few neighbors in the way of one or two of the less scrupulous developers had a bit of trouble—fire in an outbuilding, their dog found dead on the doorstep, that sort of thing. But threatening a Member, now—that's a Federal crime."

Wyatt edged around a hoof-scarred mud puddle in the middle of the path. "They were more like blackmail situations than threats of physical harm. Remarkable what the sender was able to ferret out about the peccadilloes of these fellows' family members."

Hoofbeats clip-clopped on the path behind them. They separated onto the edges of the path to let the equestrian pass. She was a straight-backed woman in an elegant black riding-habit, and to his surprise Wyatt registered the face of Senhora Pereira, the momentary spark of fearful recognition in her own eyes. The noble-looking chestnut, who must be Aurelius, blocked Macalester's view of their faces and by the time horse and rider passed, Wyatt had regained his composure.

Macalester smiled after her. "Nothin' to beat the sight of a fine-looking lassie who knows how to sit a good horse. She looked familiar…but what were we saying? Ah, yes. Blackmail. It sounds a bit refined by O'Donoghue standards, but then he's come up in the world since I knew him. There's one thing that still doesnae make sense, though—"

"Why he'd go to all that trouble to implicate Latham."

"Latham may have an idea or two about that," Macalester said. The woods were thinning as they made their way towards the Monument grounds.

"I see why you went back to the stage, by the bye. You've a gift for villainy."

Wyatt laughed. "Should I thank you for that?"

The Johnson's eager desk-clerk dug out a large bundle of Monday's mail from a pigeonhole and squared it off on the counter before handing it to Giovanna. "Bumper crop today, ma'am! You've got a legion of admirers in Washington already."

Giovanna gave him her usual beatific smile and headed for the elevator, sorting through the envelopes as the attendant slammed the cage across its entrance. A letter from Thomas, thin in its envelope but long, no doubt, on the sweet nothings, a little note in Jamie's childish scrawl which she ripped open immediately and grew misty-eyed over. There was a heavy cream-colored envelope that looked slightly familiar: the Dodge crest she'd seen on the summons the Congressman had sent to Wyatt. She slid her finger under the flap.

It wasn't from Congressman Dodge, she realized with a lurch of the gut that had nothing to do with the elevator's abrupt stop; it was from Alexis Germain, requesting a chance to talk with her alone. He didn't need to explain why. She'd known the game was up from the moment they set eyes on each other. The only question was what he meant to do with the information. Once safely back in her room, hands shaking, she pulled out a sheet of the hotel stationery from the one drawer in the spindly desk and began to write her reply.

A worried-looking, pink-faced young policeman met Macalester halfway up the stairs to his office. "Commander, Durkee's asking for you downstairs. Something to do with the Nielsen case."

Macalester consulted a turnip of a pocket-watch. "Mondays at five o'clock. Why are there always new developments on Mondays at five o'clock?"

In a small, fuggy interview room sat a solemn-looking, short-haired little Negro boy of eight or nine, trying to shrink under the shawl of a neatly but shabbily dressed young woman, presumably his mother. Between them and Officer Durkee, on the long wooden table, a soggy overcoat was spread out, gray with dark, blotchy discolorations. A mackintosh, from the looks of it.

Durkee rose as his boss entered, handing him a small, pulpy square of what had once been pink card stock. "This was in the pocket, sir."

The Commander took the card and pulled out his half-moon glasses. The print was blurry, but quite legible: a shoe repair claim ticket for a shop in Corning, New York. Richard Latham's constituency. Macalester's heart gave a little skip.

"Commander, this here's young Trudell Williams, and his mama, Mrs. Alvin Williams. They live in Foggy Bottom." The woman, who looked as scared as her son, jerked her forehead towards Macalester, who put his heels together and bowed smartly in her direction. "He found this coat fetched up against the bank of the river," Durkee went on, "down by the Heurich Brewery."

"Well, now," Macalester beamed, all twinkly-eyed and grandfatherly. He squatted down to the boy's level and held out his hand. "Master Williams. My name is Ian Macalester, and I'd like you to call me Ian."

"lo," the boy managed.

"It looks as if you've done us a good deed here, Master Williams. Or will it be all right if I call you Trudell?"

"Dell," the boy said, looking up at his mother, who nodded.

"Dell, right enough. Can you and your mummy tell me how you came upon this coat?"

The young woman took her son by the shoulders and turned him towards Macalester. "It's all right, honey, I ain't mad at you no more about goin' down to the river." She looked into Macalester's eyes and smiled ruefully. "He got these friends that take him down there with them, way home from school, you know. They was fishin' in the shallows down there by the brewery and he snagged this on his hook."

"And you brought it home to your mum," Macalester said. "Well done, lad."

The boy nodded, the beginnings of a smile at the corners of his mouth. "I tol' Mama it had *blood* on it. And Mama said—"

"Well, you know, I thought about poor Mr. Nielsen," his mother said. "Them stains could be rust or mud, but I figured maybe they could be blood like Dell says. So I brung him here to give the coat to y'all."

"We'll have to take it to the laboratory." Macalester gave the word the British pronunciation, with the stress on the first "o," and young Dell looked impressed. "We have clever scientific chaps who can tell us what these stains are. But I don't mind telling you this is a very important thing that you've done. The Metropolitan Police are grateful to you, young man."

Grateful indeed, for a piece of evidence that could explain how the suit Richard Latham had been wearing on the night of Nielsen's murder bore only the traces of a wealthy woman's perfume. If one is expecting showers—whether of water or of blood—the logical thing to wear, after all, is a mackintosh.

Strange, the coincidence that had led him to be thinking of Cornelius Dunagin—the one-time Dandy Pat O'Donoghue—as Nielsen's murderer. If Wyatt hadn't disliked the man on sight and speculated on his role in Nielsen's death, Macalester would never have learned that Dandy Pat was still alive. And if he hadn't recognized him as Dandy Pat, who was capable of anything, the notion of Dunagin as Nielsen's killer wouldn't have seemed any more likely than a dozen others of Dunagin's ilk.

Now it seemed the coincidence was just that. There had to be a way to bring Dunagin to justice for those deaths in the Mott Street cat-house all those years ago. But that history didn't mean Dunagin had had anything to do with Nielsen's death, and this new evidence lent weight to the original theory: that Richard Latham, who had means, opportunity, and a very powerful motive, had beat his colleague to death in revenge for an insufferable public insult. Superintendent Sylvester had best hear of this right away.

The Boss was in his office, plowing through paperwork like the efficient administrator he was. But he greeted Macalester cordially, his great whiskers splitting in a wide grin.

"Well, Mac, solved that Congressman's murder yet?"

"We're a step closer than we were, sir, thanks to a young chap who went fishing without his Mum's permission." Macalester gave Sylvester the details and watched his brow darken.

"Let's get the warrants ready," Sylvester said. "I don't like to arrest a sitting Congressman any more than the next man would, but I don't see that we have a choice."

Macalester closed the chief's door and left him to his papers. Wyatt would want to know of this development, but Wyatt was neither a policeman nor a prosecutor, and telling him at this stage simply would not do. He would find out soon enough, when the grand jury handed down its indictment.

CHAPTER 25

Washington Star, Extra Edition, **Wednesday, April 25, 1906**

CONGRESSMAN LATHAM INDICTED
IN MURDER OF COLLEAGUE

In a surprise move based on what a police source described as "significant new evidence," Representative Richard L. Latham, R-NY, was arrested and served with an indictment at his residence today charging him with the murder of his colleague, Populist Representative Robert H. Nielsen of Wisconsin, whose battered body was found near his Foggy Bottom residence in the early hours of April 5.

A grand jury convened by U.S. Attorney Leland K. Elphinstone handed up the indictment following presentation of evidence that established, in the prosecutor's words, "probable cause" to bring charges of first-degree murder against Representative Latham who, the document alleges, lay in wait for his victim and beat him to death near his Foggy Bottom residence on the night of April 4.

As reported in the evening edition of this newspaper on April 4, Mr. Nielsen had earlier that day offered the accused a grievous insult on the floor of the House during a debate on the victim's proposed amendment to a trade bill. Mr. Latham's initialed cane and, according to sources close to the investigation, other items of physical evidence tying him to the crime were found at or near its scene. The defendant has thus far not accounted, "in a manner satisfactory to the Department," says a police spokesman, for his whereabouts at the time interval in which the murder is estimated to have occurred.

Representative Latham will be formally arraigned in a few days, according to court officials, and the Star has confirmed a previous report that he has retained the services of Arthur O. Partridge of the firm of Partridge, Gibb, and Howland, a noted expert in criminal defense. Mr. Latham was arrested at his home and escorted by police officers to the District of Columbia Superior Court, where after a brief bail hearing he was quickly released on his own recognizance on the motion of his attorney, Mr. Partridge.

Macalester winced at the sharp smell of alcohol and vinegar that assaulted his nose inside the laboratory door. The chemical technician, a young, pale man with a shock of dark hair flopping into his eyes, looked up from his rack of test tubes and grinned at the sight of him.

"It's blood all right, Commander. Not that you couldn't tell by looking at it."

"Human?" It seemed unlikely to be anything else, but it paid to be diligent. Macalester and his men had been up against Arthur Partridge before, and the man had a genius for finding holes in the prosecution's case. It had made him rich, and Macalester had to admit that if he himself ever got round to murdering somebody, which was a sore temptation on some days, he'd want Partridge in his corner. Hiring Partridge was as good as an admission of guilt; a dozen other lawyers in the City would do if you were innocent.

The technician jerked his thumb towards an adjoining room. "I got my little sample for the Adler test. Hughes has got the coat. He's trying to get enough off one of the clots for a precipitin test to see if the blood's man or beast. He'll have to reconstitute it with saline. It's going to take some time."

There was a knock at the pebbled glass door and a young female clerk peered around it timidly. "Sorry to disturb you, Commander—there's a Mr. Wyatt here and he insists on seeing you."

Macalester sighed. He'd been expecting a visit. "Tell him I'll be up in a—" But the door swung wide behind the young woman and Wyatt's tall frame filled the doorway, his face grim and far from friendly. He nodded to the technician.

"Where's this raincoat, Commander?" he snapped.

Macalester bristled. "Latham's people will see it in due course. We're testing it at the moment."

"You'll forgive me if I prefer not to wait. Someone's setting my client up and I aim to put a stop to it." The young woman ducked under Wyatt's arm and scuttled back down the corridor.

Macalester folded his arms. "I see you've got over your reluctance to deal with the fellow."

"That's neither here nor there. I want to know what you found on that coat that made it so damn necessary to put Latham under arrest." Wyatt's glance scanned the chemical technician's row of test tubes on the laboratory bench and the doorway beyond, where it stopped on something in the next room. He was through the doorway before anyone could put a hand on him, glowering down at the hapless Hughes, a slick-haired little dandy who rose and stood protectively with his back to the coat. It had been spread out and smoothed down, but still lay in crinkles and rumples on the bench. Its silk lining was water-stained and there were patches of dried mud on a sleeve.

Macalester followed him in, laying a hand on his arm. "You're not allowed in here. You'll have to leave."

Wyatt stared past Hughes at the coat, instantly absorbed, devouring it with his eyes. "It's been stored somewhere. Look, the blood's soaked in. And gummy, which isn't easy to accomplish on a mackintosh. And look here," his finger traced a line above the surface, "it's been folded—you can see the way the spatter's mirrored between here—" he pointed to the breast of the coat, "and here, down at the hem. And there are smear patterns from the folding."

He turned back to face Macalester and lowered his voice. "Doesn't this have your Dandy Pat written all over it? The killer wants you to think Latham wore the coat to attack Nielsen, then dumped it in the river down near I Street, where it conveniently floats into the shallows down by the brewery, two weeks later. That couldn't happen if it had been thrown in near the murder site—I was just down there. The current's too fast for it to snag. Someone—I'm guessing Dunagin—has been hanging onto this to plant in case the heat came off Latham."

Macalester's nostrils flared. "How did you know where we found it?"

"It's all over Snow's Court. The kid was all excited and telling anyone who'd listen. It got back to Miss Stanstead in no time."

"It's evidence in a murder case and we'd no right to ignore it."

"I don't dispute that. It's the arrest. You caved in to the newspapers, but you know as well as I do—"

Macalester held up his hand. "I don't know anything till the evidence has been examined, which, not to put too fine a point on it, you're impedin' at the moment. As for cavin' in to the newspapers, the grand jury decided we had probable cause. In the absence of other serious suspects." The Glasgow cadences of his speech had thickened with his indignation.

"And you don't think—"

Macalester cut him off with a sweep of the hand. "I've heard nothing yet from New York about those fingerprints. Even if I had, they'd be no proof of any connection between Dunagin and this murder."

Stung, Wyatt blew out a sharp breath. He couldn't blame the police; he himself hadn't uncovered any useful evidence against Dunagin or anyone else, as both Dodge and Latham had reminded him that morning.

"That coat's been folded and stored somewhere. If it had been Latham wearing it that night, you know as well as I do it would never have been found, much less in the condition it's in. The man's not a fool."

"I'm sure the jury will take that into account," Macalester said, recovering an even tone. "Now if you'll excuse us, we have work to do."

Wyatt swept past him and stalked back down the corridor, feeling Macalester's blue eyes blazing on his retreating back. He'd got what he came for: confirmation that someone was working very hard to see Richard Latham hanged. It was hard to imagine why even Cornelius Dunagin, if it were he who'd done the deed, would go to such lengths to eliminate a man who thus far had done him only good. Outside the laboratory door, he felt weariness wash over him. Ill luck seemed to be pursuing him on this case. He was blundering around in the dark, and with Latham's arrest the sand was running through the hourglass even faster.

W.E.B. Dubois had the most riveting gaze Germain had ever seen. As the eminent social scientist spoke, his great, luminous eyes scanned the crowd in Mrs. Sarah Fleetwood's blue and rose parlor, alighting here and there on a familiar face, and for a moment his words seemed addressed to that person alone. His receding hairline, neatly trimmed beard and aquiline nose hardly compensated for the rounded cheeks which gave his face a boyish, vulnerable cast. Intellectual power though he was, Germain reflected, the man was still in his thirties.

"They will tell you, my brothers and sisters," he gave the beard a reflexive tug, "that the shape of the Negro's jaw, or the volume of his brain, or the ratio of the skull in his forebrain to the skull in its dorsal portion, are infallible indicators of his lower intelligence, of his tendencies to criminality. They will give you tables of measurements, accurate to three decimal places, from hundreds and thousands of skulls. But unless you have accepted their bigoted assumptions, they cannot tell you what any such measurement has to do with a man's capabilities or character." He tucked his hand in his pocket in a gesture that recalled James Costello's. That must be where the young man had picked it up, Germain reasoned.

"They will use these statistics to say that whites and blacks must be prevented from marrying in the interests of racial improvement. To claim that education is wasted on the Negro," Dubois concluded. "It is fear and ignorance that generate these so-called scientific theories. Education is the solution: to give the black man the tools to take his rightful place in the mainstream of American society, and to teach the white man the error of his bigoted ways. Educators of the Negro community in Washington—Mrs. Terrell, Miss Cooper, Mr. Costello—" Germain saw the younger man's face register delighted surprise with the inclusion, "I salute you here today. You know, as I do, that either the United States will destroy ignorance, or ignorance will destroy the United States."

He accepted their tumultuous applause with a diffident bend of his head. "And here is our gracious host."

For a military legend, Major Fleetwood was surprisingly tiny. Bright-eyed and handsome still behind a thick white mustache, and pressed by the appreciative crowd, he was prevailed upon to accompany his daughter on the piano as she sang a selection of popular arias.

Miss Celia Fleetwood, a virginal-looking, Gibson-haired young woman in her mid-twenties, began with "Ah, fors é lui" from *La Traviata*. Her rich, well-modulated soprano seemed to emanate from a larger and more experienced body than hers— Germain thought of the Junoesque lady he'd seen in the Violetta role at the Met—and she handled the high trills towards the end of the piece with smooth, effortless grace. She, too, might have sung on that stage, if her skin and features didn't betray her as a Negro. He could feel the weight of that injustice in his shoulders. He understood why Giovanna Treadwell, or whatever her name had been, had crossed that color line of which Dubois had so eloquently spoken.

When it was over and the applause died down, Celia's beaming father laid a hand on her shoulder.

"Friends," he boomed in the overly loud voice of a man partially deafened by cannon fire, "we all know there's a sadness hanging over our gathering tonight. Mr. Nielsen's passing was a great blow to us all. But the Lord giveth as well as taketh away; the Bible tells us that there is a time to mourn and a time to dance. Mrs. Fleetwood and I have joyous news. Our daughter Celia has accepted Mr. James Costello's offer of marriage." He gestured invitation to Costello, who rose with a shy smile and came forward to join his future bride and father-in-law. The assembly broke into applause. Dubois, now seated in the front row, caught Costello's eye and gave him an enthusiastic nod and smile.

Mrs. Hutchins, the elderly woman who had sat next to Germain at the Rankin Chapel service, elbowed him and said, "Now, isn't that something!"

"Mr. Costello came to us two weeks ago last Wednesday," Fleetwood was saying, "the very night of Mr. Nielsen's passing, as it happened—and asked me for our Celia's hand in the good old-fashioned way. Well, I don't need to tell you we couldn't have been more pleased."

Costello took his fiancée's hand and she smiled up at him with adoring eyes. Germain scanned Costello's face. The look there was hard to read. It might have been only modesty and shyness at all the attention—the man was manifestly an introvert—but he thought he saw Costello's eyes dart towards the back corner where Louisa Stanstead sat, beaming and clapping and dashing a spot of moisture from her eye. But whether he still pined for Louisa, however he'd felt about Robert Nielsen, his future father-in-law had just given him an iron-clad alibi for the time of the murder.

The streetlights of Pennsylvania Avenue glowed soft and ghostly in the night's drizzle. The light above the National's stage door was too dim for the watcher in the alley to see the woman's face clearly, but her identity was not in doubt. She pushed back the hood of her dark cloak just enough to silhouette her elegant profile. Shedding a long glove, she rapped on the door, the bared hand glowing ghostly white against the door's darkness. The door swung open. After a moment's conference she was let in, looking around as if to ensure that she hadn't been seen. To the doorman, she would be only one of a nightly stream of female would-be visitors for the leading man. But the watcher in the shadows knew that the two were acquainted, and stepped back into the deeper dark of the nearby doorway for what might be a long wait.

When the woman in the opera-cloak came out twenty minutes later, she was accompanied by the man who'd played Macbeth. The pair took a few steps north on 13th Street, avoiding Pennsylvania Avenue and the brightly lit entrance of the New Willard. The actor was walking her home. A wise precaution; the city could be perilous for an unaccompanied lady at night, especially one in possession of dangerous information.

There was time. Not much, but a few days. The watcher knew by now that the woman was in the habit of riding alone, on the Mall and in Rock Creek Park, on her splendid chestnut horse. There were plenty of opportunities along her route for what would have to be done. In the meantime, Dade Wyatt was crossing the street, heading right for the alley, his eyes scouring entrances and doorways in all directions, making sure there was no one there to follow them. The watcher hugged the wall and vanished silently down the alley, deeper into the shadows. There was no need to follow them; all that was necessary had been learned.

CHAPTER 26

Wyatt found the dressing-corridor dark and empty except for one light showing under a door. He knocked and opened it. In her tiny dressing-room, Giovanna was adjusting a handsome feathered hat and putting on her raincoat. A fresh bloom of her light jasmine scent hung in the air.

"Well, there you are! I was just about to leave."

Wyatt folded his arms and leaned against the doorjamb. "I said I'd be right back."

Giovanna's eyes widened. "Was that the Lady in the Case again?"

"It was. Forgive me for not introducing you." He pushed her gently back into the room and closed the door. "Stay a minute."

"I saw her picture in the Society pages—she's from Brazil, isn't she? I won't tell, truly," she said in response to Wyatt's alarmed look.

"I know you won't. She wants to go to the U.S. Attorney and save him."

Giovanna shrugged out of her coat and sat down, her face full of concern. "I hope you talked her out of it!"

"I'm not sure." Wyatt perched on the edge of the dressing table. "She's right to be worried about the police. And I haven't got a whole lot to show for my efforts thus far." He sighed. "Now that they've made the arrest…"

"They need to make sure it sticks."

"Exactly. So I've only got a few days to find another suspect they'll buy instead of Latham. She won't let it go to an arraignment."

Giovanna's hands flew to her face. "But she can't—she's bound to be exposed, and her husband will know, and—oh, how awful!"

Worse than that, Wyatt thought. A treaty, a nation's future… time running out, and exhaustion setting in from juggling the competing roles of villain by night and truth-seeker by day.

Giovanna squared her shoulders. "Well, I shouldn't like it a bit, but if you were accused of murder and hadn't an alibi except being with me, I'd have to—"

"There are some complications." Wyatt hopped down from the dresser and took Giovanna's hands. "Time to walk *you* home, my dear. I'm feeling gallant this evening."

"So, who do you think did it?" Giovanna took his arm.

He pulled her door shut behind them. "Someone who likes to write nasty notes, I'm guessing."

The Strivers' Mutual Advancement League and Benevolent Society had its five-story headquarters at 12th and U Streets Northwest, in the heart of the Negro commercial corridor which adjoined Howard University. LeDroit Park, a small, tree-lined and flowery neighborhood farther to the east, had at first been exclusively white. Many of the city's eminent Negroes, including the Terrells and Dr. Anna Cooper, now had spacious, ornate Victorian homes and fine brick townhouses there; the whites had fled.

A purring electric elevator conveyed Wyatt to the Strivers' offices on the fourth and fifth floors, opening to a scene of Gibson-haired clerks in striped shirtwaists and gray skirts and colored men, mostly light-skinned, in celluloid collars solemnly perusing lengthy documents at their desks. Even the click-clack of typewriters seemed disciplined and synchronized.

He was greeted in the reception area by a genteel-looking young man with pomaded hair and an air of polite bemusement at a white man's appearance in the establishment. "I'm not sure if Mr. Templeton is here this afternoon, Mr.—Wyatt, is it? If you'd care to take a seat, I'll find out."

The clerk returned with the news that Mr. Templeton had been called home on a family matter and was expected back tomorrow. "Perhaps someone else can assist you?"

Wyatt declined with thanks. Learning that his quarry lived in his mother's townhouse at Seventeenth and U Streets, just beyond the Freedmen's Hospital, "close enough to walk," Wyatt decided that Templeton, described by his colleague as "a dedicated man, and devoted to the company," might prefer to talk about a crime-related matter at his home, out of earshot of his painfully respectable colleagues.

The Templetons' three-story brick townhouse had a granite stoop flanked by neat flowerbeds. His knock was answered by the formidable Mrs. Templeton herself, frowning down at him from the doorway as straight-backed and stern as she had seemed in the Alley Relief Society's meeting at Louisa's house.

"Pardon the intrusion, ma'am—"

The frown momentarily deepened, then cleared with recognition and an Arctic glimmer of a smile. "Why, you're Mr. Wyatt. I remember you from Louisa Stanstead's."

She waved him into a tiled hallway, balustraded stairs along the left wall leading up to other floors, a doorway straight ahead to the first floor rooms beyond. Catching his upward glance, Mrs. Templeton said, "I have *tenants*," in a tone one would use to describe an infestation of cockroaches.

"I was hoping to talk with Mr. Templeton for a few minutes. His office said I might call on him here."

Her eyebrows arched. "He's with the child. Wait in the parlor, please, and I'll send him in to you." She opened a door on the right and gestured him in.

Wyatt watched her retreat through the door at the end of the hallway. He heard voices, hers and her son's, and something else: a low howl, somewhere between a moan and a wail, neither human nor animal. He stepped into the small parlor, fussy with floral wallpaper, antimacassars on overstuffed chairs, lamps rimmed with pendant crystals. A good Turkey carpet on the floor completed the image, if not of wealth, then of unimpeachable respectability.

George Templeton appeared in the doorway, his large frame filling the space. He greeted Wyatt with a smile and a strong handshake, but his eyes were clouded.

"I'm sorry to disturb you at your home," Wyatt began.

Templeton waved him vigorously to an armchair and sat himself. "No matter, Mr. Wyatt, no matter." His melodious, resonant voice would be an asset to a church choir. "Insurance men are in and out of people's houses all the time—turn about is fair play, don't you think? Is it about Mr. Nielsen? I understand they've arrested that Congressman—"

"You're sure it's not a bad time?" The corners of Templeton's mouth were drooping beneath the neat mustache. "I understand your son isn't well."

The sad look deepened. "Branford's hardly ever well. He's—he was born with a condition. They don't know what to call it." The words came in a rush. "He seemed normal enough till about, oh, fifteen months. He stopped developing, never learned to talk. Doesn't look right. He gets colds and ear infections all the time— he's in so much pain. The doctors don't know what to make of it. They're not sure how long—" Templeton's mouth tightened and he looked away. He came back smiling. "But you're not here to listen to our troubles, Mr. Wyatt."

Wyatt accepted the closing of a private door. "I had a talk with Miss Stanstead."

Templeton leaned forward eagerly. "How is she doing?"

"Well as can be expected, I'd say. She was much relieved to hear of the provision Mr. Nielsen had made for her. It means she won't have to move, on top of everything else."

"I'm glad to hear that. I was hoping it might be enough—we'd hate to lose her. She's a true friend to our people, Mr. Wyatt. There aren't so many of them left."

"Indeed. It seems Mr. Nielsen's death has put paid to the chances of his amendment to the condemnation bill. And evidently increased the chances of passage for that anti-miscegenation bill as well."

Templeton looked as if he had been struck. "Surely not," he stammered, his voice choked. "There are others in Congress— friends of the race as he was, who can carry on his work—"

"Well, as you mentioned, there aren't so many of them left. But that brings me to the reason for my call. When was it that

Mr. Nielsen came to you, to talk about taking out the life insurance policy?"

With an effort, Templeton composed himself. "Well, now, I don't remember exactly. I'd have to look at my files. I should explain, Mr. Wyatt, I'm not an underwriter—but we knew one another and he wanted to keep all this in confidence, so I agreed to handle it for him. If you're going to need details, it might be best to wait till we can talk at the office. I should be back there tomorrow, if the doctor has Branford on the mend."

"I'm more interested in the circumstances of the visit. What did he tell you about why he wanted the policy? From what I've heard, he wasn't the sort of man you'd expect to be thinking in those terms—"

Templeton leaned forward and laid an eager hand on Wyatt's sleeve. "Oh, but he was in that respect! Miss Louisa—Miss Stanstead—meant the world to him. Now, as we know, she's one of those New Women. Not about to let a man take care of her in the usual way. So Mr. Nielsen wanted to make sure that if he passed on, she'd have some way to get by. But he didn't want her to know about it—she'd have fussed, you see."

"Seems a bit unusual for a man of his years and health to be worried about dying, doesn't it?"

"Well, you know, Mr. Wyatt, things happen in life." Templeton sat back. "Just a month ago we paid out a lump sum to the wife of a young operative from the Georgetown Flour Mill. Died when he fell off a platform, broke his neck. As healthy and strapping a young fellow as you can imagine. Fortunately, he'd thought ahead, provided for his wife and two little babies. You never know."

If he'd had a wife and children, Wyatt would have thought about signing up for a policy himself. "Had you told Mr. Nielsen about this poor man?"

Templeton looked surprised. "Well, no, I wouldn't have presumed. You see, we're a colored firm and most all our clients are people of color."

"Wasn't it was a bit unusual, then, his coming to you?"

"To the Strivers'? Well, that's Mr. Nielsen for you. Patronized the colored merchants whenever he could. Putting his money where his mouth is, so to speak."

"Did he mention anything in particular that had got him thinking about insurance?"

"Not as such, no," Templeton said slowly. "Though, now you mention it, he said something about—what was it? A man with his views not making many friends in Washington society. A little joke, I thought."

"Nothing more specific? No mention of letters, threats of any kind he had received?"

"Hate mail? Not that he said, but it wouldn't surprise me. Somebody say he got threatening letters?"

"Are you sure Miss Stanstead knew nothing about the policy?"

Templeton's eyes widened at the abrupt change of tack. "She seemed mighty surprised when I told her about it...now, Mr. Wyatt, you're not thinking that fine young lady could have had anything to do with—" Templeton's eyes blazed with righteous indignation. Something else in the look: fear?

Wyatt held up a placating hand. "These are questions I have to ask, Mr. Templeton. Somebody wanted Robert Nielsen dead. And money can be a powerful motivator."

"Not for Miss Louisa, it wasn't. She could've done well for herself, with her education and talents. Married some rich fellow, could've had the house and fine clothes and all. She's from a good family."

"When someone who's insured dies," Wyatt began, "what's the usual procedure? The family comes to you with the policy papers?"

Templeton resumed his professional demeanor. "Well, a firm like ours makes a practice of knowing our clients pretty well. And it's hard to think of practical matters when you're bereaved, isn't it? So if we haven't heard from the beneficiary within a few days of the death, we'll get in touch with them. Like I did with Miss Louisa. It was on my mind, you see, after I heard about Mr. Nielsen. How fortunate it was he'd thought to make plans."

"Did you ask her for the policy papers?"

"When I told her, she was so surprised I figured she wouldn't have a clue where to find them, and I didn't want to distress her by making her go through his papers right then. We have our own fair copies, so there was no question of the coverage."

Wyatt made a mental note to tell Macalester to have his men search Nielsen's papers for a copy of the policy. If Louisa had had free access to Nielsen's office, she might well have known about the policy…perhaps living with a crusader in a perpetual state of indignation had come to be a burden. But he didn't even want to entertain that possibility.

"What you said—about Nielsen not making many friends in Washington society. Had he made any enemies that you known of?"

Templeton frowned and pursed his lips. "When I heard about Latham, I said to myself, that'll be the man, right there. Worse than a Southerner for race hatred." He grinned. "Man, I'd love to have been a fly on the wall of the House chamber when Nielsen told him off."

"So would I," Wyatt smiled in return. "But what if Latham had an alibi?"

Templeton looked startled. "They wouldn't have arrested him, surely. If he does, though, I'd be checking that very carefully."

"But if it was a good one? Who else?"

Templeton shook his head slowly. " I don't know. Friends of Latham's, maybe?"

"—who'd implicate him by leaving his cane at the scene? Doesn't sound friendly to me."

"Sure is a puzzle, Mr. Wyatt. You got your work cut out for you. But don't you even be thinking about Miss Louisa, or you'll be answering to half the colored society of Washington—" A keening wail interrupted him and grew louder as it moved from a back room into the hallway. His face clouded and he stood. "It's my boy. It's one of his ear infections, and it hurts him like the devil."

Wyatt rose. "I'll be going. Thanks for your time, Mr. Templeton. If you think of anything that could help—"

"I can find you at the theater," Templeton managed a smile. "Service door, anyway." Wyatt reddened, remembering that as a colored man Templeton wouldn't be allowed in by the main entrance.

The door burst open, pushed by a grotesque, howling dwarf with an oversized head, a flattened nose, and teeth that seemed to have migrated from an ape's mouth into a child's. His skin was leathery and thick, his hands claw-like and twisted. He shambleran over to Templeton and clung to his leg, whimpering and snuffling, tears and mucus streaming down his face. Behind him hurried Templeton's mother, her face taut with rage and embarrassment.

Templeton bent to the child, put his arms round him and rocked him, making crooning noises. "There, now, Branny, it's all right, buddy, it's all right." He took a handkerchief from his pocket and began tenderly to wipe the child's face. Wyatt and Mrs. Templeton might have vaporized. Wyatt met the mother's gaze over the crouched figures, she reading his face for the revulsion she had surely come to expect there, he searching hers for traces of compassion which he did not find.

Behind Mrs. Templeton came a white man in a frock-coat, carrying a medical bag.

"Dr. Marsden, this is Mr. Wyatt," she said stiffly. The man nodded.

"I'll be on my way, Doctor," Wyatt said, heading towards the door. "Sorry to have intruded, Mrs. Templeton."

Her response to his apology was a glare of cold fury directed towards her son. Templeton continued to ignore them all, his arms enfolding the hideous child as though it were the treasure of his heart.

CHAPTER 27

Pausing in the dimly lit front rows to contemplate the battle-field set for the opening of the Scottish Play, Wyatt caught sight of Graham, the National's manager, in the half-light of the wings, and boosted himself onto the stage to catch up with him. He was a small, portly fellow who always seemed to be running behind on some important errand, like the White Rabbit from Alice's adventures. Spotting Wyatt, he extended his hand.

"Ah, Mr. Wyatt! What brings our arch-villain here so early? Everything in order, I trust? Dressing-room suit you?"

"Very comfortable, thanks." Wyatt shook the plump, ringed hand. "I did want to ask you something. I have some friends in the city who'd like to attend a performance."

"They'll be most welcome, of course! Do you need some complimentary tickets?"

"I'm sure they'll be happy to pay. Their being colored will present no difficulty?"

Graham opened and closed his mouth, reminding Wyatt of the carp he'd seen swimming in ornamental ponds. "Ah, well, that's not possible, I'm afraid. Our Board of Directors has been very firm on that point. They're convinced we'll lose our white patrons—we used to admit the colored, oh, back about thirty years ago, but there were so many problems—" his pudgy hands opened and fell at his side.

Wyatt's frown deepened. "What sorts of problems?"

"Well, of course, I wasn't here then myself…something about noise and misbehavior in the Negro gallery—" he quailed under Wyatt's stare. "I don't know the details, but there were letters from a number of the, ah, more influential white patrons."

"Threatening letters?" Wyatt had had just about enough of those.

"Well, not in the violent sense, I'm sure."

There was a rustle in the opposite wings and Giovanna emerged on the stage, carrying a Woodward & Lothrop's shopping-bag. She was turned out in a suit of fine maroon wool with a three-quarter length jacket which emphasized her slim figure, and a broad-brimmed gray felt hat with an enormous maroon bow and great plumes dyed to match. Wyatt tried and failed to suppress a smile at the sight of her.

"Mr. Graham—Mr. Wyatt! I'm surprised to see you here." She colored prettily. "I have just achieved the shopping *coup* of the decade." She reached into the bag and emerged with something tan and furry.

"A Teddy bear!" Graham cried with delight.

"Two! One for Jamie and one for Grace. I had to trample a few dozen other mothers to get them before they ran out."

Wyatt smiled. He hadn't seen much of Giovanna's motherly side, and it was as charming as the rest of her.

"I was just talking with Mr. Graham about the Theatre's admission practices," he said. "Did you know that Negroes are not welcome here?"

"Uh, well—" Giovanna seemed abashed by the question. Wyatt wondered if the coincidence of their appearing in the theater at a time when neither had a particular reason to be there would fuel gossip about their relations.

Graham lowered his voice confidentially, gesturing them towards him. "In fact, we have a number of colored patrons, I believe—'passing,' as it's called. Some of the old colored families in the District are so light-skinned no one would ever know. And as fine-featured as any white fellows—indeed, some of the ladies are quite lovely, if a bit exotic for my tastes. We don't challenge them unless it's quite obvious, or we have a complaint from another patron. So, if your friends are of that sort—" he gave Wyatt an ingratiating wink, "I'm sure there would be no difficulty."

Giovanna was frowning at Wyatt. "You want to bring colored people to the play?"

"They've been in attendance everywhere else we've been," Wyatt told Graham. "Even in New Orleans, which is about as south as you can get." The manager shrugged and held out his hands.

Wyatt turned to Giovanna. "Germain, for one. He's the steward for Congressman Dodge," he told Graham, "and he's never had a chance to see me play a lead."

"Get the box office to give you a couple of tickets," Graham said in a conspiratorial tone. "If he's discreet about it…"

Wyatt felt a flash of anger. Graham was counting on Germain to be light-skinned. He was, relatively, but no one would mistake him for a white man.

"I don't think my friend would relish pretending to be someone he's not," he snapped, "any more than any of us would."

Graham gave him a pitying look. "It's all I can offer, I'm afraid."

Giovanna consulted her watch. "Oh, dear, I must go," she said abruptly. "The other Witches and I are going to tea at Willard's. We'll see you this evening, gentlemen."

Wyatt watched her disappear back into the wings. He'd thought himself a reasonable judge of character, but he wondered whether the woman he loved had developed a case of race-prejudice.

Giovanna was in no mood for a ladies' tea. She took a few minutes in her dressing room to recover her composure and take stock of her conversation with Alexis Germain. She picked up one of the Teddy bears and hugged it to her chest; holding it, stroking its artificial fur, felt oddly soothing.

As arranged, they had met in the back stacks of the District of Columbia Public Library, a miniature temple in white marble that still welcomed people of all colors. Germain was browsing through a volume of Audubon plates in the Natural History section when she slipped into his row, a little late and out of breath, and pulled a dusty tome out from the opposite stack. He tipped his hat, gave her a half-smile, and turned back to his book.

"Thank you for coming," he said in a library whisper.

She frowned back at him and nodded, leafing through *Principles of Industrial Chemistry* at random. It appeared to be written in ancient Egyptian.

"There were things I couldn't say in the letter," he went on.

"The letter said quite enough," she snapped.

"If I was wrong," he said, "I wanted to apologize in person. And if I'm not—what you decide to do is up to you."

"Say what you have to say." Her glance darted around the largely unpopulated stacks.

"He wants to marry you. If you're disposed to accept him, I think he deserves the truth."

"What makes you think I'd want to marry him? I have a husband and children."

Germain didn't answer, just looked steadily at her.

She bit her lip and lowered her eyes back to the book. "I don't know what I—well, all right," she looked squarely at him, "I do. Or I did. Since you know so much about me, you might as well know that."

"Does your husband know your history?"

"Nobody did. Until you somehow figured it out."

"You live in New Orleans as long as I did," Germain smiled, "you get a pretty good sense for these things. You grow up here in the District?"

Giovanna nodded and looked up at him, anguish and dim light making her eyes huge and dark. "He's met my family. He just doesn't know it. He was telling me what a cultured group of people they all are."

"Oh, Lord. This Nielsen thing." Germain scrutinized her face. "The Wilburs?"

"He's my brother. I used to tease him—I told him he got all Mama's Negro blood and I got all the white." Her smile was wistful.

"How long since you've seen him?"

"Thirteen years. Germain—" her fingers dug into his arm, "Clarence isn't a suspect, is he?"

The question startled him. "Wyatt's never mentioned him that way."

"What will Wyatt think if I tell him?"

Germain sighed. "If he'd known about it from the get-go, he would've taken it in stride." He opened his hands. "Now you've gone all this time with him thinkin' you're an Italian from New Jersey…might take him a while to deal with that."

186

"Do you think he can?"

"No way you could've gotten where you have otherwise, we both know that."

"If I'd been living as colored, he and I would never have met."

They were silent, reading the doubt in each other's eyes.

"I don't know how I can tell him," Giovanna shook her head. "It could throw him off—he's got so much else on his mind with this murder business. I wish he'd never heard of it!"

"Look," Germain said, his whisper more urgent, "He knows something's been on your nerves since you got to Washington. Might help him settle if you tell him."

"It could just make things worse."

"For what it's worth—last time he investigated a murder, something came to light about Mrs. Dodge. Something her husband hadn't known. Wyatt handled it with sympathy. And respect."

"What about Mr. Dodge?"

"He was mad all right—but at a guy who was trying to blackmail his wife."

Giovanna replaced the book and brushed dust from her hands. "I don't know what I'm going to do." She drew in a sharp breath. "But I promise you this—if I can't bring myself to tell him, I'll let him go."

She'd felt his gaze on her back as she slipped silently out of the stacks.

In the dressing-room, she hugged the Teddy bear to her breast. The origin of the prized toy, for which there was a stampede of buyers at present, was a sentimental story of how the President had refused to shoot a bear cub when on a hunt down in Mississippi. But she'd heard the real story, and it was less cheerful; the bear, full-grown, had been hunted down and mauled by dogs, and tied to a tree as a potential trophy for Roosevelt to finish off. The President declined to shoot it, but ordered the exhausted, terrified animal put out of its misery by someone else. One way or another, it had died on his account. She wasn't going to tell the children that part of the story.

CHAPTER 28

Sufficiently mollified by a friendly note in his dressing-room, Wyatt agreed to meet Commander Macalester for porter and steak at Ebbitt's after the night's performance. They perched companionably on barstools, leaning on the smudged brass rail, watched over by a row of trophy heads and the portrait of a recumbent, amply proportioned lady in diaphanous draperies.

"I thought I'd put you in the picture myself," Macalester said, "seeing as you provided us with the lead—you've a wee bit of greasepaint still, over that eyebrow—aye, that's it gone." He gave Wyatt an intense squint. "You've a couple of carpetbags under your eyes."

Wyatt scowled. "Comes with the double shifts." The porter in his belly was melting the knots out of his muscles and reminding him how badly he needed sleep.

"As to an insurance policy," Macalester went on, "there's not a trace of it among Nielsen's papers, which is a bit odd to my way of thinking. He was quite the meticulous record-keeper—a bit of a pack-rat, in fact. His will was there—not much to it—and his first wife's death certificate, his Lutheran certificate of baptism— all neat and tidy and locked away in a wooden chest under his bed. Seems to me that would've been the place for an insurance policy."

Macalester nodded to a pair of porcine Congressmen, who might to Wyatt's eyes have been Tweedledum and Tweedledee grown to adulthood. He must stop thinking of Washingtonians as characters from *Alice in Wonderland*. He finished a mouthful of tenderloin, one of the compensations of being on Dodge's payroll again, and made a mental note to decline dessert.

"Miss Stanstead gave us the key to the box," Macalester continued, "which means she could have taken the policy and tucked it away somewhere, till the heat died down, except the good Mr. Templeton made a point of bringing her the news himself."

"She told me that box was private," Wyatt said. "She'd never opened it."

Macalester raised an eyebrow. "And since when do we take people's word for it in a murder investigation?"

Wyatt's heart sank. He couldn't bear the thought of Louisa replacing Latham as the prime suspect. Especially not for so venal a motive as an insurance policy.

"There was, however, one rather interestin' item which we didn't expect to find in a gentleman's personal papers. Which Miss Stanstead says she'd never seen before." Macalester smiled and produced an envelope with the flourish of one playing a trump card. With a pair of tweezers from an inside pocket, he carefully extracted a folded piece of stationery. The same paper, Wyatt knew instantly, used for the letter he'd taken from Congressmen Chaney.

The Commander carefully spread it out between them on a napkin. Like Chaney's letter, it was typed and unsigned. "Readers of the *Wisconsin State Journal* may be interested to learn of an irregular domestic relationship involving the Member from the Second District at his Washington residence, and a 'lady' of mixed ancestry who has been his confederate in a number of legislative initiatives, in whose outcomes the pair might seem to have a more than 'passing' interest. These relations are well known to the Congressman's friends and associates…"

Wyatt's gorge rose. "Looks familiar."

"Right enough." Macalester's mouth was a thin, grim line.

"Not surprised Nielsen hadn't let Louisa see it. You get any fingerprints off it?"

"Nielsen's. And a set that matches the ones on Congressman Chaney's letter, which had Chaney's own as well, naturally."

Wyatt grinned. "He let you take his fingerprints?"

"Only 'cause I agreed to do it myself, in the privacy of his personal office, and get the ink off his fingers before his clerk saw him. He thought the whole thing was quite fascinatin'. Made him feel like a hardened criminal, he said. Gave him somethin' in common with Dick Latham at last." Macalester refolded the paper, still without touching it, and put it back in the envelope.

"And the other prints? From O'Donoghue's effects in the evidence locker?"

"Well, now, that's the interestin' thing," Macalester said with studied casualness. "I've not got the formal report, but they appear to match the ones on a certain champagne glass pilfered from the Raleigh Hotel."

Wyatt almost fell off his barstool. "They got his prints? And there's a match?"

Macalester drained his porter and tapped the glass on the bar. The barman looked up sharply from polishing a glass and Macalester signaled him for two more, overruling Wyatt's protest. "Well, we can't be absolutely sure they were Dandy Pat's, mind you, because back in those days we weren't fingerprinting people yet, so we've nothing on file to compare them to. But when you find the same prints on a fella's shaving-mug and razor, those not being items gentlemen typically pass around, it seems reasonable to conclude that they belonged to the supposed decedent."

Wyatt grinned. "That sounds like something a prosecuting attorney would say. Have you got enough to arrest him now?"

"That's one of many things about this finger-print business that isn't clear under the law. But one thing I'm sure of—we've got a match between that champagne glass, Dandy Pat O'Donoghue's personal effects, and now this letter. The murderer we thought died in the East River in 1885 is alive and well and blackmailin' Members of Congress."

"So are you ready to drop the charges against Latham?"

Macalester guffawed. "Single-minded, aren't you, laddie? Not by a long chalk. But in the circumstances I think we can see our way clear to canceling the arraignment—or postponing it, at any rate."

The two fresh beers arrived and Wyatt took a long swallow to finish his first one. A troubling thought came to him. "What did Louisa—Miss Stanstead—say when she saw the note?"

Macalester appraised him shrewdly over the rim of his glass. "You've taken a liking to the lassie, I see. Well, you're not the only one. On the one hand, it lends credence to her story of the marriage proposal. On the other—"

"The proposal may have been self-defense on Nielsen's part. Or mutual protection, at any rate."

Macalester nodded. "I wish I hadn't read it to her," he sighed. "The note, I mean. She looked stunned for a minute, then all she said was, 'Oh,' and turned her head away."

Wyatt straightened up on the barstool. "Doesn't mean he didn't want to marry her anyway. Might've just pushed things along."

"She'll never know, will she?" Macalester signaled for the check and reached for his wallet.

"I'm getting this," Wyatt said, putting a hand out to bar the reach. "Or, rather, Dodge is. Can you match those letters to a particular typewriter?"

Macalester grinned. "You anticipate me. As it happens, there's a chap who's become quite the expert at this sort of thing. We're living in an age of great advancements in forensic science. Quite the jolly time to be a homicide investigator. We got in touch with the fella—his name's Osborn, about your age, mebbe—"

"New York man? Same Osborn who was involved in the Molineux trial in '99?"

"Indeed, though that didn't go so well for the prosecution. Osborn was called in on the handwriting in that instance, but he's moved on to more advanced means of communication. Anyway, we were in touch with him as soon as Chaney handed over his note, and we've asked your Mr. Dodge to see if he can rustle up any letters sent to him from Dunagin's office. Latham too, for that matter, though he referred us to his lawyer before he'd agree to it."

"Look, even if all these prints and the typewriters match up, you still won't have enough admissible evidence to convict him on the old charges, never mind Nielsen. Did they ever find any family back in Ireland?"

"Working on it," said Macalester. "The NYPD cabled some of our Ulster colleagues and sent them off looking for a Dunagin family at the address our hero gave the Baltimore firm when he first applied for the situation. The expense will be considerable if we find them, but Chief Woods is willing to pay for a passage, in the interest of bringing an egregious criminal to justice. They'll exhume the body and do X rays as well."

"And maybe there's an old photo or two," Wyatt said. "This sounds promising."

Macalester raised a cautionary finger. "Blackmail isn't murder, laddie. You've still a job to do to bring us something we can work with on the Nielsen end of things."

"Blackmail isn't a death threat either—" Wyatt stopped and put a hand on Macalester's arm.

"What?"

"So why did Nielsen take out that insurance policy?"

Macalester's eyebrows went up. "Now there's an excellent question!"

"If the blackmail note was old enough and Nielsen hadn't backed off from his bill, maybe Dunagin decided to escalate matters and be done with it. Some physical threat we haven't found evidence for."

"If he'd got one of those I should think he'd have kept it, as he did the blackmail note. In any event, Dunagin would most likely have delegated the dirty work. We've had a couple of thugs in for questioning, I'm told, in connection with one or two assaults we can tie back to him—on competitors for some property he was after, or some troublesome tenants. But they won't admit to a connection." Macalester took a last swallow of porter and shook his head when the bartender looked up. "He pays them enough to ensure loyalty, it seems."

The porter was turning sour in Wyatt's stomach. "You need witnesses, and there don't seem to have been any. Or any willing to talk, at any rate."

But a plan was forming. He thought of Mrs. Washington, the old woman upstairs at 24th and I Streets, whom the police had questioned to no avail, whose daughter had shut the door in his own face. She'd seen or heard something, he was nearly sure of it. But how to get her to talk…

"Germain," he said aloud. Macalester looked puzzled. "The old lady on the corner—I think she saw something that night, but she's afraid. Maybe he can get something out of her. I'll talk to him."

They walked through the Ebbitt's heavy doors into the soft Washington night. "You'd best get what sleep you can, young fella," Macalester said with something like concern in his tone. "You burn that brief candle at both ends and it'll be out, out for you."

"Or at best I'll be a walking shadow," Wyatt grinned. They walked companionably towards the Johnson.

CHAPTER 29

Some nights she dreamed she was Joanna Wilbur again. She thought she'd left Joanna behind for good when she struck out for New York and crossed the color line at eighteen, shedding the constraints of her downtrodden race along with her identity, her family, and her friends. But now that she was back in Washington, the ghost of Joanna kept materializing, like Banquo before his murderer, in ever-sharpening focus.

Joanna had won prizes at the M Street School for elocution and rhetoric, all but useless to a young woman in the narrow confines of Washington's respectable Negro community. She loved Shakespeare and the stage, knew from the reactions of her directors and audiences that she had talent. The talented tenth, wasn't that what Dr. Dubois had called them? Those whose skills and intelligence would lead the race out of the wilderness.

But there was no path for her talent to take in the world where she'd been raised. So she'd fled, shedding her Negro identity and her name on the train journey north. That part had been easy. She'd been mistaken for white her whole life. Her gifts and her drive took care of the rest. But often she felt like the Little Mermaid in that tale her father had read to her as a child, dumbstruck, each step into the future the stab of a sharp knife underfoot. She'd given up everything else for that one thing, and now, fourteen years later, it wasn't enough.

There were so many things she'd had to learn, when she made that irrevocable journey. How she carried herself, how she spoke, what she wore—those were the least of it. A white woman couldn't let herself get involved with a colored man, for instance. Couldn't even initiate a conversation with one, for fear of being thought a loose woman and, if they were in the South, putting the man's safety in jeopardy. That had taken a lot of getting used to—along with the idea that white men could look at her, not just with lust, but with fellowship and respect; that they could offer her an honorable sort of love, love with marriage and children, they'd never have dreamed of with a woman they thought was black. Was it sin to have accepted that deceived love? If it was, perhaps Thomas's infidelities had been just punishment. Maybe that was why she had never called him to account, why she'd allowed the intimacy between them to wear away.

It wasn't as if one of her M Street schoolmates was going to stand up in mid-scene and cry, "Hey, that's Joanna Wilbur!", pointing at her in her Lady Macduff disguise. The National didn't officially allow colored patrons, and no colored woman who got in there would want or dare to draw such attention to herself. But the dreams wouldn't go away. In the end, she realized, it wasn't fear of public exposure that was haunting her since she'd come to Washington. It was fear of the man she'd fallen in love with, the man she was ready to leave her husband for, fear of being turned away when he found out the truth about her. Germain had brought that truth into the daylight. She had no choice now but to tell Wyatt, if she thought to make a new life with him.

What would he think when he knew, this beloved whose sleep-softened body curved around hers in futile protectiveness, the man whose gentle gaze seemed on the verge of seeing right through her? Could this white man possibly understand and accept her? He felt her fear, wanted to know its cause, to help her face it and make it go away. But he was white and she was not. If their bodies and hearts touched, there was still the dark river of history rushing between their souls whose chill, for now, only she could feel.

His involvement in investigating the death of Robert Nielsen seemed like some new judgment of Fate on her deception, taking him as it was into the heart of her old circle. He'd told her, with what sounded like admiration, about the cast of characters he was meeting: Nettie Wilbur, Nielsen's housekeeper, her husband Clarence. Joanna's brother. Witnesses in the case. When Wyatt had mentioned them, Giovanna could barely control her trembling. James Costello, who had even walked out a few times with Joanna, back in the ancient days when they were both students at the M Street School. Now, having failed in his suit to another light-skinned woman, he could be a suspect in this investigation of Wyatt's. Life was strange.

Wyatt stirred in his sleep, the first gray light of day softening the lines around his mouth and eyes. She loved his silky brown hair, its few threads of gray, the soft brush of his mustache on her lips, his taut, slender body. Loved the hint of old sadness in his eyes. Many men had wanted her, blessed as she was with beauty and high spirits, but only Wyatt had seen her whole—and yet not even he. He didn't know her history, only what she was now and had been for fourteen years. She shivered and his hands sensed it. Still mostly asleep, the arms tightened around her. Could he accept her, history and all? She longed for that more than she'd ever longed for fame.

She would find out soon. She had to tell him tonight.

"So much for the jilted lover's revenge," Wyatt said. "Poor Costello—he must think it's the most tragic case of bad timing since *Romeo and Juliet*." He plopped down beside Germain on a park bench across the Mall from the Smithsonian Castle entrance, where families in their best clothes were coming out of the Children's Wing into the bright afternoon sunlight.

"More of a Coriolanus, I'd say. Man on a mission." Germain scattered a handful of cracked corn for an attentive group of pigeons gargling wheezily at his feet. "He'd be wrong anyways—Miss Stanstead wasn't about to marry him, Nielsen or no Nielsen. He walked Miss Fleetwood home from the YMCA meeting—she's a teacher at M Street too, in music—made his declaration en route, her daddy says. She looks like a lot better fit to me than Louisa in any event."

Wyatt tilted the brim of his hat to shield his eyes from the afternoon sun. "Funny, in a way, that Louisa wouldn't have been interested in him. He's good-looking, professional, idealistic. Even seems a bit more personable than what I've heard of Nielsen."

"*La coeur a ses raisons*—" Germain began.

"—*dont la raison ne connait point.* I know. Well, the point is, there's no way he killed Nielsen."

"So I gave up my Roman histories for nothing," Germain sighed.

"Admit it—when was the last time you read Livy?"

"Oh, back at Southern, I guess, about '87. But I was gonna get back to it at some point. Not a bad trade, though—I got a couple more invitations last night. Seems I'm an acceptable addition to Washington society."

Wyatt grinned. "Don't sound so surprised. I saw those mamas sizing you up for their daughters at the Alley Relief meeting."

"I'm taken," Germain growled.

"They don't have to know that. Speaking of Washington society, I've got another favor to ask."

"What now?"

"Mrs. Washington—the old lady who lives on the corner by Nielsen's place. She probably knows more than she told the police, but the daughter won't let anybody near her. Nobody white, anyway. But Mac and I thought you might—"

"Being friends with you is costing me. How are you suggesting I get past the guard-dog daughter?"

"Miss Stanstead probably knows them. Maybe she can make an introduction."

"That'd help. What are we thinking the lady saw?"

"I've got my ideas, but we don't want to be accused of putting them in a witness's head. Just ask her about the evening, whether she saw anyone in the neighborhood she wasn't used to seeing."

"All right. I'll talk to Miz Stanstead." Germain sighed and shook his head.

Wyatt rose and adjusted his hat brim. "Going out for an early dinner before the show."

Germain smiled up at him. "Give her my regards." He watched Wyatt make his way over to Pennsylvania Avenue. Giovanna hadn't told him yet, that was apparent.

CHAPTER 30

Wyatt paused on the south side of Pennsylvania Avenue to enjoy the rosy glow of the National's massive, graceful brick facade in the late afternoon light. Lowering his gaze, he waited for his eyes to adjust to the shadows at ground level and nearly missed a dark figure that almost collided with him at the crosswalk.

"Mr. Wyatt!" It was Clarence Wilbur, the young attorney from the Strivers' insurance company.

"Sorry." Wyatt reached out to steady the smaller man. "I was wondering what's on those upper floors."

The young man, whose countenance was usually open and cheerful, looked furtive, as if he was in a hurry to get away.

"Were you looking for me?"

"Ah, uh, well—" Wilbur seemed taken aback. But he must have been at the theater, or near it; there were no shops or offices in the vicinity.

"Something to tell me about the case?" Wyatt encouraged.

Wilbur seemed to collect himself. "Well, ah, yes. Something I thought you'd want to know—though it shrinks your list of suspects."

"Shall we walk for a spell?"

"Oh—I imagine you have things to do, Mr. Wyatt—well, all right. It won't take long. It's, ah, about James Costello."

Wyatt gave him a look of polite inquiry.

"I remember you asked us to think about who we saw leaving the meeting at the Strivers,' the night Mr. Nielsen was killed. And I just thought you'd want to know—James left with Miss Celia Fleetwood. Major Fleetwood's daughter."

Wyatt had heard this from Germain, but merely smiled encouragement.

"It turns out he proposed marriage to her, while he was walking her home, and went on in to the Fleetwoods' to ask for her hand. So he couldn't have…" he trailed off.

Wyatt beamed as if he was hearing this for the first time. "Then I have two reasons to congratulate him! Anything that shrinks the list saves work, you know."

"Well, that's what I thought. We're all so anxious for you to find whoever did this, Mr. Wyatt—" Wilbur paused, "assuming it's not Latham. Mr. Nielsen's death is a great loss for our race, not to mention the Strivers' itself."

"He was a great supporter of the firm, Mr. Templeton told me."

"Oh, yes, indeed! He was on the Board—the Finances Committee. Very diligent in his oversight, I heard. Very good with numbers."

Wyatt smiled inwardly. From what he'd heard of Nielsen, that role might have made him something of a trial to the Strivers' senior management. But Wilbur's comment also tickled something at the edge of his brain. He filed it away for future examination.

"And how is your good lady?"

Wilbur looked confused, but his face cleared and he smiled broadly in his turn. "Nettie's doing very well, thank you. We're about three months away—it's our first."

"I should be very glad to hear the news, when it comes." Wyatt pulled a card from his wallet. "This is my New York address— will you let me know?" He would send a Teddy bear from F.A.O. Schwarz's; the young Master or Miss Wilbur might enjoy having one.

Wondering why Wilbur had troubled to come and tell him something he must surely have heard from Germain by now, Wyatt made his way into to the National and upstairs to Giovanna's dressing-room, where they'd arranged to meet for dinner. When he opened the door, she swiveled towards him on the stool. She wasn't dressed to go out, which registered as odd with him, since he was slightly behind time.

"So," she said in a small, trembling voice. "You must have run into my brother."

He frowned and shook his head slightly.

"My brother Clarence," she said.

He froze. "Clarence Wilbur?"

She took in a deep breath, nodded, and his world reeled from its axis.

The first question that popped out of his mouth surprised both of them.

"Who else knows?"

She bit her lip and stared at her lap. "I sent him a note, asked him to visit me. He'll tell Nettie and—and Mama. That's all, he promised me. Germain knows. He knew right away."

Wyatt shook his head. "Germain?"

"As soon as he met me, he says."

He sank into a side chair. "Was he going to tell me? If you didn't?"

She held up a hand, her eyes wide. "No! Absolutely not! We don't do that—"

We. Colored people. We don't rat on one another when one of us decides to…decides to 'pass.'

"But he thought I should tell you, if I—" she turned her head away.

Wyatt waited, knowing why she'd stopped, not wanting her to say it now, his face a mask. The moment stretched between them.

"Does your husband—?"

"No!" She shook her head. "No one else."

He swallowed. "Why?"

"Why tell you now, or why did I do it?" She closed her eyes, took another long breath. "Either way, you know the answer." The look she gave him was searing, a spotlight aimed squarely at his heart. His head hurt and his insides had turned to water.

"This is what you've been worried about, since we came here," he said at last. He didn't look up to see her nod. The silence crackled between them.

"I need some time," he said finally.

She nodded. "It's a lot to take in." She looked so small, so tiny, perched there uneasily on her stool, her great eyes dark pools in the dim light. Like a frightened but defiant child, hoping for understanding, demanding it, perhaps. He wanted to put his arms around her. He wanted to push her away.

He opened the door and stepped out into the corridor, closing it silently behind him. The woman he loved—had loved?—was a colored woman who'd been living a lie. Who'd kept a vital secret from him for all the time they'd been lovers. And she'd finally told him that secret because she loved him enough to want to stay with him, needed for all to be open between them. He had no idea, in this moment, how he felt about that.

Giovanna put her head down on the dressing-table, blindly shoving aside the bottles and jars to clear a space, and sobbed bitterly. It had been a mistake, all of it. What had possessed her to write to Clarence, to ask him to visit her, then to tell Wyatt what he clearly hadn't learned from her brother? What had she expected? That he'd break into one of his kind, loving smiles, take her hands and say, "There! I knew you were fretting over something silly. Don't you feel better now?"

She might have dreamed or fantasized that, but he was a human being, with too much on his mind. It was childish to have thought he could take it in stride. She'd thrown the dice and lost. Life was going to be so lonely without him. But Germain had been right; she'd had to tell him. If it had come out afterwards—well, that didn't bear thinking of.

Hours later, it seemed, she lifted her head and looked at her pocket-watch. She wasn't remotely interested in food, though she rarely went on stage on an empty stomach. The gray, hollowed-out feeling she had now was partly grief, but part relief too. It was done. She'd told the truth at last, and felt cleansed. No wonder the Catholics liked Confession.

It was a lovely evening. She'd go out for a little walk, over to Lafayette Park where the tulips bloomed and the trees were budding in palest green. Soon, she'd make a clandestine visit to Mama, who was ailing and not long for the world, ask forgiveness, try to explain. And then she'd go back to her old life, a life most women would envy. The children would help to fill the emptiness.

Wyatt stumbled down the hall to his own dressing-room and dropped onto its bench. He'd heard about colored people "passing;" it was the stuff of gossip, melodrama, and lurid dime novels. But until now he hadn't known—there was a fleeting sardonic smile at the thought of adding "in the Biblical sense"—anyone who'd chosen to take on that life-long secret. Its burden was off Giovanna's shoulders now, and on to his.

He'd grown up differently from most Americans, on the rural fringes of a community where whites and colored people mingled freely and on equal terms. Oberlin was founded that way, an abolitionist refuge, a major stop on the Underground Railroad. Its college had admitted Negroes—and women—almost from the beginning. People there fell in love and married across the color line—including, he remembered, Louisa Stanstead's great-grandparents. As a young boy he had played with friends of many colors, and in his youth admired the young ladies of Oberlin, some with dark skin, some with light. Nobody there had to pretend.

But Oberlin wasn't like the rest of America. Since he'd left Ohio, he'd lived in a world largely separated by color, until his short service with the Rough Riders, where white and black soldiers had fought side by side on equal terms. As he thought of his friendship with Germain, and the pleasure he was taking in meeting the community of Washington's colored elite, he realized how much he had missed the easy interactions of his younger days and his time as a soldier.

Maybe that had even attracted him to Giovanna: something about her that, somehow, he already knew. It was almost amusing that she'd been afraid to tell him what he'd have accepted without a second thought, if it had come in the beginning. Now that she'd kept it from him so long, it became a lie that had lain between them.

All those days since the troupe had come to Washington, she'd been dreading the possibility of exposure. Yet in the end, she'd taken it on herself. She might have kept it from him still. Clarence Wilbur, who had carefully not told Wyatt his real reason for visiting the National, would have gone home, Giovanna would have sneaked off to visit her ailing mother, and life would have gone on as before.

She'd told him the truth because she didn't want life-as-before. Because she wanted a new life with him, in which she could be fully herself with at least one other human being. That's what he'd wanted too, before he knew.

Maybe he'd come back to wanting it.

He'd had no qualms in the past about romantic involvement with colored women. He wanted to think that the sense of betrayal he felt was about the untruthfulness of it. That he'd been as naked with her, in all senses, as a man could be with a woman, for months now, and she'd never breathed a word.

He thought, too, of the courage it had taken to live as she did, like a spy in enemy territory, hearing or reading the latest theories that 'proved' Negroes were genetically inferior, that mixing their blood with the white would lead to racial degeneracy and the downfall of civilization. And the courage it had taken to tell him, to risk the very reaction he was experiencing: the alienation of his feelings.

He was angry with himself for not immediately rising above it, for not dismissing it, as Warren Dodge had dismissed his wife's Jewishness, as irrelevant to the character of the woman he loved. Angry with her for forcing him to acknowledge his failure to transcend race prejudice, to see past her heritage to her essence.

At least he hadn't said anything to her. Maybe, once he got used to it, once they talked about it, things could be something like what they were.

He thought about her brother Clarence and the first time they'd met. The young lawyer had been talking about a bill in Congress that would forbid blacks and whites to marry. Anyone with one-eighth or more of Negro blood would be considered a Negro. It would apply to him and Giovanna, if she hadn't crossed the color line…what was that line from *Othello*? "She hath deceiv'd her father, and may thee." Could he learn to trust a woman who had concealed her history from him for so long?

Who have I been loving all these months? Will this make our parting easier—leaving someone I never really knew?

He turned back to his dressing-table, covered his eyes with his hands, sat without moving until he heard the dresser tap on his door and reached for his box of stage makeup.

CHAPTER 31

"Why, you're the young gentleman from New Orleans Maisie Hutchins was telling me about," said Mrs. Willamina Washington, "that sat next to her in the Rankin Chapel. Will you have a cup of tea?"

"If you're making it anyways, ma'am, thank you." Alexis Germain, in a pale gray suit and immaculate white shirt, looked around the parlor while his hostess bustled in the kitchen. It was the very image of shabby respectability: spotless antimacassars on the two tiny armchairs, an oval photo in a gilded frame of a man in splendid muttonchops he took to be the late Mr. Washington. A snow-white lace panel hung before one narrow window; on the other, the curtain was pulled back, affording a clear view of the now-sunny corner where New Hampshire Avenue cut off the intersection of 24th and I Streets Northwest, steps from the area just below Washington Circle where Robert Nielsen had met his murderer.

"My daughter didn't want me talking to you." She came in smiling with the tea-tray and Germain hastily removed his derby from the pie-crust table. "'You just stay away from that business, mama,' she said. 'No good ever come a colored person from talking to the police.' But then Miss Louisa said they'd got the wrong man and Mr. Nielsen's killer could go free, so I said, well, I don't know if it'll do any good, but I'll talk to Mr. Germain."

She poured the tea and held up a sugar lump in a little pair of tongs. "You take sugar? She wants me to move in with her, says this is such a bad neighborhood with Snow's Court round the corner and all. And now Mr. Nielsen. But I've been here a long time, me and Mr. Washington raised our four children here, and

I said, 'Luella, you tend to your business and let me be. Folks 'round here know I got no money and even the bad ones got some respect for a old lady.'"

Germain sipped his tea from its flowered china cup. "You must've known Mr. Nielsen yourself, ma'am."

She put her cup down and her gaze turned towards the window. "Well, I seen him on the street often enough. He was always in a hurry, like he was late for something, you know? But he'd tip his hat if he passed a lady, just a li'l tip, but you noticed. Not what you'd call a friendly man. But a good man, a righteous man."

"Do you remember the last time you saw him?"

"Last time for sure was that very day he died. Oh, it was in the morning," she answered Germain's startled look. "He was hurrying past down here on I Street," she pointed out the window with the pulled-back curtain, "like he often did. Seemed like he was in more of a hurry than usual that day. He wouldn't even stop and talk to Mr. Templeton—"

"The insurance man?"

"That's him. You met him? He is a fine man. Everybody 'round here thinks the world of Brother Templeton. The way he takes care of that poor li'l boy of his…"

Germain contemplated interrupting the digression but decided the lady might think him rude and clam up.

"That doctor's in and out of that house 'most every day," she went on. "They say he charges colored folks more than he does white ones. And that mama of his, well, she prides herself on what a respectable woman she is, she's got plenty of money that Mr. Templeton Senior left her, but I know for a fact she doesn't spend a nickel of it helping Mr. Templeton Junior and that child." Germain widened his eyes. "No, sir, she don't, she told Miz Hutchins so herself and she don't care who knows it. Says that little boy a freak and oughta have been put away in St. Elizabeth's. Her only grandchild. Can you believe it?"

Germain shook his head slowly. "Mmph-mmph-mmph."

"Anyways, Mr. Templeton's tryin' to catch up with Mr. Nielsen, tryin' to say somethin' to him, but Mr. Nielsen, he just turns and gives Mr. T. a dirty look and walks on faster than ever. Looked like he got up on the wrong side of bed that day."

Germain recalled Wyatt's story of the quarrel between Nielsen and Louisa that morning. "And that's the day he got up on the House floor—"

Mrs. Washington chuckled. "Now, it wasn't right, what he said, but I'd'a loved to have seen the look on that Latham's face—"

"So that was the last you saw of him? Mr. Nielsen?"

"Until the next morning, when there was all the fuss up the block where they found him."

"You didn't hear anything in the night?"

"Well, now, you didn't ask me that. Things get a mite noisy 'round here, Mr. Germain, with Snow's Court right out the back," she gestured inward with her thumb, "and there's some ladies down there no better than they should be, know what I'm saying? About two, three fights a week, some of the visitors they get."

"You heard a fight?"

"I'd woken up, you know, I'd fallen asleep in this chair here. I don't sleep as good as I used to, and I had the window open, just a crack, for a little fresh air. And I heard voices, just below my window."

Germain leaned forward, cup and saucer hovering at his knee. "Could you make out what they were saying?"

"Well, they wasn't talking all that loud, but I did notice they was Irish."

"Irish, hmm?"

"So, I thought, well, we don't get many Irish 'round here— there used to be a lot of them in Snow's Court, but they moved on—so I pulled back the curtain just a li'l bit," Mrs. Washington rose and re-enacted her movements, "and I looked down, and they were stopped under that street lamp yonder, lighting cigarettes. Them two fellas that the landlord sends round to the alley for the rent when somebody's late. I don't know their names, we just call them Jekyll and Hyde. Plug-uglies, the two of 'em."

"What were they talking about, could you hear?"

"I couldn't hear them too good. Seemed like they was out of breath, you know, like they'd been running. But there was something about gone and saved them the trouble."

"Any idea what that was about?"

"Well, there was a family down in the Court, was always behind on their rent. The Demars. Man and his wife and five little ones. He drank." Mrs. Washington shook her head. "Such a shame. So we figured they was gonna get evicted. Then a couple days before Mr. Nielsen died, they up and disappeared. Took some stuff with them, left in the middle of the night, near as folks can tell. So when I saw those two plug-uglies, I figured, well, they was coming after the Demarses, but they'd left by their own selves."

"Anything else you heard?" Germain was torn between excitement at placing Dunagin's thugs near the murder scene, and the rational consideration that they might have only been there to conduct a late-night eviction.

"Something about Latham," she said suddenly. "They was movin' off—that's right. All I heard was his name. Then they kinda looked up, so I let the curtain drop right quick and they went on down I Street, that way." She pointed east. "After that I just went on to bed. Woke up with all the hubbub going on up the street. That's when we found out what had happened to poor Mr. Nielsen. Later on I figured maybe they knew Mr. Nielsen lived in the neighborhood and they were talking about what he'd said to Mr. Latham. It was all over the *Evening Star* that day."

"Miz Washington, how much of this did you tell the police?"

She shook her head slowly. "I told them I heard men's voices out my window, but that was all. I don't need no trouble from Jekyll and Hyde. That Dunagin's my landlord too."

"You were right about Miz Washington," Germain told Wyatt over a hair-of-the-dog beer in his favorite Georgetown tavern. "She saw a couple of fellas that're known for doing dirty work for Dunagin—wait a minute," he put down his tankard and looked at Wyatt, whose head was drooping. "Somethin's up, brother."

Wyatt tried for a grin and failed. "I don't want to talk about it." He scowled and took a sip of his beer.

"You'd be better off with a Bromo-Seltzer," Germain said. He waved his hand towards a shelf near the cash register where a row of the familiar little blue bottles sat.

"Stuff knocks me out," Wyatt said, holding up his hand. "I have a show tonight."

"Aspirin powder, then." Germain's expression turned serious. "She told you."

Wyatt nodded and winced at the movement. "You weren't going to."

"Wasn't my business to. 'Sides, would you have wanted me to?"

"She said you knew right away."

"Just a feeling you get lookin' at somebody, you know?"

"Can't say as I do." Wyatt put his glass down and covered his face with his hands, kneading his forehead with his fingers. "It shouldn't make any difference, I know that."

"Maybe not, if you'd known it from the start. But, then, you'd never have met her."

"I want to think that's what's bothering me. That she took all this time to tell me."

Germain held up a finger and went to the bar, returning with a mug of black coffee. "Here, this'll help. Look, somebody decides to pass, you may not like it, but you have to respect the choice. Way things are goin' these days, you're almost crazy not to if you can get away with it."

"But—it's living a lie. Your whole life is a lie." Wyatt sipped the coffee and grimaced. "Lord, you could tar rope with this."

"I've crossed the color line myself, once or twice, and I'll tell you, it scared me half to death. Felt like I'd be shot on the spot if they found me out." Germain's nostrils flared. "With all due respect, you don't know what it's like—no vote, no decent job, nobody even rent you a damn house. If you're a woman, white men thinkin' you're fair game. You think that gal would be a rising star in the theater if they knew she was colored?"

Wyatt's headache had redoubled. "I suppose not." He spread his hands out in conciliation. "The town I grew up in—it was unusual. Nobody cared what color you were, so nobody had to lie about who they were."

"That sounds like a place I should move to," Germain smiled. "And you told me once there were a lot of colored fellows in the Rough Riders. Anyways, you *know* she wouldn't have gotten anywhere if they'd known. So," Germain grinned, "you mad to find out you've been sleeping with a colored woman?"

Wyatt reddened. "You know damn well there's a colored woman I'd have married once, if she'd have had me. But she didn't pretend to be something she wasn't." He let out a long breath and shook his head. "I don't know. It wasn't supposed to be going anywhere anyway. One of those affairs that lasts the length of the run. Happens all the time with actors." He pushed the coffee mug aside and took a swallow of beer.

"But it was going somewhere."

Wyatt's head slumped onto the table. "That's why she had to tell me, isn't it?"

Germain nodded. "And take the chance you couldn't handle it. Rock and a hard place, my friend."

"If you hadn't told her she needed to, would she have—"

"She'd have got there anyway."

Wyatt sighed. "I'd never have known. Probably. If she hadn't…"

"You had to know, if it was going to be any good."

"Yeah, I suppose so."

"What will you do?"

Wyatt felt his blood rise. "Look, I may not know what it's like to be in her shoes—or yours—but don't you understand? Everything I thought I knew about her—"

"You and a lot of other folks, including the father of her kids. *And* her kids. It's not like she singled you out for deceit, brother. You think I'd be doing what I'm doing if I could pass for white?"

That stopped Wyatt in his tracks. "I can't imagine you—"

"Only 'cause I don't look white enough. It was never an option, long-term. And I'm not saying Mr. Dodge hasn't done right by me all these years. But Costello set me back with his comment about us all being tradesmen and servants."

Wyatt smiled. "I'm in that category myself, where Dodge is concerned."

"But the acting—when was the last time you saw a Negro in a Shakespeare play?"

Wyatt shook his head. "Never. Not even *Othello*," he added ruefully. What would you have done, if you'd been able to—" He stopped. "Music. Composing. I've heard your violin, and they weren't just pieces I knew."

Germain shrugged. "I've got a little stack of pieces piling up. Maybe I can get one of Miss Louisa's friends to recommend me to the MuSoLit Club one of these days. I'm light enough to get in there, from what I hear. Maybe they'd even want to try my music." He picked up his derby and flicked a speck of dust from it. "But back to the topic. That lady's having a rough time right now."

Wyatt rocked back on his chair. "I should just let her go back to her husband and kids, uncomplicate both our lives—" He smiled at the challenge in Germain's face. "Of course I'll talk to her. I'm just not ready yet."

"Back to this old lady—"

"You didn't take Miss Stanstead, did you?"

"Course not. What kind of side-kick do you take me for?"

That got a smile out of Wyatt. "Macalester hasn't ruled her out. I can't believe she's capable of it, but—"

"No alibi, *hein*? If she did it, she'd have to be a better actor than you, *mon vieux*. And a brazen piece, too, making that fuss at the funeral."

Wyatt grinned. "That's one of the things I like about her. So, what did Mrs. Washington have to say after you charmed your way into her house?"

Germain told him about her sighting of Jekyll and Hyde. "Thing is, there's a Dunagin link, all right—but what she said she saw doesn't sound to me like guys on their way back from a murder."

"I'm betting Macalester will think otherwise. So do I. Dunagin had every reason—" Wyatt broke off. Germain was sitting back and giving him a long look.

"What?"

Germain tapped his glass on the table. "Next to Mr. Dodge, you've got less race-prejudice than any white man I ever met—"

"But…?"

Germain sighed. "What the hell. I'm just wondering whether that might be getting in the way, with this situation. Wait—don't get mad, hear me out."

The pounding in Wyatt's temples intensified.

"Just because this Nielsen fella was up there in Congress trying to do right by the race, doesn't mean everybody had to be grateful. Or that he didn't do some harm. We know it wasn't Costello, but that doesn't mean there couldn't have been others—"

"We've got some pretty damning evidence against Dunagin now," Wyatt persisted.

Germain shrugged. "Maybe that'll pan out. But in case it doesn't—think of all the ways one man can get in another man's way. Women, money, power, who knows. Colored people aren't plaster saints just 'cause they're colored, any more than they're low-lifes or imbeciles."

"You thinking of anyone in particular?"

Germain shook his head. "Just don't be walking around with blinders on, is all I'm saying."

Wyatt made his way back to the hotel. He didn't know what he wanted to say to Giovanna, or when. Even in the one night they'd spent apart, he missed her touch, her breath on his neck, the sleepy blink of her deep brown eyes in the morning light. Would he have been better off not knowing? It was a pointless question.

She was still the same woman she had been yesterday. All that had changed was what he knew of her, how he thought of her. Whatever she'd been once, she was someone else now, and had been for a long time. That's why people crossed the seas to America, why country boys like him came to New York City—for a chance to reinvent themselves.

In her situation, what would he have done?

CHAPTER 32

Washington Post, **Monday, April 30,**
1906, late morning edition

TOP DIPLOMAT'S WIFE KILLED
IN RIDING ACCIDENT

Senhora Pereira, Wife of Brazilian Ambassador,
Dies after Horse Bolts in Rock Creek Park

Washington society and the Capital's diplomatic corps lost a gracious and luminous ornament yesterday with the tragic death of Senhora Isabel Barros Alves Almeida e Pereira de Lima, wife of the Brazilian Ambassador. Senhora Pereira, according to shocked witnesses, died instantly upon being thrown from her horse which shied, reared and bolted on a bridle-path in Rock Creek Park on Monday at about four o'clock in the afternoon. She had been riding alone, as was her custom, according to Brazilian Embassy staff.

Ambassador Pereira, visiting his homeland in connection with arrangements for the forthcoming Third Conference of American States, received the heavy news by cable in Rio de Janeiro and is reported by Embassy aides to have made arrangements for his wife's body to be embalmed and conveyed to Recife, her birthplace, where a state funeral will be held. Alfonso Antonio da Silva, the Embassy's chargé d'affaires, informed the press in a statement that Ambassador Pereira would not return to the United States until after his wife's funeral and burial, but stated that the progress of the Pan-American Conference is "unlikely to be significantly delayed" by the tragedy.

The accident occurred along a narrow section of a Rock Creek bridle path, densely wooded in evergreens and other trees. An Embassy aide gave it as his opinion that Sra. Pereira's horse, a chestnut named Aurelius, was a spirited, intelligent animal of a steady temperament and unlikely to have reacted as it did without "serious provocation," such as a sudden attack from the rear or an unexpected danger in its path.

"Had there been any fears whatever as to the disposition of the creature, the ambassadress would never have been allowed to ride him," the aide stated, adding that the horse had been in the household for many years and had been brought to Washington when Sr. Pereira assumed the ambassadorship.

No evidence of what provoked the accident was reported by the witnesses, who included several others riding on the path and two gentlemen rambling in the nearby woods. One of the riders, who gave her name as Madame Antónia Kóhary, spoke tearfully to reporters of following, on her own mount, the same steep and rocky path to the creek bed as Sra. Pereira's horse, and watching in horror as the ambassadress began urging her mount over a waist-high rock wall at a dip in the narrow path. Suddenly the horse started violently to the right, and its front hooves left the ground. Sra. Pereira, riding with an old-fashioned side-saddle that did not incorporate a leaping-horn, lost her grip and was thrown, her head striking the stones of the wall as the horse bolted, with fatal results.

One of the hiking gentlemen recaptured the horse while his companion and a male rider went to the ambassadress' aid. She was taken to the George Washington University Hospital. Sadly, there was nothing to be done.

A Funeral Mass is to be held this coming Wednesday, April 25 at the Roman Catholic church of St. Matthew the Apostle, where the Ambassador and his wife were communicants...

Wyatt slumped onto a park bench in Lafayette Square, the newspaper sliding from his hands. Senhora Pereira dead. It couldn't be. The woman for whose sake, and against every inclination, he had taken on Latham's case. Who held—had held—the key to his acquittal, who'd been prepared to risk all to save her unworthy lover, if it had come to that.

He had spent half the night drinking away the aftertaste of a mediocre performance. Giovanna's had been fiery and flawless, as if something trapped inside her had been turned loose. They had avoided each other backstage for the whole evening.

When he'd arrived at the Embassy in hopes of a private audience with Senhora Pereira, the doorway was hung with crape and a black-bowed wreath. The embassy guard, red-eyed, told him in halting English that "we have lost our dear lady yesterday." The morning newspaper told him the rest.

An accident, the paper said, but it wouldn't have taken much to get her horse to bolt. Aim a good-sized pebble in a slingshot at the horse's rump, then disappear into the woods, leaving nothing for evidence but another rock in a rocky path. In Cuba, he'd seen the most steady-tempered horses, who'd face down anything they could see in front of them, shy and bolt at an attack from behind. Aurelius, a noble-looking beast whose good character was attested to by the Embassy witness, had looked anything but skittish on the Mall's bridle path.

From behind…he went back to the newspaper column. The tearful witness, Madame Kóhary—Dunagin's wife, the vampire-woman, the Hungarian "countess" who had oozed flattery over him after his performance. Dunagin enlisting his wife to silence Senhora Pereira—the brazenness of it was astounding. Dandy Pat O'Donoghue, clearing another minor obstacle out of his way. Germain's report on the Irishmen seen by Mrs. Washington supplied the last link: Dunagin's thugs had been on the scene of Nielsen's murder. Dunagin must have set up Latham so carefully that he was aware of Latham's potential alibi and had taken steps to eliminate it.

He thought he had saved her. Hot tears sprang to his eyes along with a rising anger—with Latham, for whose sake she had died, with the Dunagins, real-life Macbeths, the pair of them; most of all with himself, for failing to foresee and protect her from this. Some d'Artagnan. Some gallant knight rescuing the damsel in distress. He'd thought the danger was to her reputation, to her country's relations with the United States, not to her life.

It didn't help to recall her assurances that no one had observed her movements and Latham's on the night of the killing. The murderer *had* seen, and knew. Must have followed her, or had her followed, from the Embassy to the stage door on one of the nights she came to see him, realized she was prepared to go to the authorities to save Latham. And coldly taken steps to ensure that his scheme to pin the crime on Latham would remain undetected. Not knowing about the fingerprint evidence that would render Latham, at least for the moment, safe from prosecution.

The waste of it.

Wyatt folded the hateful headline away and stood up. Since he could not save her, the least he could do would be to avenge her death.

Commander Macalester looked up from the Washington *Post* and regarded Miss Blumenhofer, breathless and agog, bustling through his office doorway.

"It's the actor, sir—Macbeth! I mean—Mr. Wyatt come to see you." She clasped her hands together, eyes shining. "He knew me! He asked me how I did, and what I thought of the play, and when I'd like to come and see the rest of it—"

Macalester smiled. "Ssshhh! Don't let on he's here. He's on a secret mission for us."

"Oh, uh, of course, sir. I'll show him in."

Wyatt closed the door behind her and turned, a look of bleak sorrow on his face. "To what do I owe—" Macalester began.

Wyatt pointed to the headline. "You've seen the story."

"Ah, that photograph," Macalester said, "The Ambassador's wife—she passed us on the Mall the other day, didn't she? I'd no idea who she was. What a shame."

"Commander—I've something to tell you, and I need your assurance that it will go no farther."

"What are you, daft, laddie? If it's a criminal matter—"

"It is that. And it couldn't be more pertinent to this murder investigation. But it can't be in the record—please, it'll be clear to you in a minute. The Dodges know, and Germain, but that's all."

Macalester folded his arms and raised an eyebrow. "Let's have it, then. But I don't like you asking me to put my job on the line."

"Senhora Pereira was Latham's alibi."

"You what??" Macalester grabbed the paper.

Wyatt nodded. "When Dodge asked me to take this thing on, I agreed to meet Latham. It didn't go well and I told him to go hang. The next night she came to me at the theater. Told me everything. That's what got me into this—for her, not him."

"Dear God, the implications...the Pan-American Treaty—he meant that much to her?"

"After the raincoat business—" Wyatt saw Macalester's eyes drop, "she was going to come in—to talk with the U.S. Attorney. I begged her to let me work on things. She thought she'd not been observed, that last time she came to see me, but obviously she was wrong." The last words caught in his throat. "She's been in agony—"

"I can well imagine." Macalester looked stricken.

"She cared for him. The prospect of his being hanged for something he didn't do—she couldn't bear it. *He'd* begged her not to come forward, I'll credit him for that. I think she'd have waited, in hopes that I'd come up with something." Wyatt dropped into the visitor's chair. "I found out about this when I went to the Embassy. To tell her about the fingerprints you've found. Did you notice the name of the supposed witness?"

Macalester picked up the paper and scanned the story again. "Madame Kóhary...that rings a wee bell..." Macalester let the paper fall. "Mrs. Dunagin?"

"Germain visited your witness Mrs. Washington on Saturday and got some new information out of her. A pair of Dunagin's goons was on the scene that night."

"Now that's interestin.'" Macalester folded his arms and looked shrewdly at him. "That horse didn't look like a bolter to me. And the Embassy aide makes a point of saying he wouldn't have bolted without provocation."

"A small rock from behind will spook the best horse in the world."

"And this Kóhary woman was right behind her." Macalester stared out the window, then turned back. "She couldn't have counted on it killing the lassie."

"Wouldn't have had to, if she was laid up badly enough to keep her away from the police."

Macalester shook his head. "Seems like a chancy way to handle it. But it has the advantage of simplicity—as well as difficulty of proof, I'm sorry to say." He picked up the paper again. "None of the witnesses seems to have noticed anything hitting the beastie."

"Think they were asked?" Wyatt kneaded the space between his eyebrows.

"Maybe not till she was at the morgue and some of the witnesses had dispersed." Macalester frowned. "Isn't it a bit odd that this Kóhary would identify herself for the papers? If you'd done this, wouldn't you have made yourself scarce?"

"Not if she got hemmed in by riders behind her. Best to brazen it out, in that case. The lady struck me as having a flair for the dramatic."

Macalester dropped back into his chair. "If Dunagin put her up to this, it's clear he'll go to any length he has to, to protect himself."

"No surprise there, if we're dealing with Dandy Pat, is it? If I'd just been more careful—"

Macalester regarded him gravely and shook his head. "No use bashin' yourself in the head, laddie. Our villain must've had her in his sights for a long time before she came to you." He was silent for a long moment. "Here's a puzzle, though—if she *was* murdered, it can only have been because the murderer knows you're involved in the investigation—that she was coming to you to tell you something about the case. And how would Cornelius Dunagin have come by that knowledge?"

Wyatt straightened in his chair. "That's a damn good question. I warned Dodge about not telling Dunagin anything, but maybe—" He shook his head. "No. He'd have told me then if he'd already said anything to the man. And he'd never have done so after I warned him off—"

"You'd best have a chat with Mr. Dodge, just to be sure."

Wyatt shrugged. "All right, but—d'you suppose Dunagin has an informant at police headquarters? Don't take offense—"

"Oh, 'deed I'm not!" Macalester said, raising a hand. "I've never yet known an HQ that wasn't a leaky bucket. Nobody on my immediate staff, I don't think, but..."

They sat silent for a while. "It seems to add up to Dunagin," Wyatt said, "but it does involve a few complicated assumptions."

"So we'd best invoke good old Occam and his razor," Macalester said. "Who else knows you're helping Latham?"

Their eyes met. "Louisa Stanstead," Wyatt said as a cavern opened in his gut, "and anyone who's anybody in the Washington colored population." Germain's words came back to him. *Don't be walking around with blinders on.*

As if reading his thoughts, Macalester asked, "Exactly what did the good Mrs. Washington say about the fellas she saw?"

"She called them Jekyll and Hyde. Regular enforcers when the rent's overdue, apparently."

Macalester nodded. "That'll be Jeffords and Clyde—I've heard the nicknames. I don't wonder she was reluctant to finger them to us."

"Germain seems to think they may just have been on an eviction expedition. She thought she heard something about saving them the trouble, which could mean the renters had moved out—"

"—or that they stumbled on Nielsen's body," Macalester said, his face turning grim. "Which would take us back to the colored community, given what you've told me about Latham's alibi."

Wyatt hung his head. "You're thinking about the insurance policy."

"There's something not quite right about all that," Macalester said. "It's odd that we've found no trace of the original policy, and that Miss Stanstead claims to have known nothing of it."

"If she did kill him for that, wouldn't she have at least produced the paperwork when Templeton—the insurance fellow—went to see her about it?"

"You'd think so, right enough," Macalester said. "But if it wasn't her, who else had enough of a grudge against both Nielsen and

Latham to kill the one and frame the other?" He folded his arms and stared at Wyatt.

"Templeton got upset at even a hint from me that Louisa might've known about the policy, never mind been motivated to kill by it," Wyatt said. "Maybe he'd be a bit more forthcoming with Germain—" he sighed. Macalester wasn't going to let him off the hook. "I'll ask him to talk to him. And while he's at it, he can rule out—well, check out some of the people who were at the YMCA meeting just before Nielsen died."

Macalester nodded his satisfaction. "The pattern's highly suggestive that Dandy Pat's been up to his old tricks, but we've still nothing we can move forward from. And till we do, if Dunagin or whoever did for Nielsen has somehow learned what you're about, you'd best be very careful in dark alleys."

"I could say the same to you," Wyatt said. "He's got you in his sights for other reasons." He got up and headed for the door.

"I'll keep my own phizog out of it—for the moment, at any rate. I don't want to queer the pitch for the NYPD, once they get the real Cornelius Dunagin's elder brother over to this side of the Pond. He set sail a couple of days ago, they tell me. By the way, when you had your little champagne supper at the Raleigh, what did our man say about the family he'd left behind?"

CHAPTER 33

Dodge's study, papered in deep green and gold, still smelled of new paint and wallpaper paste. Wyatt buried his nose in a cup of Germain's ambrosial coffee and sniffed deeply. Dodge hurried in, tossing his hat on a side chair. "Why didn't you come down to the Hill?"

"You heard the news."

Dodge strode over to the window and yanked it open. Soft spring air poured in, dissipating the chemical vapors. "Latham's a wreck. Worst is he can't talk about it."

"I can imagine. Had any dealings with Cornelius Dunagin lately?"

"What's he—"

"You notice who was behind Senhora Pereira on the path?"

"His wife. The Countess." Dodge's brow furrowed. "Dun agin said she was in hysterics when she came home from Rock Creek."

"Wasn't muttering 'Out, damn'd spot,' by any chance?"

Dodge stared. "My God, you don't think—" He deflated into a swivel chair.

Germain came in with two more cups of coffee, placing one on a coaster on Dodge's desk. "First thing I thought too. You talked to Macalester?"

"Somebody knew she was Latham's alibi," Wyatt said.

Germain moved Dodge's hat and perched on the side chair. "The killer, you mean."

"And must've followed her that last night she came to see me at the theater, figured she was getting ready to go to the police."

Dodge leaned forward, elbows on the desk. "Which means the killer knows you're involved in investigating this."

"That's why I asked about Dunagin. Any chance you'd let anything slip?"

"What do you take me for? As it happens, he came by yesterday to push me to commit myself on Columbia Heights. The Pereira thing came up, naturally. They'd got invited to a soirée at the Embassy last year. Quite a social coup for them."

"What'd you decide about the investment?"

Dodge walked to the window and took in a deep breath. "Told him one of our Fourdriniers up in Rumford had thrown a cylinder. Very expensive proposition, our replacement reserve not being what it should be. So I was going to have to see how the repair estimates came in, before I made any more capital commitments."

"What the hell is a Fourdrinier?" Germain asked.

"Big paper-making machine," Dodge grinned. "Truth is, I had a clerk go down to the District Building and check on the ownership of Snow's Court. Not the sort of property management I want my name associated with."

Wyatt suppressed a smile. "So Dunagin's shy a hundred thousand dollars."

"Thing is, Wyatt, he was sidling round to a lot of questions about you. He and the wife were quite taken with you, he said, wondered how you were spending your daylight hours, whether you were sight-seeing on off days, did you have a lady-friend. And something about getting in touch to invite you to some tea party or other."

"What else?"

"Said you seemed to have some odd ideas about businessmen, no surprise in an artistic type, people like him and me didn't pay such things any mind, did we?"

"He mention Macalester?" Germain asked sharply.

"Said he was afraid the Nielsen investigation would come to nothing with Macalester running it. He'd heard some stories from New York that Macalester was known for being a bit on the paranoid side. Seeing anarchists behind every bush, wasting investigators' time, so forth. He heard the NYPD commissioner called in a favor with Roosevelt to get him transferred down here."

Wyatt glowered. "With a promotion to Commander. That sound likely to you?"

"Why's he interested in discrediting Macalester?"

"I would be, too," Wyatt said, "if I were in the man's sights."

Red-eyed and haggard, Richard Latham seemed to have aged another twenty years since Wyatt had last seen him. "You think she was murdered, then?" he whispered. "Dear God." He put his head in his hands and leaned his elbows on his massive desk. The greening, woody paths of the Mall were framed in the window behind him.

Wyatt finished the soda water Latham's secretary had offered him while the Congressman was getting rid of a lobbyist. "The police hadn't even told *you* yet that the arraignment was being called off. Someone out there knows you were with her the night Nielsen died. Someone who followed her to the theater when she came to talk to me Thursday night—and who knows I'm helping you. Whoever it is must have concluded—correctly—that she'd go to the U.S. Attorney to save you from being arraigned."

Latham's head came up and he stared at Wyatt in horror. "You'd have talked her out of that, surely."

Wyatt shrugged. "Told her I was working on something, and begged her not to do anything till she heard from me. By the time I got her back to Lafayette Square, I think I'd talked sense into her. But the killer wouldn't have known that."

"And you saw nobody following *you* that night?" Latham's tone had taken on some of its old belligerence. "Isn't it likely this killer followed the two of you back to the Embassy?"

"Absolutely not." Wyatt's nostrils flared, but it was a fair question. "Before we went half a block I'd reconnoitered the area, and I kept checking as we went. But he might have followed her to the theater, saw her head for the stage door after the performance, and figured out what she was up to."

"Why did they cancel the arraignment? The police wouldn't tell me anything."

"That's what I came to talk with you about. And—" Wyatt cleared his throat, " to offer you my sympathy, for what it's worth."

Latham looked sharply at him, gave a small, affirmative jerk of the head. "Thank you." He turned away, picking up the cane with the gold lion's head she'd given him, leaning on it as he stared out the window towards the half-built House office building taking shape to the east.

"Will you attend the funeral?"

"Mrs. Latham knows nothing." The words came out in a rush. "As far as she's concerned, I was at home in bed, which is what I told the police. We have, ah, separate rooms," he added unnecessarily, giving Wyatt a defiant look. "As for the funeral—I'll have to go. The entire House and Senate leadership—she's lying in state, in the Embassy foyer. Open casket, not a mark on her, they said. Dear God, I don't know how I'm going to stand it. If it hadn't been for me—"

Remorse. Regret. Wyatt hadn't thought Richard Latham capable of those feelings. He turned awkwardly away, his own eyes prickling, feeling a kindly instinct to comfort a man he'd hated for decades. And instantly suppressing it.

"Why would Cornelius Dunagin be trying to frame you for this murder?"

Latham swung round. "What did you say?"

"He's been sending nasty notes to some of your more charitably inclined colleagues. Nielsen included. About what dirt would surface on them, or their families, if they pushed for Nielsen's amendment to the condemnation bill."

"That nonsense about not giving development permits if someone's got violations? Who doesn't, with the kind of trash that lives in those places? You can't keep up with it."

"You knew about these notes?"

"I did not." Latham stalked over to a side table and poured himself water from a carafe. "How could you know Dunagin had anything to do with them?"

"The wonders of science. He left his finger-prints all over them."

Latham snorted. "People write threatening letters to their Congressman all the time. We're talking about some monster here. Dunagin might be rough around the edges, but he's a businessman, not a killer."

"So you think that Dunagin's wife's being right behind Senhora Pereira on that bridle-path was mere coincidence?"

"She's an avid horsewoman, Dunagin's told me. A social climber who likes to be seen with the gentry. She's called on my wife a few times—"

"And the witness who's placed two goons of his at the scene of the murder, that's coincidence too?"

"What are you talking about?" Latham's hand trembled around the water glass.

"He employs a pair of enforcers, we're told. The locals call them Jekyll and Hyde. They collect late rents, throw out deadbeat tenants, who knows what other nuisances they get rid of for him."

"And you infer from this that Dunagin had Nielsen—and Isabel—" Latham turned his head away and shut his eyes tight, then glared at Wyatt. "For God's sake, if you think it's murder, go and find the fiend who did this to her. And to me."

"That's just what I mean to do. But it would help if you faced reality and told me why Dunagin would want to set you up for this."

"Cornelius Dunagin has done nothing but good to me," Latham said. "I won't listen to you slander a man who's treated me with honesty and respect."

Wyatt shrugged. "We'll see what the police come up with when they question his associates. In the meantime, if you don't think Dunagin's involved, who else is out to get you?"

Latham dropped back into his chair and his head slumped on his desk. "Leave me alone, please." His voice was muffled. "I can't think right now. I haven't any idea who could have done this. I don't know what else to tell you."

Wyatt turned and left, closing the door quietly behind him. "The Congressman asked not to be disturbed for an hour," he told the secretary.

CHAPTER 34

From the sidewalk Wyatt spotted the jovial, star-struck desk clerk on duty and slipped into the hotel through the saloon bar's entrance to avoid him. He wasn't in a mood for superficial exchanges. He climbed to the acting troupe's floor by the back stairs. His knock on Giovanna's door was hesitant, but he used their old signal. No response for a long moment, then the door opened a crack and her face, carefully expressionless, peered out at him and into the gloom of the hallway.

"May I come in?"

She opened the door wider and closed it behind him. A pen lay across a half-written letter on the room's spindly desk.

"I saw the newspaper yesterday." She was wearing a light afternoon dress, soft peach with a low bodice framed in muslin and lace. Her hair rippled loose down to a bow at its back. "I'm so sorry."

"I'd gone to see her at the Embassy that morning." He swallowed. "I should've thought of—I could have protected her."

She stood near the door, arms awkward at her sides. He turned and took her hands, searching her face as she did his. He drew her hands together and lifted them to his lips. She closed her eyes and shivered as the soft mustache brushed them.

"I sat on a park bench and thought, what if it had been you?"

A little sob broke from her. He folded her in his arms. "You've had a lot of shocks this week," she finally managed.

He led her to the embroidered loveseat under the window, his gaze fixed on her face, his fingers caressing her cheek, pushing the great tumble of hair back from her brow.

"When I was in the third grade, there was a girl in my class named Christine—Christine Brooks. She had brown skin and crinkly hair, mostly brown but in the summer it looked gold sometimes. She broke my heart."

"She was colored?"

Wyatt gave her a crooked smile. "Nobody around Oberlin took any account of such things. I picked daffodils from my mother's garden and took them to school one day. I hid them in the schoolyard until recess and I gave them to her."

"She wasn't charmed?"

"She wrinkled up her nose and said, 'They smell funny.' Then she dropped them on the ground and let Bobby Schmidt help her onto the tree-swing. He was in *fifth* grade. And I got a paddling for picking Ma's flowers."

Giovanna squeezed his hands and made a sad face. "And you were scarred for life."

"When I grew up," he said, "I left for the city as soon as I could. If I'd stayed, I'd have been stuck being a farmhand my whole life. But there were some things about that place, some good things I'd forgotten."

Her hand traced his cheek and rested under his chin.

"I've missed you," he said. "I wanted to tell you I'm—"

She held up her hand. "No—give me a chance. Let me explain—"

"You've got nothing to explain." He pinned her in his arms and rained kisses on her mouth, her cheeks, her throat. His face grew wet with her tears, and he felt a strangled sob rise in his own throat. "I'm sorry."

"Me too." Her voice was rough, half-choked. He shook his head. She pushed his arms away but held him by the forearms, her gaze on him unguarded now, he realized with a pang, as it had never been. All the fear and anxiety of the last few weeks gone. God, she was beautiful.

"Who else here knows," he said, "besides your brother."

"He told Nettie. And I'm going to see my mother."

"I'm glad for that. But—"

"They wouldn't give me away. I'll become a new family secret," she laughed ruefully. "I promised to stay in touch, and I will, somehow. She'll want to see her grandchildren." Her face fell. "I'm not sure how I'll manage that part."

He kissed her neck, just below and behind the ear, where she loved it so. His lips moved to the nape and he felt her shiver as they brushed the line of her backbone. He took her nipples under their thin muslin and squeezed them gently. She moaned and turned to him, her own lips moving up his neck, her small teeth fastening on the lobe of his ear, her tongue flicking in and out of the opening. He pressed against her.

"Not much time before call." Her voice was husky.

He rose and turned the lock on her door. "Just enough." He carried her from the settee to the bed, pushed up the thin folds of the tea-gown and rolled her over on top of him. "We'll talk more later." He bathed his face in her hair, buried his nose in the silky cleft between her breasts. "God, I missed you so much."

"Your own damn fault," she gasped, while she still had the breath for it.

CHAPTER 35

Messrs. Jeffords and Clyde were not cooperating. Macalester, watching them through one-way mirrors in the darkened space between two interrogation rooms, marveled at the pair's resistance even to the most basic questions. They didn't know about any damn dead Congressman, they said in almost identical phrasing. They'd been home in their beds that night.

The interrogating officers didn't bring up the due-to-be-evicted Demars family, not wanting to give the men an easy out. As far as Macalester knew, they'd had no warning of being brought in for questioning. It was unlikely that Mrs. Washington had either imagined or misidentified the pair; clamming up must be their standard response to police inquiries.

So, after several fruitless hours during which the two Irishmen were denied access to food, drink, smokes, and toilet facilities, Macalester instructed each pair of interrogators to tell their quarry that the other had admitted to being in the area that night and seeing Nielsen on 24th Street Northwest.

The porcine, muscle-bound Jeffords gave a good imitation of a grudging admission that they'd gone to Snow's Court to evict a deadbeat tenant. Snake-thin Clyde said they'd been coming back from a Foggy Bottom saloon, adding that they'd seen a man fitting Nielsen's description going up the walkway of a townhouse—it might have been on 25th Street. Jeffords said he saw a prone body on the street, figured it was a drunk. Neither remembered anything about a fight, or anybody else skulking around "other than them nigger lowlifes from the alley," Clyde said, "that would knock you on the head for a dime soon as look at you. Musta got to him before he made it into the house."

It occurred to Macalester that if Jekyll and Hyde had attacked Nielsen, they should have robbed him as well so as to throw the blame on the alley lowlifes. Nevertheless, they'd been caught in a lie.

"You lyin' bag a shit," Officer Durkee laid about Clyde's head and shoulders with a rubber hose. "You bastids beat that poor guy to death an' left him lyin' in the street like a heap a garbage. Why'd your boss want him dead?"

"I never touched the fella, I swear ta God," Clyde whined through bruised lips. "He was dead when we got there—I mean, when we went by on our way home from the bar."

In the opposite room, Officer Cuddy was having similar results. "I tell ya the fella was dead already, just like I said," Jeffords moaned.

"Don't lie to me, creep!" Cuddy whacked him in the solar plexus and knocked him over gasping. "You said you saw a passed-out drunk. Drunks ain't usually lyin' in a pool o' blood."

"I thought it was puke, honest ta God," wheezed Jeffords. "Ask me mate. He'll tell ya."

Macalester stepped into the room and waved Cuddy aside. "Have a seat, Mr. Jeffords," he said kindly. He nodded towards the hose in Cuddy's hand. "No need for that. We just need an answer or two and we can let this poor fella go. Now, tell me—anyone would know why your boss wanted Mr. Nielsen out of the way, but we're havin' a hard time understanding why he'd pin it on his business partner. What had he and Mr. Latham disagreed about? A trusted fella like you would be in his confidence on such a matter."

Jeffords spat on the floor. "I don't know what yez are talkin' about. We didn't do nothin' to that Nielsen. Mr. Dunagin's got nothin' to do with this."

Macalester shook his head sorrowfully. "What a shame. I thought you were going to tell us the truth—that your partner got carried away."

"You're fulla shite."

Cuddy stepped forward but Macalester held up a hand.

"You were supposed to rough him up a bit, give him a good fright. Show him the letters your boss had sent weren't just an empty threat. But Clyde there's got a temper and he went too far. That's what happened, isn't it? He says it was you, but that doesn't make sense to me."

Jeffords squinted up at Macalester through a half-closed eye. "Balls! He didn't say nothin' like that because it didn't happen, I'm tellin' ya…" But there was a slight quaver in his voice. "He said anythin' like that, it's only 'cause your bulls beat it into him."

"Well, now," Macalester said placidly, "we have an interestin' situation here. There's an eminent Member of Congress, a valued acquaintance of your employer, brought up on charges of murder. But except for his cane near the scene, no evidence to tie him to the crime. Meanwhile, you two are seen leaving the street where by your own admission you saw Mr. Nielsen's dead body. And a boss whose antipathy—pardon me, dislike, for the victim was well known—a man who'd sent him threatening notes. *That* we know for a fact. Now, what would you think, in my position?"

Jeffords glared at him, sullen and silent.

"Well, I'll tell you what I think: he's had a falling-out with Mr. Latham and saw the chance to kill two birds with one stone. So he calls on his faithful retainers—that'd be you and Clyde—for a wee spot of work. It'll go a lot easier with you, Mr. Jeffords, if you'd let me know why Mr. Dunagin was trying to get Mr. Latham blamed for this."

"Maybe Latham did it," Jeffords growled. "Aye, that's what musta happened. 'Cause it wasn't us. Why'n't you ask *him*?"

Macalester sighed. "They've had their chance," he told Cuddy. "We'll have to put them downstairs for a while."

"The cooler?" Cuddy asked with a piggy-eyed smile.

Macalester shrugged and left the room. Wyatt would have to find out from Latham why Dunagin would want him out of the way. Meanwhile, he wondered how Dandy Pat had reacted to the news that his henchmen were in custody. Just as well he'd phoned to warn Wyatt…

"She's back to her old form," Mrs. Marlowe whispered with a sideways smile. "You've settled things between you?" In the dark

231

wings she and Wyatt were watching Giovanna as Lady Macduff, railing against her absent husband while Fred Lewis as the Earl of Ross tried to justify him. It was one of the things Wyatt missed about leaving the Ross role for the lead: their emotional connection in the scene, absent in the few they now shared as Macbeth and the First Witch. She was giving it her all tonight, the fiery contempt for Ross's excuses on her husband's behalf, the fearful tenderness lying beneath the whip-cracks of wit in her dialogue with Billy Harris, playing her little son. She was living the part again, and he registered the audience's gasps of horror as the murderers came for her and her children.

Wyatt didn't confirm Mrs. Marlowe's suppositions. There hadn't been time to raise the question of marriage, but there was the walk back to the hotel to come…he smiled inwardly. There'd be no need for Giovanna to introduce him to her family; they'd already met. Jamie and Grace's future cousin would soon have a Teddy bear like theirs. Once he and Giovanna were married, maybe she'd feel safe enough to resume the connection, even introduce the children to one another.

Sill flushed with excitement over their riotous curtain call, she took Wyatt's arm and they stepped out from the circle of light around the stage door into a dense spring fog.

"What do you say to a stroll around the White House?" he asked. "Though I doubt Mr. Roosevelt will ask us in for a nightcap."

"Poor man! I dare say he's a bit preoccupied, between the earthquakes and riots." The cataclysmic quake in San Francisco had been the talk of the green room. Giovanna squeezed Wyatt's arm. "Was he very dashing as a commander?" Wyatt hadn't told her much about his time as a Rough Rider, insisting there wasn't much to tell, but in their new spirit of openness she wanted to know everything about him.

"I wonder," she said, "whether having been a soldier helps you imagine your way into the heart of Macbeth. I think you play him with more—this will sound odd—understanding than Mr. Sothern did."

Wyatt had worried about being less flamboyant in the role than the famous leading man. Grandiloquence like Sothern's wasn't his strength; he liked to find his way into a character's heart, figure out why he did what he did. But audiences often came for the spectacle, not the subtleties.

"Somebody once asked me what it was like. That charge up Kettle Hill. I said it was fun." He took Giovanna's elbow and steered her across the street. "Battle's like that, until people start getting hurt. A man never feels more alive than when he's in danger of dying in an instant." Wyatt was almost talking to himself, remembering. Giovanna squeezed his arm.

"I think Macbeth misses that," he went on. "He's grown used to killing; that's how you got to be a king, in his world. But it's like what happens to drug-fiends. You can't stop so easily."

"But that kind of killing—his king, his friends—that wouldn't feel like fun, would it?" Giovanna pulled her faille cape closer with a little shiver. Wyatt wrapped an arm around her shoulder and pulled her close.

"It's as if he's forgotten other ways of handling difficulties," he said. "He brings that murderous spirit, that blood-lust, home with him from the battlefield."

"And she eggs him on," Giovanna said, "without any idea of what she's unleashing. That's why she goes crazy, isn't it?"

Wyatt stopped, impressed by the insight. "Perhaps we can play them, some day, in a run of our own—you and me."

"I'd be afraid to," she whispered, holding a finger over his lips. "When he decides to kill Banquo and Fleance, he stops confiding in her. She's completely alone, she can't reach him any more."

Mrs. Marlowe had never played her that way, Wyatt realized.

"Julia's way is good too," Giovanna said, as if reading his thoughts. "It's as if she takes our friendship onto the stage in the sleepwalking scene—thinking it's Mrs. Treadwell her husband has murdered, not Lady Macduff. Someone she can't help but have sympathy for."

The fog made gold haloes around the street lamps, the moist air holding the scent of hyacinth from the edges of the White House lawn. Cool vapors caressed their faces. A few hansom cabs, the horses' hooves mist-muffled, clip-clopped their way softly up and down the streets and avenues in search of customers. Wyatt waved them off when they slowed down near them.

They promenaded along Pennsylvania Avenue, where the darkened windows of the Executive Mansion attested that its occupants had retired for the evening, and had walked down 17th Street past the Corcoran Gallery before Wyatt finished his account of his more recent encounter with Theodore Roosevelt, on Heron Island in Vermont.

"You could've been killed!" Giovanna pulled his arm tighter.

Wyatt smiled. "She loves me for the dangers I have pass'd, and I love her that she does pity them." They were on E Street, walking by a great equestrian statue of General Sherman. He drew her into the shadows behind a statue of an artilleryman at its base and took her in his arms.

Giovanna giggled. "He'll see us!"

"Not to worry. He's looking the other way."

"Some sentinel."

"War's over," Wyatt said, cupping her chin in his hands and bending to her. "God, you make me so happy," he said when they broke the kiss. "I want us to go on forever."

In the misty light from a streetlamp, her eyes searched his and she nodded. "So do I."

There was no hesitation after, no "but." *Now might I do it...* The night breeze had freshened and she shivered again. "We should head back," he said, taking her hand up and kissing it. "But I want to ask you something first, if you're willing to hear it." He took her hands in his and turned to face her.

She drew a deep breath. "Are you sure? Knowing what you know?"

He nodded, unsmiling, squeezed her fingers. "Giovanna, I want to marry you."

She swallowed and returned the pressure of his fingers. "All right." Her face was grave, but the light in her eyes reassured him.

Hand in hand, they made their way along E Street towards 13th, which ran between the theater and their hotel. As they passed 15th Street he was saying, "I know it may take time to sort things out—"

There was a clatter of hoofbeats from behind them, advancing rapidly, and they turned to see what had put a coachman in such a hurry with the visibility so poor. From a block away a two-horse hansom was looming up on them through the mist, the driver a dark figure whipping the horses frantically along the wrong side of the street, the side they were walking on.

"He's going too fast," Wyatt shouted, getting between Giovanna and the coach and seizing her around the waist. "Coming too close. Run!"

He began pulling her across the street. To his horror the coach veered to the right, picking up even more speed and heading right at them. This wasn't a runaway. His brain registered the fact that the coach had no lights. He heard Giovanna's terrified gasp, the clatter of the wheels, the crack of the whip, the horses' frantic breath. They gained the other sidewalk just as the horses' hooves hit it and the wheels skittered on and off its edge. Beyond, deep in the fog, was a brush-strewn vacant lot. He tripped on a sidewalk crack and went flying, but managed to keep his grip on Giovanna. They fell into the weeds and rolled, barely out of the path of the coach, which passed in a great rush of air and noise.

Wyatt sat up, panting and staring after it. It raced on up 15th Street and disappeared in a black blur. Giovanna had curled herself into a ball, gasping and sobbing. Her hat was halfway over her eye, its feathered cockade askew.

"Giovanna!"

She propped herself up on one arm. "I'm all right. I think." Her voice was wobbly. Something was wrong with his foot and the side he'd fallen on was a battered mass of pain. He crawled to his knees and bent over her.

"Don't move," he said. "Let me look at you."

There was a dark spot on her forehead but there wasn't enough light to tell whether it was an abrasion or an opened cut. His hands ran over her neck and shoulders, eliciting a wince or two, and down her back.

"Can you stand up?" He went to rise himself, and a searing pain shot up his leg. The ankle was wrenched, and badly. "Sweet Jesus!" He doubled over and sat down again.

"Wyatt!" She scrambled to her feet and swayed.

"Twisted ankle," he said through gritted teeth. "You all right?"

She took a few tentative steps. "Really, I'm fine. Just shaky." Her breath was coming ragged and fast, but her voice was strengthening. "Can you stand? I'll help."

She put her arm under his and with difficulty they got him on his feet. Wyatt put the injured foot down again. It throbbed like the devil, but he could walk if he leaned on her shoulder.

They brushed leaves and twigs off each other and straightened their ripped and rumpled clothes. Thankfully, the hotel was only a block away, but at the pace he could go it felt like a mile. Arm in arm they crossed the fog-dimmed, uneven lot on the diagonal, Giovanna testing the terrain underfoot before letting him step. Back among the lights and traffic of Pennsylvania Avenue, they felt safe at last.

"Can you walk in by yourself?" she asked as they approached the hotel entrance. He nodded. In the lobby, she marched up ahead of him to the desk clerk, the same friendly plump fellow who'd been trying to engage her in chat since their arrival.

"Mr. Wyatt has had a slight accident," she said. "Can you have some ice sent up to his room?"

"Oh, dear," the clerk's welcoming smile dimmed as he bustled out from behind the desk. "Shall I send for a doctor?"

"Not necessary, thanks," Wyatt said, forcing a smile that came out as a wince. "Just a sprain. Some ice—and a bandage, if you can find one. Good night, Mrs. Treadwell. Thank you for your help." He nodded her towards the elevator. The attendant clanged the cage shut and she disappeared behind it.

"Let me get that ice sent up," the clerk said, ringing a bell on the desk. "Oh, Mr. Wyatt, I nearly forgot—a telephone message came for you earlier this evening."

Wyatt started limping towards the elevator. "I'll get it in the morning."

"Do let me get it for you—the gentleman said it was important, but I couldn't find you before the show."

Wyatt opened the note while he leaned against the elevator wall. "Took the boyos in today. D. will know soon, so be careful."

The caller had been a Mr. Macalester.

CHAPTER 36

"It's all highly suggestive," Commander Macalester sighed, "but that's all it is, including your rogue hansom, in the absence of identifyin' information." Germain took a sip of police-issue coffee, grimaced and set it aside.

"We could have been killed—" Wyatt protested, but Macalester held up a hand.

"We've got nothing useful so far out of Jekyll and Hyde. And nobody from Rock Creek Park saw this Countess make so much as an untoward movement. The Ambassador's lady could have met with a genuine accident. Or someone else entirely could have spooked the horse."

"And the blackmail notes?" Wyatt said.

"—while also highly suggestive, can't convict Dunagin of Nielsen's murder. I'm not prepared to haul him in at this stage, given what's due to happen in New York."

"But you know Latham's innocent now!" Wyatt's vehemence drew a surprised look from Germain.

"I'll see about postponing the arraignment further, keeping in mind what I'm not supposed to know."

"That'll help. I appreciate it."

"You've still not given me any motive for Dunagin, even if he is our murderous Dandy Pat, to want to ruin a powerful and well-connected business partner." Macalester tapped his pen on the desk-blotter. "I could buy him as the murderer—directly or otherwise—but why pin it on Latham?"

Wyatt shrugged, conceding the point. "There may be someone we haven't put at the scene yet."

"Commander, you've got his operatives on the scene, presumably around the right time," Germain added. "Why not go on the assumption you have a new set of prime suspects?"

Macalester gave him a thoughtful frown. "Just so, just so. But I think you'd best be looking for the other party you mentioned. Someone working very hard to see that Latham swings for this. I can't think why Dunagin would want that."

"Neither can I at the moment," Wyatt rose awkwardly and retrieved his new cane, removing his hat from a peg behind the door, "but you know who we're dealing with, and I'd bet any amount he's responsible for this." He nodded towards his ankle.

Germain fetched his own hat from the other peg. "I 'spect we'd all like for it to be him. Gotta get back to my day job."

"I'm much obliged to you, Germain," Macalester said, opening the door. "We'll let you know if we get any more from our discussions with the gents."

On the steps of the District Building, Germain paused. "I don't know that I should keep putting ideas in your head, but I got a feeling this is more about personal than business interests."

Wyatt leaned on the walking-stick and turned back to stare up at him. "You're not back to Louisa, are you?"

Germain held up his hand. "Not necessarily. But there was something I forgot to mention in there."

"Forgot, or decided not to?"

"I'm not sure," Germain smiled, then turned serious. "Miz Washington saw Nielsen from her window on his way to the Hill, the morning he went off half-cocked on the House floor. Said he was always pretty brisk going by in the mornings but this day he was in a real hurry. George Templeton came up and tried talking to him, but he more or less shoved him aside. Wouldn't even slow down, Miz Washington said."

Wyatt shifted on the walking-stick, wondering how he was going to get through the duel with Macduff on his throbbing ankle. "That fits with what Louisa said about the quarrel. He stormed out and that was the last time she saw him."

"Point being, Templeton might be able to shed some more light on that, depending on what Nielsen said when he was brushin' him off. "

"Let me talk to Louisa first." Wyatt winced as he descended the last step.

"First we're gonna limp you over to the People's Drug Store and get some of those Bayer Aspirin pills. Supposed to help with this sorta thing."

Wyatt shrugged. "Worth a try."

"I should've thought of it when you had that crapulous attack. Anyway, like I was saying, folks might get upset about a fella like Nielsen puttin' a crimp in their profits," Germain gestured to Wyatt to set the pace. "But I can't see them killing over it."

"But look who we're dealing with—"

"He's been trying to go straight for twenty years, far as we know. Straight for him, anyways. He'd have beat out Nielsen in the end over the alley business. Money talks in this town, just like any place else. Maybe more so."

"I'd been wondering about that," Wyatt confessed. "The blackmail threats are one thing. But you'd think there'd be some roughing up or property damage first. That's often enough to scare people off."

"I bet that's what happened with that cab last night. Dunagin got on to you somehow, and you messed with him just enough to get him mad and wantin' to show you what he can do to you. But if he'd wanted you dead he'd've found a better way. Giovanna all right?"

"A few bruises and a good-sized scrape on her forehead. She can hide it with greasepaint. Scared the dickens out of her, though."

"You can be a dangerous man to associate with, my friend."

"Seems stupid to incriminate himself further," Wyatt said, "but he also struck me as a fellow who couldn't let an insult pass." He shivered. If Dunagin was Dandy Pat O'Donoghue, he and Giovanna were lucky to be alive. He walked with Germain along Pennsylvania Avenue, his glance straying north to the crape-hung door on Lafayette Square. "Nielsen wasn't the type to scare off easily, though," he added.

"I was those fellas, I'd have gone after the lady-friend. Miss Louisa," Germain said. "I suspect that would have got him to back off better than a threat to himself. But there was nothing like that, was there?"

"Not directly." Wyatt told him about the ugly note the police had found in the box Louisa gave them. "So who are you thinking of, if it wasn't a business interest, or Louisa herself?"

Germain frowned. "I wondered if there might've been somebody he knew locally. Say somebody like *your* lady-friend—" Wyatt reddened and Germain held up a placatory hand, "with a big secret they couldn't afford to be public. Something that could ruin them, you know?"

"Something Nielsen found out, you're saying."

"What else was he into? In the community, I mean. The neighborhood. He go to church?"

"I doubt it—he was a Goldmanite, they say. But he was involved with a lot of charities. The construction committee for the YMCA, and some Board Committee at the Strivers'." Clarence Wilbur had told him that, but there was something odd, something he'd meant to follow up on…for the moment, he couldn't recall. The pain in his ankle was distracting. "He may not have been religious but he was certainly capable of self-righteousness. I wouldn't have wanted to be on the south side of that man's moral compass."

Germain stepped ahead of him and pulled open the drugstore's heavy wood and glass door, standing aside to let Wyatt through. "Maybe Miss Louisa will have some ideas for you."

Wyatt gave him a rueful smile. "I'll talk to her. Last time I got fixed on somebody as the murderer because he seemed so perfect for it, I got in trouble."

"That singer from New York," Germain smiled back. "Well, he did have something to hide."

"Nothing like murder, though," Wyatt said. "In any event, I'd best not make that mistake again."

241

CHAPTER 37

In the offices of the *Washington Bee*, Wyatt found Louisa Stanstead engaged in a lively speculation with Calvin Chase, dapper in his signature white cravat and an amethyst tie-pin, over who might have sent the attempted blackmail note to Robert Nielsen.

Louisa's eyes widened at the sight of Wyatt's walking stick. "What happened to you?"

"Twisted my ankle. Nothing some aspirin pills and a little Sloan's liniment won't cure."

"Thought that was for horses," Chase said.

"'Good for man or beast,' they say," Wyatt smiled. "Smells something wicked, though. Like that note in Mr. Nielsen's box."

"A number of his allies in Congress received such letters, I hear." The publisher led Wyatt and Louisa to chairs in his inner office. "Naturally, no one will confirm it."

"Have you an idea of who might be behind them?" Wyatt was wondering how far Chase's intelligence network extended.

Chase's brow wrinkled. "The sad part, Mr. Wyatt—Miss Stanstead and I were just discussing it—is that the author of these threats may not be Bob's killer. The note Bob got didn't hint at outright violence, after all."

"That's true enough." Wyatt thought again of Germain's comment about blinders and wondered what he was failing to see.

"Calvin—Mr. Chase—and I were wondering about Latham's cane being found nearby," Louisa said, "if he had no involvement in the crime. We're racking our brains to think of someone who wished both of them ill."

"Let's try one at a time," Wyatt said. "Can you think of anyone in your circle who was at odds with Mr. Nielsen?"

Louisa looked bewildered. "The prevailing view of him was admiration and—shall I say gratitude?"

Chase nodded. "It's hard to conceive of anyone in our community with a reason to hurt him."

Wyatt sat forward and steepled his hands under his chin. "Tell me, please—everything you can think of about the man outside of his Congressional service. His charitable and, ah, social involvements—"

Chase smiled wryly, but Louisa responded first. "His views on the rights of the Negro made him unwelcome in the white men's social clubs—but, then, Robert was never a 'joiner.'"

"He had such associations in the colored community," Chase put in. "He was an honorary member of the MuSoLit Club, and he was on the governing board of the Strivers' Mutual—"

"The insurance company," Wyatt recalled. "Where Clarence Wilbur works, and Mr. Templeton."

"'By the Negro, for the Negro,'" Chase said with pride. "That Board's comprised of the most eminent colored men of the City—renowned for the probity of its dealings and its benefits to the race. Which is more than could be said of the Freedmen's Bank that was set up after the war." He shook his head sadly. "My father lost his life savings in that one."

Louisa's face brightened. "I'd quite forgotten that—it was hard to keep track of all of Robert's doings. He *was* on the Strivers' board—their one white man. He considered it a distinct honor. Why, that would explain the insurance policy." Chase looked politely puzzled. "I learned a few days after his death that I was the beneficiary of a life insurance annuity which he had taken out recently," Louisa explained.

"Then perhaps he had received more direct threats, and took them to heart," Chase said. "I'm glad of that policy for your sake, 'Ouisa."

Louisa turned away and went to the window. It had begun to rain lightly, and she watched the drops falling on the new young leaves of the sidewalk locust tree.

Something surfaced in Wyatt's memory. "What was the nature of the board?"

"Well," Chase said, "nominally fiduciary—overseeing the organization's finances and such. But the managing directors are all well-qualified men, Howard graduates, mostly—the best that our race or any race can supply. There's little need for looking over *their* shoulders."

A touching testimonial coming from a journalist as skeptical as Chase. "From what I've heard of Mr. Nielsen, though," Wyatt said, "that wouldn't have stopped him from doing so, would it?"

Louisa turned from the window, giving her steel-rimmed glasses a surreptitious wipe on her skirts. "He was the chairman of their Finances Committee," she smiled. "I'm sure he concerned himself with every aspect of the operation."

Wyatt had heard about Nielsen's role on the Committee from Clarence Wilbur, but Giovanna's subsequent revelation had driven the detail out of his head. It was surprising in retrospect that no one had mentioned it as a reason for Nielsen to buy his life insurance policy from the Strivers'. That was the missing detail that had been puzzling him.

"Miss Stanstead, did Mr. Nielsen share with you any details of that Board work? Had he any concerns about the company's finances, for instance?" He saw Chase bristle at the question. "I don't mean to suggest there was anything irregular. But from what I've heard of Mr. Nielsen, it sounds as if he was—ah, extremely conscientious in such matters."

Louisa's brows knit in recollection. "Something he said a while ago—a month or two, maybe—about paying more attention on the disbursement end of things. He thought their expenses were on the high side, something like that."

"Could that mean that claimants were defrauding the company, or receiving more than they were due?"

"I can't remember, other than—something about needing to be more careful with out-of-town claims."

Chase's eyebrows went up. "First I've heard of that," he said. "The Strivers' has policy-holders up and down the Eastern Seaboard," he added for Wyatt's benefit.

"How would they verify a claim from someone who lived in upstate New York, say? Or Georgia?"

Chase rocked back in his swivel chair. "They have field men on contract—claims adjusters. They're only brought in past a certain point—a big house-fire, for instance. If a claim's on the small side, and the customer provides receipts for the repairs, they'd most likely dispense with that."

"You could talk to Mr. Templeton," Louisa suggested. "He's in the confidence of the managing directors. I must get hold of him soon—he offered to come and help me clear out Robert's office. So many papers—the police went through them and brought them back, but I just haven't been able to face them—"

"Congressional papers?"

Louisa waved a dismissive hand. "All sorts—from the House, the Strivers', the YMCA, everything he was involved with. A mountain of stuff! It makes me tired just to think of it."

Wyatt made a mental note to check on what Macalester's people had found.

"The police examiners went through everything and found nothing useful to the investigation," Louisa sighed, answering the unspoken question. "Same for what they took from his desk and cabinet in the House. Wyatt, are you suggesting that Robert's involvement with the Strivers' may have had something to do with his death?"

"I'm fishing," Wyatt admitted. "Is there anywhere else Mr. Nielsen might have kept records? Did he have a safe-deposit box at a bank, for instance?"

"If he did, he never mentioned it."

"Miss Stanstead—forgive me—have you gone through his effects? Other than his papers, I mean?" Something heavy was starting to stir and settle in the back of Wyatt's mind.

"Not yet." Louisa drooped visibly.

"You thinking there might've been a box?" Chase said.

"And if so, a key somewhere. A pocket, maybe, or a drawer. As long as we're branching out in this direction, had he other involvements of this kind?"

"Well, you know he'd just joined the fundraising committee for the new YMCA," Chase replied. "Terrell could tell you something about that. But I can't think of any shady dealings or controversy associated with that *or* the Strivers'—and believe me, the *Bee* keeps a close eye on such things."

"The YMCA," Wyatt said. "You were at that meeting, weren't you, Mr. Chase?"

"I was, yes…" Chase looked uncomfortable.

"I think you told me you stayed a little while at the end—"

"I did," said Chase cautiously. "Why do you ask?"

"Was anyone from the Strivers' still there?"

"Well, sure, Clarence was, and Roy DeYoung—Clarence locked up behind me, matter of fact."

"Everyone else had left by then?"

Chase bit his lip and nodded.

Wyatt changed tack. "About that safe-deposit box—"

"I can look for a key," Louisa said, as if hoping to be forestalled.

"I'm sorry to ask it of you," Wyatt said. "And I must also ask, for safety's sake, that neither of you mention the possibility of its existence to anyone."

Chase took his meaning at once and nodded in response to Louisa's puzzled look.

Wyatt remembered George Templeton's gentleness with his damaged child, the cold rage of the matriarch whose house he shared. A decent man, universally respected, a man in continual difficulties…he had handled both the origination of Nielsen's insurance policy and the settlement of the survivor's claim with the annuity to Louisa. He'd told Wyatt he wasn't an underwriter, the day Wyatt visited him and met little Branford.

"I'll talk to Mr. Templeton as you suggested, Miss Stanstead. What did you say his title is with the Strivers'?"

"He's head of the Claims Department," Chase said. "A very senior position."

"I wonder, then," he chose his words carefully, "if there were anything irregular among the executives of the Strivers', might his loyalty to the company bind him to silence?"

"Oh, no!" Louisa laid a hand on his arm. "George would give anything to find the guilty party. You saw how distressed he was at the meeting, about the effects of Robert's death on the bills they'd been working on. He's been up to the Hill several times since then, with Mrs. Terrell and Reverend Grimké and the others, trying to get Robert's alley amendment moving again. I know he'll help you all he can."

Tears glimmered behind the steel spectacles. "Oh, dear, I don't know what to think—could it really be that a man of color was capable of..." her voice broke. "I'm sorry, it's still so new. It catches me unawares sometimes." She took the handkerchief produced by Chase from a vest-pocket and noisily blew her nose. Wyatt liked the artlessness of it. Her eyes were red-rimmed when the handkerchief came away.

"What *I'm* hoping for," he said, "is that Commander Macalester finds some way of tying Mr. Dunagin and his crew to what happened that night." The alternative that was taking shape in his mind was too painful to contemplate. He'd learned all too well in the past that murder could be an act of purest love.

CHAPTER 38

"For my own good," Wyatt said, turning away from Lady Macbeth and retreating into Macbeth's private hell, "All causes shall give way. I am in blood stepp'd in so far that, should I wade no more, Returning were as tedious as go o'er." He paused for a long moment, raising an alarmed look from Mrs. Marlowe. What had stopped him was the thought that the speech could have been uttered by Nielsen's murderer. Who would do whatever was necessary for the good of his own, who might not yet be finished with killing.

"Strange things I have in head…" he went on, and the smooth flow of the scene carried him offstage.

He and Sydney Mather had rehearsed an alternative duel between Macbeth and Macduff, trying to keep the stress on his battered ankle to a minimum. "Seems that curse is the real thing, old boy," Mather had said. "No understudy left to fall back on!"

Now, in performance, the ankle sent fiery spears shooting up his leg. He hoped the pain twisting his features gave the stage combat authenticity.

After the curtain call, with a stagehand standing by with ice for the sprain, Mrs. Marlowe pulled him aside.

"Good news!" she beamed. "Edward's coming back!"

Wyatt stopped in his tracks and let the wave of pain wash over him. "Oh…I'm glad to hear it," he said. "Right away?"

"Night after next!" she turned to the rest of the cast. "Quick run-through at four tomorrow—you'll be back to Young Siward," she flashed a sympathetic look at Fred Lewis, who looked chagrined, "and Wyatt, you're all right with Ross, aren't you?"

Wyatt wasn't all right with Ross. In spite of the complications, distractions, and even the pain, he'd finally been making the role of Macbeth his own. He was going to miss it. At least he'd have Lady Macduff to run lines with overnight.

Germain's gaze, which had swept proudly around the Dodges' newly completed ground-floor kitchen, turned troubled when it landed back on Wyatt. Stacks of dishes gleamed behind the glass fronts of cabinets, and a vase of yellow tulips graced the latest design of Chicago-Williams soapstone counters. The room smelled of floor wax and baked apples.

"Looks good." Wyatt helped himself to a mug of coffee from the stove.

"Why have I got to be the one to go checking up on this 'alternative hypothesis' of yours?" Germain passed Wyatt a warm slice of Cook's apple tart.

"I can't see anyone opening up to *me* about it," Wyatt said through a sweet, tangy mouthful.

"If I get anywhere near it, why's Templeton going to give me anything to work from?"

"Start somewhere else. Isn't he in some club you were interested in joining?"

"That was Costello. Look, Templeton's a nice fella. We hit it off—"

"I like him too. If this disbursements thing has anything to do with the murder, it doesn't have to have been him."

"If it's not him, and I tip him off that something's fishy, he's going to try to fix it himself, isn't he? How does that help you home in on the killer?"

"I'm taking a flyer," Wyatt admitted. "Louisa gets an insurance annuity, courtesy of George Templeton. When I ask him about Nielsen buying the policy, he doesn't mention Nielsen's role on the Board, much less the Finances Committee. Louisa does, and tells me Nielsen was worried about excessive claims expenses or some such. Templeton's struggling with all his child's medical bills and no help from his mother. On the morning before he dies, he accosts Nielsen on the street, wants to talk to him about something, and Nielsen shoves him aside. It may all mean nothing—but if it does, there's nobody else at the Strivers' whose name has come into this."

"Clarence Wilbur?" *Your future brother-in-law.*

"He's the one who told me Nielsen chaired the Finances Committee. Which Templeton did not."

Germain took a swig of coffee. "Templeton's in the MuSoLit too, come to think. But how do I *segué* from there into problems in the company?"

"Maybe tell him you're thinking about buying some insurance, but you've heard street talk that Nielsen was worried about them paying out too much claim money—"

Germain heaved a sigh and shook his head. "I don't like it."

"You're the one that got me thinking about it," Wyatt shrugged. "What do you think he'll do? If he's…"

"Just a guess—Louisa hasn't cleaned out Nielsen's papers yet. If Templeton's innocent, he'll go back and raise hell at the Strivers' till he finds out what Nielsen was worried about. If he isn't, and thinks there's something incriminating in Nielsen's papers, he'll suggest he take them and sort them out for her."

"Wouldn't the cops have found anything like that?"

"Might not have known what they were looking at. Or Nielsen kept the information somewhere more secure. I've got Louisa looking for a safe-deposit key but I've told her not to do anything with it without having us along. Or even tell anyone else she's found it."

"So if Templeton's guilty—" Germain's face was troubled.

"I don't like the idea either. But if he comes looking for whatever Nielsen might've had, Louisa can truthfully say there's nothing else she knows of besides the papers in the study."

"You think that'll keep her safe?"

"He wouldn't hurt her unless he felt he had no choice. If my hypothesis proves out, keep in mind he tried to make it up to her by getting her an insurance settlement."

"Which, if you're right, would be fraudulent. So, what am I getting out of this again?"

Wyatt grinned. "Besides my undying gratitude—and Mr. Dodge's?"

"Hell, I got that already. All right, I have it. You get me in to see the play."

Wyatt owed Germain far more than that, for bringing Giovanna's truth to light and setting them both free. But he had no idea how he could make it happen.

He gave Germain his hand. "Deal."

Germain rinsed out his mug in the new sink. "They still can't make a case against Dunagin's hoodlums?"

"Both of them insist Nielsen was dead when they found him. They're holding them, but so far there's no physical evidence linking them to the scene."

Germain shook his head gloomily. "Where will I find you, after my li'l chat with George?"

"I'm going to the Hill to push Latham on the Dunagin theory. Then back to the National. This is my last night as Macbeth."

"Thought you had full houses."

"We have," Wyatt shrugged. "But Sothern's back tomorrow. We're rehearsing our old roles this afternoon."

"Busy man," Germain's smile faded to dejection. "I'm not gonna get to see you in the lead. I'm sorry to hear that."

"You and me both," Wyatt said.

"You're still harping on that nonsense? That Dunagin has something against me?" Latham hissed at Wyatt in a corner of the walnut-paneled Republican cloakroom. "This is neither the time nor the place—" A number of his colleagues darted glances in their direction.

"We've got two of his operatives at the scene," Wyatt hissed back. "We know he sent blackmail letters to Nielsen and allies of his."

"You told me that. Over here, for God's sake." Latham waved Wyatt to a pair of well-worn leather chairs near a defunct fireplace. "Dodge got you in here?"

"They're preparing warrants for Dunagin and the two thugs," Wyatt said. "Your testimony on the state of your relations is critical. It might come down to you or him." He was bluffing, but if he couldn't give Macalester a motive to work with, Dunagin would slip the hook—for Nielsen's death, at least.

Latham's brow furrowed. "As far as I know, Dunagin considers my involvement, and certainly my good name, critical to his success with Columbia Heights. He came to see me about it—"

"When?"

"Keep your voice down! Two days ago. It wasn't long after your visit—" Latham's gaze went far away suddenly.

"Go on."

Latham shook his head. "He asked me if I knew you. He thinks you're dissuading Dodge from the investment."

"What did you tell him?"

"Said I'd heard of you as an actor, that was all. I don't think he believed me. I told him I'd talk to Dodge."

"Was he satisfied with that?"

"I had to go and vote, so that was the end of the conversation. What on earth could he—" he drummed his fingers on the arm.

Wyatt leaned across to him. "How far along are the sales?"

"He has commitments in hand for over ninety percent of the lots," Latham said. "It's been a roaring success—"

"And how were you to be compensated for your assistance?"

"Contingent on sales—payouts to begin once deposits are secured. I have about twenty thousand due in the next..." Latham stopped, his face going pale. "No. No, he has other developments in mind—he'll want my help—"

Wyatt looked at him steadily. "He owes you a lot of money."

"It can't be," Latham said in a lost, wondering tone. His jaw set. "The man may be a little rough around the edges, but he'd never do such a thing. It's not in his interest. I've been an asset to him—"

"Have been. Don't people dispose of assets when their useful life is ending?"

Shrill electric bells began ringing for a floor vote. Latham rose, red-faced, and stalked towards the door to the House chamber, turning to Wyatt. "It won't wash. Slandering my friend, turning us against one another. That's no answer. Go and get me a better one."

"You don't think it's odd that he came to ask you about me?" Wyatt shook his head. "It's your funeral, Congressman."

"Damn you—that's what you're being paid to prevent." The etched-glass door swung wildly behind Latham's retreating back.

CHAPTER 39

George Templeton looked up from a jumble of papers on his desk and broke into a wide smile. "Mr. Germain! This is a pleasant surprise!"

Germain shook his hand but remained standing when Templeton gestured him to a chair. "Don't want to interrupt your work, friend. But if you might have some time in the next couple of days, would you let me buy you a cup of coffee and discuss a—a social matter? A personal matter, that is."

Templeton closed a manila file. "Happens I could use a little pick-me-up." He led him around the corner to the lunch counter of a People's Drug Store, where Germain was intrigued to see white and colored patrons seemingly at ease in one another's presence.

Templeton caught his look. "They don't let the darker folks in. I probably shouldn't even be coming here, knowing that. My mama's glad of it, though—she doesn't like to mix with the darkies, she calls them. Cherry pie's good here."

Germain smiled, thinking of the fine distinctions New Orleans storekeepers made about skin color. They sat in a booth off the hexagonal-tiled floor, thick mugs in hand, amid the comings and goings of high-collared clerks, young matrons with children in hand, and brisk businessmen.

Membership in the MuSoLit Club would present no difficulty, Germain learned. Costello had mentioned his generosity with his Roman histories, and to find out in addition that he not only played the violin but composed—he was just the sort of man they were looking for. The next membership round would be in four months or so, but…Templeton himself would be honored to put his name forward.

Germain felt a rush of gratitude. Accomplished and educated as he was, he had yet to find a place in the colored world of New York, which scorned Southern migrants with slaves in their family trees. He warmed to Templeton even as his heart sagged from the weight of what Wyatt had asked him to do.

His host took their mugs to the counterman for refills. "You're a friend of Mr. Wyatt's, aren't you? I hope he's making progress with his investigation?"

There. The man himself had brought it up. "He hasn't said much to me," Germain said slowly. "What I hear of this Latham, he sure sounds like the one who did it. But Mr. Wyatt doesn't seem to think they have the right man."

Templeton frowned. "If that had been a colored man's walking-stick they found, he'd have been arrested in a New York minute."

"A Congressman as powerful as that, they'd want to be sure," Germain mused. "He could make a lot of trouble for the D.C. Police. And somebody might've wanted to set him up."

"Surely somebody who disliked Mr. Nielsen enough to kill him would be friendly with Latham. Or at least have common interests, political or business-wise."

"Well, you'd think so. So, how do you like working for the Strivers'?"

"You thinking about a change of profession, my friend?" Templeton beamed. "There's an opening—"

"Oh, uh, no." The mental picture of himself as an insurance man chilled Germain's blood. "It's just—I was thinking maybe about a policy. I got a sister back home, single gal. Schoolteacher. I'd like to make sure she's taken care of if, you know, something happened to me. But my daddy got burned in the '73 business, so we're kinda—conservative about where we put our money. And—" he looked away, "I guess I shouldn't be repeating loose gossip, but seems like a few folks in town are wondering about the, ah, financial situation at the Strivers'."

Templeton's brow darkened. "Now where'd you hear a thing like that, brother?"

"Lemme see—somebody had been talking to Mr. Chase, I believe it was."

"The newspaper-man?" Templeton's hands tightened around his mug. "Isn't that just typical. Colored folks are their own worst enemies in this town, I swear. Bandying about the name of a fine institution like the Strivers', that takes care of them when the white firms won't even let them in the door—" He half-rose in his seat, his big frame constrained by the booth table.

"Now, I shouldn't have said anything. It's just that—"

Templeton mastered himself. "No, no. It's important to know that that kind of talk is out there. But there's not a shred of truth to it. Our Statements of Affairs are prepared by the most capable and scrupulous men in the business. The policy-holders' surplus is well within the industry standards—Mr. Germain, we need to follow up on this. Can you tell me anything more?"

Germain made a show of trying to remember. The coffee was burning in his gut. "Seems like it was something about paying out too much on claims, maybe?"

Templeton's voice was low, but urgent. "Mr. Germain, I am the head of the Claims Department. That's a very serious allegation indeed. It reflects particularly on me and the good people that work with me, in my own department and the Finance Department."

If there were problems with claims payments, they could just as easily have arisen in the department that cut the actual checks as in Templeton's bailiwick. Germain wondered if Wyatt had thought of that. Any man in Templeton's position might react this way upon learning that there might be a bad apple among his trusted colleagues. Germain cursed Wyatt inwardly for putting him onto this, causing more distress to a kindly man whose life already had enough for a dozen.

"It's my obligation to get to the bottom of this," Templeton was saying, "and, believe me, I will! Was there mention of any evidence of this supposed problem?"

"Lord, Mr. Templeton, I'm sorry I even brought it up. All I know is what I heard from Mr. Chase. Want me to see if I can find out a little more? Discreetly, of course."

"Let me look around some on my own first," Templeton said. "If something's amiss, I'm more likely to be able to ferret it out than anyone else. I've got a better idea of what to look for."

"Well, that makes sense," Germain smiled. "And in the meantime, maybe one of your folks could help me with that policy."

Templeton rose and smiled in his turn, extending his hand. "Thank you for that faith. I'll put one of our best agents in touch. He'll fix you right up. And—I'd appreciate it if you didn't mention this other business to anybody. If there is a problem, I assure you it'll be taken care of."

When Templeton had gone, Germain stood on the drugstore steps and consulted his pocket watch. He was due back on Belmont Road to supervise the arrival of a shipment of new drawing-room furniture. Wyatt would be onstage by the time they were done. His report on the interview with Templeton could wait until morning.

Wyatt awoke with Giovanna spooned at his back. It had been a strong night for everyone, the sort of night that made you forget all the drudgery of the acting life. He'd surprised himself by tapping into something new, towards the end, on his last night in the role: Macbeth wanted to die. He'd lost the woman whose love, however twisted, however polluted by lust for power, gave his life energy and purpose. As he himself had lost Rose, as he hoped never to lose Giovanna. On stage, he'd drawn his sword and turned towards Macduff, thinking of him as a savior, a bringer of release. It was a subtle shift, but it came across to Mather, an intelligent player, and to the audience. The long pause at the blackout before the applause began was gratifying; the audience, mesmerized, had needed a few seconds to pull themselves back to the world.

He grasped the slender hand that lay around his waist and twisted back to look at her. One sleepy brown eye opened and she groaned a little. His wife...? His *Negro* wife. He smiled. She pulled her hand away to push at a drooping curl.

There was a knock at the door.

The bellboy handed him a note from Germain asking him to meet at the Dodge house at nine o'clock. *Tell you about my talk with T.* He came back to the bed. Giovanna, awake and sitting up now, took the note from his hand.

"Who's T?"

"Templeton. The insurance man." Wyatt wound his fingers through the hair at the back of her neck.

"Oh, that poor man. Clarence and I were talking about him. He works with him at the Strivers', you know. How he manages, with that poor child and all those medical bills and that Gorgon mother of his—do you know, she even charges him rent?"

Wyatt shook his head. The Templeton matriarch was not a woman he would care to cross.

"Now there's a woman who's worse than a white man for color lines," Giovanna went on. "When George came home married to that black girl, she threw a fit, Clarence says." Now that her secret was out, Wyatt was picking up faint cadences of Negro speech he'd missed before.

"He wasn't likely to have married a white woman, was he?"

"No, but this girl was really dark. Mrs. T. is one of those people who won't have anything to do with folk who are darker than her. It didn't help when the girl ran away, when the little boy was—three or four, I think Clarence said. She couldn't handle it. 'Just like a damn nigger,' Mrs. Templeton said." Giovanna laughed at the shocked look on Wyatt's face.

He held her by both hands across the bedclothes. "You caught up on a lot of the neighborhood gossip, I see."

"I've missed them," she said, her eyes dark and sad. "I hadn't let myself feel how much. I made myself forget them. But when I saw Mama in that bed…" she dropped her head and a little sob came out. "Oh, Wyatt, I *am* frightened about all this!"

Wyatt folded her in his arms and pulled her close. "Do you want some more time?"

"No!" she said quickly. "I can't go back. There are four people now—Mama, Clarence and Nettie, and you—who really know who I am. And don't hate me for it. It's so funny…"

"What?"

"How you know more about me than Thomas and my own children do."

"Can you ever tell them—the children, I mean?"

"I can't imagine. What kind of lives would they have?"

Wyatt tilted her chin up with a finger, "How safe do you feel now? Can you think of anyone who'd tell on you or try to blackmail you, if they found out?"

"Why do you ask?"

"Well—I promised my friend Germain he'd see us perform. But the National won't admit colored people. I thought I'd talk to Mr. Sothern about an extra performance."

"At the National? You mean, a Jim Crow performance?"

"No!" Wyatt said hastily. "I don't like that idea any more than you. I was thinking—there must be venues in town where colored people are welcome. Their own theaters, maybe? We'd have to dispense with some of the set—but that doesn't signify much with Shakespeare, if it's done well."

"And we know we would!" Her face grew serious. "You know how scared I've been…" she said, "but I've never known *personally* of anyone who passed who was given away. Or blackmailed. People may not like it, but they understand." She sat up straight among the rumpled sheets and pillows. "Besides, with the makeup and that headdress and all—I'm willing to take a chance."

"You are the gutsiest woman I ever met," Wyatt smiled, nuzzling her neck. "Some day we need to be in a play together where I don't have to murder you."

"Antony and Cleopatra?" she said, giving him a lopsided smile. "But—" she shook her head.

"I hate snakes," they chorused.

Wyatt replaced his coffee mug on the Dodges' kitchen table. "How'd he take it when you raised the claims thing?"

"Sure seemed indignant at the idea of somebody questioning the Strivers' integrity," Germain said. "Said he was gonna look into it himself, asked me not to say anything."

"An innocent man might react that way too," Wyatt frowned. "If he's not—" his heart lurched. "we'd best get to Miss Stanstead right away before he gets in touch with her." They might have put Louisa in more danger than he'd realized. "We should've warned her he might be coming by."

"Oh, Lord, I should've got you word last night." Germain rose and tossed the dregs of his coffee in the sink. "Let me get my coat. I'm going with you."

CHAPTER 40

They found Louisa at home with a headache and what she called "a touch of the vapors." "It's odd," she said, putting the kettle on for coffee. "I fell asleep in my clothes again. Evidently I'd had a spot of sherry, and I haven't much of a head for the stuff. But I don't even remember fetching myself any, and there are two fingers gone from the bottle—you'll think me a terrible souse!"

Wyatt pushed past her to the shelf above the sink. "What glass did you use?"

"There were two in the dish drainer. They'd been washed," she said. "I must've forgotten the first and poured myself another." She pointed to a shelf where she'd replaced them. "But why would I have been so slatternly about *using* the glasses, then washed them and put them away? And the bottle—I know it was in this cupboard, with the little teacakes for ladies' visits, but I found it in this other one, with the whiskey and brandy."

Wyatt took the glasses down, sniffed them and passed them to Germain. "This one smells a little funny," Germain said. "Kinda—sharp."

"Louisa, forgive me—let me smell your breath."

The urgency in Wyatt's tone convinced her. He waited through two long exhalations. "I think someone has slipped Miss Stanstead a mickey—chloral hydrate drops," he told Germain. "Please—Louisa—try to remember. Who was here? Did someone call on you last night?"

Louisa collapsed into the easy chair where she had slept. "I can't think…my head is throbbing. There was somebody—Robert's papers…I can't be sure—they were rather a muddle when the police brought them back, but even so they looked different this morning…"

Germain stared at Wyatt and the realization struck them both. "Please try to remember," Wyatt said carefully, "Where did Mr. Nielsen keep his notes from the Strivers' Finances Committee?"

She passed a hand over her eyes. "Why is everyone so interested in those papers? George Templeton's been by…" Her eyes grew wide. "Why, that's who it was. He was here last night… good heavens, Wyatt, you don't think *he*…"

"We have to find those papers," Wyatt said grimly.

"That's what George said too," Louisa said with some asperity. "There's a lot of confidential information that the Strivers' Board asked him to retrieve. He was quite anxious about it, poor man. He's so conscientious…"

But you haven't found them," Germain said.

"I hadn't really looked yet. Oh, that reminds me, Wyatt—I did find this." Louisa pulled a small green square of cardboard from her pocket with "Riggs National Bank" embossed on it in bold capitals. "This looks like the key to a safe-deposit box, doesn't it? I found it in one of Robert's vest-pockets yesterday."

"Did you mention this to Templeton?"

"Well, no, I didn't—you told me not to. Besides, there might be personal items in there, and I wanted to check on it myself first."

Wyatt blew out a breath. "That was wise."

"Sounds like a good place to stash important papers," Germain said.

Louisa reached for her hat, which hung on a peg by the door. "Let's go and have a look, shall we?"

Germain settled his derby on his head as Louisa preceded them out the door. "Should we be saying something to Mr. Mac?"

Wyatt paused. "Not just yet."

President Roosevelt was incredulous. "O'Donoghue's alive?" He stabbed at the hearth logs with a poker, producing a few anemic flickers.

"Living not two miles from here, sir," Commander Macalester said. They were meeting in the President's Room in the new temporary Executive Office Building.

"Didn't they fish him out of the East River after that Mott Street business?"

"We thought so, sir," Macalester said.

"It now appears he got hold of a poor immigrant fellow who'd just landed at Castle Garden," said Arthur Woods, New York's new detective chief. "Did him in and assumed his identity."

"Which was—?"

"Cornelius Dunagin."

"The developer?" Macalester hadn't thought anything could shock Theodore Roosevelt. "That half of Congress has money into?" Woods and Macalester nodded, and Roosevelt's eyes narrowed. "There isn't any doubt, I take it."

"Very little, sir," said Woods. "There being no trial for the Mott Street murders, it was a cold case, not a closed one, so the Department kept the evidence. We got some fingerprints."

"With a little help from Wyatt," Macalester added.

"Our old friend from Heron Island?" Roosevelt grinned. "Thought he'd gone back to acting. "

"So did he."

"Hasn't he been doing *Macbeth* here? Edith and I were hoping to see it—"

"Mr. Dodge persuaded him to help get Richard Latham off the hook for Congressman Nielsen's murder."

Roosevelt raised an eyebrow. "And has he?"

"Things are moving in that direction."

"Thing is, sir," said Woods, "you having been something of a nemesis to the Whyos as Police Commissioner, we were wondering if you'd like to give us a hand wrapping up the O'Donoghue business."

Roosevelt sat down behind his desk and waved them to chairs. "Tell me more."

After she read its contents, Louisa had carefully re-sealed the envelope she'd retrieved from the safe-deposit box. It sat beside her on a gate-leg table. Robert Nielsen had been careful to keep his evidence safe. Not careful enough to save his own life, but it wouldn't have occurred to him that the object of his investigations would grow desperate enough to kill. That man sat across from her now. She kept her own countenance a pleasant blank.

"These seem to be very important to the company, George," she said, lifting the envelope into her lap. "But surely there would be plenty of copies of anything that a Board member would receive?"

"Just so. But our President specifically asked me to get them back—he doesn't want confidential company records, ah, floating around."

Louisa smiled. "You told me how important they were, and I was never going to be careless with them, once I'd found them."

"Of course not." Templeton glanced at his watch. "So I'll just take the envelope and get back to the office—"

"You won't stay for a glass of sherry?" Louisa's eyebrows arched. "I suppose not. It can make a person uncommonly sleepy when there's work to be done."

He rose with a little laugh and came towards her with his hand extended. His shadow blocked out the morning sunlight.

She picked up the envelope and slit it open with her forefinger. "I must say—I suppose it's a female trait—I'm wondering why Robert considered these important enough to put in a safe-deposit box." She slid the papers from the envelope. Templeton's hand shot towards hers but she snatched them back, half-rising from the chair.

"You really mustn't—" he said, his voice darkening, "these are company property."

"They're actually more than that," Louisa said quietly. "An affidavit by Robert with supporting documents, dated the day before his death, detailing the history of your embezzlements from the Strivers' Mutual."

Templeton froze. "You read them?"

Louisa nodded, revulsion showing on her face at last. "The fake claims examining firm in Baltimore. Fees sent to the post-office box on Calvert Street. Checks cashed at the National Bank by a 'Mr. Branford.' 'Oh, yes, that nice Negro gentleman who comes in every week.' That's what they told Robert when he went up there and described you."

Templeton's jaw tightened.

"You killed my Robert, Mr. Templeton. You beat him and smashed his head until he died. You filled his last moments on earth with terror and pain. And you filled my life with nightmares I can't wake up from." Louisa laughed mirthlessly. "I should thank you for the chloral hydrate. It's the first decent night's sleep I've had since Robert died."

Templeton snapped back into movement. "I had no choice. Give me those papers."

"No choice but to kill?" Louisa skittered behind her chair and began backing away from him, clutching the papers to her breast.

"I'll do it again, if I have to." Templeton's face was a mask of rage as he advanced on her. "I'll do anything to take care of my boy. He said, 'Pay it back. Pay all the money back by next week and show me the proof of it or I'll go to the Chairman.' He could document what I'd been doing, he said. He wouldn't listen. If I'd had the money to pay it back I wouldn't have had to take it in the first place."

He leapt on Louisa like a big cat and his hands closed around her throat, tightening till she began sinking to the floor.

CHAPTER 41

The guests for Mrs. Roosevelt's musicale filed into the East Room from the new portico. Waiters circulated with champagne and hors d'oeuvres while the latest piano prodigy from Curtis played Chopin on the Steinway Gold Grand. From his vantage point behind Secret Service Chief Wilkie, Macalester watched the Roosevelts shake hands with Congressional leaders and their wives, members of the diplomatic corps, and prominent area businessmen—one of whom, Cornelius Dunagin, had received his first-ever invitation to the White House. He was at the head of the receiving line now, resplendent in the requisite white tie and tails, his black curls smoothed with oil, his wife high-colored in an off-the-shoulder cobalt blue gown layered with beaded black lace.

In the adjoining Green Room, Wilkie had settled Chief Arthur Woods with two of his New York detectives, one carrying a voluminous briefcase, and three Secret Service agents. Harder to settle had been a gangling, underfed-looking man in his forties, his face raw with recent shaving, dressed in a threadbare black suit. He had refused all refreshment except for a cup of strong tea on the train from New York.

As the musicale guests were being shown to chairs, Wilkie approached his quarry. "Mr. Dunagin, the President would like a word with you. Follow me, please?" Macalester slipped into the Green Room, retreating behind a Japanese screen in the far corner. Wilkie and a puzzled but pleased-looking Dunagin came in a few moments later.

Roosevelt stood in front of a blazing fire, hands in his pockets. Woods and his men lined the walls, two Secret Service men standing on either side of a wicker couch which sat at an angle a few feet back from the fireplace.

"I won't keep you long, Mr. Dunagin," the President said. "But I couldn't resist an opportunity that's come my way. To officiate at a family reunion."

"Reunion, sir?" Dunagin's look of polite puzzlement deepened.

"I'm told it's been many years since you saw your native turf," Roosevelt smiled, "and that your family back there, by misfortune, fell out of touch with you. Well, we've found them." He gestured towards the wicker couch.

"You've, ah—?"

The gangling stranger rose slowly from the couch and turned towards Dunagin, scrutinizing his face as if seeking something he had lost there.

"Cornelius?"

From the edge of the screen, Macalester watched the play of expressions on Dunagin's face: a bolt of pure panic, a flash of rage, a flare of resolve settling into wary impassivity.

"Cornelius, d'you not know me?"

Silence.

"It's Daniel." The accent was Ulster, rural Ulster at that, if Macalester was any judge.

"Daniel," Dunagin repeated, like a child learning a new word. "My... brother Daniel, you'd be?"

The stranger smiled sadly. "Twenty-one years." Neither man made a move toward the other. "We thought you were dead. How did you never get word to us in all that time?"

Dunagin seemed to stagger, steadied himself on a chair. "Well, now, I did, at first, but I heard nothing back, and—"

The man's voice was soft, but firm now. "And what address did you send your letters to?"

"Why, to home, of course, in—in Armagh."

Daniel Dunagin shook his head sadly. "Ah, they must all have gone astray," he said, "and all the years, and Mam gone with never a word from you—"

"How long?" Dunagin croaked.

"Five years. It was the heart that got her, as you'd foreseen."

"God rest her," Dunagin said, looking away. "I'm heart-sorry for it."

"There's happy news too. Deirdre got married to that O'Hara fella from Ballyjamesduff, that works at Bushmill's now, and they've two young ones. They named the boy for you."

"Did they now," Cornelius Dunagin said, letting out a long breath. "Well! I'll have to be sending the lad something, to set him up, like."

"I'm wonderin', though—how did you get your leg fixed? " Daniel Dunagin said. "How'd they manage to get rid of the limp for you?"

"The limp…"

"From that break that never healed right," Daniel Dunagin said, "though I'm not rememberin' now which leg it was—?"

"The break. Yes, I got it fixed. Amazing what they can do now."

"Which leg was it, again?" Daniel Dunagin's eyes never left the other's face.

A log popped in Roosevelt's fireplace and a blue flame shot up. The men ringing the room stiffened and their hands reflexively went to their waistbands, dropping slowly back to their sides.

"The right," said Cornelius Dunagin.

Woods' detective reached into the briefcase he was carrying and extracted a large file folder.

"Funny," said Daniel Dunagin. "I was nearly positive it was the left."

"Ah—well, sometimes it's hard to remember myself. And how is the old place? The farm still going strong?" Cornelius Dunagin's tone had recovered some of its assertiveness.

"The farm struggles as it always did," Daniel Dunagin said. "We were hoping you'd get to America and be able to send something back to help us. It was so hard for Mam to let you go, having lost Deirdre so young."

Cornelius Dunagin took a step or two back. "Lost Deirdre," he echoed.

"At five and a half years of age, to typhus, which my real brother would have known, and never let me away with telling him she was married," Daniel Dunagin said, trembling now from head to foot.

266

He pointed a shaking finger. "This man is not my brother."

Theodore Roosevelt stepped towards Daniel, put an arm around his shoulder and led him to the fireplace. The man's shoulders heaved and he began to sob.

Woods took the file folder from his detective. It splayed open to a ghostly negative, shadowy white on a black ground. "The break you described, Mr. Dunagin," he said, nodding towards Daniel, "is in the left tibia. It healed improperly, which produced the limp you remember in your brother. Something no surgeon can fix."

Roosevelt took the X-ray from Woods' hand. "Where did this image come from, Mr. Woods?"

"From the remains exhumed on Hart's Island last week, sir. Buried there in 1885 as Patrick Joseph O'Donoghue, having surfaced in the East River wearing O'Donoghue's clothes and a silver ring in the form of a skull." Woods reached into a pocket, extracted a small metal object, and tossed it in the air.

"You might as well have it back."

Cornelius Dunagin's eyes flew wide and followed its perfect arc. His hand reached out and snatched it.

"Patrick Joseph O'Donoghue, I arrest you for the murders of Cornelius Dunagin, Sarah McKinstry, Effie VanSlyke, Bridie O'Donnell, and Terence McNab." As Woods spoke, his New York detectives, the Secret Service men, and Commander Macalester converged like a pride of lions on the man who had stolen Cornelius Dunagin's life and identity. From the briefcase, the detective produced a set of handcuffs.

"You—!"

O'Donoghue, the feral light now blazing from his eyes, lunged towards Macalester, seizing him by a sleeve with one arm and hooking the other round his neck. Six men came at him, six pairs of arms pulled him off kicking and flailing, the New York detective cuffing him from behind. Six revolvers pointed at his head.

"Take him out the north door," Roosevelt said. "Now if you'll excuse me, gentlemen, I'll get back to my guests. Ian," he added, turning to Macalester and pumping his hand, "it's a good thing I brought you down here."

Which led Macalester to wonder how Wyatt was getting on with finding Nielsen's killer.

Wyatt and Germain sprang from the coat closet. Germain covered the room in two strides and seized George Templeton's arms. Wyatt flanked him on the other side and pulled Louisa to her feet from Templeton's loosening grip.

"That's enough now, brother," Germain said.

"You all right?" Wyatt asked Louisa. She nodded shakily, hands at her neck.

The man in the three-piece suit slumped to his knees, watch falling from his pocket, its chain puddling on the floor. He burst into wracking sobs, his distorted face reminding Wyatt of the damaged child for whose sake all this murder had been done.

"It was all for Branny," Templeton gasped, "that's the only reason, I swear. That doctor's bills have been running me two hundred dollars a month." He covered his face with his hands. "God in heaven, what's going to happen to my child?"

The three stared at one another across Templeton's heaving shoulders. Louisa was the first to recover her voice.

"What about your family? Your friends? The church? They could have helped you."

"Family." Templeton spat out the word. "My beloved mother charges me rent. She's been after me to put Branny away in the Government Hospital since before Bessie left. He's a low-grade idiot, she says. Served me right for marrying that black gal. She'd've thrown us out in the street if I'd so much as mentioned our situation outside the house." He took a great, sniffing inward breath and let it out.

"So I did what I had to do."

He started to rise. Wyatt and Germain snapped forward to restrain him but he shook his head and waved them off. "Just let me sit." He slumped onto a chair.

Louisa sat on the arm of the easy chair, her face a mixture of pity and horror. "Robert would have *helped* you."

"Oh, he was going to help me all right," Templeton said bitterly. "He was giving me a chance to make it right with the Strivers' Mutual. 'Cheating your own people,' he said. 'Stealing from your own race.' He gave me a week to put it all back, didn't care what story I made up as long as there was cold, hard cash back in the claims reserve. Where was I supposed to get it?"

"And if you didn't?" Wyatt asked.

Templeton nodded towards the envelope in the crook of Louisa's arm. "He'd take it to the Chairman and the company president. I'd go to jail. And Branny," his voice shook, "would go to the Government Hospital, die there all alone with nobody to give a damn about him." He shot Louisa an apologetic look for the profanity. "By God, I'd have killed President Roosevelt himself to keep that from happening."

Wyatt was the first to break the tense silence. "Senhora Pereira did nothing to you."

Templeton's head bowed. "I never meant for her to die. That was an unlucky thing."

"Unlucky!" The word scalded Wyatt's heart. "She couldn't incriminate you. All she could do was exonerate Latham."

"I'm not used to killing, Mr. Wyatt. I wasn't thinking straight. I haven't slept a good night myself, since I…after I did it, I didn't know what might lead back to me if they took the heat off Latham. I figured getting that lady out of commission would be my best—"

"—insurance policy," Germain finished.

"How did you get Latham's cane?"

"If anyone at Latham's house had seen me, I'd've asked for one of the servants. Most all of them have policies with the Strivers'. It was their dinner hour and the vestibule door was open, so I took that cane with his initials from the stand and walked off. Took one of his raincoats, too. Waited on the street till his carriage went out. Wasn't going fast, so I could keep up. Followed him from Willard's to Lafayette Square, saw him go in the back and that house all quiet, so I knew what kind of visit it was, and figured he'd be in there a long while."

"And then you went to the YMCA meeting," Wyatt said, "at the Strivers' Hall." Templeton didn't answer.

"That quarrel on the House floor—you'd seen the evening paper," Germain said from the doorpost where he was leaning.

Templeton nodded. "Must've seemed like too good a chance to pass up, Latham being an enemy of the race."

"I was careful," Templeton said, directing an earnest gaze towards Louisa, who sat rigid with her eyes half-closed. "I hated that man but I didn't want him to suffer. I gave him a good hard whack from behind with a lead-filled sap. Knocked him right out. Then a hit to the temple. That bled a lot. That's the one that must have killed him. He never made a sound. Then I took Latham's cane and beat him about the head and shoulders till I got some blood on the cane head. Took it off a little ways, threw it in the bushes. Figured they'd come across it when they found him."

"What would you have done," Louisa opened her eyes slowly, "if not for learning of Robert's quarrel with Latham on the House floor?"

"I heard he and some other folks that were pushing his alley amendment were getting hate mail. I'd been thinking I could do something and make it look like some hired hooligans."

"I'd tried talking to him that morning," Templeton went on. "When he left here to go to the Capitol, before he called Latham out. But he just shoved me aside. 'You know what you have to do,' he said."

Wyatt shot a look at Louisa, who gasped as if she'd been daggered in the heart. He thought of her quarrel with Nielsen that last morning, and his own heart lurched with near-nauseated relief. He'd had the chance to go back to Giovanna and make amends, as Louisa Stanstead never would with her Robert. She would never know whether, absent their quarrel, Nielsen would have given Templeton a response that might have saved his life.

But from what he'd heard of Nielsen, he doubted it. Why were so many people of his sort, passionate advocates for the masses of the downtrodden, such cold and priggish judges of the frailties of individuals? As if they could deal in compassion only in wholesale quantities, or in the abstract.

"That annuity," Louisa said. "There never was any insurance policy."

Templeton shook his head.

"I found nothing in the safe-deposit box or anywhere else. That money's been stolen from the Strivers' too. You were trying to—" a little cry came out, somewhere between a sob and a laugh. "You were trying to make it up to me."

"I never wished you any harm, Louisa. I couldn't let what I'd done drive you out of your home, on top of all the rest."

"Shall I telephone for the police?" Louisa asked Wyatt.

Templeton stood up and forced her gaze onto his. "The doctor says my boy's not long for the world. They can't tell me what he's got, but his heart and his lungs aren't right. They can't fix him. The doctor says the next infection could kill him—pneumonia or heart failure." He looked wildly from Louisa to Germain to Wyatt. "Let me stay with him—I'll sign a letter myself, saying everything in that envelope is true. That I was the one that killed Mr. Nielsen. And the Brazilian lady. Then, if—" his voice shook, "when the Lord takes Branny home, I'll turn myself in. The hangman won't have long to wait."

Wyatt remembered the day he'd visited the Templeton home, the father's tenderness with his damaged son. Could there be a purer love? It wasn't the animal instinct of mother-love, nor a treasuring of beauty, grace, accomplishment. George Templeton had killed—twice—for his child. He would die for him too.

He pulled himself back. "And what about the innocent men in police custody? The Congressman you've tainted with the name of murderer?"

"If they haven't arraigned Latham by now, they must not think they can pin it on him," Templeton said defiantly. "He'll get some expensive lawyer who can show how anybody could have taken that cane and that raincoat. But if they arrest me now—I'll tell them what I know about him and that Brazilian lady."

"No!" Germain and Louisa looked startled at Wyatt's outburst. "You murdered her—that was bad enough. You won't drag her reputation and her country's future down with you."

"Then you'd best take my bargain, Mr. Wyatt."

CHAPTER 42

Louisa's eyes flickered to Wyatt and settled back on Templeton. "You killed the man I loved most in this world, and you'd have murdered me for this envelope if—" she nodded at Wyatt and Germain, "—my friends hadn't been here to protect me. But what you say is true—your mother would put Branford away. I see no reason to destroy one more harmless life. I'll take your bargain, if these men will.

"We'll go to Reverend Grimké and ask him for help with Branford's medical bills. I'm sure he'll ask no questions about your mother; we all know her. When your son dies—" there was the slightest twisting of a knife in that adverb, Wyatt thought, "there will be time enough for justice. And what you owe the Strivers' can be settled eventually. A good lawyer may win you life in prison. And when you inherit, when your mother dies, you can make restitution. In that respect, at least."

Templeton's head fell and his eyes closed. "Sounds like you got it all figured out."

"It's a lot to ask of you, to be party to this," Louisa said to Wyatt and Germain. "I dare say it goes against your instincts, if not your ethics."

"Justice delayed, justice denied," Germain said. "Where does that leave Latham?"

Wyatt leaned on the wall, his arms folded. Germain was right; the job he'd taken on was to exonerate Richard Latham. A delayed confession by George Templeton didn't accomplish that.

"It's not my choice to make," he said finally. "It's Latham's. His name cleared right away, or Senhora Pereira's memory and the future of her country's relations with ours. Hell of a bargain. Have you pen and ink, Miss Stanstead?"

Louisa nodded. Wyatt unholstered the Army-issue Colt .38 he'd brought as a precaution, and gestured Templeton to Nielsen's desk, watching him while he settled in the chair and took the pen and paper Louisa gave him. He handed the revolver to Germain, nodding in Templeton's direction. "Keep an eye him till I get back."

"This is blackmail," Richard Latham snarled, his hands curling into fists. He and Wyatt walked in bright afternoon sun on the Capitol terrace, above a frothy sea of apple and cherry blossom on its west lawn that sent perfumed waves over the light breeze.

"Of a sort. I don't like it any more than you. How good is your lawyer?"

"That's not the point. He'll likely win if it comes to that, but…"

Wyatt stopped at the corner of the terrace. "The killer tracked you to Senhora Pereira's. And killed her when he thought she'd go to the police to save you. If he's arrested now and discloses that—well, it's up to you."

Grief and pain replaced the anger in Latham's face. "Is she to have no rest? Can't they leave her in peace?"

"I'll talk to Macalester," Wyatt said. "Maybe he can find a way to drop the case against you."

Latham stared across the sea of blossoms. "You can't ask me to risk this and not tell me who did it. Who killed her."

"The same man who killed Nielsen. To protect a family member who depends on him. You'll know it all eventually."

Latham's eyes narrowed. "A Negro?"

"No guessing games."

Latham dropped his eyes and let out a long breath. "I owe her that much. Her—and her husband."

And her country, and ours. "I'll say this," Wyatt added, "If I can't get some kind of assurance from Macalester, the deal's off. She wasn't going to let you die for her, and I won't either."

"Even after everything—"

Wyatt turned his back on Latham's astonished gaze and walked away. It was as close to an apology as he was ever likely to get from the man.

Germain took two porters from the bartender and sat them down on a scarred wooden tabletop. "Don't suppose Mr. Mac was any happier than Latham about all this. How'd you get him to go along with it?"

Wyatt shrugged and smiled. "I didn't, exactly."

After Louisa Stanstead had taken new envelopes to the Riggs safe-deposit box, and Germain had taken Templeton's confession to be stored in his own bank, George Templeton had returned home to his child.

Wyatt sipped his beer. "He and the U.S. Attorney have been talking about the autopsy results and the analysis on that coat the kid found in the Potomac. It wouldn't be an easy one to win on the forensics—which is all they have. Mac himself told me that the blows that killed Nielsen came from something bigger and heavier than Latham's cane. And young Hughes at the police lab—despite my bursting in and terrorizing him—confirmed that Latham's old raincoat had been folded and kept somewhere for a while before it was put in the river. The bloodstains were long soaked in."

"Hmmph. So it looks obvious somebody was setting Latham up. They gonna let those plug-uglies go too, or d'you leave Mac with the impression they were part of the set-up?"

Wyatt grinned. "Jekyll and Hyde? He'll have to let them out eventually." He wiped foam from his mustache. "In any event, Macalester's going to visit Latham and tell him they're dropping the case against him."

"He taking you on faith, or what?"

"The politics are sensitive. That's one of the reasons Roosevelt wanted him on the force down here. He bought my argument that good hemispheric relations are a fair trade for a delay in solving Nielsen's murder."

"This has got to leave Latham wondering who set him up," Germain mused, signaling the barkeep for one of the big salty pretzels from a jar behind the taps. "Serve 'em all right if he and Dunagin fell out over it and put paid to their development scheme."

Wyatt grinned. "By now he knows it wasn't Dunagin, but it's too late. After I put the bug in his ear about how Dunagin might be trying to cut him out of the payoff, which I sincerely believed to be a possibility—don't laugh, you'd have thought so too—he sent him a note terminating their arrangement and demanding payment of what was due him. 'Course, that's the least of Dunagin's—uh, O'Donoghue's—problems at this point." Macalester had related the story of the Green Room encounter.

"Seriously," Germain sighed, shaking his head, "It's all such a shame. The one fella who cared enough to get something done to force that lowlife and his kind to clean up the alleys is gone."

"That's the worst of it," Wyatt agreed. A murder for personal reasons had had the effect of an assassination. Robert Nielsen's causes had all but died, with him; Dunagin's blackmail letters, taking advantage of his death, had made sure of that. No relief for the poverty-stricken folk in their foul, pestilential alleys; the looming threat of a bill banning marriages between the races that would push the rights of Negroes that much farther back towards the days of slavery. A bill that, among others, would have forbidden Nielsen himself to marry the woman he loved, prevented the union of Thomas Treadwell and the woman who had once been Joanna Wilbur of Washington, D.C., and—prevented that same woman and Wyatt himself from making their love legal.

"I can't see that marriage bill passing," Germain said, as if reading his thoughts. "Might get through the Senate, but the House is mostly Northerners now, and it just won't matter to them as much. 'Specially with Commissioner Macfarland opposing it out of respect for Mr. Nielsen's memory."

"Which is more than he might have felt for the living Nielsen," Wyatt smiled. "It's easier to kill a bill than pass one—and that's a good thing, sometimes." He drained his beer. "Gotta go to work. I must admit Ross is easier, particularly on a hurt leg."

Germain reached for his derby. "So how come you don't look thrilled about it?"

"I hate matinees," Giovanna said. She and Wyatt were promenading around the Washington Monument's grounds between shows, drinking in the sweet air of an idyllic spring Saturday. The sky's deep blue vibrated against the new greens of grass and trees, almost hurting their eyes. In the lively breeze, the circle of flags that surrounded the monument snapped and flapped. Giovanna was in pale sea-blue, the feathers of a jaunty bonnet nodding with each step.

She'd bought the ensemble to go with the ring Wyatt had given her, a square-cut aquamarine set in white gold and surrounded by tiny diamonds. "A love-token," he'd said, kissing her fingers when he slipped it on. "A promise." It sparkled on her right ring finger.

Wyatt patted the arm that sat atop his. "Extra shows are the price of popularity. Well, actually—the price of having Sothern back in the lead." He felt the twinge in his leg again. "Two hours before evening call. How about going back to the hotel for a rejuvenating nap?"

She raised an eyebrow and grinned. "Sleep seems unlikely."

"Worse ways to murder it."

She stopped and seized him by the hands. "Dearest. We have to make a plan."

"That we do, love." Wyatt breathed deeply and nodded. "When does his run end?"

"Tonight. I was going to meet him at his sister's in New Haven on Wednesday, pick up the children—"

"Might be easier on some neutral ground. A restaurant, maybe, in the City?"

"Tell him before we go to get the children?" She looked doubtful. "I could wire him to meet me…"

Wyatt shrugged. "It might be more difficult otherwise."

"I guess—I'm hoping Miss Wellington might have stuck—"

"The latest ingenue?"

"And he'll be relieved to go off with her. They haven't up until now, he's always tired of them, but when a man like him gets older, actors especially, sometimes it seems…ah…"

"They need a change of pace. Or change of—something."

"They want youthful blood," she smiled. "Like Count Dracula."

"Good Lord, I didn't know you read that sort of thing," Wyatt laughed.

She colored and hung her head. "I shouldn't have said that—Thomas isn't a bit like Count Dracula. She is a lot younger than me, though—only twenty or so." They were alone in a grove of young trees. She came into his arms and buried her face in his chest. "I can't expect it to be that easy."

The one advantage of widowerhood, Wyatt thought wryly, stepping back to cup her face in his hands. No one to break it off with. "Does he know you know? About this one, and, uh, the others?"

"Unwritten rules," Giovanna gave him a sad smile. "It never came up. Maybe it's time it did." She rose on tiptoe and kissed him, a long, lingering embrace from which she stood back, reluctant, at last, holding him at arm's length, her great brown eyes brimming with something that could have been joy or sadness. She squeezed his hand. "Let's go back."

Wyatt held the heavy door and followed Giovanna into the hotel, his eyes too sun-dazzled at first to register more than dark shapes near the front desk.

"Giovanna! Darling!" a male voice boomed with delight across the lobby.

"Mama!" two childish voices chorused, and four small feet came clattering towards them across the terrazzo. They were upon Giovanna in an instant, and as Wyatt's vision adjusted he saw a small sailor-suited boy with golden curls throwing his arms around her skirts while a tiny girl in a white pinafore took a flying leap, ringlets bouncing, into her arms.

"Grace! Jamie! Give your mummy a chance to breathe!" the male voice said. The little girl slid to the floor and chuckled at the smiling Apollo in spring tweeds who sauntered towards them, masses of tulips and irises in his arms. "You nearly bowled her over. Hold these a moment, would you, old man?" He thrust the flowers into Wyatt's arms, picked up Giovanna by the waist and kissed her effusively on each cheek.

"God, you're more beautiful than ever! I've missed you so much!" He gave off a sort of golden light that enveloped the woman in his embrace and the children in hers. Everyone else in the lobby, Wyatt included, seemed to evaporate into gray dusk. His eyes adjusting now, he noted with dark amusement the chagrined expression of the plump desk clerk who'd been so smitten with the luminous Mrs. Treadwell.

Giovanna, her feathered hat hanging askew and her hair tumbling loose, gave her husband a tremulous, baffled smile as her hands reflexively tightened around her children. She drew in a sharp breath. "Tom! Uh, what a—what a surprise!"

"Oh, good!" he beamed. "I hoped it would be!"

CHAPTER 43

Wyatt sat with his back to the cluttered dressing-table, trying vainly to control the racing of his heart and the blood pounding in his temples.

After a perfunctory, distracted introduction and apology for loading him up with his extravagant bouquets, Thomas Treadwell had informed Giovanna that he'd got her out of "this rat-hole they call a hotel"—at which the desk clerk's look of chagrin darkened—and they were installed in the Lincoln Suite at Willard's. Not knowing of the added matinee, he'd arrived earlier in the afternoon, and had already seen to having all her things packed up and moved over to the luxury hotel.

"It's a *fait accompli*, darling—no arguments!" he'd smiled, pleased with himself, over her protests. "Your last night—no worries about *esprit de corps* any more, surely?" He'd filled her arms with blooms, slipped a proprietary hand around her waist and steered her out the door, the children trailing at her skirts.

"Break a leg, old man," he'd said over his shoulder. "Heard you did a fine job filling in for the lead."

Wyatt had loathed him on sight.

Now he sat wondering what form the reunion between Mr. and Mrs. Thomas Treadwell might be taking. And how he was going to get through his scenes tonight. He would, of course; that's what you did, no matter what, whether your mother had just died or your house had burned down.

There was a soft knock on his dressing-room door. Could it be her? Too early for her call—his heart skipped with hope. "Come in," he said, his voice half-choked.

It was Mrs. Marlowe, and her look of stricken sympathy was worse than a death sentence. "I hear he's in town," she said, perching opposite him and taking his hand.

Wyatt shook his head. "We had no idea. There wasn't time to—"

"They cut the run short. Word is La Wellington had a nervous collapse after she told him she thought she was *enceinte* and he didn't react well."

"He dropped her?"

"Said of course he'd pay for the operation, is what she confessed to a girl-friend of hers who knows a girl-friend of mine. The baby business may have been a bluff, in any event. Naturally what she'd been after for the whole run was a proposal, silly girl—I'd hoped for your sake and Giovanna's he might actually do it this time, but I should have known better. So she went up on her lines in the middle of Act Two and fell to the floor in a faint. I think this one has scared him good and proper."

"He wants Giovanna back."

"As far as he's concerned, she's never been away," Mrs. Marlowe said. "But I must say, bringing the children with him like that was downright underhanded."

"As if he thought he might need them…"

"I suppose he knows her better than anybody." She stood and turned back with her hand on the doorknob. "What will you do, do you think?"

The look Wyatt gave her was more blood-chilling than any she'd seen on his Macbeth. "It's not really up to me now, is it?"

There was no time for them to talk until the end of Act Four. Giovanna had raced back to the National with barely enough time to get into her First Witch costume and makeup. Their one scene together, as Ross and Lady Macduff, seemed riddled with ironies tonight: Wyatt as Ross assuring the doomed wife that "your husband…is noble, wise, judicious and best knows the fits o'th'season." Well, the last part was true, at least; Thomas Treadwell knew when to dispense with a losing proposition. Giovanna, for her part, seemed to hover over little Billy Harris, her stage son, as if she were truly afraid of losing him forever.

After Wyatt as Ross had delivered his ill news to the newly widowed Macduff, he and Giovanna retreated to the momentarily deserted green room. Her role was finished for the evening; he had one more scene, greeting Macduff's triumphant entry with Macbeth's head.

"Is he here?"

"Seventh row center," she whispered. "With Jamie. We thought Grace would have nightmares at the sight of me as an evil old witch. She wasn't happy about being left with Roisin. The nanny," she added.

"What happened?"

"Miss Wellington was taken ill, it seems." She gave him a crooked smile. "During a performance. So they cut the run short—but the tour still made a fortune."

He kept his distance. "You haven't talked to him yet."

She bit her lip and turned her head from him. "He wants to start a new troupe. I'm to be his leading lady. A little Shakespeare, for my sake, he says, but mostly, ah, modern stuff. He's all excited about G.B. Shaw. Wants to do *Caesar and Cleopatra* with me."

"No snakes in that one, at any rate."

"And some drawing-room comedies, and some of those heroic medieval melodramas everyone's so mad about these days…oh, Wyatt!" Her shoulders heaved and she came to him, collapsing into his arms and sobbing. His arms closed around her and he rubbed her back gently. Someone in armor-plate and a plaid looked in at the door and quickly withdrew.

"What do you want?" he said at last.

She looked up, shaking her head, her stage makeup tear-stained. "When we got to the room, Jamie—my manly little Jamie—he just *dissolved*, Wyatt. Dissolved in tears. 'Oh, Mama, I've missed you so much. Please don't ever go away again, promise you won't.' He wouldn't let go of me. And Grace—"

She stopped, gulped, fished for a handkerchief in a pocket of her costume, sniffed loudly. "Grace just sat there and looked up at me. Didn't say a word. Never took her eyes off me for a minute."

"You've left them before," Wyatt said.

"I don't know why it was so different this time."

"Their father realized he missed you too."

"That's a generous interpretation."

Wyatt shrugged. "There are all kinds of ways to miss someone."

A great shudder passed through her, and gaze she gave him was full of pain. "Wyatt, I—"

He didn't finish it for her. He had to hear her say it. He hoped to God she wouldn't.

She stepped back from him. "I can't. Not just yet. Not just—now."

His head spun with desperate fantasies. He'd spirit her and the children out of the Willard, catch a train to Oberlin. Or Heron Island. Dodge would lend it to him…He'd tell Treadwell the truth about his wife's origins. Then Thomas would divorce her, and…no, he'd use it against her if she crossed him in any way, or tried to divorce him; he'd threaten to take the children. That secret would bind the couple closer, in a way that would only imprison Giovanna.

He closed his eyes and bowed his head. After a moment he lifted it.

"I've no business asking, but did you and he—"

She shook her head. "I told him," she said, giving him a bleak smile, "that I had my monthlies."

"Wyatt!" Rowland Buckstone hissed from the doorway. "You're on!"

He raced for the stage, his mind registering the image of the aquamarine ring still sparkling on her finger.

CHAPTER 44

Edward Sothern, restored to health and reveling in the role of the Scottish Play's arch-villain, took Mrs. Marlowe's hand and marched triumphantly downstage for his curtain-call. Flanking them on either side, the supporting cast joined in the audience's wild applause. The end of the last, unscheduled performance, put together on three days' notice, before an audience unlike any other the troupe had played to in Washington—and on the stage, not of the National Theatre, but of the Strivers' Mutual Hall in the heart of Negro Washington.

Except for Louisa Stanstead and Charles Weller, there was not a white face to be seen in the audience, which stood clapping and cheering until Sothern bowed and swept offstage, only to return for two more curtain calls. From their positions on opposite sides of the stage, Wyatt and Giovanna Treadwell, as Lord Ross and Lady Macduff, caught each other's eyes through a sparkle of tears. He would take the train north tomorrow. She would stay in Washington for a few days with her husband and children, showing them the sights of the capital.

Under the heavy makeup and medieval headgear, no one in the audience recognized Mrs. Thomas Treadwell as Joanna Wilbur—except Alexis Germain, and her brother and sister-in-law, and they were telling no one.

Wyatt caught Germain's eye and jerked his head backwards. "Ten minutes," he mouthed. Germain paused for a minute, understanding dawning in his eyes, and he nodded.

Bullock's was unusually empty for a week-night. Germain slid a foaming porter towards Wyatt and watched as his friend downed half of it in one swallow.

"So the husband came to town—"

"Trailing glory and a greenhouse's worth of tulips," Wyatt said, wiping his mustache on his sleeve. "And that was just the beginning. He and the boy came up to her after the last show at the National and buried her and Mrs. Marlowe in roses."

"Owns stock in a florist, huh? Man, Wyatt, if you didn't have bad luck, you'd have no luck at all."

Wyatt snorted. "That sounds like some Negro proverb."

"Common theme in the blues songs from the Delta plantations. I learned a few of them when I lived in N'awlins. Gimme that. I'll get you another one." He took their glasses to the bar. "She gone back to him for good, you think?" he said when he returned.

"He's starting a new troupe," Wyatt said between long swallows. "Wants her to be the leading lady. Word is he got a scare with the last female he took up with and decided there's no place like home."

"Can't fault the man's taste, anyway."

"It's the kids, mainly. This was the longest she'd been gone and it was too much for them."

"So your real rival for her affections is a seven-year-old."

"Eight. And six if you count the little girl."

"I saw how she was looking at you, at the curtain call. My guess is you won't have long to wait."

"If she doesn't leave him soon, she won't." Wyatt drained the glass and rose. "So, if you'll excuse me," the laugh in his voice turned to a quaver, "I'm going out and drown myself in the Potomac."

Germain looked genuinely alarmed and he got up quickly. "Don't be doing that! That river's so nasty down here, all the bodies come up black. Poor coroner can't tell the white corpses from the Negroes."

He held Wyatt's gaze for a long moment and they exploded in laughter. "Come on, then, walk me home and save me from myself," Wyatt said.

He and Giovanna took a last, furtive embrace the next morning in his dressing-room at the National.

"Will you come to see me?" She was wearing the maroon sacque suit, his favorite, and the matching plumed hat sat on his dressing-table. His heart ached at the beauty of her.

He tilted her chin and gazed into her eyes. "How badly do you want to complicate your life?"

"We can meet—at the Metropolitan, or—the Brooklyn Museum has a subway line now. I could bring the children. You should meet them properly."

He smiled, closed his eyes, opened them again. "Mr. Sothern was talking about a tour out west, since we did so well with this one. You could bring them—the Harrises manage fine with Billy. And when we go through Reno—"

She held up her hands. "I need some time." She started to turn away, turned back and crushed him in her arms. "Oh, God, Wyatt, don't let me go!"

He stroked her hair and pulled her closer. His eyes stung. "All right," he managed. "I won't."

She disentangled herself and shook her head. "I have to. For the children. For now, at any rate."

Wyatt thought of the sepia photo of the little pair she'd kept on her dressing-table throughout the run. The originals so alive, so full of energy and love and need. What did he know of children? Would these children ever know their mother's secret, the truth that ran in their blood? Best if they didn't. If Giovanna Treadwell's star kept rising, their lives would be complicated enough.

After she'd gone he closed his little dressing-case and let himself out by the National's stage door, his heavy steps turning west towards Foggy Bottom. There was one more woman to say goodbye to, bereaved but moving on, guided by the light of her own ideals and by the love she bore for the race whose blood flowed so lightly in her own veins. Love freely given, and as freely returned.

EPILOGUE

Washington Bee, May 12, 1906

WINS AND LOSSES FOR THE RACE ON CAPITOL HILL

Marriage ban and alley relief amendment both defeated in committee

It is often said by those in the know that it is far easier to kill legislation than to pass it. In this regard, friends of the Negro race must simultaneously applaud and deplore two instances of legislative demise that occurred last week in Congress.

In a surprising development, the House Judiciary Committee failed by one vote to release the so-called 'miscegenation bill' for action by the full House, effectively killing this insult to the race for the duration of the 59th Congress. The bill, which would have forbidden marriage in the District and U.S. Territories between whites and anyone with more than one-eighth Negro blood, had been the subject of a discharge petition spearheaded by its original sponsor, Congressman Milton of Florida.

Observers attributed the failure of the vote to the absence of one of the bill's most influential co-sponsors, Representative Richard Latham, R-Corning, New York, who had been widely expected to make a statement in favor of releasing the bill for action on the House floor, where it had been given a "greater than even" chance of passage, according to a source close to the Committee.

Latham, who returned to the Committee after debate on the petition concluded, "took a walk," according to a disgruntled colleague, thereby denying the measure a majority vote which would have released it for House action.

Mrs. Mary Church Terrell, a leader and educator in the Negro community, hailed the Committee vote as one that "we trust will put paid once and for all to the legalized inferiority of our race in the District of Columbia."

Unhappily for the less fortunate residents of the District, a measure sponsored by the late Representative Robert Nielsen of Wisconsin failed a D.C. Committee vote to attach an amendment to the condemnation bill.

The bill itself, widely expected to pass, would require demolition of alley-dwellings which persistently fail to meet basic standards of decency and habitability. Mr. Nielsen's amendment would have required that owners of such properties bring the structures into compliance with building codes before being issued additional building permits in the District of Columbia.

Vociferous objections by real estate development interests were cited by several members of the Committee, speaking on condition of anonymity, as the reason for the failure of the Nielsen amendment. "However," said one of its co-sponsors, "we shall try again in the next Congress, you may be assured."

The *Bee* respectfully suggests that as long as Members of Congress are permitted to make investments in D.C. development schemes, there will be little incentive for the kind of oversight and protection of the public interest that Mr. Nielsen's amendment would have required.

THE END

HISTORICAL NOTES

Though more than one decade could qualify as "the nadir of American race relations" (a term coined by Rayford W. Logan), the first decade of the twentieth century may have the strongest claim on that dubious distinction. From 1900 to 1908, the Southern states completed a program of systematic disenfranchisement of African Americans through mechanisms ranging from onerous poll taxes to impossible "literacy" tests. The formal extinction of black civil rights was accompanied by systematic denial of economic and educational opportunity that all but re-enslaved the black population of the Deep South. Lynching as an enforcement tool for white supremacy reached epidemic levels.

As the last black post-Reconstruction Member of Congress still in office in 1901, George Henry White, "disfranchised" by his native North Carolina in 1899, made a poignant farewell to Capitol Hill: "I cannot live in North Carolina and be a man and be treated as a man...This is perhaps the Negroes' temporary farewell to the American Congress, but let me say, Phoenix-like he will rise up some day and come again. These parting words are in behalf of an outraged, heart-broken, bruised and bleeding, but God-fearing people; faithful, industrious, loyal, rising people—full of potential force." Until the election of Oscar De Priest from Illinois in 1928, there would be no other black Representatives.

The Supreme Court's 1896 decision in the infamous *Plessy v. Ferguson* case had institutionalized racial segregation laws. By 1913 over half the states, as far north as Oregon and the Dakotas, had passed laws prohibiting intermarriage between whites and

"Negroes" or variously defined "colored" people, in some cases with as little as one-sixteenth non-white blood. The pseudo-scientific theories of the eugenics movement—to which Theodore Roosevelt, among others, subscribed—reinforced existing race prejudice from slavery days and spread fears about white "race suicide" due to supposedly higher birthrates among the "inferior" races. Sociologist W.E.B. Du Bois, the first African American to receive a doctorate, was one of the most articulate critics of this form of "scientific racism."

While for purposes of this story I have invented a District of Columbia anti-miscegenation bill making its way through the House of Representatives in the 58th Congress, and a Congressional career for William Hall Milton of Florida that preceded his brief, appointive service in the U.S. Senate, Milton did in fact introduce such a bill in the Senate, S. 8462, during the 60th Congress. It was tabled on a motion by Ohio Senator Joseph B. Foraker, described by biographer Edmund Morris as a man with "a passion for racial justice," known also for his public challenge to Theodore Roosevelt's action in dishonorably discharging members of a black garrison following the late 1906 "Brownsville Affair." That wrong on Roosevelt's part was not remedied until 1972.

Though nothing came of Milton's 1909 bill, an anti-miscegenation bill for the District sponsored by another Floridian, Frank Clark, passed the House of Representatives in the "lame duck" session of 1915 by a vote of 238 to 60. Sent to the Senate, it was referred to the District of Columbia Committee and never taken up.

The altercation I have depicted between Robert Nielsen and Richard Latham on the floor of the House of Representatives was a mild exchange compared with the fisticuffs that broke out in the Senate in February of 1902 when South Carolina Senator John McLaurin rushed into the Senate chamber and accused his senior Benjamin "Pitchfork Ben" Tillman of maliciously lying. Tillman punched McLaurin in the jaw and it required several colleagues to separate the two. The brutal caning of abolitionist Senator Charles Sumner by Representative Preston Brooks of

South Carolina in 1856 is the most notorious instance of Congressional violence.

Representatives George Pearre, Benjamin Birdsall, John Lacey, and Walter Smith, along with Senators William Warner and Foraker, won regular praise from the *Washington Bee*, published by William Calvin Chase between 1880 and 1920, as true Congressional "friends of the race." The Member from the Second District of Wisconsin, Robert Nielsen, bears no resemblance to his real-life counterpart Henry Cullen Adams apart from the fact that both were Progressive followers of Robert LaFollette and both died in 1906 (naturally, in Adams' case).

Within the confines of their rigidly re-segregated world, members of Washington's educated black elite came to feel increasing solidarity with the race which they had been encouraged to transcend or even try to escape by "passing" if their skin color permitted. A desire to improve conditions for "the race" as a whole led W.E.B. Du Bois and other members of the Niagara Movement to encourage talented blacks to aim for education in elite white-dominated institutions and become leaders in the drive for racial uplift.

Washington educators such as Robert and Mary Church Terrell and Anna Julia Cooper were Du Bois' allies in this effort, building a reputation for academic excellence at the M Street School (later renamed Dunbar High School in honor of poet Paul Laurence Dunbar, a one-time resident of LeDroit Park) which lasted for decades. "Lady Mollie" Terrell was a founding member of the NAACP, successfully filed suit to end segregation in Washington restaurants and other public places, and lived just long enough to see the *Brown v. Board of Education* decision handed down in 1954.

The Strivers' Mutual Advancement League and Benevolent Society is a fictional counterpart to the Grand Fountain of the United Order of True Reformers, a mutual insurance agency which during the period covered by this novel comprised "the largest and most successful black business enterprise in the United States." It went into decline following an embezzlement scandal in 1910. The True Reformers building at 12th and U

Streets NW in the heart of Black Washington, built in 1903, is now the headquarters of the Public Welfare Foundation and is listed on the National Register of Historic Places.

Charles Weller was a real-life crusader for improving conditions in the squalor-ridden alley dwellings of Washington on behalf of that city's Associated Charities, which he served as General Secretary from 1900 to 1908. Louisa Stanstead's Alley Relief Society is a fictional version of the Associated Charities' Committee on Improvement of Housing Conditions, on which Weller also served between 1902 and 1907. So influential was Weller in his efforts on behalf of the District's poor that Theodore Roosevelt appointed him to chair the President's Homes Commission, "a special commission to investigate housing and health conditions in the National Capital," and wrote the introduction to his 1909 book on alley conditions, *Neglected Neighbors*. My depictions of Snow's Court and other Capital slums drew heavily from Weller's narrative.

The investigation and report on alley conditions which I have attributed to Louisa Stanstead was actually the work of Janet E. Kemp, whose remarkable career as an investigator of the living conditions of the poor took her over the years to Baltimore, Washington, New York City, Louisville, and coastal South Carolina. The Washington report came out in March of 1906 in a special edition of the journal *Charities and the Commons* and was sent to all members of Congress, resulting in the enactment of a condemnation-or-compulsory-repair bill (to which I have appended a fictional Alley Relief Bill which did not pass) on May 1, 1906. Sadly, the provisions of that Act were invalidated by a 1907 Supreme Court decision.

At least two First Ladies were sufficiently appalled by living conditions in Washington's alleys that they became activists for improved conditions. James Borchert cites the dying words of Woodrow Wilson's first wife, Ellen Axson Wilson, in 1914: "I should be happier if I knew the Alley Bill had passed." Eleanor Roosevelt also worked to eliminate the "menace" of alley dwellings.

The row of gracious townhouses on Belmont Road where Congressman Warren Dodge finds a temporary Washington home and a lucrative investment were built in 1909, not 1906 as I have depicted them. Columbia Heights was indeed the focus of real estate speculation in this period and only the extension of a streetcar line beyond its boundaries brought inflated land values there back into line.

I have replaced the real-life Evelina Torres Soares Ribeiro and her spouse, Brazilian Ambassador Joaquim Aurélio Barreto Nabuco de Araújo, with an entirely fictional couple. While Ambassador Pereira's public life and history correspond closely to those of Ambassador Nabuco, the private doings of Senhora Pereira and her ultimate fate are entirely my own invention.

Edward H. Sothern (1859–1933), the leading Shakespearean actor of his era, made regular appearances at the National Theatre from the early 1880s on, performing with his first wife Virginia Harned there in the late 1890s and as late as 1901. His first appearance with Julia Marlowe (1865-1950) as his partner took place in February of 1905. Marlowe filed for divorce from her first husband, actor Robert Taber, in 1899 and he died in 1904. Sothern and Harned were not divorced until 1910 and he married Marlowe the following year. But by 1906, Sothern & Marlowe were already considered the pre-eminent interpreters of Shakespeare in the U.S.

I have delayed the troupe's 1906 engagement in Washington, DC by two months and changed their repertoire from a quartet (*Romeo & Juliet*, *Twelfth Night*, *The Merchant of Venice*, and *Taming of the Shrew*) to a single presentation of *Macbeth*, in which they did not in fact perform together until 1910. The February 1906 repertory session was their last appearance at the National until a February 1921 benefit for the Medical Society of Washington.

So far as I know, Mr. Sothern was never stricken with the debilitating case of pneumonia which I have inflicted on him for purposes of this narrative.

FURTHER READING: *MURDERED SLEEP* SOURCES

Although this work is strictly fictional, the following were invaluable sources for providing historical context and such authenticity as it conveys:

Anacostia Museum and Center for African American History and Culture, *The Black Washingtonians: the Anacostia Museum Illustrated Chronology*, J. Wiley, 2005

Grace Vawter Bicknell, *The Inhabited Alleys of Washington, D.C.* Committee on Housing, Women's Welfare Department, Press of the Ideal Printery, 1912

Douglas A. Blackmon, *Slavery by Another Name: The Re-Enslavement of Black Americans from the Civil War to World War II*, Anchor Books, 2008

James Borchert, *Alley Life in Washington: Family, Community, Religion, and Folklife in the City, 1850-1970*, University of Illinois Press, 1980

James Borchert, "Alley Life in Washington: An Analysis of 600 Photographs," *Records of the Columbia Historical Society, Washington, D.C.*, Vol. 49, pp. 244-259, Historical Society of Washington, D.C.

James Borchert, "The Rise and Fall of Washington's Inhabited Alleys," *Records of the Columbia Historical Society, Washington, D.C.*, Vol. 71/72, pp. 267-288.

Karl John Byrand, *Changing Race, Changing Place: Racial, Occupational, and Residential Patterns in Shaw, Washington, D.C., 1880-1920*, University of Maryland, 1999

Senator Robert C. Byrd, "The Capitol Police," in *Addresses on the History of the U.S. Senate, Vol. 2*, U.S. Senate Historical Office, 1976

Charles W. Chesnutt, *The Wife of His Youth and Other Stories*, Houghton Mifflin, 1899

Charles W. Chesnutt, *The House Behind the Cedars*, Houghton Mifflin, 1900

Thomas G. Dyer, *Theodore Roosevelt and the Idea of Race*, LSU Press, 1992

W.E.B.Du Bois, *The Souls of Black Folk*, 1903

W.E.B.Du Bois, "Health and Physique of the Negro American," Proceedings of the 11th Atlanta Conference, May 29, 1906

Federal Writers Project, *Washington: City and Capital,* Works Progress Administration, 1937

Sandra Fitzpatrick and Maria R. Goodwin, *The Guide to Black Washington: Places and Events of Historical and Cultural Significance in the Nation's Capital,* Hippocrene Books, 1990

Willard B. Gatewood, *Aristocrats of Color: The Black Elite, 1880-1920,* University of Arkansas Press, 2000

Joseph R. Gay, *Progress and Achievements of the 20th Century Negro,* 1913

Constance McLaughlin Green, *The Secret City: A History of Race Relations in the Nation's Capital,* Princeton University Press, 1967

Jinny Huh, *The Arresting Eye: Race and the Detection of Deception,* University of Southern California Ph.D. dissertation, 2005

Albert Ernest Jenks, "The Legal Status of Negro-White Amalgamation in the United States," *The American Journal of Sociology,* Vol. 21 No. 5, 1916

Rayford W. Logan, *The Betrayal of the Negro, from Rutherford B. Hayes to Woodrow Wilson,* Collier Books, 1965

August Meier, *Negro Thought in America, 1880-1915,* University of Michigan Press, 1963

Jacqueline M. Moore, *Leading the Race: The Transformation of the Black Elite in the Nation's Capital,* University of Virginia Press, 1999

Sharon Ann Murphy, "Life Insurance in the United States through World War I," at http://eh.net/encyclopedia/article/murphy.life.insurance.us

William L. O'Neill, "Divorce in the Progressive Era," *American Quarterly,* Summer 1965, pp. 203-217

Nell Irwin Painter, *Creating Black Americans: African-American History and its Meanings, 1619 to the Present,* Oxford University Press, 2006

Gary Schuman, "Life insurance and the homicidal beneficiary: The insurer's responsibilities under state slayer laws and statutes," *FICC Quarterly,* Spring 2001

Charles H. Shattuck, *Shakespeare on the American Stage: from Booth and Barrett to Sothern and Marlowe,* Associated University Presses, 1987

John David Smith, editor, *Anti-Black Thought: 1863-1925,* vols. 1-11, Garland Publishing, 1993

Mary Church Terrell, *A Colored Woman in a White World,* Ransdell, Inc., 1940

Charles Weller and Eugenia Winston Weller, *Neglected Neighbors: Stories of Life in the Alleyways, Tenements, and Shanties of the National Capital,* J.C. Winston, 1909

ACKNOWLEDGEMENTS

I'm once again deeply in debt to my Fearless Readers, whose generous critiques have (from my perspective, at least) improved this book immeasurably: Don Rowe, Bob Swierczek, Catherine Hughes, the late Kit Ward of Christina Ward Literary Agency, and most particularly for services above and beyond the call on numerous later drafts, Mary Hays and George Spaulding.

I'm also indebted to Mr. Alfred Austin, great-grandson of William Calvin Chase, founder and publisher of the *Washington Bee*, for introducing me to his distinguished ancestor's publication in early 2006. At that time, Mr. Austin had had the extant issues of the *Bee* digitized onto compact disks; since then, the Library of Congress has archived them at http://chroniclingamerica.loc. gov/lccn/sn84025891/. They make fascinating reading.

Senate Historical Office Historian Donald Ritchie provided valuable guidance on Congressional procedures in the period; Kristen Wilhelm and Judy Adkins of the National Archives and Records Administration were most helpful regarding legislation on racial matters in the first decade of the 20th century.

The staff of the Kiplinger Library of the District of Columbia Historical Society was extremely helpful in directing me to materials that helped illuminate the lives of African-Americans in Washington at the turn of the last century.

Lieutenant Kimberley Schneider of the U.S. Capitol Police Information Office provided valuable information about security on the Capitol grounds in the period of the novel.

Kitty Werner of RSBPress is a magician who turns manuscripts into finished books. *Murdered Sleep* would quite literally not be a book without her expertise, good humor and commitment to making sure that a work of literature presents its best possible face to the world.

As always, my deepest thanks and best love to my husband, Wayne Fawbush, who kept me going through many difficult periods and dry spells with his generous heart and positive outlook.

ABOUT THE AUTHOR

Roberta Harold is at work on her third novel, a re-imagining of the life of a Civil War widow. Her first two books, *Heron Island* and *Murdered Sleep*, mysteries set in the early 1900s and published under her pen name of R.A. Harold, feature security agent and sometime Shakespearean actor Dade Wyatt.

A 2001 graduate of the Bread Loaf School of English at Middlebury College, she studied fiction writing with novelist Jonathan Strong and poetry with Paul Muldoon, winning the 1999 Poetry Competition there. She was a 2009 finalist for the Orlando Award in Short Fiction of the A Room of Her Own Foundation. A member of Sisters in Crime and of Grub Street, Boston's creative writing center, she blogs about life in Vermont and her former residence in Brooklyn at http://raharold.com.

A native of Scotland whose family emigrated to the Washington, DC area when she was twelve, Harold was among the first women graduates of Princeton University in 1973. While a Presidential campaign aide and Congressional staffer for environmentalist and government reformer Representative Morris K. "Mo" Udall in the mid-1970s, she lived and worked on Capitol Hill. She and her husband live in Montpelier, Vermont.